THE
GREY FAIRY BOOK

The Dervish drowning the Pigs

THE
GREY FAIRY BOOK

Edited by

ANDREW LANG

With Numerous Illustrations by

H. J. Ford

DOVER PUBLICATIONS, INC.

NEW YORK

Published in Canada by General Publishing Company, Ltd., 30 Lesmill Road, Don Mills, Toronto, Ontario.

Published in the United Kingdom by Constable and Company, Ltd., 10 Orange Street, London WC 2.

This Dover edition, first published in 1967, is an unabridged and unaltered republication of the work originally published by Longmans, Green and Company in 1900.

Standard Book Number: 486-21791-4

Library of Congress Catalog Card Number: 67-17983

Manufactured in the United States of America
Dover Publications, Inc.
180 Varick Street
New York, N. Y. 10014

PREFACE

THE tales in the Grey Fairy Book are derived from many countries—Lithuania, various parts of Africa, Germany, France, Greece, and other regions of the world. They have been translated and adapted by Mrs. Dent, Mrs. Lang, Miss Eleanor Sellar, Miss Blackley, and Miss Lang. 'The Three Sons of Hali' is from the last century 'Cabinet des Fées,' a very large collection. The French author may have had some Oriental original before him in parts; at all events he copied the Eastern method of putting tale within tale, like the Eastern balls of carved ivory. The stories, as usual, illustrate the method of popular fiction. A certain number of incidents are shaken into many varying combinations, like the fragments of coloured glass in the kaleidoscope. Probably the possible combinations, like possible musical combinations, are not unlimited in number, but children may be less sensitive in the matter of fairies than Mr. John Stuart Mill was as regards music.

CONTENTS

ILLUSTRATIONS

PLATES

IN TEXT

THE
GREY FAIRY BOOK

DONKEY SKIN

THERE was once upon a time a king who was so much beloved by his subjects that he thought himself the happiest monarch in the whole world, and he had everything his heart could desire. His palace was filled with the rarest of curiosities, and his gardens with the sweetest flowers, while in the marble stalls of his stables stood a row of milk-white Arabs, with big brown eyes.

Strangers who had heard of the marvels which the king had collected, and made long journeys to see them, were, however, surprised to find the most splendid stall of all occupied by a donkey, with particularly large and drooping ears. It was a very fine donkey; but still, as far as they could tell, nothing so very remarkable as to account for the care with which it was lodged; and they went away wondering, for they could not know that every night, when it was asleep, bushels of gold pieces tumbled out of its ears, which were picked up each morning by the attendants.

After many years of prosperity a sudden blow fell upon the king in the death of his wife, whom he loved dearly. But before she died, the queen, who had always thought first of his happiness, gathered all her strength, and said to him:

'Promise me one thing: you must marry again, I know, for the good of your people, as well as of yourself. But do not set about it in a hurry. Wait until you have found a woman more beautiful and better formed than myself.'

'Oh, do not speak to me of marrying,' sobbed the king; 'rather let me die with you!' But the queen only smiled faintly, and turned over on her pillow and died.

For some months the king's grief was great; then gradually he began to forget a little, and, besides, his counsellors were always urging him to seek another wife. At first he refused to listen to them, but by-and-by he allowed himself to be persuaded to think of it, only stipulating that the bride should be more beautiful and attractive than the late queen, according to the promise he had made her.

Overjoyed at having obtained what they wanted, the counsellors sent envoys far and wide to get portraits of all the most famous beauties of every country. The artists were very busy and did their best, but, alas! nobody could even pretend that any of the ladies could compare for a moment with the late queen.

At length, one day, when he had turned away discouraged from a fresh collection of pictures, the king's eyes fell on his adopted daughter, who had lived in the palace since she was a baby, and he saw that, if a woman existed on the whole earth more lovely than the queen, this was she! He at once made known what his wishes were, but the young girl, who was not at all ambitious, and had not the faintest desire to marry him, was filled with dismay, and begged for time to think about it. That night, when everyone was asleep, she started in a little car drawn by a big sheep, and went to consult her fairy godmother.

'I know what you have come to tell me,' said the fairy, when the maiden stepped out of the car; 'and if you don't wish to marry him, I will show you how to avoid it. Ask him to give you a dress that exactly matches the sky. It will be impossible for him to get one, so you will be quite safe.' The girl thanked the fairy and returned home again.

The next morning, when her father (as she had always

called him) came to see her, she told him that she could
give him no answer until he had presented her with a

The King's Pet Donkey

dress the colour of the sky. The king, overjoyed at this
answer, sent for all the choicest weavers and dressmakers
in the kingdom, and commanded them to make a robe

the colour of the sky without an instant's delay, or he
would cut off their heads at once. Dreadfully frightened
at this threat, they all began to dye and cut and sew, and
in two days they brought back the dress, which looked
as if it had been cut straight out of the heavens! The
poor girl was thunderstruck, and did not know what to
do ; so in the night she harnessed her sheep again, and
went in search of her godmother.

'The king is cleverer than I thought,' said the fairy ;
' but tell him you must have a dress of moonbeams.'

And the next day, when the king summoned her into
his presence, the girl told him what she wanted.

' Madam, I can refuse you nothing,' said he ; and he
ordered the dress to be ready in twenty-four hours, or
every man should be hanged.

They set to work with all their might, and by dawn
next day, the dress of moonbeams was laid across her
bed. The girl, though she could not help admiring its
beauty, began to cry, till the fairy, who heard her, came
to her help.

' Well, I could not have believed it of him ! ' said she ;
' but ask for a dress of sunshine, and I shall be surprised
indeed if he manages that ! '

The goddaughter did not feel much faith in the fairy
after her two previous failures ; but not knowing what else
to do, she told her father what she was bid.

The king made no difficulties about it, and even gave his
finest rubies and diamonds to ornament the dress, which
was so dazzling, when finished, that it could not be looked
at save through smoked glasses !

When the princess saw it, she pretended that the
sight hurt her eyes, and retired to her room, where she
found the fairy awaiting her, very much ashamed of
herself.

' There is only one thing to be done now,' cried she ;
' you must demand the skin of the ass he sets such
store by. It is from that donkey he obtains all his

The Fairy, the Princess & The Donkey's Skin

vast riches, and I am sure he will never give it to you.'

The princess was not so certain ; however, she went to the king, and told him she could never marry him till he had given her the ass's skin.

The king was both astonished and grieved at this new request, but did not hesitate an instant. The ass was sacrificed, and the skin laid at the feet of the princess.

The poor girl, seeing no escape from the fate she dreaded, wept afresh, and tore her hair ; when, suddenly, the fairy stood before her.

'Take heart,' she said, 'all will now go well ! Wrap yourself in this skin, and leave the palace and go as far as you can. I will look after you. Your dresses and your jewels shall follow you underground, and if you strike the earth whenever you need anything, you will have it at once. But go quickly : you have no time to lose.'

So the princess clothed herself in the ass's skin, and slipped from the palace without being seen by anyone.

Directly she was missed there was a great hue and cry, and every corner, possible and impossible, was searched. Then the king sent out parties along all the roads, but the fairy threw her invisible mantle over the girl when they approached, and none of them could see her.

The princess walked on a long, long way, trying to find some one who would take her in, and let her work for them ; but though the cottagers, whose houses she passed, gave her food from charity, the ass's skin was so dirty they would not allow her to enter their houses. For her flight had been so hurried she had had no time to clean it.

Tired and disheartened at her ill-fortune, she was wandering, one day, past the gate of a farmyard, situated just outside the walls of a large town, when she heard a voice calling to her. She turned and saw the farmer's wife standing among her turkeys, and making signs to her to come in.

' I want a girl to wash the dishes and feed the turkeys, and clean out the pig-sty,' said the woman, 'and, to judge by your dirty clothes, you would not be too fine for the work.'

The girl accepted her offer with joy, and she was at once set to work in a corner of the kitchen, where all the farm servants came and made fun of her, and the ass's skin in which she was wrapped. But by-and-by they got so used to the sight of it that it ceased to amuse them, and she worked so hard and so well, that her mistress grew quite fond of her. And she was so clever at keeping sheep and herding turkeys that you would have thought she had done nothing else during her whole life !

One day she was sitting on the banks of a stream bewailing her wretched lot, when she suddenly caught sight of herself in the water. Her hair and part of her face was quite concealed by the ass's head, which was drawn right over like a hood, and the filthy matted skin covered her whole body. It was the first time she had seen herself as other people saw her, and she was filled with shame at the spectacle. Then she threw off her disguise and jumped into the water, plunging in again and again, till she shone like ivory. When it was time to go back to the farm, she was forced to put on the skin which disguised her, and now seemed more dirty than ever ; but, as she did so, she comforted herself with the thought that to-morrow was a holiday, and that she would be able for a few hours to forget that she was a farm girl, and be a princess once more.

So, at break of day, she stamped on the ground, as the fairy had told her, and instantly the dress like the sky lay across her tiny bed. Her room was so small that there was no place for the train of her dress to spread itself out, but she pinned it up carefully when she combed her beautiful hair and piled it up on the top of her head, as she had always worn it. When she had done, she was so pleased with herself that she determined never to let a chance pass of putting on her splendid clothes, even if she had to wear them in the fields, with no one to admire her but the sheep and turkeys.

Now the farm was a royal farm, and, one holiday, when 'Donkey Skin' (as they had nicknamed the princess) had locked the door of her room and clothed herself in her dress of sunshine, the king's son rode through the gate, and asked if he might come and rest himself a little after hunting. Some food and milk were set before him in the garden, and when he felt rested he got up, and began to explore the house, which was famous throughout the whole kingdom for its age and beauty. He opened one door after the other, admiring the old rooms, when he came to a handle that would not turn. He stooped and peeped through the keyhole to see what was inside, and was greatly astonished at beholding a beautiful girl, clad in a dress so dazzling that he could hardly look at it.

The dark gallery seemed darker than ever as he turned away, but he went back to the kitchen and inquired who slept in the room at the end of the passage. The scullery maid, they told him, whom everybody laughed at, and called ' Donkey Skin ; ' and though he perceived there was some strange mystery about this, he saw quite clearly there was nothing to be gained by asking any more questions. So he rode back to the palace, his head filled with the vision he had seen through the keyhole.

All night long he tossed about, and awoke the next morning in a high fever. The queen, who had no other child, and lived in a state of perpetual anxiety about this one, at once gave him up for lost, and indeed his sudden illness puzzled the greatest doctors, who tried the usual remedies in vain. At last they told the queen that some secret sorrow must be at the bottom of all this, and she threw herself on her knees beside her son's bed, and implored him to confide his trouble to her. If it was ambition to be king, his father would gladly resign the cares of the crown, and suffer him to reign in his stead ; or, if it was love, everything should be sacrificed to get for him the wife he desired, even if she were daughter of a king with whom the country was at war at present !

'Madam,' replied the prince, whose weakness would hardly allow him to speak, 'do not think me so unnatural as to wish to deprive my father of his crown. As long as he lives I shall remain the most faithful of his subjects ! And as to the princesses you speak of, I have seen none that I should care for as a wife, though I would always obey your wishes, whatever it might cost me.'

'Ah ! my son,' cried she, 'we will do anything in the world to save your life—and ours too, for if you die, we shall die also.'

'Well, then,' replied the prince, 'I will tell you the only thing that will cure me—a cake made by the hand of "Donkey Skin." '

'Donkey Skin?' exclaimed the queen, who thought her son had gone mad ; 'and who or what is that ? '

'Madam,' answered one of the attendants present, who had been with the prince at the farm, '"Donkey Skin" is, next to the wolf, the most disgusting creature on the face of the earth. She is a girl who wears a black, greasy skin, and lives at your farmer's as hen-wife.'

'Never mind,' said the queen ; 'my son seems to have eaten some of her pastry. It is the whim of a sick man, no doubt ; but send at once and let her bake a cake.'

The attendant bowed and ordered a page to ride with the message.

Now it is by no means certain that 'Donkey Skin' had not caught a glimpse of the prince, either when his eyes looked through the keyhole, or else from her little window, which was over the road. But whether she had actually seen him or only heard him spoken of, directly she received the queen's command, she flung off the dirty skin, washed herself from head to foot, and put on a skirt and bodice of shining silver. Then, locking herself into her room, she took the richest cream, the finest flour, and the freshest eggs on the farm, and set about making her cake.

As she was stirring the mixture in the saucepan a ring that she sometimes wore in secret slipped from her finger and fell into the dough. Perhaps 'Donkey Skin' saw it, or perhaps she did not; but, any way, she went on stirring, and soon the cake was ready to be put in the oven. When it was nice and brown she took off her dress and put on her dirty skin, and gave the cake to the page, asking at the same time for news of the prince. But the page turned his head aside, and would not even condescend to answer.

The page rode like the wind, and as soon as he arrived at the palace he snatched up a silver tray and hastened to present the cake to the prince. The sick man began to eat it so fast that the doctors thought he would choke; and, indeed, he very nearly did, for the ring was in one of the bits which he broke off, though he managed to extract it from his mouth without anyone seeing him.

The moment the prince was left alone he drew the ring from under his pillow and kissed it a thousand times. Then he set his mind to find how he was to see the owner—for even he did not dare to confess that he had only beheld 'Donkey Skin' through a keyhole, lest they should laugh at this sudden passion. All this worry brought back the fever, which the arrival of the cake had diminished for the time; and the doctors, not knowing what else to say, informed the queen that her son was simply dying of love. The queen, stricken with horror, rushed into the king's presence with the news, and together they hastened to their son's bedside.

' My boy, my dear boy !' cried the king, ' who is it you want to marry? We will give her to you for a bride, even if she is the humblest of our slaves. What is there in the whole world that we would not do for you? '

The prince, moved to tears at these words, drew the ring, which was an emerald of the purest water, from under his pillow.

' Ah, dear father and mother, let this be a proof that she whom I love is no peasant girl. The finger which that ring fits has never been thickened by hard work. But be her condition what it may, I will marry no other.'

The king and queen examined the tiny ring very closely, and agreed, with their son, that the wearer could be no mere farm girl. Then the king went out and ordered heralds and trumpeters to go through the town, summoning every maiden to the palace. And she whom the ring fitted would some day be queen.

First came all the princesses, then all the duchesses' daughters, and so on, in proper order. But not one of them could slip the ring over the tip of her finger, to the great joy of the prince, whom excitement was fast curing. At last, when the high-born damsels had failed, the shopgirls and chambermaids took their turn ; but with no better fortune.

' Call in the scullions and shepherdesses,' commanded the prince ; but the sight of their fat, red fingers satisfied everybody.

' There is not a woman left, your Highness,' said the chamberlain ; but the prince waved him aside.

' Have you sent for " Donkey Skin," who made me the cake? ' asked he, and the courtiers began to laugh, and replied that they would not have dared to introduce so dirty a creature into the palace.

' Let some one go for her at once,' ordered the king. ' I commanded the presence of every maiden, high or low, and I meant it.'

The princess had heard the trumpets and the proclamations, and knew quite well that her ring was at the bottom of it all. She, too, had fallen in love with the prince in the brief glimpse she had had of him, and trembled with fear lest someone else's finger might be

The Donkey-skin falls off.

as small as her own. When, therefore, the messenger from the palace rode up to the gate, she was nearly beside herself with delight. Hoping all the time for such a summons, she had dressed herself with great care, putting on the garment of moonlight, whose skirt was scattered over with emeralds. But when they began calling to her to come down, she hastily covered herself with her donkey-skin and announced she was ready to present herself before his Highness. She was taken straight into the hall, where the prince was awaiting her, but at the sight of the donkey-skin his heart sank. Had he been mistaken after all?

'Are you the girl,' he said, turning his eyes away as he spoke, ' are you the girl who has a room in the furthest corner of the inner court of the farmhouse?'

' Yes, my lord, I am,' answered she.

' Hold out your hand then,' continued the prince, feeling that he must keep his word, whatever the cost, and, to the astonishment of every one present, a little hand, white and delicate, came from beneath the black and dirty skin. The ring slipped on with the utmost ease, and, as it did so, the skin fell to the ground, disclosing a figure of such beauty that the prince, weak as he was, fell on his knees before her, while the king and queen joined their prayers to his. Indeed, their welcome was so warm, and their caresses so bewildering, that the princess hardly knew how to find words to reply, when the ceiling of the hall opened, and the fairy godmother appeared, seated in a car made entirely of white lilac. In a few words she explained the history of the princess, and how she came to be there, and, without losing a moment, preparations of the most magnificent kind were made for the wedding.

The kings of every country in the earth were invited, including, of course, the princess's adopted father (who by this time had married a widow), and not one refused.

But what a strange assembly it was! Each monarch travelled in the way he thought most impressive ; and some came borne in litters, others had carriages of every shape and kind, while the rest were mounted on ele-

phants, tigers, and even upon eagles. So splendid a
wedding had never been seen before; and when it was
over the king announced that it was to be followed by a
coronation, for he and the queen were tired of reigning,
and the young couple must take their place. The
rejoicings lasted for three whole months, then the new
sovereigns settled down to govern their kingdom, and
made themselves so much beloved by their subjects, that
when they died, a hundred years later, each man mourned
them as his own father and mother.

[From *Le Cabinet des Fées.*]

THE GOBLIN PONY

'Don't stir from the fireplace to-night,' said old Peggy, 'for the wind is blowing so violently that the house shakes; besides, this is Hallow-e'en, when the witches are abroad, and the goblins, who are their servants, are wandering about in all sorts of disguises, doing harm to the children of men.'

'Why should I stay here?' said the eldest of the young people. 'No, I must go and see what the daughter of old Jacob, the rope-maker, is doing. She wouldn't close her blue eyes all night if I didn't visit her father before the moon had gone down.'

'I must go and catch lobsters and crabs,' said the second, 'and not all the witches and goblins in the world shall hinder me.'

So they all determined to go on their business or pleasure, and scorned the wise advice of old Peggy. Only the youngest child hesitated a minute, when she said to him, 'You stay here, my little Richard, and I will tell you beautiful stories.'

But he wanted to pick a bunch of wild thyme and some blackberries by moonlight, and ran out after the others. When they got outside the house they said: 'The old woman talks of wind and storm, but never was the weather finer or the sky more clear; see how majestically the moon stalks through the transparent clouds!'

Then all of a sudden they noticed a little black pony close beside them.

' Oh, ho ! ' they said, ' that is old Valentine's pony ; it must have escaped from its stable, and is going down to drink at the horse-pond.'

' My pretty little pony,' said the eldest, patting the creature with his hand, ' you mustn't run too far ; I'll take you to the pond myself.'

With these words he jumped on the pony's back and was quickly followed by his second brother, then by the third, and so on, till at last they were all astride the little

beast, down to the small Richard, who didn't like to be left behind.

On the way to the pond they met several of their companions, and they invited them all to mount the pony, which they did, and the little creature did not seem to mind the extra weight, but trotted merrily along.

The quicker it trotted the more the young people enjoyed the fun ; they dug their heels into the pony's sides and called out, ' Gallop, little horse, you have never had such brave riders on your back before ! '

In the meantime the wind had risen again, and the waves began to howl; but the pony did not seem to mind the noise, and instead of going to the pond, cantered gaily towards the sea-shore.

Richard began to regret his thyme and blackberries, and the eldest brother seized the pony by the mane and tried to make it turn round, for he remembered the blue eyes of Jacob the rope-maker's daughter. But he tugged and pulled in vain, for the pony galloped straight on into the sea, till the waves met its forefeet. As soon as it felt the water it neighed lustily and capered about with glee, advancing quickly into the foaming billows. When the waves had covered the children's legs they repented their careless behaviour, and cried out: ' The cursed little black pony is bewitched. If we had only listened to old Peggy's advice we shouldn't have been lost.'

The further the pony advanced, the higher rose the sea; at last the waves covered the children's heads and they were all drowned.

Towards morning old Peggy went out, for she was anxious about the fate of her grandchildren. She sought them high and low, but could not find them anywhere. She asked all the neighbours if they had seen the children, but no one knew anything about them, except that the eldest had not been with the blue-eyed daughter of Jacob the rope-maker.

As she was going home, bowed with grief, she saw a little black pony coming towards her, springing and curveting in every direction. When it got quite near her it neighed loudly, and galloped past her so quickly that in a moment it was out of her sight.

[From the French, Kletke.]

AN IMPOSSIBLE ENCHANTMENT

THERE once lived a king who was much loved by his people, and he, too, loved them warmly. He led a very happy life, but he had the greatest dislike to the idea of marrying, nor had he ever felt the slightest wish to fall in love. His subjects begged him to marry, and at last he promised to try to do so. But as, so far, he had never cared for any woman he had seen, he made up his mind to travel in hopes of meeting some lady he could love.

So he arranged all the affairs of state in an orderly manner, and set out, attended by only one equerry, who, though not very clever, had most excellent good sense. These people indeed generally make the best fellow-travellers.

The king explored several countries, doing all he could to fall in love, but in vain; and at the end of two years' journeys he turned his face towards home, with as free a heart as when he set out.

As he was riding along through a forest he suddenly heard the most awful miawing and shrieking of cats you can imagine. The noise drew nearer, and nearer, and at last they saw a hundred huge Spanish cats rush through the trees close to them. They were so closely packed together that you could easily have covered them with a large cloak, and all were following the same track. They were closely pursued by two enormous apes, dressed in purple suits, with the prettiest and best made boots you ever saw.

The apes were mounted on superb mastiffs, and spurred them on in hot haste, blowing shrill blasts on little toy trumpets all the time.

The king and his equerry stood still to watch this strange hunt, which was followed by twenty or more little dwarfs, some mounted on wolves, and leading relays, and others with cats in leash. The dwarfs were all dressed in purple silk liveries like the apes.

A moment later a beautiful young woman mounted on a tiger came in sight. She passed close to the king, riding at full speed, without taking any notice of him ; but he was at once enchanted by her, and his heart was gone in a moment.

To his great joy he saw that one of the dwarfs had fallen behind the rest, and at once began to question him.

The dwarf told him that the lady he had just seen was the Princess Mutinosa, the daughter of the king in whose country they were at that moment. He added that the princess was very fond of hunting, and that she was now in pursuit of rabbits.

The king then asked the way to the court, and having been told it, hurried off, and reached the capital in a couple of hours.

As soon as he arrived, he presented himself to the king and queen, and on mentioning his own name and that of his country, was received with open arms. Not long after, the princess returned, and hearing that the hunt had. been very successful, the king complimented her on it, but she would not answer a word.

Her silence rather surprised him, but he was still more astonished when he found that she never spoke once all through supper-time. Sometimes she seemed about to speak, but whenever this was the case her father or mother at once took up the conversation. However, this silence did not cool the king's affection, and when he retired to his rooms at night he confided his feelings to

The King sees
Princess Mutinosa
out hunting

his faithful equerry. But the equerry was by no means delighted at his king's love affair, and took no pains to hide his disappointment.

'But why are you vexed?' asked the king. 'Surely the princess is beautiful enough to please anyone?'

'She is certainly very handsome,' replied the equerry, 'but to be really happy in love something more than beauty is required. To tell the truth, sire,' he added, 'her expression seems to me hard.'

'That is pride and dignity,' said the king, 'and nothing can be more becoming.'

'Pride or hardness, as you will,' said the equerry; 'but to my mind the choice of so many fierce creatures for her amusements seems to tell of a fierce nature, and I also think there is something suspicious in the care taken to prevent her speaking.'

The equerry's remarks were full of good sense; but as opposition is only apt to increase love in the hearts of men, and especially of kings who hate being contradicted, this king begged, the very next day, for the hand of the Princess Mutinosa. It was granted him on two conditions.

The first was that the wedding should take place the very next day; and the second, that he should not speak to the princess till she was his wife; to all of which the king agreed, in spite of his equerry's objections, so that the first word he heard his bride utter was the 'Yes' she spoke at their marriage.

Once married, however, she no longer placed any check on herself, and her ladies-in-waiting came in for plenty of rude speeches—even the king did not escape scolding; but as he was a good-tempered man, and very much in love, he bore it patiently. A few days after the wedding the newly married pair set out for their kingdom without leaving many regrets behind.

The good equerry's fears proved only too true, as the king found out to his cost. The young queen made her-

self most disagreeable to all her court, her spite and bad
temper knew no bounds, and before the end of a month
she was known far and wide as a regular vixen.

One day, when riding out, she met a poor old woman
walking along the road, who made a curtsy and was
going on, when the queen had her stopped, and cried:
' You are a very impertinent person ; don't you know
that I am the queen ? And how dare you not make me a
deeper curtsy ? '

' Madam,' said the old woman, ' I have never learnt
how to measure curtsies ; but I had no wish to fail in
proper respect.'

' What ! ' screamed the queen ; ' she dares to answer !
Tie her to my horse's tail and I'll just carry her at once
to the best dancing-master in the town to learn how to
curtsy.'

The old woman shrieked for mercy, but the queen
would not listen, and only mocked when she said she
was protected by the fairies. At last the poor old
thing submitted to be tied up, but when the queen urged
her horse on he never stirred. In vain she spurred him,
he seemed turned to bronze. At the same moment the
cord with which the old woman was tied changed into
wreaths of flowers, and she herself into a tall and stately
lady.

Looking disdainfully at the queen, she said, ' Bad
woman, unworthy of your crown ; I wished to judge for
myself whether all I heard of you was true. I have now
no doubt of it, and you shall see whether the fairies are to
be laughed at.'

So saying the fairy Placida (that was her name) blew
a little gold whistle, and a chariot appeared drawn by six
splendid ostriches. In it was seated the fairy queen,
escorted by a dozen other fairies mounted on dragons.

All having dismounted, Placida told her adventures,
and the fairy queen approved all she had done, and
proposed turning Mutinosa into bronze like her horse.

Placida, however, who was very kind and gentle, begged for a milder sentence, and at last it was settled that Mutinosa should become her slave for life unless she should have a child to take her place.

The king was told of his wife's fate and submitted to it, which, as he could do nothing to help it, was the only course open to him.

The fairies then all dispersed, Placida taking her slave with her, and on reaching her palace she said : 'You ought by rights to be scullion, but as you have been delicately brought up the change might be too great for you. I shall therefore only order you to sweep my rooms carefully, and to wash and comb my little dog.'

Mutinosa felt there was no use in disobeying, so she did as she was bid and said nothing.

After some time she gave birth to a most lovely little girl, and when she was well again the fairy gave her a good lecture on her past life, made her promise to behave better in future, and sent her back to the king, her husband.

Placida now gave herself up entirely to the little princess who was left in her charge. She anxiously thought over which of the fairies she would invite to be godmothers, so as to secure the best gift, for her adopted child.

At last she decided on two very kindly and cheerful fairies, and asked them to the christening feast. Directly it was over the baby was brought to them in a lovely crystal cradle hung with red silk curtains embroidered with gold.

The little thing smiled so sweetly at the fairies that they decided to do all they could for her. They began by naming her Graziella, and then Placida said : 'You know, dear sisters, that the commonest form of spite or punishment amongst us consists of changing beauty to ugliness, cleverness to stupidity, and oftener still to change a person's form altogether. Now, as we can only each bestow one gift, I think the best plan will be for one of you to give her beauty, the other good understanding, whilst I will undertake that she shall never be changed into any other form.'

The two godmothers quite agreed, and as soon as the little princess had received their gifts, they went home, and Placida gave herself up to the child's education. She succeeded so well with it, and little Graziella grew so lovely, that when she was still quite a child her fame was spread abroad only too much, and one day Placida was surprised by a visit from the Fairy Queen, who was attended by a very grave and severe-looking fairy.

The queen began at once : ' I have been much surprised by your behaviour to Mutinosa ; she had insulted our whole race, and deserved punishment. You might forgive your own wrongs if you chose, but not those of others. You treated her very gently whilst she was with you, and I come now to avenge our wrongs on her daughter. You have ensured her being lovely and clever, and not subject to change of form, but I shall place her in an enchanted prison, which she shall never leave till she finds herself in the arms of a lover whom she herself loves. It will be my care to prevent anything of the kind happening.'

The enchanted prison was a large high tower in the midst of the sea, built of shells of all shapes and colours. The lower floor was like a great bathroom, where the water was let in or off at will. The first floor contained the princess's apartments, beautifully furnished. On the second was a library, a large wardrobe-room filled with beautiful clothes and every kind of linen, a music-room, a pantry with bins full of the best wines, and a store-room with all manner of preserves, bonbons, pastry and cakes, all of which remained as fresh as if just out of the oven.

The top of the tower was laid out like a garden, with beds of the loveliest flowers, fine fruit trees, and shady arbours and shrubs, where many birds sang amongst the branches.

The fairies escorted Graziella and her governess, Bonnetta, to the tower, and then mounted a dolphin which was waiting for them. At a little distance from the tower the queen waved her wand and summoned two thousand great fierce sharks, whom she ordered to keep close guard, and not to let a soul enter the tower.

The good governess took such pains with Graziella's education that when she was nearly grown up she was not only most accomplished, but a very sweet, good girl.

One day, as the princess was standing on a balcony, she saw the most extraordinary figure rise out of the sea. She quickly called Bonnetta to ask her what it could be. It looked like some kind of man, with a bluish face and long sea-green hair. He was swimming towards the tower, but the sharks took no notice of him.

'It must be a merman,' said Bonnetta.

'A *man*, do you say?' cried Graziella; 'let us hurry down to the door and see him nearer.'

When they stood in the doorway the merman stopped to look at the princess and made many signs of admiration. His voice was very hoarse and husky, but when he found that he was not understood he took to signs. He carried a little basket made of osiers and filled with rare shells, which he presented to the princess.

She took it with signs of thanks; but as it was getting dusk she retired, and the merman plunged back into the sea.

When they were alone, Graziella said to her governess: 'What a dreadful-looking creature that was! Why do those odious sharks let him come near the tower? I suppose all men are not like him?'

'No, indeed,' replied Bonnetta. 'I suppose the sharks look on him as a sort of relation, and so did not attack him.'

A few days later the two ladies heard a strange sort

of music, and looking out of the window, there was the merman, his head crowned with water plants, and blowing a great sea-shell with all his might.

They went down to the tower door, and Graziella politely accepted some coral and other marine curiosities he had brought her. After this he used to come every evening, and blow his shell, or dive and play antics under the princess's window. She contented herself with bowing to him from the balcony, but she would not go down to the door in spite of all his signs.

Some days later he came with a person of his own kind, but of another sex. Her hair was dressed with great taste, and she had a lovely voice. This new arrival induced the ladies to go down to the door. They were surprised to find that, after trying various languages, she at last spoke to them in their own, and paid Graziella a very pretty compliment on her beauty.

The mermaid noticed that the lower floor was full of water. ' Why,' cried she, ' that is just the place for us, for we can't live quite out of water.' So saying, she and her brother swam in and took up a position in the bathroom, the princess and her governess seating themselves on the steps which ran round the room.

' No doubt, madam,' said the mermaid, ' you have given up living on land so as to escape from crowds of lovers ; but I fear that even here you cannot avoid them, for my brother is already dying of love for you, and I am sure that once you are seen in our city he will have many rivals.'

She then went on to explain how grieved her brother was not to be able to make himself understood, adding : ' I interpret for him, having been taught several languages by a fairy.'

' Oh, then, you have fairies, too ? ' asked Graziella, with a sigh.

' Yes, we have,' replied the mermaid ; ' but if I am not mistaken you have suffered from the fairies on earth.'

The princess, on this, told her entire history to the mermaid, who assured her how sorry she felt for her, but begged her not to lose courage; adding, as she took her

The Sea-People visit Graziella

leave: 'Perhaps, some day, you may find a way out of your difficulties.'

The princess was delighted with this visit and with the hopes the mermaid held out. It was something to meet some one fresh to talk to.

'We will make acquaintance with several of these

people,' she said to her governess, ' and I dare say they
are not all as hideous as the first one we saw.   Anyhow,
we shan't be so dreadfully lonely.'

' Dear me,' said Bonnetta, ' how hopeful young people
are to be sure !   As for me I feel afraid of these folk.
But what do you think of the lover you have
captivated ? '

' Oh, I could never love him,' cried the princess ; ' I
can't bear him.   But, perhaps, as his sister says they
are related to the fairy Marina, they may be of some use
to us.'

The mermaid often returned, and each time she
talked of her brother's love, and each time Graziella
talked of her longing to escape from her prison, till at
length the mermaid promised to bring the fairy Marina
to see her, in hopes she might suggest something.

Next day the fairy came with the mermaid, and the
princess received her with delight.   After a little talk she
begged Graziella to show her the inside of the tower and
let her see the garden on the top, for with the help of
crutches she could manage to move about, and being a
fairy could live out of water for a long time, provided she
wetted her forehead now and then.

Graziella gladly consented, and Bonnetta stayed below
with the mermaid.

When they were in the garden the fairy said : ' Let us
lose no time, but tell me how I can be of use to you.'
Graziella then told all her story and Marina replied :
' My dear princess, I can do nothing for you as regards
dry land, for my power does not reach beyond my own
element.   I can only say that if you will honour my
cousin by accepting his hand, you could then come and
live amongst us.   I could teach you in a moment to swim
and dive with the best of us.   I can harden your skin
without spoiling its colour.   My cousin is one of the
best matches in the sea, and I will bestow so many gifts
on him that you will be quite happy.'

The fairy talked so well and so long that the princess was rather impressed, and promised to think the matter over.

Just as they were going to leave the garden they saw a ship sailing nearer the tower than any other had done before. On the deck lay a young man under a splendid awning, gazing at the tower through a spy-glass; but before they could see anything clearly the ship moved away, and the two ladies parted, the fairy promising to return shortly.

As soon as she was gone Graziella told her governess what she had said. Bonnetta was not at all pleased at the turn matters were taking, for she did not fancy being turned into a mermaid in her old age. She thought the matter well over, and this was what she did. She was a very clever artist, and next morning she began to paint a picture of a handsome young man, with beautiful curly hair, a fine complexion, and lovely blue eyes. When it was finished she showed it to Graziella, hoping it would show her the difference there was between a fine young man and her marine suitor.

The princess was much struck by the picture, and asked anxiously whether there could be any man so good-looking in the world. Bonnetta assured her that there were plenty of them; indeed, many far handsomer.

'I can hardly believe that,' cried the princess; 'but, alas! if there are, I don't suppose I shall ever see them or they me, so what is the use? Oh, dear, how unhappy I am!'

She spent the rest of the day gazing at the picture, which certainly had the effect of spoiling all the merman's hopes or prospects.

After some days, the fairy Marina came back to hear what was decided; but Graziella hardly paid any attention to her, and showed such dislike to the idea of the proposed marriage that the fairy went off in a regular huff.

Without knowing it, the princess had made another

conquest. On board the ship which had sailed so near was the handsomest prince in the world. He had heard of the enchanted tower, and determined to get as near it as he could. He had strong glasses on board, and whilst looking through them he saw the princess quite clearly, and fell desperately in love with her at once. He wanted to steer straight for the tower and to row off to it in a small boat, but his entire crew fell at his feet and begged him not to run such a risk. The captain, too, urged him not to attempt it. 'You will only lead us all to certain death,' he said. 'Pray anchor nearer land, and I will then seek a kind fairy I know, who has always been most obliging to me, and who will, I am sure, try to help your Highness.'

The prince rather unwillingly listened to reason. He landed at the nearest point, and sent off the captain in all haste to beg the fairy's advice and help. Meantime he had a tent pitched on the shore, and spent all his time gazing at the tower and looking for the princess through his spyglass.

After a few days the captain came back, bringing the fairy with him. The prince was delighted to see her, and paid her great attention. 'I have heard about this matter,' she said; 'and, to lose no time, I am going to send off a trusty pigeon to test the enchantment. If there is any weak spot he is sure to find it out and get in. I shall bid him bring a flower back as a sign of success, and if he does so I quite hope to get you in too.'

'But,' asked the prince, 'could I not send a line by the pigeon to tell the princess of my love?'

'Certainly,' replied the fairy, 'it would be a very good plan.'

So the prince wrote as follows :—

'Lovely Princess,—I adore you, and beg you to accept my heart, and to believe there is nothing I will not do to end your misfortunes.—BLONDEL.'

This note was tied round the pigeon's neck, and he

flew off with it at once. He flew fast till he got near the
tower, when a fierce wind blew so hard against him that he
could not get on. But he was not to be beaten, but flew
carefully round the top of the tower till he came to one
spot which, by some mistake, had not been enchanted like
the rest. He quickly slipped into the arbour and waited
for the princess.

Before long Graziella appeared alone, and the pigeon
at once fluttered to meet her, and seemed so tame that
she stopped to caress the pretty creature. As she did so
she saw it had a pink ribbon round its neck, and tied to
the ribbon was a letter. She read it over several times
and then wrote this answer :—

'You say you love me ; but I cannot promise to love
you without seeing you. Send me your portrait by this
faithful messenger. If I return it to you, you must give
up hope ; but if I keep it you will know that to help me
will be to help yourself.—GRAZIELLA.'

Before flying back the pigeon remembered about the
flower, so, seeing one in the princess's dress, he stole it
and flew away.

The prince was wild with joy at the pigeon's return
with the note. After an hour's rest the trusty little bird
was sent back again, carrying a miniature of the prince,
which by good luck he had with him.

On reaching the tower the pigeon found the princess
in the garden. She hastened to untie the ribbon, and on
opening the miniature case what was her surprise and
delight to find it very like the picture her governess had
painted for her. She hastened to send the pigeon back,
and you can fancy the prince's joy when he found she
had kept his portrait.

'Now,' said the fairy, 'let us lose no more time. I
can only make you happy by changing you into a bird,
but I will take care to give you back your proper shape
at the right time.'

The prince was eager to start, so the fairy, touching

him with her wand, turned him into the loveliest hum-
ming-bird you ever saw, at the same time letting him
keep the power of speech. The pigeon was told to show
him the way.

Graziella was much surprised to see a perfectly
strange bird, and still more so when it flew to her saying,
'Good-morning, sweet princess.'

She was delighted with the pretty creature, and let
him perch on her finger, when he said, 'Kiss, kiss, little
birdie,' which she gladly did, petting and stroking him at
the same time.

After a time the princess, who had been up very early,
grew tired, and as the sun was hot she went to lie down
on a mossy bank in the shade of the arbour. She held
the pretty bird near her breast, and was just falling
asleep, when the fairy contrived to restore the prince to
his own shape, so that as Graziella opened her eyes she
found herself in the arms of a lover whom she loved in
return!

At the same moment her enchantment came to an
end. The tower began to rock and to split. Bonnetta
hurried up to the top so that she might at least perish
with her dear princess. Just as she reached the garden,
the kind fairy who had helped the prince arrived with
the fairy Placida, in a car of Venetian glass drawn by six
eagles.

'Come away quickly,' they cried, 'the tower is about
to sink!' The prince, princess, and Bonnetta lost no
time in stepping into the car, which rose in the air
just as, with a terrible crash, the tower sank into
the depths of the sea, for the fairy Marina and the
mermen had destroyed its foundations to avenge themselves on Graziella. Luckily their wicked plans were
defeated, and the good fairies took their way to the
kingdom of Graziella's parents.

They found that Queen Mutinosa had died some
years ago, but her kind husband lived on peaceably,

The Fairy-Car Arrives.

ruling his country well and happily. He received his daughter with great delight, and there were universal rejoicings at the return of the lovely princess.

The wedding took place the very next day, and, for many days after, balls, dinners, tournaments, concerts and all sorts of amusements went on all day and all night.

All the fairies were carefully invited, and they came in great state, and promised the young couple their protection and all sorts of good gifts. Prince Blondel and Princess Graziella lived to a good old age, beloved by every one, and loving each other more and more as time went on.

THE STORY OF
DSCHEMIL AND DSCHEMILA

THERE was once a man whose name was Dschemil, and he had a cousin who was called Dschemila. They had been betrothed by their parents when they were children, and now Dschemil thought that the time had come for them to be married, and he went two or three days' journey, to the nearest big town, to buy furniture for the new house.

While he was away, Dschemila and her friends set off to the neighbouring woods to pick up sticks, and as she gathered them she found an iron mortar lying on the ground. She placed it on her bundle of sticks, but the mortar would not stay still, and whenever she raised the bundle to put it on her shoulders it slipped off sideways. At length she saw the only way to carry the mortar was to tie it in the very middle of her bundle, and had just unfastened her sticks, when she heard her companions' voices.

'Dschemila, what are you doing? it is almost dark, and if you mean to come with us you must be quick!'

But Dschemila only replied, 'You had better go back without me, for I am not going to leave my mortar behind, if I stay here till midnight.'

'Do as you like,' said the girls, and started on their walk home.

The night soon fell, and at the last ray of light the mortar suddenly became an ogre, who threw Dschemila on his back, and carried her off into a desert place, distant a whole month's journey from her native town. Here he shut her into a castle, and told her not to fear, as her life was safe. Then he went back to his wife, leaving Dschemila weeping over the fate that she had brought upon herself.

Meanwhile the other girls had reached home, and Dschemila's mother came out to look for her daughter.

'What have you done with her?' she asked anxiously.

'We had to leave her in the wood,' they replied, 'for she had picked up an iron mortar, and could not manage to carry it.'

So the old woman set off at once for the forest, calling to her daughter as she hurried along.

'Do go home,' cried the townspeople, as they heard her; 'we will go and look for your daughter; you are only a woman, and it is a task that needs strong men.'

But she answered, 'Yes, go; but I will go with you! Perhaps it will be only her corpse that we shall find after all. She has most likely been stung by asps, or eaten by wild beasts.'

The men, seeing her heart was bent on it, said no more, but told one of the girls she must come with them, and show them the place where they had left Dschemila. They found the bundle of wood lying where she had dropped it, but the maiden was nowhere to be seen.

'Dschemila! Dschemila!' cried they; but nobody answered.

'If we make a fire, perhaps she will see it,' said one of the men. And they lit a fire, and then went, one this way, and one that, through the forest, to look for her, whispering to each other that if she had been killed by a lion they would be sure to find some trace of it; or if she had fallen asleep, the sound of their voices would wake her; or if a snake had bitten her, they would at least come on her corpse.

All night they searched, and when morning broke and

they knew no more than before what had become of the maiden, they grew weary, and said to the mother:

'It is no use. Let us go home, nothing has happened to your daughter, except that she has run away with a man.'

'Yes, I will come,' answered she, 'but I must first look in the river. Perhaps some one has thrown her in there.' But the maiden was not in the river.

For four days the father and mother waited and watched for their child to come back; then they gave up hope, and said to each other: 'What is to be done? What are we to say to the man to whom Dschemila is betrothed? Let us kill a goat, and bury its head in the grave, and when the man returns we must tell him Dschemila is dead.'

Very soon the bridegroom came back, bringing with him carpets and soft cushions for the house of his bride. And as he entered the town Dschemila's father met him, saying, 'Greeting to you. She is dead.'

At these words the young man broke into loud cries, and it was some time before he could speak. Then he turned to one of the crowd who had gathered round him, and asked: 'Where have they buried her?'

'Come to the churchyard with me,' answered he; and the young man went with him, carrying with him some of the beautiful things he had brought. These he laid on the grass and then began to weep afresh. All day he stayed, and at nightfall he gathered up his stuffs and carried them to his own house. But when the day dawned he took them in his arms and returned to the grave, where he remained as long as it was light, playing softly on his flute. And this he did daily for six months.

One morning, a man who was wandering through the desert, having lost his way, came upon a lonely castle. The sun was very hot, and the man was very tired, so he said to himself, 'I will rest a little in the shadow of this castle.' He stretched himself out comfortably, and was almost asleep, when he heard a voice calling to him softly :

'Are you a ghost,' it said, ' or a man ? '

He looked up, and saw a girl leaning out of a window, and he answered :

'I am a man, and a better one, too, than your father or your grandfather.'

' May all good luck be with you,' said she ; ' but what has brought you into this land of ogres and horrors ? '

' Does an ogre really live in this castle ? ' asked he.

' Certainly he does,' replied the girl, ' and as night is not far off he will be here soon. So, dear friend, depart quickly, lest he return and snap you up for supper.'

' But I am so thirsty ! ' said the man. ' Be kind, and give me some drink, or else I shall die ! Surely, even in this desert there must be some spring ? '

'Well, I have noticed that whenever the ogre brings back water he always comes from that side ; so if you follow the same direction perhaps you may find some.'

The man jumped up at once and was about to start, when the maiden spoke again :

' Tell me, where are you going ? '

' Why do you want to know ? '

' I have an errand for you ; but tell me first whether you go east or west.'

' I travel to Damascus.'

' Then do this for me. As you pass through our village, ask for a man called Dschemil, and say to him : " Dschemila greets you, from the castle, which lies far away, and is rocked by the wind. In my grave lies only a goat. So take heart." '

And the man promised, and went his way, till he came to a spring of water. And he drank a great draught and then lay on the bank and slept quietly. When he woke he said to himself, ' The maiden did a good deed when she told me where to find water. A few hours

more, and I should have been dead. So I will do her
bidding, and seek out her native town and the man for
whom the message was given.'

For a whole month he travelled, till at last he reached
the town where Dschemil dwelt, and as luck would have
it, there was the young man sitting before his door with
his beard unshaven and his shaggy hair hanging over his
eyes.

'Welcome, stranger,' said Dschemil, as the man
stopped. 'Where have you come from?'

'I come from the west, and go towards the east,' he
answered.

'Well, stop with us awhile, and rest and eat!' said
Dschemil. And the man entered; and food was set before
him, and he sat down with the father of the maiden and
her brothers, and Dschemil. Only Dschemil himself was
absent, squatting on the threshold.

'Why do you not eat too?' asked the stranger. But
one of the young men whispered hastily:

'Leave him alone. Take no notice! It is only at
night that he ever eats.'

So the stranger went on silently with his food.
Suddenly one of Dschemil's brothers called out and said:
'Dschemil, bring us some water!' And the stranger
remembered his message and said:

'Is there a man here named "Dschemil"? I lost
my way in the desert, and came to a castle, and a maiden
looked out of the window and——'

'Be quiet,' they cried, fearing that Dschemil might
hear. But Dschemil had heard, and came forward and
said:

'What did you see? Tell me truly, or I will cut off
your head this instant!'

'My lord,' replied the stranger, 'as I was wandering,
hot and tired, through the desert, I saw near me a great
castle, and I said aloud, "I will rest a little in its
shadow." And a maiden looked out of a window and

said, " Are you a ghost or a man ? " And I answered, " I
am a man, and a better one, too, than your father or your
grandfather." And I was thirsty and asked for water, but
she had none to give me, and I felt like to die. Then she
told me that the ogre, in whose castle she dwelt, brought
in water always from the same side, and that if I too went
that way most likely I should come to it. But before I
started she begged me to go to her native town, and if I
met a man called Dschemil I was to say to him, " Dschemila greets you, from the castle which lies far away, and
is rocked by the wind. In my grave lies only a goat. So
take heart." '

Then Dschemil turned to his family and said :
' Is this true ? and is Dschemila not dead at all, but
simply stolen from her home ? '

' No, no,' replied they, ' his story is a pack of lies.
Dschemila is really dead. Everybody knows it.'

' That I shall see for myself,' said Dschemil, and,
snatching up a spade, hastened off to the grave where the
goat's head lay buried.

And they answered, ' Then hear what really happened..
When you were away, she went with the other maidens
to the forest to gather wood. And there she found an
iron mortar, which she wished to bring home ; but she
could not carry it, neither would she leave it. So the
maidens returned without her, and as night was come, we
all set out to look for her, but found nothing. And we
said, " The bridegroom will be here to-morrow, and when
he learns that she is lost, he will set out to seek her, and
we shall lose him too. Let us kill a goat, and bury it in
her grave, and tell him she is dead." Now you know, so
do as you will. Only, if you go to seek her, take with you
this man with whom she has spoken that he may show
you the way.'

' Yes ; that is the best plan,' replied Dschemil ; ' so give
me food, and hand me my sword, and we will set out
directly.'

But the stranger answered: 'I am not going to waste a whole month in leading you to the castle! If it were only a day or two's journey I would not mind; but a month—no!'

'Come with me then for three days,' said Dschemil, 'and put me in the right road, and I will reward you richly.'

'Very well,' replied the stranger, 'so let it be.'

For three days they travelled from sunrise to sunset, then the stranger said: 'Dschemil?'

'Yes,' replied he.

'Go straight on till you reach a spring, then go on a little farther, and soon you will see the castle standing before you.'

'So I will,' said Dschemil.

'Farewell, then,' said the stranger, and turned back the way he had come.

It was six and twenty days before Dschemil caught sight of a green spot rising out of the sandy desert, and knew that the spring was near at last. He hastened his steps, and soon was kneeling by its side, drinking thirstily of the bubbling water. Then he lay down on the cool grass, and began to think. 'If the man was right, the castle must be somewhere about. I had better sleep here to-night, and to-morrow I shall be able to see where it is.' So he slept long and peacefully. When he awoke the sun was high, and he jumped up and washed his face and hands in the spring, before going on his journey. He had not walked far, when the castle suddenly appeared before him, though a moment before not a trace of it could be seen. 'How am I to get in?' he thought. 'I dare not knock, lest the ogre should hear me. Perhaps it would be best for me to climb up the wall, and wait to see what will happen. So he did, and after sitting on the top for about an hour, a window above him opened, and a voice said: 'Dschemil!' He looked up, and at the sight of Dschemila, whom he had so long believed to be dead, he began to weep.

'Dear cousin,' she whispered, 'what has brought you here?'

'My grief at losing you.'

'Oh! go away at once. If the ogre comes back he will kill you.'

'I swear by your head, queen of my heart, that I have not found you only to lose you again! If I must die, well, I must!'

'Oh, what can I do for you?'

'Anything you like!'

'If I let you down a cord, can you make it fast under your arms, and climb up?'

'Of course I can,' said he.

So Dschemila lowered the cord, and Dschemil tied it round him, and climbed up to her window. Then they embraced each other tenderly, and burst into tears of joy.

'But what shall I do when the ogre returns?' asked she.

'Trust to me,' he said.

Now there was a chest in the room, where Dschemila kept her clothes. And she made Dschemil get into it, and lie at the bottom, and told him to keep very still.

He was only hidden just in time, for the lid was hardly closed when the ogre's heavy tread was heard on the stairs. He flung open the door, bringing men's flesh for himself and lamb's flesh for the maiden. 'I smell the smell of a man!' he thundered. 'What is he doing here?'

'How could any one have come to this desert place?' asked the girl, and burst into tears.

'Do not cry,' said the ogre; 'perhaps a raven has dropped some scraps from his claws.'

'Ah, yes, I was forgetting,' answered she. 'One did drop some bones about.'

'Well, burn them to powder,' replied the ogre, 'so that I may swallow it.'

So the maiden took some bones and burned them, and gave them to the ogre, saying, 'Here is the powder, swallow it.'

And when he had swallowed the powder the ogre stretched himself out and went to sleep.

In a little while the man's flesh, which the maiden was cooking for the ogre's supper, called out and said:

> 'Hist! Hist!
> A man lies in the kist!'

And the lamb's flesh answered:

> 'He is your brother,
> And cousin of the other.'

The ogre moved sleepily, and asked, 'What did the meat say, Dschemila?'

'Only that I must be sure to add salt.'

'Well, add salt.'

'Yes, I have done so,' said she.

The ogre was soon sound asleep again, when the man's flesh called out a second time:

> 'Hist! Hist!
> A man lies in the kist!'

And the lamb's flesh answered:

> 'He is your brother,
> And cousin of the other.'

'What did it say, Dschemila?' asked the ogre.

'Only that I must add pepper.'

'Well, add pepper.'

'Yes, I have done so,' said she.

The ogre had had a long day's hunting, and could not keep himself awake. In a moment his eyes were tight shut, and then the man's flesh called out for the third time:

> 'Hist! Hist!
> A man lies in the kist.'

DSCHEMILA·OUTWITS·THE·OGRE

And the lamb's flesh answered :

> ' He is your brother,
> And cousin of the other.'

' What did it say, Dschemila ? ' asked the ogre.

' Only that it was ready, and that I had better take it off the fire.'

' Then if it is ready, bring it to me, and I will eat it.'

So she brought it to him, and while he was eating she supped off the lamb's flesh herself, and managed to put some aside for her cousin.

When the ogre had finished, and had washed his hands, he said to Dschemila : ' Make my bed, for I am tired.'

So she made his bed, and put a nice soft pillow for his head, and tucked him up.

' Father,' she said suddenly.

' Well, what is it ? '

' Dear father, if you are really asleep, why are your eyes always open ? '

' Why do you ask that, Dschemila ? Do you want to deal treacherously with me ? '

' No, of course not, father. How could I, and what would be the use of it ? '

' Well, why do you want to know ? '

' Because last night I woke up and saw the whole place shining in a red light, which frightened me.'

' That happens when I am fast asleep.'

' And what is the good of the pin you always keep here so carefully ? '

' If I throw that pin in front of me, it turns into an iron mountain.'

' And this darning needle ? '

' That becomes a sea.'

' And this hatchet ? '

' That becomes a thorn hedge, which no one can pass

through. But why do you ask all these questions? I am
sure you have something in your head.'

'Oh, I just wanted to know; and how could anyone
find me out here?' and she began to cry.

'Oh, don't cry, I was only in fun,' said the ogre.

He was soon asleep again, and a yellow light shone
through the castle.

'Come quick!' called Dschemil from the chest; 'we
must fly now while the ogre is asleep.'

'Not yet,' she said, 'there is a yellow light shining.
I don't think he is asleep.'

So they waited for an hour. Then Dschemil whispered
again: 'Wake up! There is no time to lose!'

'Let me see if he is asleep,' said she, and she peeped
in, and saw a red light shining. Then she stole back to
her cousin, and asked, 'But how are we to get out?'

'Get the rope, and I will let you down.'

So she fetched the rope, the hatchet, and the pin
and the needles, and said, 'Take them, and put them
in the pocket of your cloak, and be sure not to lose
them.'

Dschemil put them carefully in his pocket, and tied
the rope round her, and let her down over the wall.

'Are you safe?' he asked.

'Yes, quite.'

'Then untie the rope, so that I may draw it up.

And Dschemila did as she was told, and in a few
minutes he stood beside her.

Now all this time the ogre was asleep, and had heard
nothing. Then his dog came to him and said, 'O, sleeper,
are you having pleasant dreams? Dschemila has for-
saken you and run away.'

The ogre got out of bed, gave the dog a kick, then
went back again, and slept till morning.

When it grew light, he rose, and called, 'Dschemila!
Dschemila!' but he only heard the echo of his own voice!
Then he dressed himself quickly; buckled on his sword

and whistled to his dog, and followed the road which he
knew the fugitives must have taken.

'Cousin,' said Dschemila suddenly, and turning round
as she spoke.

DSCHEMILA GETS AN ASS'S HEAD

'What is it?' answered he.
'The ogre is coming after us. I saw him.'
'But where is he? I don't see him.'
'Over there. He only looks about as tall as a needle.'
Then they both began to run as fast as they could,

while the ogre and his dog kept drawing always nearer.
A few more steps, and he would have been by their side,
when Dschemila threw the darning needle behind her.
In a moment it became an iron mountain between them
and their enemy.

'We will break it down, my dog and I,' cried the ogre
in a rage, and they dashed at the mountain till they had
forced a path through, and came ever nearer and nearer.

'Cousin!' said Dschemila suddenly.

'What is it?'

'The ogre is coming after us with his dog.'

'You go on in front then,' answered he; and they
both ran on as fast as they could, while the ogre and the
dog drew always nearer and nearer.

'They are close upon us!' cried the maiden, glancing
behind, 'you must throw the pin.'

So Dschemil took the pin from his cloak and threw it
behind him, and a dense thicket of thorns sprang up
round them, which the ogre and his dog could not pass
through.

'I will get through it somehow, if I burrow underground,' cried he, and very soon he and the dog were on
the other side.

'Cousin,' said Dschemila, 'they are close to us
now.'

'Go on in front, and fear nothing,' replied Dschemil.

So she ran on a little way, and then stopped.

'He is only a few yards away now,' she said, and
Dschemil flung the hatchet on the ground, and it turned
into a lake.

'I will drink, and my dog shall drink, till it is dry,'
shrieked the ogre, and the dog drank so much that it
burst and died. But the ogre did not stop for that, and
soon the whole lake was nearly dry. Then he exclaimed,
'Dschemila, let your head become a donkey's head, and
your hair fur!'

But when it was done, Dschemil looked at her in

horror, and said, ' She is really a donkey, and not a woman at all ! '

And he left her, and went home.

For two days poor Dschemila wandered about alone, weeping bitterly. When her cousin drew near his native town, he began to think over his conduct, and to feel ashamed of himself.

' Perhaps by this time she has changed back to her proper shape,' he said to himself, ' I will go and see ! '

So he made all the haste he could, and at last he saw her seated on a rock, trying to keep off the wolves, who longed to have her for dinner. He drove them off and said, ' Get up, dear cousin, you have had a narrow escape.'

Dschemila stood up and answered, ' Bravo, my friend. You persuaded me to fly with you, and then left me helplessly to my fate.'

' Shall I tell you the truth ? ' asked he.

' Tell it.'

' I thought you were a witch, and I was afraid of you.'

' Did you not see me before my transformation ? and did you not watch it happen under your very eyes, when the ogre bewitched me ? '

' What shall I do ? ' said Dschemil. ' If I take you into the town, everyone will laugh, and say, "Is that a new kind of toy you have got ?   It has hands like a woman, feet like a woman, the body of a woman ; but its head is the head of an ass, and its hair is fur." '

' Well, what do you mean to do with me ? ' asked Dschemila. ' Better take me home to my mother by night, and tell no one anything about it.'

' So I will,' said he.

They waited where they were till it was nearly dark, then Dschemil brought his cousin home.

' Is that Dschemil ? ' asked the mother when he knocked softly.

'Yes, it is.'

'And have you found her?

'Yes, and I have brought her to you.'

'Oh, where is she? let me see her!' cried the mother.

'Here, behind me,' answered Dschemil.

But when the poor woman caught sight of her daughter, she shrieked, and exclaimed, 'Are you making fun of me? When did I ever give birth to an ass?'

'Hush!' said Dschemil, 'it is not necessary to let the whole world know! And if you look at her body, you will see two scars on it.'

'Mother,' sobbed Dschemila, 'do you really not know your own daughter?'

'Yes, of course I know her.'

'What are her two scars then?'

'On her thigh is a scar from the bite of a dog, and on her breast is the mark of a burn, where she pulled a lamp over her when she was little.'

'Then look at me, and see if I am not your daughter,' said Dschemila, throwing off her clothes and showing her two scars.

And at the sight her mother embraced her, weeping.

'Dear daughter,' she cried, 'what evil fate has befallen you?'

'It was the ogre who carried me off first, and then bewitched me,' answered Dschemila.

'But what is to be done with you?' asked her mother.

'Hide me away, and tell no one anything about me. And you, dear cousin, say nothing to the neighbours, and if they should put questions, you can make answer that I have not yet been found.'

'So I will,' replied he.

Then he and her mother took her upstairs and hid her in a cupboard, where she stayed for a whole month, only going out to walk when all the world was asleep.

Meanwhile Dschemil had returned to his own home,

where his father and mother, his brothers and neighbours, greeted him joyfully.

'When did you come back?' said they, 'and have you found Dschemila?'

'No, I searched the whole world after her, and could hear nothing of her.'

'Did you part company with the man who started with you?'

'Yes; after three days he got so weak and useless he could not go on. It must be a month by now since he reached home again. I went on and visited every castle, and looked in every house. But there were no signs of her; and so I gave it up.'

And they answered him: 'We told you before that it was no good. An ogre or an ogress must have snapped her up, and how can you expect to find her?'

'I loved her too much to be still,' he said.

But his friends did not understand, and soon they spoke to him again about it.

'We will seek for a wife for you. There are plenty of girls prettier than Dschemila.'

'I dare say; but I don't want them.'

'But what will you do with all the cushions and carpets, and beautiful things you bought for your house?'

'They can stay in the chests.'

'But the moths will eat them! For a few weeks, it is of no consequence, but after a year or two they will be quite useless.'

'And if they have to lie there ten years I will have Dschemila, and her only, for my wife. For a month, or even two months, I will rest here quietly. Then I will go and seek her afresh.'

'Oh, you are quite mad! Is she the only maiden in the world? There are plenty of others better worth having than she is.'

'If there are I have not seen them! And why do

you make all this fuss ? Every man knows his own
business best.

'Why, it is you who are making all the fuss yourself——'

But Dschemil turned and went into the house, for he
did not want to quarrel.

Three months later a Jew, who was travelling across
the desert, came to the castle, and laid himself down
under the wall to rest.

In the evening the ogre saw him there and said to
him, 'Jew, what are you doing here ? Have you anything
to sell ? '

'I have only some clothes,' answered the Jew, who
was in mortal terror of the ogre.

'Oh, don't be afraid of me,' said the ogre, laughing.
'I shall not eat you. Indeed, I mean to go a bit of the
way with you myself.'

'I am ready, gracious sir,' replied the Jew, rising to his
feet.

'Well, go straight on till you reach a town, and in
that town you will find a maiden called Dschemila and a
young man called Dschemil. Take this mirror and this
comb with you, and say to Dschemila, " Your father, the
ogre, greets you, and begs you to look at your face in this
mirror, and it will appear as it was before, and to comb
your hair with this comb, and it will be as formerly." If
you do not carry out my orders, I will eat you the next
time we meet.'

'Oh, I will obey you punctually,' cried the Jew.

After thirty days the Jew entered the gate of the town,
and sat down in the first street he came to, hungry, thirsty,
and very tired.

Quite by chance, Dschemil happened to pass by, and
seeing a man sitting there, full in the glare of the sun, he
stopped, and said, 'Get up at once, Jew ; you will have a
sunstroke if you sit in such a place.'

DSCHEMILA GETS RID OF THE ASS'S HEAD

'Ah, good sir,' replied the Jew, 'for a whole month I have been travelling, and I am too tired to move.'

'Which way did you come?' asked Dschemil.

'From out there,' answered the Jew pointing behind him.

'And you have been travelling for a month, you say? Well, did you see anything remarkable?'

'Yes, good sir; I saw a castle, and lay down to rest under its shadow. And an ogre woke me, and told me to come to this town, where I should find a young man called Dschemil, and a girl called Dschemila.'

'My name is Dschemil. What does the ogre want with me?'

'He gave me some presents for Dschemila. How can I see her?'

'Come with me, and you shall give them into her own hands.'

So the two went together to the house of Dschemil's uncle, and Dschemil led the Jew into his aunt's room.

'Aunt!' he cried, 'this Jew who is with me has come from the ogre, and has brought with him, as presents, a mirror and a comb which the ogre has sent her.'

'But it may be only some wicked trick on the part of the ogre,' said she.

'Oh, I don't think so,' answered the young man, 'give her the things.'

Then the maiden was called, and she came out of her hiding place, and went up to the Jew, saying, 'Where have you come from, Jew?'

'From your father the ogre.'

'And what errand did he send you on?'

'He told me I was to give you this mirror and this comb, and to say "Look in this mirror, and comb your hair with this comb, and both will become as they were formerly."'

And Dschemila took the mirror and looked into it,

and combed her hair with the comb, and she had no longer an ass's head, but the face of a beautiful maiden.

Great was the joy of both mother and cousin at this wonderful sight, and the news that Dschemila had returned soon spread, and the neighbours came flocking in with greetings.

' When did you come back? '

' My cousin brought me.'

' Why, he told us he could not find you! '

' Oh, I did that on purpose,' answered Dschemil. ' I did not want everyone to know.'

Then he turned to his father and his mother, his brothers and his sisters-in-law, and said, ' We must set to work at once, for the wedding will be to-day.'

A beautiful litter was prepared to carry the bride to her new home, but she shrank back, saying, ' I am afraid, lest the ogre should carry me off again.'

' How can the ogre get at you when we are all here? ' they said. ' There are two thousand of us all told, and every man has his sword.'

' He will manage it somehow,' answered Dschemila, ' he is a powerful king! '

' She is right,' said an old man. ' Take away the litter, and let her go on foot if she is afraid.'

' But it is absurd! ' exclaimed the rest; ' how can the ogre get hold of her? '

' I will not go,' said Dschemila again. ' You do not know that monster; I do.'

And while they were disputing the bridegroom arrived.

' Let her alone. She shall stay in her father's house. After all, I can live here, and the wedding feast shall be made ready.'

And so they were married at last, and died without having had a single quarrel.

[Märchen und Gedichte aus der Stadt Tripolis.]

JANNI AND THE DRAKEN

ONCE there was a man who shunned the world, and lived in the wilderness. He owned nothing but a flock of sheep, whose milk and wool he sold, and so procured himself bread to eat; he also carried wooden spoons, and sold them. He had a wife and one little girl, and after a long time his wife had another child. The evening it was born the man went to the nearest village to fetch a nurse, and on the way he met a monk who begged him for a night's lodging. This the man willingly granted, and took him home with him. There being no one far nor near to baptize the child, the man asked the monk to do him this service, and the child was given the name of Janni.

In the course of time Janni's parents died, and he and his sister were left alone in the world ; soon affairs went badly with them, so they determined to wander away to seek their fortune. In packing up, the sister found a knife which the monk had left for his godson, and this she gave to her brother.

Then they went on their way, taking with them the three sheep which were all that remained of their flocks. After wandering for three days they met a man with three dogs who proposed that they should exchange animals, he taking the sheep, and they the dogs. The brother and sister were quite pleased at this arrangement, and after the exchange was made they separated, and went their different ways.

Janni and his sister in course of time came to a great castle, in which dwelt forty Draken, who, when they heard that Janni had come, fled forty fathoms underground.

So Janni found the castle deserted, and abode there with his sister, and every day went out to hunt with the weapons the Draken had left in the castle.

One day, when he was away hunting, one of the Draken came up to get provisions, not knowing that there was anyone in the castle. When he saw Janni's sister he was terrified, but she told him not to be afraid, and by-and-by they fell in love with each other, for every time that Janni went to hunt the sister called the Drakos up. Thus they went on making love to each other till at length, unknown to Janni, they got married. Then, when it was too late, the sister repented, and was afraid of Janni's wrath when he found it out.

One day the Drakos came to her, and said : 'You must pretend to be ill, and when Janni asks what ails you, and what you want, you must answer : " Cherries," and when he inquires where these are to be found, you must say : " There are some in a garden a day's journey from here." Then your brother will go there, and will never come back, for there dwell three of my brothers who will look after him well.'

Then the sister did as the Drakos advised, and next day Janni set out to fetch the cherries, taking his three dogs with him. When he came to the garden where the cherries grew he jumped off his horse, drank some water from the spring, which rose there, and fell directly into a deep sleep. The Draken came round about to eat him, but the dogs flung themselves on them and tore them in pieces, and scratched a grave in the ground with their paws, and buried the Draken so that Janni might not see their dead bodies. When Janni awoke, and saw his dogs all covered with blood, he believed that they had caught, somewhere, a wild beast, and was angry because they had left none of it for him. But he plucked the cherries, and took them back to his sister.

When the Drakos heard that Janni had come back, he fled for fear forty fathoms underground. And the sister ate the cherries and declared herself well again.

The next day, when Janni was gone to hunt, the Drakos came out, and advised the sister that she should pretend to be ill again, and when her brother asked her what she would like, she should answer 'Quinces,' and when he inquired where these were to be found, she should say : ' In a garden distant about two days' journey.' Then would Janni certainly be destroyed, for there dwelt six brothers of the Drakos, each of whom had two heads.

The sister did as she was advised, and next day Janni again set off, taking his three dogs with him. When he came to the garden he dismounted, sat down to rest a little, and fell fast asleep. First there came three Draken round about to eat him, and when these three had been worried by the dogs, there came three others who were worried in like manner. Then the dogs again dug a grave and buried the dead Draken, that their master might not see them. When Janni awoke and beheld the dogs all covered with blood, he thought, as before, that they had killed a wild beast, and was again angry with them for leaving him nothing. But he took the quinces and brought them back to his sister, who, when she had eaten them, declared herself better. The Drakos, when he heard that Janni had come back, fled for fear forty fathoms deeper underground.

Next day, when Janni was hunting, the Drakos went to the sister and advised that she should again pretend to be ill, and should beg for some pears, which grew in a garden three days' journey from the castle. From this quest Janni would certainly never return, for there dwelt nine brothers of the Drakos, each of whom had three heads.

The sister did as she was told, and next day Janni,

taking his three dogs with him, went to get the pears. When he came to the garden he laid himself down to rest, and soon fell asleep.

Then first came three Draken to eat him, and when the dogs had worried these, six others came and fought the dogs a long time. The noise of this combat awoke Janni, and he slew the Draken, and knew at last why the dogs were covered with blood.

After that he freed all whom the Draken held prisoners, amongst others, a king's daughter. Out of gratitude she would have taken him for her husband ; but he put her off, saying : ' For the kindness that I have been able to do to you, you shall receive in this castle all the blind and lame who pass this way.' The princess promised him to do so, and on his departure gave him a ring.

So Janni plucked the pears and took them to his sister, who, when she had eaten them, declared she felt better. When, however, the Drakos heard that Janni had come back yet a third time safe and sound, he fled for fright forty fathoms deeper underground ; and, next day, when Janni was away hunting, he crept out and said to the sister : ' Now are we indeed both lost, unless you find out from him wherein his strength lies, and then between us we will contrive to do away with him.'

When, therefore, Janni had come back from hunting, and sat at evening with his sister by the fire, she begged him to tell her wherein lay his strength, and he answered : ' It lies in my two fingers; if these are bound together then all my strength disappears.'

' That I will not believe,' said the sister, ' unless I see it for myself.'

Then he let her tie his fingers together with a thread, and immediately he became powerless. Then the sister called up the Drakos, who, when he had come forth, tore out Janni's eyes, gave them to his dogs to eat, and threw him into a dry well.

Now it happened that some travellers, going to draw water from this well, heard Janni groaning at the bottom. They came near, and asked him where he was, and he begged them to draw him up from the well, for he was a poor unfortunate man.

The travellers let a rope down and drew him up to

JANNI AND HIS DOGS FIGHT THE THREE-HEADED DRAKEN

daylight. It was not till then that he first became aware that he was blind, and he begged the travellers to lead him to the country of the king whose daughter he had freed, and they would be well repaid for their trouble.

When they had brought him there he sent to beg the princess to come to him; but she did not recognise him till he had shown her the ring she had given him.

Then she remembered him, and took him with her into the castle.

When she learnt what had befallen him she called together all the sorceresses in the country in order that they should tell her where the eyes were. At last she found one who declared that she knew where they were, and that she could restore them. This sorceress then went straight to the castle where dwelt the sister and the Drakos, and gave something to the dogs to eat which caused the eyes to reappear. She took them with her and put them back in Janni's head, so that he saw as well as before.

Then he returned to the castle of the Drakos, whom he slew as well as his sister; and, taking his dogs with him, went back to the princess and they were immediately married.

THE PARTNERSHIP OF THE THIEF
AND THE LIAR.

THERE was once upon a time a thief, who, being out of
a job, was wandering by himself up and down the sea-
shore. As he walked he passed a man who was standing
still, looking at the waves.

'I wonder,' said the thief, addressing the stranger, 'if
you have ever seen a stone swimming?'

'Most certainly I have,' replied the other man, 'and,
what is more, I saw the same stone jump out of the
water and fly through the air.'

'This is capital,' replied the thief. 'You and I must
go into partnership. We shall certainly make our
fortunes. Let us start together for the palace of the king
of the neighbouring country. When we get there, I will
go into his presence alone, and will tell him the most
startling thing I can invent. Then you must follow and
back up my lie.'

Having agreed to do this, they set out on their travels.
After several days' journeying, they reached the town
where the king's palace was, and here they parted for a
few hours, while the thief sought an interview with the
king, and begged his majesty to give him a glass of beer.

'That is impossible,' said the king, 'as this year
there has been a failure of all the crops, and of the hops
and the vines ; so we have neither wine nor beer in the
whole kingdom.'

'How extraordinary!' answered the thief. 'I have
just come from a country where the crops were so fine

that I saw twelve barrels of beer made out of one branch of hops.'

'I bet you three hundred florins that is not true,' answered the king.

'And I bet you three hundred florins it is true,' replied the thief.

Then each staked his three hundred florins, and the king said he would decide the question by sending a servant into that country to see if it was true.

So the servant set out on horseback, and on the way he met a man, and he asked him whence he came. And the man told him that he came from the self-same country to which the servant was at that moment bound.

'If that is the case,' said the servant, 'you can tell me how high the hops grow in your country, and how many barrels of beer can be brewed from one branch?'

'I can't tell you that,' answered the man, 'but I happened to be present when the hops were being gathered in, and I saw that it took three men with axes three days to cut down one branch.'

Then the servant thought that he might save himself a long journey; so he gave the man ten florins, and told him he must repeat to the king what he had just told him. And when they got back to the palace, they came together into the king's presence.

And the king asked him: 'Well, is it true about the hops?'

'Yes, sire, it is,' answered the servant; 'and here is a man I have brought with me from the country to confirm the tale.'

So the king paid the thief the three hundred florins; and the partners once more set out together in search of adventures. As they journeyed, the thief said to his comrade: 'I will now go to another king, and will tell him something still more startling; and you must follow and back up my lie, and we shall get some money out of him; just see if we don't.'

When they reached the next kingdom, the thief presented himself to the king, and requested him to give him a cauliflower. And the king answered : ' Owing to a blight among the vegetables we have no cauliflower.'

' That is strange,' answered the thief. ' I have just come from a country where it grows so well that one head of cauliflower filled twelve water-tubs.'

' I don't believe it,' answered the king.

' I bet you six hundred florins it is true,' replied the thief.

' And I bet you six hundred florins it is not true,' answered the king. And he sent for a servant, and ordered him to start at once for the country whence the thief had come, to find out if his story of the cauliflower was true. On his journey the servant met with a man. Stopping his horse he asked him where he came from, and the man replied that he came from the country to which the other was travelling.

' If that is the case,' said the servant, ' you can tell me to what size cauliflower grows in your country? Is it so large that one head fills twelve water-tubs?'

' I have not seen that,' answered the man. ' But I saw twelve waggons, drawn by twelve horses, carrying one head of cauliflower to the market.'

And the servant answered : ' Here are ten florins for you, my man, for you have saved me a long journey. Come with me now, and tell the king what you have just told me.'

' All right,' said the man, and they went together to the palace ; and when the king asked the servant if he had found out the truth about the cauliflower, the servant replied : ' Sire, all that you heard was perfectly true ; here is a man from the country who will tell you so.'

So the king had to pay the thief the six hundred florins. And the two partners set out once more on their travels, with their nine hundred florins. When they reached the country of the neighbouring king, the thief entered the royal presence, and began conversation by asking if his majesty knew that in an adjacent kingdom there was a town with a church steeple on which a bird had alighted, and that the steeple was so high, and the bird's beak so long, that it had pecked the stars till some of them fell out of the sky.

'I don't believe it,' said the king.

'Nevertheless I am prepared to bet twelve hundred florins that it is true,' answered the thief.

'And I bet twelve hundred florins that it is a lie,' replied the king. And he straightway sent a servant into the neighbouring country to find out the truth.

As he rode, the servant met a man coming in the opposite direction. So he hailed him and asked him where he came from. And the man replied that he came out of the very town to which the man was bound. Then the servant asked him if the story they had heard about the bird with the long beak was true.

'I don't know about that,' answered the man, 'as I have never seen the bird; but I once saw twelve men shoving all their might and main with brooms to push a monster egg into a cellar.'

'That is capital,' answered the servant, presenting the man with ten florins. 'Come and tell your tale to the king, and you will save me a long journey.'

So, when the story was repeated to the king, there was nothing for him to do but to pay the thief the twelve hundred florins.

Then the two partners set out again with their ill-gotten gains, which they proceeded to divide into two equal shares; but the thief kept back three of the florins that belonged to the liar's half of the booty. Shortly afterwards they each married, and settled down in homes of their own with their wives. One day the liar discovered that he had been done out of three florins by his partner, so he went to his house and demanded them from him.

'Come next Saturday, and I will give them to you,' answered the thief. But as he had no intention of giving the liar the money, when Saturday morning came he stretched himself out stiff and stark upon the bed, and told his wife she was to say he was dead. So the wife rubbed her eyes with an onion, and when the liar appeared at the door, she met him in tears, and told him that as her husband was dead he could not be paid the three florins.

"I ONCE SAW" 12 MEN SHOVING ALL THEIR MIGHT AND MAIN WITH BROOMS TO PUSH A MONSTER EGG INTO A CELLAR

But the liar, who knew his partner's tricks, instantly suspected the truth, and said: 'As he has not paid me, I will pay him out with three good lashes of my riding whip.'

At these words the thief sprang to his feet, and, appearing at the door, promised his partner that if he would return the following Saturday he would pay him. So the liar went away satisfied with this promise.

But when Saturday morning came the thief got up

early and hid himself under a truss of hay in the hay-loft.

When the liar appeared to demand his three florins, the wife met him with tears in her eyes, and told him that her husband was dead.

' Where have you buried him ? ' asked the liar.

' In the hay-loft,' answered the wife.

' Then I will go there, and take away some hay in payment of his debt,' said the liar. And proceeding to the hay-loft, he began to toss about the hay with a pitch-fork, prodding it into the trusses of hay, till, in terror of his life, the thief crept out and promised his partner to pay him the three florins on the following Saturday.

When the day came he got up at sunrise, and going down into the crypt of a neighbouring chapel, stretched himself out quite still and stiff in an old stone coffin. But the liar, who was quite as clever as his partner, very soon bethought him of the crypt, and set out for the chapel, confident that he would shortly discover the hiding-place of his friend. He had just entered the crypt, and his eyes were not yet accustomed to the darkness, when he heard the sound of whispering at the grated windows. Listening intently, he overheard the plotting of a band of robbers, who had brought their treasure to the crypt, meaning to hide it there, while they set out on fresh adventures. All the time they were speaking they were removing the bars from the window, and in another minute they would all have entered the crypt, and dis-covered the liar. Quick as thought he wound his mantle round him and placed himself, standing stiff and erect, in a niche in the wall, so that in the dim light he looked just like an old stone statue. As soon as the robbers entered the crypt, they set about the work of dividing their treasure. Now, there were twelve robbers, but by mistake the chief of the band divided the gold into thirteen heaps. When he saw his mistake he said they had not time to count it all over again, but that the thirteenth heap should belong to whoever among them could strike off the head of the old stone statue in the niche with one stroke. With these words he took up an axe, and approached the niche where the liar was standing. But, just as he had waved the axe over his head ready to strike, a voice was heard from the stone coffin saying, in sepulchral tones : ' Clear out of this, or the dead will arise from their coffins, and the statues will descend from the walls, and you will be driven out more dead than alive.' And with a bound the thief jumped out of his coffin and the liar from his niche, and the robbers were so terrified that they ran helter-skelter out of the crypt, leaving all their gold behind them, and vowing that they would never put foot inside the haunted place again. So the partners divided the gold between them, and carried it to their homes ; and history tells us no more about them.

FORTUNATUS AND HIS PURSE

ONCE upon a time there lived in the city of Famagosta, in the island of Cyprus, a rich man called Theodorus. He ought to have been the happiest person in the whole world, as he had all he could wish for, and a wife and little son whom he loved dearly; but unluckily, after a short time he always grew tired of everything, and had to seek new pleasures. When people are made like this the end is generally the same, and before Fortunatus (for that was the boy's name) was ten years old, his father had spent all his money and had not a farthing left.

But though Theodorus had been so foolish he was not quite without sense, and set about getting work at once. His wife, too, instead of reproaching him sent away the servants and sold their fine horses, and did all the work of the house herself, even washing the clothes of her husband and child.

Thus time passed till Fortunatus was sixteen. One day when they were sitting at supper, the boy said to Theodorus, 'Father, why do you look so sad. Tell me what is wrong, and perhaps I can help you.'

'Ah, my son, I have reason enough to be sad; but for me you would now have been enjoying every kind of pleasure, instead of being buried in this tiny house.'

'Oh, do not let that trouble you,' replied Fortunatus, 'it is time I made some money for myself. To be sure I have never been taught any trade. Still there must be something I can do. I will go and walk on the seashore and think about it.'

Very soon—sooner than he expected—a chance came, and Fortunatus, like a wise boy, seized on it at once. The post offered him was that of page to the Earl of Flanders, and as the Earl's daughter was just going to be married, splendid festivities were held in her honour, and at some of the tilting matches Fortunatus was lucky enough to win the prize. These prizes, together with presents from the lords and ladies of the court, who liked him for his pleasant ways, made Fortunatus feel quite a rich man.

But though his head was not turned by the notice taken of him, it excited the envy of some of the other pages about the Court, and one of them, called Robert, invented a plot to move Fortunatus out of his way. So he told the young man that the Earl had taken a dislike to him and meant to kill him; Fortunatus believed the story, and packing up his fine clothes and money, slipped away before dawn.

He went to a great many big towns and lived well, and as he was generous and not wiser than most youths of his age, he very soon found himself penniless. Like his father, he then began to think of work, and tramped half over Brittany in search of it. Nobody seemed to want him, and he wandered about from one place to another, till he found himself in a dense wood, without any paths, and not much light. Here he spent two whole days, with nothing to eat and very little water to drink, going first in one direction and then in another, but never being able to find his way out. During the first night he slept soundly, and was too tired to fear either man or beast, but when darkness came on for the second time, and growls were heard in the distance, he grew frightened and looked about for a high tree out of reach of his enemies. Hardly had he settled himself comfortably in one of the forked branches, when a lion walked up to a spring that burst from a rock close to the tree, and crouching down drank greedily. This was bad enough, but after all, lions do not climb trees, and as long as Fortunatus stayed up on his perch, he was quite safe. But no sooner was the lion out of sight, than his place was taken by a bear, and bears, as Fortunatus knew very well, *are* tree-climbers. His heart beat fast, and not without reason, for as the bear turned away he looked up and saw Fortunatus !

Now in those days every young man carried a sword slung to his belt, and it was a fashion that came in very handily for Fortunatus. He drew his sword, and when the bear got within a yard of him he made a fierce lunge forward. The bear, wild with pain, tried to spring, but the bough he was standing on broke with his weight, and he fell heavily to the ground. Then Fortunatus descended from his tree (first taking good care to see no other wild animals were in sight) and killed him with a single blow. He was just thinking he would light a fire and make a hearty dinner off bear's flesh, which is not at all bad eating, when he beheld a beautiful lady standing by his side leaning on a wheel, and her eyes hidden by a bandage.

' I am Dame Fortune,' she said, ' and I have a gift for you. Shall it be wisdom, strength, long life, riches, health, or beauty? Think well, and tell me what you will have.'

But Fortunatus, who had proved the truth of the proverb that ' It's ill thinking on an empty stomach,' answered quickly, ' Good lady, let me have riches in such plenty that I may never again be as hungry as I am now.'

And the lady held out a purse and told him he had only to put his hand into it, and he and his children would always find ten pieces of gold. But when they were dead it would be a magic purse no longer.

At this news Fortunatus was beside himself with joy, and could hardly find words to thank the lady. But she told him that the best thing he could do was to find his way out of the wood, and before bidding him farewell pointed out which path he should take. He walked

THE GIFT OF FORTUNE

along it as fast as his weakness would let him, until a welcome light at a little distance showed him that a house was near. It turned out to be an inn, but before entering Fortunatus thought he had better make sure of the truth of what the lady had told him, and took out the purse and looked inside. Sure enough there were the ten pieces of gold, shining brightly. Then Fortunatus walked boldly up to the inn, and ordered them to get ready a good supper at once, as he was very hungry, and to bring him the best wine in the house. And he seemed to care so little what he spent that everybody thought he was a great lord, and vied with each other who should run quickest when he called.

After a night passed in a soft bed, Fortunatus felt so much better that he asked the landlord if he could find him some men-servants, and tell him where any good horses were to be got. The next thing was to provide himself with smart clothes, and then to take a big house where he could give great feasts to the nobles and beautiful ladies who lived in palaces round about.

In this manner a whole year soon slipped away, and Fortunatus was so busy amusing himself that he never once remembered his parents whom he had left behind in Cyprus. But though he was thoughtless, he was not bad-hearted. As soon as their existence crossed his mind, he set about making preparations to visit them, and as he was not fond of being alone he looked round for some one older and wiser than himself to travel with him. It was not long before he had the good luck to come across an old man who had left his wife and children in a far country many years before, when he went out into the world to seek the fortune which he never found. He agreed to accompany Fortunatus back to Cyprus, but only on condition he should first be allowed to return for a few weeks to his own home before venturing to set sail for an island so strange and distant. Fortunatus agreed to his

proposal, and as he was always fond of anything new,
said that he would go with him.

The journey was long, and they had to cross many
large rivers, and climb over high mountains, and find
their way through thick woods, before they reached at
length the old man's castle. His wife and children had
almost given up hopes of seeing him again, and crowded
eagerly round him. Indeed, it did not take Fortunatus
five minutes to fall in love with the youngest daughter,
the most beautiful creature in the whole world, whose
name was Cassandra.

'Give her to me for my wife,' he said to the old man,
'and let us all go together to Famagosta.'

So a ship was bought big enough to hold Fortunatus,
the old man and his wife, and their ten children—
five of them sons and five daughters. And the day before
they sailed the wedding was celebrated with magnificent
rejoicings, and everybody thought that Fortunatus must
certainly be a prince in disguise. But when they reached
Cyprus, he learned to his sorrow that both his father and
mother were dead, and for some time he shut himself up in
his house and would see nobody, full of shame at having
forgotten them all these years. Then he begged that the
old man and his wife would remain with him, and take
the place of his parents.

For twelve years Fortunatus and Cassandra and their
two little boys lived happily in Famagosta. They had a
beautiful house and everything they could possibly want,
and when Cassandra's sisters married the purse provided
them each with a fortune. But at last Fortunatus grew
tired of staying at home, and thought he should like to
go out and see the world again. Cassandra shed many
tears at first when he told her of his wishes, and he had
a great deal of trouble to persuade her to give her consent. But on his promising to return at the end of two
years she agreed to let him go. Before he went away
he showed her three chests of gold, which stood in a

room with an iron door, and walls twelve feet thick.
'If anything should happen to me,' he said, 'and I should
never come back, keep one of the chests for yourself, and
give the others to our two sons.' Then he embraced them
all and took ship for Alexandria.

The wind was fair and in a few days they entered the
harbour, where Fortunatus was informed by a man whom
he met on landing, that if he wished to be well received
in the town, he must begin by making a handsome
present to the Sultan. 'That is easily done,' said Fortunatus, and went into a goldsmith's shop, where he
bought a large gold cup, which cost five thousand pounds.
This gift so pleased the Sultan that he ordered a hundred
casks of spices to be given to Fortunatus ; Fortunatus
put them on board his ship, and commanded the captain
to return to Cyprus and deliver them to his wife,
Cassandra. He next obtained an audience of the Sultan,
and begged permission to travel through the country,
which the Sultan readily gave him, adding some letters
to the rulers of other lands which Fortunatus might wish
to visit.

Filled with delight at feeling himself free to roam
through the world once more, Fortunatus set out on his
journey without losing a day. From court to court he
went, astonishing everyone by the magnificence of his
dress and the splendour of his presents. At length he grew
as tired of wandering as he had been of staying at home,
and returned to Alexandria, where he found the same
ship that had brought him from Cyprus lying in the
harbour. Of course the first thing he did was to pay his
respects to the Sultan, who was eager to hear about his
adventures.

When Fortunatus had told them all, the Sultan observed : 'Well, you have seen many wonderful things,
but I have something to show you more wonderful still ; '
and he led him into a room where precious stones lay
heaped against the walls. Fortunatus' eyes were quite

dazzled, but the Sultan went on without pausing and
opened a door at the farther end.   As far as Fortunatus
could see, the cupboard was quite bare, except for a little
red cap, such as soldiers wear in Turkey.

'Look at this,' said the Sultan.

'But there is nothing very valuable about it,' answered
Fortunatus. 'I've seen a dozen better caps than that, this
very day.'

'Ah,' said the Sultan, 'you do not know what you are
talking about. Whoever puts this cap on his head and
wishes himself in any place, will find himself there in a
moment.'

'But who made it?' asked Fortunatus.

'That I cannot tell you,' replied the Sultan.

'Is it very heavy to wear?' asked Fortunatus.

'No, quite light,' replied the Sultan, 'just feel it.'

Fortunatus took the cap and put it on his head, and
then, without thinking, wished himself back in the ship that
was starting for Famagosta.   In a second he was standing at the prow, while the anchor was being weighed, and
while the Sultan was repenting of his folly in allowing
Fortunatus to try on the cap, the vessel was making fast
for Cyprus.

When it arrived, Fortunatus found his wife and
children well, but the two old people were dead and
buried. His sons had grown tall and strong, but unlike
their father had no wish to see the world, and found their
chief pleasure in hunting and tilting.   In the main, Fortunatus was content to stay quietly at home, and if a restless
fit did seize upon him, he was able to go away for a few
hours without being missed, thanks to the cap, which he
never sent back to the Sultan.

By-and-by he grew old, and feeling that he had not
many days to live, he sent for his two sons, and showing
them the purse and cap, he said to them: 'Never part
with these precious possessions. They are worth more
than all the gold and lands I leave behind me.   But

never tell their secret, even to your wife or dearest friend. That purse has served me well for forty years, and no one knows whence I got my riches.' Then he died and was buried by his wife Cassandra, and he was mourned in Famagosta for many years.

THE GOAT-FACED GIRL

THERE was once upon a time a peasant called Masaniello who had twelve daughters. They were exactly like the steps of a staircase, for there was just a year between each sister. It was all the poor man could do to bring up such a large family, and in order to provide food for them he used to dig in the fields all day long. In spite of his hard work he only just succeeded in keeping the wolf from the door, and the poor little girls often went hungry to bed.

One day, when Masaniello was working at the foot of a high mountain, he came upon the mouth of a cave which was so dark and gloomy that even the sun seemed afraid to enter it. Suddenly a huge green lizard appeared from the inside and stood before Masaniello, who nearly went out of his mind with terror, for the beast was as big as a crocodile and quite as fierce looking.

But the lizard sat down beside him in the most friendly manner, and said : ' Don't be afraid, my good man, I am not going to hurt you ; on the contrary, I am most anxious to help you.'

When the peasant heard these words he knelt before the lizard and said : ' Dear lady, for I know not what to call you, I am in your power ; but I beg of you to be merciful, for I have twelve wretched little daughters at home who are dependent on me.'

' That's the very reason why I have come to you,' replied the lizard. ' Bring me your youngest daughter to-morrow morning. I promise to bring her up as if she

The Lizard takes charge of Renzolla

were my own child, and to look upon her as the apple of
my eye.'

When Masaniello heard her words he was very
unhappy, because he felt sure, from the lizard's wanting
one of his daughters, the youngest and tenderest too, that
the poor little girl would only serve as dessert for the
terrible creature's supper. At the same time he said to
himself, ' If I refuse her request, she will certainly eat me
up on the spot. If I give her what she asks she does
indeed take part of myself, but if I refuse she will take
the whole of me. What am I to do, and how in the
world am I to get out of the difficulty?'

As he kept muttering to himself the lizard said,
' Make up your mind to do as I tell you at once. I
desire to have your youngest daughter, and if you won't
comply with my wish, I can only say it will be the worse
for you.'

Seeing that there was nothing else to be done,
Masaniello set off for his home, and arrived there looking
so white and wretched that his wife asked him at once :
' What has happened to you, my dear husband? Have
you quarrelled with anyone, or has the poor donkey
fallen down?'

' Neither the one nor the other,' answered her
husband, ' but something far worse than either. A terrible
lizard has nearly frightened me out of my senses, for
she threatened that if I did not give her our youngest
daughter, she would make me repent it. My head is
going round like a mill-wheel, and I don't know what to
do. I am indeed between the Devil and the Deep Sea.
You know how dearly I love Renzolla, and yet, if I fail to
bring her to the lizard to-morrow morning, I must say
farewell to life. Do advise me what to do.'

When his wife had heard all he had to say, she said
to him : ' How do you know, my dear husband, that the
lizard is really our enemy? May she not be a friend
in disguise? And your meeting with her may be the

beginning of better things and the end of all our misery. Therefore go and take the child to her, for my heart tells me that you will never repent doing so.'

Masaniello was much comforted by her words, and next morning as soon as it was light he took his little daughter by the hand and led her to the cave.

The lizard, who was awaiting the peasant's arrival, came forward to meet him, and taking the girl by the hand, she gave the father a sack full of gold, and said: 'Go and marry your other daughters, and give them dowries with this gold, and be of good cheer, for Renzolla will have both father and mother in me; it is a great piece of luck for her that she has fallen into my hands.'

Masaniello, quite overcome with gratitude, thanked the lizard, and returned home to his wife.

As soon as it was known how rich the peasant had become, suitors for the hands of his daughters were not wanting, and very soon he married them all off; and even then there was enough gold left to keep himself and his wife in comfort and plenty all their days.

As soon as the lizard was left alone with Renzolla, she changed the cave into a beautiful palace, and led the girl inside. Here she brought her up like a little princess, and the child wanted for nothing. She gave her sumptuous food to eat, beautiful clothes to wear, and a thousand servants to wait on her.

Now, it happened, one day, that the king of the country was hunting in a wood close to the palace, and was overtaken by the dark. Seeing a light shining in the palace he sent one of his servants to ask if he could get a night's lodging there.

When the page knocked at the door the lizard changed herself into a beautiful woman, and opened it herself. When she heard the king's request she sent him a message to say that she would be delighted to see him, and give him all he wanted.

The king, on hearing this kind invitation, instantly
betook himself to the palace, where he was received in
the most hospitable manner. A hundred pages with
torches came to meet him, a hundred more waited on
him at table, and another hundred waved big fans in the
air to keep the flies from him. Renzolla herself poured
out the wine for him, and, so gracefully did she do it, that
his Majesty could not take his eyes off her.

When the meal was finished and the table cleared,
the king retired to sleep, and Renzolla drew the shoes
from his feet, at the same time drawing his heart from
his breast. So desperately had he fallen in love with
her, that he called the fairy to him, and asked her for
Renzolla's hand in marriage. As the kind fairy had
only the girl's welfare at heart, she willingly gave her
consent, and not her consent only, but a wedding portion
of seven thousand golden guineas.

The king, full of delight over his good fortune, prepared to take his departure, accompanied by Renzolla,
who never so much as thanked the fairy for all she had
done for her. When the fairy saw such a base want of
gratitude she determined to punish the girl, and, cursing
her, she turned her face into a goat's head. In a moment
Renzolla's pretty mouth stretched out into a snout, with
a beard a yard long at the end of it, her cheeks sank in,
and her shining plaits of hair changed into two sharp
horns. When the king turned round and saw her he
thought he must have taken leave of his senses. He
burst into tears, and cried out: ' Where is the hair that
bound me so tightly, where are the eyes that pierced
through my heart, and where are the lips I kissed? Am
I to be tied to a goat all my life? No, no! nothing will
induce me to become the laughing-stock of my subjects
for the sake of a goat-faced girl!'

When they reached his own country he shut Renzolla
up in a little turret chamber of his palace, with a
waiting-maid, and gave each of them ten bundles of flax

to spin, telling them that their task must be finished by the end of the week.

The maid, obedient to the king's commands, set at once to work and combed out the flax, wound it round the spindle, and sat spinning at her wheel so diligently that her work was quite done by Saturday evening. But Renzolla, who had been spoilt and petted in the fairy's house, and was quite unaware of the change that had taken place in her appearance, threw the flax out of the window and said : ' What is the king thinking of that he should give me this work to do? If he wants shirts he can buy them. It isn't even as if he had picked me out of the gutter, for he ought to remember that I brought him seven thousand golden guineas as my wedding portion, and that I am his wife and not his slave. He must be mad to treat me like this.'

All the same, when Saturday evening came, and she saw that the waiting-maid had finished her task, she took fright lest she should be punished for her idleness. So she hurried off to the palace of the fairy, and confided all her woes to her. The fairy embraced her tenderly, and gave her a sack full of spun flax, in order that she might show it to the king, and let him see what a good worker she was. Renzolla took the sack without one word of thanks, and returned to the palace, leaving the kind fairy very indignant over her want of gratitude.

When the king saw the flax all spun, he gave Renzolla and the waiting-maid each a little dog, and told them to look after the animals and train them carefully.

The waiting-maid brought hers up with the greatest possible care, and treated it almost as if it were her son. But Renzolla said : ' I don't know what to think. Have I come among a lot of lunatics ? Does the king imagine that I am going to comb and feed a dog with my own hands ? ' With these words she opened the window and threw the poor little beast out, and he fell on the ground as dead as a stone.

When a few months had passed the king sent
a message to say he would like to see how the dogs
were getting on. Renzolla, who felt very uncomfortable
in her mind at this request, hurried off once more to the

RENZOLLA SEES HER FACE IN THE MIRROR

fairy. This time she found an old man at the door of
the fairy's palace, who said to her: 'Who are you, and
what do you want?'

When Renzolla heard his question she answered

angrily : 'Don't you know me, old Goat-beard? And how dare you address me in such a way?'

'The pot can't call the kettle black,' answered the old man, 'for it is not I, but you who have a goat's head. Just wait a moment, you ungrateful wretch, and I will show you to what a pass your want of gratitude has brought you.'

With these words he hurried away, and returned with a mirror, which he held up before Renzolla. At the sight of her ugly, hairy face, the girl nearly fainted with horror, and she broke into loud sobs at seeing her countenance so changed.

Then the old man said : 'You must remember, Renzolla, that you are a peasant's daughter, and that the fairy turned you into a queen ; but you were ungrateful, and never as much as thanked her for all she had done for you. Therefore she has determined to punish you. But if you wish to lose your long white beard, throw yourself at the fairy's feet and implore her to forgive you. She has a tender heart, and will, perhaps, take pity on you.'

Renzolla, who was really sorry for her conduct, took the old man's advice, and the fairy not only gave her back her former face, but she dressed her in a gold embroidered dress, presented her with a beautiful carriage, and brought her back, accompanied by a host of servants, to her husband. When the king saw her looking as beautiful as ever, he fell in love with her once more, and bitterly repented having caused her so much suffering.

So Renzolla lived happily ever afterwards, for she loved her husband, honoured the fairy, and was grateful to the old man for having told her the truth.

[From the Italian. *Kletke.*]

WHAT CAME OF PICKING FLOWERS

THERE was once a woman who had three daughters whom she loved very much. One day the eldest was walking in a water-meadow, when she saw a pink growing in the stream. She stooped to pick the flower, but her hand had scarcely touched it, when she vanished altogether. The next morning the second sister went out into the meadow, to see if she could find any traces of the lost girl, and as a branch of lovely roses lay trailing across her path, she bent down to move it away, and in so doing, could not resist plucking one of the roses. In a moment she too had disappeared. Wondering what could have become of her two sisters, the youngest followed in their footsteps, and fell a victim to a branch of delicious white jessamine. So the old woman was left without any daughters at all.

She wept, and wept, and wept, all day and all night, and went on weeping so long, that her son, who had been a little boy when his sisters disappeared, grew up to be a tall youth. Then one night he asked his mother to tell him what was the matter.

When he had heard the whole story, he said, 'Give me your blessing, mother, and I will go and search the world till I find them.'

So he set forth, and after he had travelled several miles without any adventures, he came upon three big boys fighting in the road. He stopped and inquired what they were fighting about, and one of them answered :

'My lord! our father left to us, when he died, a pair of

boots, a key, and a cap. Whoever puts on the boots and wishes himself in any place, will find himself there. The key will open every door in the world, and with the cap on your head no one can see you. Now our eldest brother wants to have all three things for himself, and we wish to draw lots for them.'

'Oh, that is easily settled,' said the youth. 'I will throw this stone as far as I can, and the one who picks it up first, shall have the three things.' So he took the stone and flung it, and while the three brothers were running after it, he drew hastily on the boots, and said, 'Boots, take me to the place where I shall find my eldest sister.'

The next moment the young man was standing on a steep mountain before the gates of a strong castle guarded by bolts and bars and iron chains. The key, which he had not forgotten to put in his pocket, opened the doors one by one, and he walked through a number of halls and corridors, till he met a beautiful and richly-dressed young lady who started back in surprise at the sight of him, and exclaimed, 'Oh, sir, how did you contrive te get in here?' The young man replied that he was her brother, and told her by what means he had been able to pass through the doors. In return, she told him how happy she was, except for one thing, and that was, her husband lay under a spell, and could never break it till there should be put to death a man who could not die.

They talked together for a long time, and then the lady said he had better leave her as she expected her husband back at any moment, and he might not like him to be there; but the young man assured her she need not be afraid, as he had with him a cap which would make him invisible. They were still deep in conversation when the door suddenly opened, and a bird flew in, but he saw nothing unusual, for, at the first noise, the youth had put on his cap. The lady jumped up and brought a large golden basin, into which the bird flew,

What Came of Picking Jessamine

reappearing directly after as a handsome man. Turning
to his wife, he cried, 'I am sure someone is in the room!'
She got frightened, and declared that she was quite alone,
but her husband persisted, and in the end she had to
confess the truth.

'But if he is really your brother, why did you hide
him?' asked he. 'I believe you are telling me a lie, and
if he comes back I shall kill him!'

At this the youth took off his cap, and came forward.
Then the husband saw that he was indeed so like his wife
that he doubted her word no longer, and embraced his
brother-in-law with delight. Drawing a feather from his
bird's skin, he said, 'If you are in danger and cry, "Come
and help me, King of the Birds," everything will go well
with you.'

The young man thanked him and went away, and
after he had left the castle he told the boots that they
must take him to the place where his second sister was
living. As before, he found himself at the gates of a huge
castle, and within was his second sister, very happy with
her husband, who loved her dearly, but longing for the
moment when he should be set free from the spell that
kept him half his life a fish. When he arrived and had
been introduced by his wife to her brother, he welcomed
him warmly, and gave him a fish-scale, saying, 'If you
are in danger, call to me, "Come and help me, King of
the Fishes," and everything will go well with you.'

The young man thanked him and took his leave, and
when he was outside the gates he told the boots to take
him to the place where his youngest sister lived. The boots
carried him to a dark cavern, with steps of iron leading
up to it. Inside she sat, weeping and sobbing, and as she
had done nothing else the whole time she had been there,
the poor girl had grown very thin. When she saw a man
standing before her, she sprang to her feet and exclaimed,
'Oh, whoever you are, save me and take me from this
horrible place!' Then he told her who he was, and how

he had seen her sisters, whose happiness was spoilt by the spell under which both their husbands lay, and she, in turn, related her story. She had been carried off in the water-meadow by a horrible monster, who wanted to make her marry him by force, and had kept her a prisoner all these years because she would not submit to his will. Every day he came to beg her to consent to his wishes, and to remind her that there was no hope of her being set free, as he was the most constant man in the world, and besides that he could never die. At these words the youth remembered his two enchanted brothers-in-law, and he advised his sister to promise to marry the old man, if he would tell her why he could never die. Suddenly everything began to tremble, as if it was shaken by a whirlwind, and the old man entered, and flinging himself at the feet of the girl, he said : ' Are you still determined never to marry me ? If so you will have to sit there weeping till the end of the world, for I shall always be faithful to my wish to marry you ! ' ' Well, I will marry you,' she said, ' if you will tell me why it is that you can never die.'

Then the old man burst into peals of laughter. ' Ah, ah, ah ! You are thinking how you would be able to kill me ? Well, to do that, you would have to find an iron casket which lies at the bottom of the sea, and has a white dove inside, and then you would have to find the egg which the dove laid, and bring it here, and dash it against my head.' And he laughed again in his certainty that no one had ever got down to the bottom of the sea, and that if they did, they would never find the casket, or be able to open it. When he could speak once more, he said, ' Now you will be obliged to marry me, as you know my secret.' But she begged so hard that the wedding might be put off for three days, that he consented, and went away rejoicing at his victory. When he had disappeared, the brother took off the cap which had kept him invisible all this time, and told his sister not to lose heart as he hoped in three days she would be

HOW THE WHITE DOVE ESCAPED

free. Then he drew on his boots, and wished himself at
the seashore, and there he was directly. Drawing out
the fish-scale, he cried, ' Come and help me, King of the
Fishes! ' and his brother-in-law swam up, and asked
what he could do. The young man related the story,
and when he had finished his listener summoned all
the fishes to his presence. The last to arrive was a little
sardine, who apologised for being so late, but said she
had hurt herself by knocking her head against an iron
casket that lay in the bottom of the sea. The king
ordered several of the largest and strongest of his subjects to take the little sardine as a guide, and bring him
the iron casket. They soon returned with the box
placed across their backs and laid it down before him.
Then the youth produced the key and said ' Key, open
that box ! ' and the key opened it, and though they were
all crowding round, ready to catch it, the white dove
within flew away.

It was useless to go after it, and for a moment the
young man's heart sank. The next minute, however, he
remembered that he had still his feather, and drew it out
crying, ' Come to me, King of the Birds! ' and a rushing
noise was heard, and the King of the Birds perched on
his shoulder, and asked what he could do to help him.
His brother-in-law told him the whole story, and when
he had finished the King of the Birds commanded all
his subjects to hasten to his presence. In an instant the
air was dark with birds of all sizes, and at the very
last came the white dove, apologising for being so late
by saying that an old friend had arrived at his nest, and
he had been obliged to give him some dinner. The King
of the Birds ordered some of them to show the young
man the white dove's nest, and when they reached it, there
lay the egg which was to break the spell and set them all
free. When it was safely in his pocket, he told the boots
to carry him straight to the cavern where his youngest
sister sat awaiting him.

Now it was already far on into the third day, which the old man had fixed for the wedding, and when the youth reached the cavern with his cap on his head, he found the monster there, urging the girl to keep her word and let the marriage take place at once. At a sign from her brother she sat down and invited the old monster to lay his head on her lap. He did so with delight, and her brother standing behind her back passed her the egg unseen. She took it, and dashed it straight at the horrible head, and the monster started, and with a groan that people took for the rumblings of an earthquake, he turned over and died.

As the breath went out of his body the husbands of the two eldest daughters resumed their proper shapes, and, sending for their mother-in-law, whose sorrow was so unexpectedly turned into joy, they had a great feast, and the youngest sister was rich to the end of her days with the treasures she found in the cave, collected by the monster.

[From the Portuguese.]

THE STORY OF BENSURDATU

THERE was once a king and a queen who had three wonderfully beautiful daughters, and their one thought, from morning till night, was how they could make the girls happy.

One day the princesses said to the king, 'Dear father, we want so much to have a picnic, and eat our dinner in the country.'

'Very well, dear children, let us have a picnic by all means,' answered he, and gave orders that everything should be got ready.

When luncheon was prepared it was put into a cart, and the royal family stepped into a carriage and drove right away into the country. After a few miles they reached a house and garden belonging to the king, and close by was their favourite place for lunch. The drive had made them very hungry, and they ate with a hearty appetite, till almost all the food had disappeared.

When they had quite done, they said to their parents : ' Now we should like to wander about the garden a little, but when you want to go home, just call to us.' And they ran off, laughing, down a green glade, which led to the garden.

But no sooner had they stepped across the fence, than a dark cloud came down and covered them, and prevented them seeing whither they were going.

Meanwhile the king and queen sat lazily among the heather, and an hour or two slipped away. The sun was dropping towards the horizon, and they began to think it

was time to go home. So they called to their daughters
and called again, but no one answered them.

Frightened at the silence, they searched every corner
of the garden, the house, and the neighbouring wood,
but no trace of the girls was to be found anywhere. The
earth seemed to have swallowed them up. The poor
parents were in despair. The queen wept all the way
home, and for many days after, and the king issued a
proclamation that whoever should bring back his lost
daughters should have one of them to wife, and should,
after his death, reign in his stead.

Now two young generals were at that time living at
the court, and when they heard the king's declaration,
they said one to the other : ' Let us go in search of them ;
perhaps we shall be the lucky persons.'

And they set out, each mounted on a strong horse,
taking with them a change of raiment and some money.

But though they inquired at every village they rode
through, they could hear nothing of the princesses, and
by-and-by their money was all spent, and they were forced
to sell their horses, or give up the search. Even this
money only lasted a little while longer, and nothing but
their clothes lay between them and starvation. They
sold the spare garments that were bound on their sad-
dles, and went in the coats they stood up in to the inn, to
beg for some food, as they were really starving. When,
however, they had to pay for what they had eaten and
drank, they said to the host : ' We have no money, and
naught but the clothes we stand up in. Take these, and
give us instead some old rags, and let us stay here and
serve you.' And the innkeeper was content with the bargain, and the generals remained, and were his servants.

All this time the king and queen remained in their
palace hungering for their children, but not a word was
heard of either of them or of the generals who had gone
to seek for them.

Now there was living in the palace a faithful servant

NOW THE THREE PRINCESSES WERE LOST

of the king's called Bensurdatu, who had served him for many years, and when Bensurdatu saw how grieved the king was, he lifted up his voice and said to him : ' Your majesty, let me go and seek your daughters.'

' No, no, Bensurdatu,' replied the king. ' Three daughters have I lost, and two generals, and shall I lose you also ? '

But Bensurdatu said again : ' Let me now go, your majesty; trust me, and I will bring you back your daughters.'

Then the king gave way, and Bensurdatu set forth, and rode on till he came to the inn, where he dismounted and asked for food. It was brought by the two generals, whom he knew at once in spite of their miserable clothes, and, much astonished, asked them how in the world they came there.

They told him all their adventures, and he sent for the innkeeper, and said to him : ' Give them back their garments, and I will pay everything that they owe you.'

And the innkeeper did as he was bid, and when the two generals were dressed in their proper clothes, they declared they would join Bensurdatu, and with him seek for the king's daughters.

The three companions rode on for many miles, and at length they came to a wild place, without sign of a human being. It was getting dark, and fearing to be lost on this desolate spot they pushed on their horses, and at last saw a light in the window of a tiny hut.

' Who comes there ?' asked a voice, as they knocked at the door.

' Oh ! have pity on us, and give us a night's shelter,' replied Bensurdatu ; ' we are three tired travellers who have lost our way.'

Then the door was opened by a very old woman who stood back, and beckoned them to enter. ' Whence do you come, and whither do you go ? ' said she.

' Ah, good woman, we have a heavy task before us,'

answered Bensurdatu, 'we are bound to carry the king's daughters back to the palace!'

'Oh, unhappy creatures,' cried she, 'you know not what you are doing! The king's daughters were covered by a thick cloud, and no one knows where they may now be.'

'Oh, tell us, if you know, my good woman,' entreated Bensurdatu, 'for with them lies all our happiness.'

'Even if I were to tell you,' answered she, 'you could not rescue them. To do that you would have to go to the very bottom of a deep river, and though certainly you would find the king's daughters there, yet the two eldest are guarded by two giants, and the youngest is watched by a serpent with seven heads.'

The two generals, who stood by listening, were filled with terror at her words, and wished to return immediately; but Bensurdatu stood firm, and said : 'Now we have got so far we must carry the thing through. Tell us where the river is, so that we may get there as soon as possible.' And the old woman told them, and gave them some cheese, wine, and bread, so that they should not set forth starving; and when they had eaten and drunk they laid themselves down to sleep.

The sun had only just risen above the hills next morning before they all woke, and, taking leave of the wise woman who had helped them, they rode on till they came to the river.

'I am the eldest,' said one of the generals, 'and it is my right to go down first.'

So the others fastened a cord round him, and gave him a little bell, and let him down into the water. But scarcely had the river closed above his head when such dreadful rushing sounds and peals of thunder came crashing round about him that he lost all his courage, and rang his bell, if perchance it might be heard amidst all this clamour. Great was his relief when the rope began slowly to pull him upwards.

Then the other general plunged in; but he fared no better than the first, and was soon on dry ground again.

'Well, you are a brave pair!' said Bensurdatu, as he tied the rope round his own waist; 'let us see what will happen to me.' And when he heard the thunder and clamour round about him he thought to himself, 'Oh, make as much noise as you like, it won't hurt me!' When his feet touched the bottom he found himself in a large, brilliantly lighted hall, and in the middle sat the eldest princess, and in front of her lay a huge giant, fast asleep. Directly she saw Bensurdatu she nodded to him, and asked with her eyes how he had come there.

For answer he drew his sword, and was about to cut off the giant's head, when she stopped him quickly, and made signs to hide himself, as the giant was just beginning to wake. 'I smell the flesh of a man!' murmured he, stretching his great arms.

'Why, how in the world could any man get down here?' replied she; 'you had better go to sleep again.'

So he turned over and went to sleep. Then the princess signed to Bensurdatu, who drew his sword and cut off the giant's head with such a blow that it flew into the corner. And the heart of the princess leapt within her, and she placed a golden crown on the head of Bensurdatu, and called him her deliverer.

'Now show me where your sisters are,' he said, 'that I may free them also.'

So the princess opened a door, and led him into another hall, wherein sat her next sister, guarded by a giant who was fast asleep. When the second princess saw them, she made a sign to them to hide themselves, for the giant was showing symptoms of waking.

'I smell man's flesh!' murmured he, sleepily.

'Now, how could any man get down here?' asked she; 'go to sleep again.' And as soon as he closed his eyes, Bensurdatu stole out from his corner, and struck such a blow at his head that it flew far, far away. The princess could not find words to thank Bensurdatu for what he had done, and she too placed in his hand a golden crown.

'Now show me where your youngest sister is,' said he, 'that I may free her also.'

'Ah! that I fear you will never be able to do,' sighed they, 'for she is in the power of a serpent with seven heads.'

'Take me to him,' replied Bensurdatu. 'It will be a splendid fight.'

Then the princess opened a door, and Bensurdatu passed through, and found himself in a hall that was even larger than the other two. And there stood the youngest sister, chained fast to the wall, and before her was stretched a serpent with seven heads, horrible to see. As Bensurdatu came forward it twisted all its seven heads in his direction, and then made a quick dart to snatch him within its grasp. But Bensurdatu drew his sword and laid about him, till the seven heads were rolling on the floor. Flinging down his sword he rushed to the princess and broke her chains, and she wept for joy, and embraced him, and took the golden crown from off her head, and placed it in his hand.

'Now we must go back to the upper world,' said Bensurdatu, and led her to the bottom of the river. The other princesses were waiting there, and he tied the rope round the eldest, and rung his bell. And the generals above heard, and drew her gently up. They then unfastened the cord and threw it back into the river, and in a few moments the second princess stood beside her sister.

So now there were left only Bensurdatu and the youngest princess. 'Dear Bensurdatu,' said she, 'do me a kindness, and let them draw you up before me. I dread the treachery of the generals.

'No, no,' replied Bensurdatu, 'I certainly will not

BENSURDATU ATTACKS THE SEVEN-HEADED SERPENT.

leave you down here. There is nothing to fear from my comrades.'

' If it is your wish I will go up then ; but first I swear that if you do not follow to marry me, I shall stay single for the rest of my life.' Then he bound the rope round her, and the generals drew her up.

But instead of lowering the rope again into the river, envy at the courage and success of Bensurdatu so filled the hearts of the two generals, that they turned away and left him to perish. And, more than that, they threatened the princesses, and forced them to promise to tell their parents that it was the two generals who had set them free. ' And if they should ask you about Bensurdatu, you must say you have never seen him,' they added ; and the princesses, fearing for their lives, promised everything, and they rode back to court together.

The king and queen were beside themselves with joy when they saw their dear children once more. But when the generals had told their story, and the dangers they had run, the king declared that they had gained their reward, and that the two eldest princesses should become their wives.

And now we must see what poor Bensurdatu was doing.

He waited patiently a long, long time, but when the rope never came back he knew he had been right, and that his comrades had betrayed him. ' Ah, now I shall never reach the world again,' murmured he ; but being a brave man, and knowing that moaning his fate would profit him nothing, he rose and began to search through the three halls, where, perhaps, he might find something to help him. In the last one stood a dish, covered with food, which reminded him that he was hungry, and he sat down and ate and drank.

Months passed away, when, one morning, as he was walking through the halls, he noticed a purse hanging on the wall, which had never been there before. He took it down to examine it, and nearly let it fall with surprise when a voice came from the purse saying : ' What commands have you ? '

' Oh, take me out of this horrible place, and up into the world again ; ' and in a moment he was standing by the river bank, with the purse tightly grasped in his hand.

' Now let me have the most beautiful ship that ever was built, all manned and ready for sea.' And there was the ship, with a flag floating from its mast on which were the words, ' King with the three crowns.' Then Bensurdatu climbed on board, and sailed away to the city where the three princesses dwelt; and when he reached the harbour he blew trumpets and beat drums, so that every one ran to the doors and windows. And the king heard too, and saw the beautiful vessel, and said to himself : ' That must indeed be a mighty monarch, for he has three crowns while I have only one.' So he hastened to greet the stranger, and invited him to his castle, for, thought he, ' this will be a fine husband for my youngest daughter.' Now, the youngest princess had never married, and had turned a deaf ear to all her wooers.

Such a long time had passed since Bensurdatu had left the palace, that the king never guessed for a moment that the splendidly clad stranger before him was the man whom he had so deeply mourned as dead. ' Noble lord,' said he, ' let us feast and make merry together, and then, if it seem good to you, do me the honour to take my youngest daughter to wife.'

And Bensurdatu was glad, and they all sat down to a great feast, and there were great rejoicings. But only the youngest daughter was sad, for her thoughts were with Bensurdatu. After they arose from the table the king said to her, ' Dear child, this mighty lord does you the honour to ask your hand in marriage.'

' Oh, father,' answered she, ' spare me, I pray you, for I desire to remain single.'

Then Bensurdatu turned to her, and said: 'And if I were Bensurdatu, would you give the same answer to me?'

And as she stood silently gazing at him, he added: 'Yes, I am Bensurdatu; and this is my story.'

The king and queen had their hearts stirred within them at the tale of his adventures, and when he had ended the king stretched out his hand, and said: 'Dear Bensurdatu, my youngest daughter shall indeed be your wife; and when I die my crown shall be yours. As for the men who have betrayed you, they shall leave the country and you shall see them no more.'

And the wedding feast was ordered, and rejoicings were held for three days over the marriage of Bensurdatu and the youngest princess.

[From the *Sicilianische Märchen.*]

THE MAGICIAN'S HORSE

ONCE upon a time, there was a king who had three sons. Now it happened that one day the three princes went out hunting in a large forest at some distance from their father's palace, and the youngest prince lost his way, so his brothers had to return home without him.

For four days the prince wandered through the glades of the forest, sleeping on moss beneath the stars at night, and by day living on roots and wild berries. At last, on the morning of the fifth day, he came to a large open space in the middle of the forest, and here stood a stately palace ; but neither within nor without was there a trace of human life. The prince entered the open door and wandered through the deserted rooms without seeing a living soul. At last he came on a great hall, and in the centre of the hall was a table spread with dainty dishes and choice wines. The prince sat down, and satisfied his hunger and thirst, and immediately afterwards the table disappeared from his sight. This struck the prince as very strange ; but though he continued his search through all the rooms, upstairs and down, he could find no one to speak to. At last, just as it was beginning to get dark, he heard steps in the distance and he saw an old man coming towards him up the stairs.

' What are you doing wandering about my castle ? ' asked the old man.

To whom the prince replied : ' I lost my way hunting in the forest. If you will take me into your

service, I should like to stay with you, and will serve you
faithfully.'

'Very well,' said the old man. 'You may enter my
service. You will have to keep the stove always lit, you
will have to fetch the wood for it from the forest, and you
will have the charge of the black horse in the stables. I
will pay you a florin a day, and at meal times you will always
find the table in the hall spread with food and wine, and
you can eat and drink as much as you require.'

The prince was satisfied, and he entered the old man's
service, and promised to see that there was always wood
on the stove, so that the fire should never die out. Now,
though he did not know it, his new master was a magician,
and the flame of the stove was a magic fire, and if it had
gone out the magician would have lost a great part of his
power.

One day the prince forgot, and let the fire burn so
low that it very nearly burnt out. Just as the flame
was flickering the old man stormed into the room.

'What do you mean by letting the fire burn so low?'
he growled. 'I have only arrived in the nick of time.'
And while the prince hastily threw a log on the stove and
blew on the ashes to kindle a glow, his master gave him
a severe box on the ear, and warned him that if ever it
happened again it would fare badly with him.

One day the prince was sitting disconsolate in the
stables when, to his surprise, the black horse spoke to
him.

'Come into my stall,' it said, 'I have something to say
to you. Fetch my bridle and saddle from that cupboard
and put them on me. Take the bottle that is beside
them; it contains an ointment which will make your hair
shine like pure gold; then put all the wood you can
gather together on to the stove, till it is piled quite high up.'

So the prince did what the horse told him; he saddled
and bridled the horse, he put the ointment on his hair
till it shone like gold, and he made such a big fire in the

stove that the flames sprang up and set fire to the roof, and in a few minutes the palace was burning like a huge bonfire.

Then he hurried back to the stables, and the horse said to him : 'There is one thing more you must do. In the cupboard you will find a looking-glass, a brush and a riding-whip. Bring them with you, mount on my back, and ride as hard as you can, for now the house is burning merrily.'

The prince did as the horse bade him. Scarcely had he got into the saddle than the horse was off and away, galloping at such a pace that, in a short time, the forest and all the country belonging to the magician lay far behind them.

In the meantime the magician returned to his palace, which he found in smouldering ruins. In vain he called for his servant. At last he went to look for him in the stables, and when he discovered that the black horse had disappeared too, he at once suspected that they had gone together; so he mounted a roan horse that was in the next stall, and set out in pursuit.

As the prince rode, the quick ears of his horse heard the sound of pursuing feet.

'Look behind you,' he said, 'and see if the old man is following.' And the prince turned in his saddle and saw a cloud like smoke or dust in the distance.

'We must hurry,' said the horse.

After they had galloped for some time, the horse said again : 'Look behind, and see if he is still at some distance.'

'He is quite close,' answered the prince.

'Then throw the looking-glass on the ground,' said the horse. So the prince threw it; and when the magician came up, the roan horse stepped on the mirror, and crash ! his foot went through the glass, and he stumbled and fell, cutting his feet so badly that there was nothing for the old man to do but to go slowly back with him to the

stables, and put new shoes on his feet. Then they started
once more in pursuit of the prince, for the magician
set great value on the horse, and was determined not to
lose it.

How the Magician was Thwarted by the Brush

In the meanwhile the prince had gone a great distance ; but the quick ears of the black horse detected the
sound of following feet from afar.

'Dismount,' he said to the prince; 'put your ear to
the ground, and tell me if you do not hear a sound.'

So the prince dismounted and listened. 'I seem to
hear the earth tremble,' he said; 'I think he cannot be
very far off.'

'Mount me at once,' answered the horse, 'and I will gallop as fast as I can.' And he set off so fast that the earth seemed to fly from under his hoofs.

'Look back once more,' he said, after a short time, 'and see if he is in sight.'

'I see a cloud and a flame,' answered the prince; 'but a long way off.'

'We must make haste,' said the horse. And shortly after he said: 'Look back again; he can't be far off now.'

The prince turned in his saddle, and exclaimed: 'He is close behind us, in a minute the flame from his horse's nostrils will reach us.'

'Then throw the brush on the ground,' said the horse. And the prince threw it, and in an instant the brush was changed into such a thick wood that even a bird could not have got through it, and when the old man got up to it the roan horse came suddenly to a stand-still, not able to advance a step into the thick tangle. So there was nothing for the magician to do but to retrace his steps, to fetch an axe, with which he cut himself a way through the wood. But it took him some time, during which the prince and the black horse got on well ahead.

But once more they heard the sound of pursuing feet. 'Look back,' said the black horse, 'and see if he is following.'

'Yes,' answered the prince, 'this time I hear him distinctly.

'Let us hurry on,' said the horse. And a little later he said: 'Look back now, and see if he is in sight.'

'Yes,' said the prince, turning round, 'I see the flame; he is close behind us.'

'Then you must throw down the whip,' answered the horse.' And in the twinkling of an eye the whip was changed into a broad river. When the old man got up to it he urged the roan horse into the water, but as the water

mounted higher and higher, the magic flame which gave
the magician all his power grew smaller and smaller, till,
with a fizz, it went out, and the old man and the roan
horse sank in the river and disappeared. When the
prince looked round they were no longer to be seen.

'Now,' said the horse, 'you may dismount; there is
nothing more to fear, for the magician is dead. Beside
that brook you will find a willow wand. Gather it, and
strike the earth with it, and it will open and you will see
a door at your feet.'

When the prince had struck the earth with the wand
a door appeared, and opened into a large vaulted stone
hall.

'Lead me into that hall,' said the horse, 'I will stay
there; but you must go through the fields till you reach
a garden, in the midst of which is a king's palace. When
you get there you must ask to be taken into the king's
service. Good-bye, and don't forget me.'

So they parted; but first the horse made the prince
promise not to let anyone in the palace see his golden
hair. So he bound a scarf round it, like a turban, and the
prince set out through the fields, till he reached a beautiful
garden, and beyond the garden he saw the walls and
towers of a stately palace. At the garden gate he met
the gardener, who asked him what he wanted.

'I want to take service with the king,' replied the
prince.

'Well, you may stay and work under me in the garden,'
said the man; for as the prince was dressed like a
poor man, he could not tell that he was a king's son. 'I
need someone to weed the ground and to sweep the dead
leaves from the paths. You shall have a florin a day, a
horse to help you to cart the leaves away, and food and
drink.'

So the prince consented, and set about his work. But
when his food was given to him he only ate half of it;
the rest he carried to the vaulted hall beside the brook,

and gave to the black horse. And this he did every day, and the horse thanked him for his faithful friendship.

One evening, as they were together, after his work in the garden was over, the horse said to him : 'To-morrow a large company of princes and great lords are coming to your king's palace. They are coming from far and near, as wooers for the three princesses. They will all stand in a row in the courtyard of the palace, and the three princesses will come out, and each will carry a diamond apple in her hand, which she will throw into the air. At whosesoever feet the apple falls he will be the bridegroom of that princess. You must be close by in the garden at your work. The apple of the youngest princess, who is much the most beautiful of the sisters, will roll past the wooers and stop in front of you. Pick it up at once and put it in your pocket.'

The next day, when the wooers were all assembled in the courtyard of the castle, everything happened just as the horse had said. The princesses threw the apples into the air, and the diamond apple of the youngest princess rolled past all the wooers, out on to the garden, and stopped at the feet of the young gardener, who was busy sweeping the leaves away. In a moment he had stooped down, picked up the apple and put it in his pocket. As he stooped the scarf round his head slipped a little to one side, and the princess caught sight of his golden hair, and loved him from that moment.

But the king was very sad, for his youngest daughter was the one he loved best. But there was no help for it ; and the next day a threefold wedding was celebrated at the palace, and after the wedding the youngest princess returned with her husband to the small hut in the garden where he lived.

Some time after this the people of a neighbouring country went to war with the king, and he set out to battle, accompanied by the husbands of his two eldest daughters mounted on stately steeds. But the husband of the

The Gardener gets the Apple

youngest daughter had nothing but the old broken-down horse which helped him in his garden work; and the king, who was ashamed of this son-in-law, refused to give him any other.

So as he was determined not to be left behind, he went into the garden, mounted the sorry nag, and set out. But scarcely had he ridden a few yards before the horse stumbled and fell. So he dismounted and went down to the brook, to where the black horse lived in the vaulted hall. And the horse said to him: 'Saddle and bridle me, and then go into the next room and you will find a suit of armour and a sword. Put them on, and we will ride forth together to battle.'

And the prince did as he was told; and when he had mounted the horse his armour glittered in the sun, and he looked so brave and handsome, that no one would have recognised him as the gardener who swept away the dead leaves from the paths. The horse bore him away at a great pace, and when they reached the battle-field they saw that the king was losing the day, so many of his warriors had been slain. But when the warrior on his black charger and in glittering armour appeared on the scene, hewing right and left with his sword, the enemy were dismayed and fled in all directions, leaving the king master of the field. Then the king and his two sons-in-law, when they saw their deliverer, shouted, and all that was left of the army joined in the cry: 'A god has come to our rescue!' And they would have surrounded him, but his black horse rose in the air and bore him out of their sight.

Soon after this, part of the country rose in rebellion against the king, and once more he and his two sons-in-law had to fare forth to battle. And the son-in-law who was disguised as a gardener wanted to fight too. So he came to the king and said: 'Dear father, let me ride with you to fight your enemies.'

'I don't want a blockhead like you to fight for me,

answered the king. 'Besides, I haven't got a horse fit for you. But see, there is a carter on the road carting hay, you may take his horse.'

So the prince took the carter's horse, but the poor beast was old and tired, and after it had gone a few yards it stumbled and fell. So the prince returned sadly to the garden and watched the king ride forth at the head of the army accompanied by his two sons-in-law. When they were out of sight the prince betook himself to the vaulted chamber by the brook-side, and having taken counsel of the faithful black horse, he put on the glittering suit of armour, and was borne on the back of the horse through the air, to where the battle was being fought. And once more he routed the king's enemies, hacking to right and left with his sword. And again they all cried: 'A god has come to our rescue!' But when they tried to detain him the black horse rose in the air and bore him out of their sight.

When the king and his sons-in-law returned home they could talk of nothing but the hero who had fought for them, and all wondered who he could be.

Shortly afterwards the king of a neighbouring country declared war, and once more the king and his sons-in-law and his subjects had to prepare themselves for battle, and once more the prince begged to ride with them, but the king said he had no horse to spare for him. 'But,' he added, 'you may take the horse of the woodman who brings the wood from the forest, it is good enough for you.'

So the prince took the woodman's horse, but it was so old and useless that it could not carry him beyond the castle gates. So he betook himself once more to the vaulted hall, where the black horse had prepared a still more magnificent suit of armour for him than the one he had worn on the previous occasions, and when he had put it on, and mounted on the back of the horse, he bore him straight to the battle-field, and once more he scattered the king's enemies, fighting single-handed in their

ranks, and they fled in all directions. But it happened
that one of the enemy struck with his sword and wounded
the prince in the leg. And the king took his own pocket-
handkerchief, with his name and crown embroïdered on it,

The Hero discovered

and bound it round the wounded leg. And the king would
fain have compelled him to mount in a litter and be
carried straight to the palace, and two of his knights
were to lead the black charger to the royal stables. But
the prince put his hand on the mane of his faithful

horse, and managed to pull himself up into the saddle, and the horse mounted into the air with him. Then they all shouted and cried: 'The warrior who has fought for us is a god! He must be a god.'

And throughout all the kingdom nothing else was spoken about, and all the people said: 'Who can the hero be who has fought for us in so many battles? He cannot be a man, he must be a god.'

And the king said: 'If only I could see him once more, and if it turned out that after all he was a man and not a god, I would reward him with half my kingdom.'

Now when the prince reached his home—the gardener's hut where he lived with his wife—he was weary, and he lay down on his bed and slept. And his wife noticed the handkerchief bound round his wounded leg, and she wondered what it could be. Then she looked at it more closely and saw in the corner that it was embroidered with her father's name and the royal crown. So she ran straight to the palace and told her father. And he and his two sons-in-law followed her back to her house, and there the gardener lay asleep on his bed. And the scarf that he always wore bound round his head had slipped off, and his golden hair gleamed on the pillow. And they all recognised that this was the hero who had fought and won so many battles for them.

Then there was great rejoicing throughout the land, and the king rewarded his son-in-law with half of his kingdom, and he and his wife reigned happily over it.

THE LITTLE GRAY MAN

A NUN, a countryman, and a blacksmith were once wandering through the world together. One day they lost their way in a thick, dark forest, and were thankful when they saw, in the distance, the walls of a house, where they hoped they might obtain refuge for the night. When they got close to the house they found that it was an old deserted castle, fast falling into ruins, but with some of the rooms in it still habitable. As they were homeless they determined to take up their abode in the castle, and they arranged that one of them should always stay at home and keep house, while the other two went out into the world to seek their fortunes.

The lot of remaining at home fell first to the nun, and when the countryman and the blacksmith had gone out into the wood, she set to work, tidied up the house, and prepared all the food for the day. As her companions did not come home for their mid-day meal, she ate up her own portion and put the rest in the oven to keep warm. Just as she was sitting down to sew, the door opened and a little gray man came in, and, standing before her, said: 'Oh! how cold I am!'

The nun was very sorry for him, and said at once: 'Sit down by the fire and warm yourself.'

The little man did as he was told, and soon called out: 'Oh! how hungry I am!'

The nun answered: 'There is food in the oven, help yourself.'

The little man did not need to be told twice, for he set to work and ate up everything with the greatest possible despatch. When the nun saw this she was very angry, and scolded the dwarf because he had left nothing for her companions.

The little man resented her words, and flew into such a passion that he seized the nun, beat her, and threw her first against one wall and then against the other. When he had nearly killed her he left her lying on the floor, and hastily walked out of the house.

In the evening the countryman and the blacksmith returned home, and when they found, on demanding their dinner, that there was nothing left for them, they reproached the nun bitterly, and refused to believe her when she tried to tell them what had happened.

The next day the countryman asked to be left in charge of the house, and promised that, if he remained at home, no one should go hungry to bed. So the other two went out into the forest, and the countryman having prepared the food for the day, ate up his own portion, and put the rest in the oven. Just as he had finished clearing away, the door opened and the little gray man walked in, and this time he had two heads. He shook and trembled as before, and exclaimed : 'Oh! how cold I am.'

The countryman, who was frightened out of his wits, begged him to draw near the fire and warm himself.

Soon after the dwarf looked greedily round, and said : 'Oh! how hungry I am!'

'There is food in the oven, so you can eat,' replied the countryman.

Then the little man fell to with both his heads, and soon finished the last morsel.

When the countryman scolded him for this proceeding he treated him exactly as he had done the nun, and left the poor fellow more dead than alive.

Now when the blacksmith came home with the nun

THE LITTLE GRAY MAN

"HE DEMANDED MORE"

in the evening, and found nothing for supper, he flew into
a passion; and swore that he would stay at home the
following day, and that no one should go supperless to
bed.

When day dawned the countryman and the nun set
out into the wood, and the blacksmith prepared all
the food for the day as the others had done. Again the
gray dwarf entered the house without knocking, and this
time he had three heads. When he complained of cold,
the blacksmith told him to sit near the fire ; and when he
said he was hungry, the blacksmith put some food on a
plate and gave it to him. The dwarf made short work of
what was provided for him, and then, looking greedily
round with his six eyes, he demanded more. When the
blacksmith refused to give him another morsel, he flew
into a terrible rage, and proceeded to treat him in the
same way as he had treated his companions.

But the blacksmith was a match for him, for he seized
a huge hammer and struck off two of the dwarf's heads
with it. The little man yelled with pain and rage, and
hastily fled from the house. The blacksmith ran after
him, and pursued him for a long way ; but at last they
came to an iron door, and through it the little creature
vanished. The door shut behind him, and the blacksmith
had to give up the pursuit and return home. He found
that the nun and the countryman had come back in the
meantime, and they were much delighted when he placed
some food before them, and showed them the two heads
he had struck off with his hammer. The three companions determined there and then to free themselves
from the power of the gray dwarf, and the very next day
they set to work to find him.

They had to walk a long way, and to search for many
hours, before they found the iron door through which the
dwarf had disappeared ; and when they had found it they
had the greatest difficulty in opening it. When at last
they succeeded in forcing the lock, they entered a large hall,

in which sat a young and lovely girl, working at a table. The moment she saw the nun, the blacksmith, and the countryman, she fell at their feet, thanking them with tears in her eyes for having set her free. She told them that she was a king's daughter, who had been shut up in the castle by a mighty magician. The day before, just about noon, she had suddenly felt the magic power over her disappear, and ever since that moment she had eagerly awaited the arrival of her deliverers. She went on to say that there was yet another princess shut up in the castle, who had also fallen under the might of the magician.

They wandered through many halls and rooms till at last they found the second princess, who was quite as grateful as the first, and thanked the three companions most warmly for having set her free.

Then the princesses told their rescuers that a great treasure lay hidden in the cellars of the castle, but that it was carefully guarded by a fierce and terrible dog.

Nothing daunted, they all went down below at once, and found the fierce animal mounting guard over the treasure as the princesses had said. But one blow from the blacksmith's hammer soon made an end of the monster, and they found themselves in a vaulted chamber full of gold and silver and precious stones. Beside the treasure stood a young and handsome man, who advanced to meet them, and thanked the nun, the blacksmith, and the countryman, for having freed him from the magic spell he was under. He told them that he was a king's son, who had been banished to this castle by a wicked magician, and that he had been changed into the three-headed dwarf. When he had lost two of his heads the magic power over the two princesses had been removed, and when the blacksmith had killed the horrible dog, then he too had been set free.

To show his gratitude he begged the three companions to divide the treasure between them, which they did;

but there was so much of it that it took a very long time.

The princesses, too, were so grateful to their rescuers, that one married the blacksmith, and the other the countryman.

Then the prince claimed the nun as his bride, and they all lived happily together till they died.

[From the German. *Kletke.*]

HERR LAZARUS AND THE DRAKEN

ONCE upon a time there was a cobbler called Lazarus, who was very fond of honey. One day, as he ate some while he sat at work, the flies collected in such numbers that with one blow he killed forty. Then he went and ordered a sword to be made for him, on which he had written these words : ' With one blow I have slain forty.' When the sword was ready he took it and went out into the world, and when he was two days' journey from home he came to a spring, by which he laid himself down and slept.

Now in that country there dwelt Draken, one of whom came to the spring to draw water ; there he found Lazarus sleeping, and read what was written on his sword. Then he went back to his people and told them what he had seen, and they all advised him to make fellowship with this powerful stranger. So the Draken returned to the spring, awoke Lazarus, and said that if it was agreeable to him they should make fellowship together.

Lazarus answered that he was willing, and after a priest had blessed the fellowship, they returned together to the other Draken, and Lazarus dwelt among them. After some days they told him that it was their custom to take it in turns to bring wood and water, and as he was now of their company, he must take his turn. They went first for water and wood, but at last it came to be Lazarus's turn to go for water. The Draken had a great leathern bag, holding two hundred measures of

water. This Lazarus could only, with great difficulty,
drag empty to the spring, and because he could not carry
it back full, he did not fill it at all, but, instead, he dug up
the ground all round the spring.

As Lazarus remained so long away, the Draken sent

HOW THE DRAKEN FOUND HERR LAZARUS ASLEEP by the SPRING

one of their number to see what had become of him, and
when this one came to the spring, Lazarus said to him :
'We will no more plague ourselves by carrying water
every day. I will bring the entire spring home at once,
and so we shall be freed from this burden.'

But the Draken called out : ' On no account, Herr Lazarus, else we shall all die of thirst ; rather will we carry the water ourselves in turns, and you alone shall be exempt.'

Next it comes to be Lazarus's turn to bring the wood. Now the Draken, when they fetched the wood, always took an entire tree on their shoulder, and so carried it home. Because Lazarus could not imitate them in this, he went to the forest, tied all the trees together with a thick rope, and remained in the forest till evening. Again the Draken sent one of them after him to see what had become of him, and when this one asked what he was about, Lazarus answered : ' I will bring the entire forest home at once, so that after that we may have rest.'

But the Draken called out : ' By no means, Herr Lazarus, else we shall all die of cold ; rather will we go ourselves to bring wood, and let you be free.' And then the Draken tore up one tree, threw it over his shoulder, and so carried it home.

When they had lived together some time, the Draken became weary of Lazarus, and agreed among themselves to kill him ; each Draken, in the night while Lazarus slept, should strike him a blow with a hatchet. But Lazarus heard of this scheme, and when the evening came, he took a log of wood, covered it with his cloak, laid it in the place where he usually slept, and then hid himself. In the night the Draken came, and each one hit the log a blow with his hatchet, till it flew in pieces.

Then they believed their object was gained, and they lay down again.

Thereupon Lazarus took the log, threw it away, and laid himself down in its stead. Towards dawn, he began to groan, and when the Draken heard that, they asked what ailed him, to which he made answer : ' The gnats have stung me horribly.'

This terrified the Draken, for they believed that Lazarus took their blows for gnat-stings, and they determined at any price to get rid of him. Next morning, therefore, they asked him if he had not wife or child, and said that if he would like to go and visit them they would give him a bag of gold to take away with him. He agreed willingly to this, but asked further that one of the Draken should go with him to carry the bag of gold. They consented, and one was sent with him.

When they had come to within a short distance of Lazarus's house, he said to the Draken : ' Stop here, in the meantime, for I must go on in front and tie up my children, lest they eat you.'

So he went and tied his children with strong ropes, and said to them : ' As soon as the Draken comes in sight, call out as loud as you can, " Drakenflesh ! Drakenflesh ! " '

So, when the Draken appeared, the children cried out : ' Drakenflesh ! Drakenflesh ! ' and this so terrified the Draken that he let the bag fall and fled.

On the road he met a fox, which asked him why he seemed so frightened. He answered that he was afraid of the children of Herr Lazarus, who had been within a hair-breadth of eating him up.

But the fox laughed, and said : ' What ! you were afraid of the children of Herr Lazarus ? He had two fowls, one of which I ate yesterday, the other I will go and fetch now—if you do not believe me, come and see for yourself ; but you must first tie yourself on to my tail.'

The Draken then tied himself on to the fox's tail, and went back thus with it to Lazarus's house, in order to see what it would arrange. There stood Lazarus with his gun raised ready to fire, who, when he saw the fox coming along with the Draken, called out to the fox : ' Did I not tell you to bring me all the Draken, and you bring me only one ? '

When the Draken heard that he made off to the right-about at once, and ran so fast that the fox was dashed in pieces against the stones.

When Lazarus had got quit of the Draken he built himself, with their gold, a magnificent house, in which he spent the rest of his days in great enjoyment.

THE STORY OF THE QUEEN OF THE FLOWERY ISLES

THERE once lived a queen who ruled over the Flowery Isles, whose husband, to her extreme grief, died a few years after their marriage. On being left a widow she devoted herself almost entirely to the education of the two charming princesses, her only children. The elder of them was so lovely that as she grew up her mother greatly feared she would excite the jealousy of the Queen of all the Isles, who prided herself on being the most beautiful woman in the world, and insisted on all rivals bowing before her charms.

In order the better to gratify her vanity she had urged the king, her husband, to make war on all the surrounding islands, and as his greatest wish was to please her, the only conditions he imposed on any newly-conquered country was that each princess of every royal house should attend his court as soon as she was fifteen years old, and do homage to the transcendent beauty of his queen.

The queen of the Flowery Isles, well aware of this law, was fully determined to present her daughter to the proud queen as soon as her fifteenth birthday was past.

The queen herself had heard a rumour of the young princess's great beauty, and awaited her visit with some anxiety, which soon developed into jealousy, for when the interview took place it was impossible not to be dazzled by such radiant charms, and she was obliged to admit that she had never beheld anyone so exquisitely lovely.

Of course she thought in her own mind ' excepting myself! ' for nothing could have made her believe it possible that anyone could eclipse her.

But the outspoken admiration of the entire court soon undeceived her, and made her so angry that she pretended illness and retired to her own rooms, so as to avoid witnessing the princess's triumph. She also sent word to the Queen of the Flowery Isles that she was sorry not to be well enough to see her again, and advised her to return to her own states with the princess, her daughter.

This message was entrusted to one of the great ladies of the court, who was an old friend of the Queen of the Flowery Isles, and who advised her not to wait to take a formal leave but to go home as fast as she could.

The queen was not slow to take the hint, and lost no time in obeying it. Being well aware of the magic powers of the incensed queen, she warned her daughter that she was threatened by some great danger if she left the palace for any reason whatever during the next six months.

The princess promised obedience, and no pains were spared to make the time pass pleasantly for her.

The six months were nearly at an end, and on the very last day a splendid fête was to take place in a lovely meadow quite near the palace. The princess, who had been able to watch all the preparations from her window, implored her mother to let her go as far as the meadow; and the queen, thinking all risk must be over, consented, and promised to take her there herself.

The whole court was delighted to see their much-loved princess at liberty, and everyone set off in high glee to join in the fête.

The princess, overjoyed at being once more in the open air, was walking a little in advance of her party

The Princess is swallowed up by the Earth.

when suddenly the earth opened under her feet and closed again after swallowing her up!

The queen fainted away with terror, and the younger princess burst into floods of tears and could hardly be dragged away from the fatal spot, whilst the court was overwhelmed with horror at so great a calamity.

Orders were given to bore the earth to a great depth, but in vain; not a trace of the vanished princess was to be found.

She sank right through the earth and found herself in a desert place with nothing but rocks and trees and no sign of any human being. The only living creature she saw was a very pretty little dog, who ran up to her and at once began to caress her. She took him in her arms, and after playing with him for a little put him down again, when he started off in front of her, looking round from time to time as though begging her to follow.

She let him lead her on, and presently reached a little hill, from which she saw a valley full of lovely fruit trees, bearing flowers and fruit together. The ground was also covered with fruit and flowers, and in the middle of the valley rose a fountain surrounded by a velvety lawn.

The princess hastened to this charming spot, and sitting down on the grass began to think over the misfortune which had befallen her, and burst into tears as she reflected on her sad condition.

The fruit and clear fresh water would, she knew, prevent her from dying of hunger or thirst, but how could she escape if any wild beast appeared and tried to devour her?

At length, having thought over every possible evil which could happen, the princess tried to distract her mind by playing with the little dog. She spent the whole day near the fountain, but as night drew on she wondered what she should do, when she noticed that the little dog was pulling at her dress.

She paid no heed to him at first, but as he continued

to pull her dress and then run a few steps in one particular direction, she at last decided to follow him; he stopped before a rock with a large opening in the centre, which he evidently wished her to enter.

The princess did so and discovered a large and beautiful cave lit up by the brilliancy of the stones with which it was lined, with a little couch covered with soft moss in one corner. She lay down on it and the dog at once nestled at her feet. Tired out with all she had gone through she soon fell asleep.

Next morning she was awakened very early by the songs of many birds. The little dog woke up too, and sprang round her in his most caressing manner. She got up and went outside, the dog as before running on in front and turning back constantly to take her dress and draw her on.

She let him have his way and he soon led her back to the beautiful garden where she had spent part of the day before. Here she ate some fruit, drank some water of the fountain, and felt as if she had made an excellent meal. She walked about amongst the flowers, played with her little dog, and at night returned to sleep in the cave.

In this way the princess passed several months, and as her first terrors died away she gradually became more resigned to her fate. The little dog, too, was a great comfort, and her constant companion.

One day she noticed that he seemed very sad and did not even caress her as usual. Fearing he might be ill she carried him to a spot where she had seen him eat some particular herbs, hoping they might do him good, but he would not touch them. He spent all the night, too, sighing and groaning as if in great pain.

At last the princess fell asleep, and when she awoke her first thought was for her little pet, but not finding him at her feet as usual, she ran out of the cave to look for him. As she stepped out of the cave she caught

SHE·SPENT·THE·WHOLE·DAY·NEAR THE·FOUNTAIN·

sight of an old man, who hurried away so fast that she had barely time to see him before he disappeared.

This was a fresh surprise and almost as great a shock as the loss of her little dog, who had been so faithful to her ever since the first day she had seen him. She wondered if he had strayed away or if the old man had stolen him.

Tormented by all kinds of thoughts and fears she wandered on, when suddenly she felt herself wrapped in a thick cloud and carried through the air. She made no resistance and before very long found herself, to her great surprise, in an avenue leading to the palace in which she had been born. No sign of the cloud anywhere.

As the princess approached the palace she perceived that everyone was dressed in black, and she was filled with fear as to the cause of this mourning. She hastened on and was soon recognised and welcomed with shouts of joy. Her sister hearing the cheers ran out and embraced the wanderer, with tears of happiness, telling her that the shock of her disappearance had been so terrible that their mother had only survived it a few days. Since then the younger princess had worn the crown, which she now resigned to her sister to whom it by right belonged.

But the elder wished to refuse it, and would only accept the crown on condition that her sister should share in all the power.

The first acts of the new queen were to do honour to the memory of her dear mother and to shower every mark of generous affection on her sister. Then, being still very grieved at the loss of her little dog, she had a careful search made for him in every country, and when nothing could be heard of him she was so grieved that she offered half her kingdom to whoever should restore him to her.

Many gentlemen of the court, tempted by the thought of such a reward, set off in all directions in search of the dog; but all returned empty-handed to the queen, who, in despair announced that since life was unbearable without her little dog, she would give her hand in marriage to the man who brought him back.

The prospect of such a prize quickly turned the court into a desert, nearly every courtier starting on the quest. Whilst they were away the queen was informed one day that a very ill-looking man wished to speak with her. She desired him to be shown into a room where she was sitting with her sister.

On entering her presence he said that he was prepared to give the queen her little dog if she on her side was ready to keep her word.

The princess was the first to speak. She said that the queen had no right to marry without the consent of the nation, and that on so important an occasion the general council must be summoned. The queen could not say anything against this statement ; but she ordered an apartment in the palace to be given to the man, and desired the council to meet on the following day.

Next day, accordingly, the council assembled in great state, and by the princess's advice it was decided to offer the man a large sum of money for the dog, and should he refuse it, to banish him from the kingdom without seeing the queen again. The man refused the price offered and left the hall.

The princess informed the queen of what had passed, and the queen approved of all, but added that as she was her own mistress she had made up her mind to abdicate ner throne, and to wander through the world till she had found her little dog.

The princess was much alarmed by such a resolution, and implored the queen to change her mind. Whilst they were discussing the subject, one of the chamberlains appeared to inform the queen that the bay was covered with ships. The two sisters ran to the balcony, and saw a large fleet in full sail for the port.

In a little time they came to the conclusion that the

ships must come from a friendly nation, as every vessel
was decked with gay flags, streamers, and pennons, and
the way was led by a small ship flying a great white flag
of peace.

The queen sent a special messenger to the harbour,
and was soon informed that the fleet belonged to the Prince
of the Emerald Isles, who begged leave to land in her
kingdom, and to present his humble respects to her. The
queen at once sent some of the court dignitaries to
receive the prince and bid him welcome.

She awaited him seated on her throne, but rose on
his appearance, and went a few steps to meet him ; then
begged him to be seated, and for about an hour kept him
in close conversation.

The prince was then conducted to a splendid suite of
apartments, and the next day he asked for a private
audience. He was admitted to the queen's own sitting-
room, where she was sitting alone with her sister.

After the first greetings the prince informed the queen
that he had some very strange things to tell her, which
she only would know to be true.

'Madam,' said he, 'I am a neighbour of the Queen
of all the Isles ; and a small isthmus connects part of my
states with hers. One day, when hunting a stag, I had
the misfortune to meet her, and not recognising her, I
did not stop to salute her with all proper ceremony. You,
Madam, know better than anyone how revengeful she
is, and that she is also a mistress of magic. I learnt
both facts to my cost. The ground opened under my
feet, and I soon found myself in a far distant region
transformed into a little dog, under which shape I had
the honour to meet your Majesty. After six months, the
queen's vengeance not being yet satisfied, she further
changed me into a hideous old man, and in this form I
was so afraid of being unpleasant in your eyes, Madam,
that I hid myself in the depths of the woods, where I
spent three months more. At the end of that time I was

so fortunate as to meet a benevolent fairy who delivered me from the proud queen's power, and told me all your adventures and where to find you. I now come to offer you a heart which has been entirely yours, Madam, since first we met in the desert.'

A few days later a herald was sent through the kingdom to proclaim the joyful news of the marriage of the Queen of the Flowery Isles with the young prince. They lived happily for many years, and ruled their people well.

As for the bad queen, whose vanity and jealousy had caused so much mischief, the Fairies took all her power away for a punishment.

['Cabinet des Fées.']

UDEA AND HER SEVEN BROTHERS

ONCE upon a time there was a man and his wife who had seven boys. The children lived in the open air and grew big and strong, and the six eldest spent part of every day hunting wild beasts. The youngest did not care so much about sport, and he often stayed with his mother.

One morning, however, as the whole seven were going out for a long expedition, they said to their aunt, ' Dear aunt, if a baby sister comes into the world to-day, wave a white handkerchief, and we will return immediately ; but if it is only a boy, just brandish a sickle, and we will go on with what we are doing.'

Now the baby when it arrived really proved to be a girl, but as the aunt could not bear the boys, she thought it was a good opportunity to get rid of them. So she waved the sickle. And when the seven brothers saw the sign they said, ' Now we have nothing to go back for,' and plunged deeper into the desert.

The little girl soon grew to be a big girl, and she was called by all her friends (though she did not know it) ' Udea, who had driven her seven brothers into strange lands.'

One day, when she had been quarrelling with her playmates, the oldest among them said to her, ' It is a pity you were born, as ever since, your brothers have been obliged to roam about the world.'

Udea did not answer, but went home to her mother and asked her, ' Have I really got brothers ? '

' Yes,' replied her mother, ' seven of them. But they

went away the day you were born, and I have never
heard of them since.'

Then the girl said, ' I will go and look for them till I
find them.'

' My dear child,' answered her mother, ' it is fifteen
years since they left, and no man has seen them. How
will you know which way to go ? '

' Oh, I will follow them, north and south, east and
west, and though I may travel far, yet some day I will
find them.'

Then her mother said no more, but gave her a camel
and some food, and a negro and his wife to take care of
her, and she fastened a cowrie shell round the camel's
neck for a charm, and bade her daughter go in peace.

During the first day the party journeyed on without
any adventures, but the second morning the negro said to
the girl, ' Get down, and let the negress ride instead of
you.'

' Mother,' cried Udẹa.

' What is it ? ' asked her mother.

' Barka wants me to dismount from my camel.'

' Leave her alone, Barka,' commanded the mother,
and Barka did not dare to persist.

But on the following day he said again to Udea, ' Get
down, and let the negress ride instead of you,' and though
Udea called to her mother she was too far away, and the
mother never heard her. Then the negro seized her roughly
and threw her on the ground, and said to his wife, ' Climb
up,' and the negress climbed up, while the girl walked by the
side. She had meant to ride all the way on her camel as
her feet were bare and the stones cut them till the blood
came. But she had to walk on till night, when they
halted, and the next morning it was the same thing again.
Weary and bleeding the poor girl began to cry, and implored the negro to let her ride, if only for a little. But
he took no notice, except to bid her walk a little faster.

By-and-by they passed a caravan, and the negro

stopped and asked the leader if they had come across
seven young men, who were thought to be hunting some-

THE NEGRO COMPELS UDEA TO WALK

where about. And the man answered, 'Go straight on,
and by midday you will reach the castle where they live.'

When he heard this, the black melted some pitch in
the sun, and smeared the girl with it, till she looked as

much a negro as he did.   Next he bade his wife get down
from the camel, and told Udea to mount, which she was
thankful to do.   So they arrived at her brothers' castle.

Leaving the camel kneeling at the entrance for Udea
to dismount, the negro knocked loudly at the door, which
was opened by the youngest brother, all the others being
away hunting.   He did not of course recognise Udea,
but he knew the negro and his wife, and welcomed
them gladly, adding, 'But who does the other negress
belong to?'

'Oh, that is your sister!' said they.

'My sister! but she is coal black!'

'That may be, but she is your sister for all that.'

The young man asked no more questions, but took
them into the castle, and he himself waited outside till
his brothers came home.

As soon as they were alone, the negro whispered to
Udea, 'If you dare to tell your brothers that I made you
walk, or that I smeared you with pitch, I will kill you.'

'Oh, I will be sure to say nothing,' replied the girl,
trembling, and at that moment the six elder brothers
appeared in sight.

'I have some good news for you,' said the youngest,
hastening to meet them; 'our sister is here!'

'Nonsense,' they answered.   'We have no sister; you
know the child that was born was a boy.'

'But that was not true,' replied he, 'and here she is
with the negro and his wife.   Only—she too is black,' he
added softly, but his brothers did not hear him, and
pushed past joyfully.

'How are you, good old Barka?' they said to the
negro; 'and how comes it that we never knew that we
had a sister till now?' and they greeted Udea warmly,
while she shed tears of relief and gladness.

The next morning they all agreed that they would not
go out hunting.   And the eldest brother took Udea on his
knee, and she combed his hair and talked to him of their

home till the tears ran down his cheeks and dropped on her bare arm. And where the tears fell a white mark was made. Then the brother took a cloth and rubbed the place, and he saw that she was not black at all.

'Tell me, who painted you over like this?' cried he.

'I am afraid to tell you,' sobbed the girl, 'the negro will kill me.'

'Afraid! and with seven brothers!'

'Well, I will tell you then,' she answered. 'The negro forced me to dismount from the camel and let his wife ride instead. And the stones cut my feet till they bled and I had to bind them. And after that, when we heard your castle was near by, he took pitch and smeared my body with it.'

Then the brother rushed in wrath from the room, and seizing his sword, cut off first the negro's head and then his wife's. He next brought in some warm water, and washed his sister all over, till her skin was white and shining again.

'Ah, now we see that you are our sister!' they all said. 'What fools the negro must have thought us, to believe for an instant that we could have a sister who was black!' And all that day and the next they remained in the castle.

But on the third morning they said to their sister: 'Dear sister, you must lock yourself into this castle, with only the cat for company. And be very careful never to eat anything which she does not eat too. You must be sure to give her a bit of everything. In seven days we shall be back again.'

'All right,' she answered, and locked herself into the castle with the cat.

On the eighth day the brothers came home. 'How are you?' they asked. 'You have not been anxious?'

'No, why should I be anxious? The gates were fast locked, and in the castle are seven doors, and the seventh is of iron. What is there to frighten me?'

'No one will try to hurt *us*,' said the brothers, 'for they fear us greatly. But for yourself, we implore you to do nothing without consulting the cat, who has grown up in the house, and take care never to neglect her advice.'

'All right,' replied Udea, 'and whatever I eat she shall have half.'

'Capital! and if ever you are in danger the cat will come and tell us—only elves and pigeons, which fly round your window, know where to find us.'

'This is the first I have heard of the pigeons,' said Udea. 'Why did you not speak of them before?'

We always leave them food and water for seven days,' replied the brothers.

'Ah,' sighed the girl, 'if I had only known, I would have given them fresh food and fresh water; for after seven days anything becomes bad. Would it not be better if I fed them every day?'

'Much better,' said they, 'and we shall feel any kindnesses you do towards the cat or the pigeons exactly as if they were shown to ourselves.'

'Set your minds at ease,' answered the girl, 'I will treat them as if they were my brothers.'

That night the brothers slept in the castle, but after breakfast next morning they buckled on their weapons and mounted their horses, and rode off to their hunting grounds, calling out to their sister, 'Mind you let nobody in till we come back.'

'Very well,' cried she, and kept the doors carefully locked for seven days and on the eighth the brothers returned as before. Then, after spending one evening with her, they departed as soon as they had done breakfast.

Directly they were out of sight Udea began to clean the house, and among the dust she found a bean which she ate.

'What are you eating?' asked the cat.

'Nothing,' said she.

'Open your mouth, and let me see.' The girl did as

she was told, and then the cat said 'Why did you not give me half?'

'I forgot,' answered she, 'but there are plenty of beans about, you can have as many as you like.'

'No, that won't do. I want half of that particular bean.'

'But how can I give it you? I tell you I have eaten it. I can roast you a hundred others.'

'No, I want half of that one.'

'Oh! do as you like, only go away!' cried she.

So the cat ran straight to the kitchen fire, and spit on it and put it out, and when Udea came to cook the supper she had nothing to light it with. 'Why did you put the fire out?' asked she.

'Just to show you how nicely you would be able to cook the supper. Didn't you tell me to do what I liked?'

The girl left the kitchen and climbed up on the roof of the castle and looked out. Far, far away, so far that she could hardly see it, was the glow of a fire. 'I will go and fetch a burning coal from there and light my fire,' thought she, and opened the door of the castle. When she reached the place where the fire was kindled, a hideous man-eater was crouching over it.

'Peace be with you, grandfather,' said she.

'The same to you,' replied the man-eater. 'What brings you here, Udea?'

'I came to ask for a lump of burning coal, to light my fire with.'

'Do you want a big lump or a little lump?'

'Why, what difference does it make?' said she.

'If you have a big lump you must give me a strip of your skin from your ear to your thumb, and if you have a little lump, you must give me a strip from your ear to your little finger.'

Udea, who thought that one sounded as bad as the other, said she would take the big lump, and when the man-eater had cut the skin, she went home again.

And as she hastened on a raven beheld the blood on the ground, and plastered it with earth, and stayed by her till she reached the castle. And as she entered the door he flew past, and she shrieked from fright, for up to that moment she had not seen him. In her terror she called after him. 'May you get the same start as you have given me!'

'Why should you wish me harm,' asked the raven pausing in his flight, 'when I have done you a service?'

'What service have you done me?' said she.

'Oh, you shall soon see,' replied the raven, and with his bill he scraped away all the earth he had smeared over the blood and then flew away.

In the night the man-eater got up, and followed the blood till he came to Udea's castle. He entered through the gate which she had left open, and went on till he reached the inside of the house. But here he was stopped by the seven doors, six of wood and one of iron, and all fast locked. And he called through them 'Oh Udea, what did you see your grandfather doing?'

'I saw him spread silk under him, and silk over him, and lay himself down in a four-post bed.'

When he heard that, the man-eater broke in one door, and laughed and went away.

And the second night he came back, and asked her again what she had seen her grandfather doing, and she answered him as before, and he broke in another door, and laughed and went away, and so each night till he reached the seventh door. Then the maiden wrote a letter to her brothers, and bound it round the neck of a pigeon, and said to it, 'Oh, thou pigeon that served my father and my grandfather, carry this letter to my brothers, and come back at once.' And the pigeon flew away.

It flew and it flew and it flew till it found the brothers. The eldest unfastened the letter from the pigeon's neck, and read what his sister had written : 'I am in a great strait, my brothers. If you do not rescue me to-night, to-morrow I shall be no longer living, for the man-eater has broken open six doors, and only the iron door is left. So haste, haste, post haste.'

'Quick, quick ! my brothers,' cried he.

'What is the matter?' asked they.

'If we cannot reach our sister to-night, to-morrow she will be the prey of the man-eater.'

And without more words they sprang on their horses, and rode like the wind.

The gate of the castle was thrown down, and they entered the court and called loudly to their sister. But the poor girl was so ill with fear and anxiety that she

could not even speak. Then the brothers dismounted
and passed through the six open doors, till they stood
before the iron one, which was still shut. ' Udea, open! '
they cried, ' it is only your brothers! ' And she arose
and unlocked the door, and throwing herself on the neck
of the eldest burst into tears.

' Tell us what has happened,' he said, ' and how the
man-eater traced you here.'

' It is all the cat's fault,' replied Udea. ' She put out
my fire so that I could not cook. All about a bean! I
ate one and forgot to give her any of it.'

' But we told you so particularly,' said the eldest
brother, ' never to eat anything without sharing it with
the cat.'

' Yes, but I tell you I forgot,' answered Udea.

' Does the man-eater come here every night? ' asked
the brothers.

' Every night,' said Udea, ' and he breaks one door in
and then goes away.'

Then all the brothers cried together, ' We will dig a
great hole, and fill it with burning wood, and spread a
covering over the top; and when the man-eater arrives
we will push him into it.' So they all set to work and
prepared the great hole, and set fire to the wood, till
it was reduced to a mass of glowing charcoal. And
when the man-eater came, and called as usual, ' Udea,
what did you see your grandfather doing? ' she answered,
' I saw him pull off the ass' skin and devour the ass, and
he fell in the fire, and the fire burned him up.'

Then the man-eater was filled with rage, and he flung
himself upon the iron door and burst it in. On the other
side stood Udea's seven brothers, who said, ' Come, rest
yourself a little on this mat.' And the man-eater sat
down, and he fell right into the burning pit which was
under the mat, and they heaped on more wood, till
nothing was left of him, not even a bone. Only one of
his finger-nails was blown away, and fell into an upper

UDEA · FOUND · LIFELESS ·
BY · HER · SEVEN · BROTHERS ·

chamber where Udea was standing, and stuck under one of the nails of her own fingers. And she sank lifeless to the earth.

Meanwhile her brothers sat below waiting for her and wondering why she did not come. ' What can have happened to her ! ' exclaimed the eldest brother. ' Perhaps she has fallen into the fire, too.' So one of the others ran upstairs and found his sister stretched on the floor. ' Udea ! Udea ! ' he cried, but she did not move or reply. Then he saw that she was dead, and rushed down to his brothers in the courtyard and called out, ' Come quickly, our sister is dead ! ' In a moment they were all beside her and knew that it was true, and they made a bier and laid her on it, and placed her across a camel, and said to the camel, ' Take her to her mother, but be careful not to halt by the way, and let no man capture you, and see you kneel down before no man, save him who shall say " string " [1] to you. But to him who says " string," then kneel.'

So the camel started, and when it had accomplished half its journey it met three men, who ran after it in order to catch it ; but they could not. Then they cried ' Stop ! ' but the camel only went the faster. The three men panted behind till one said to the others, ' Wait a minute ! The string of my sandal is broken ! ' The camel caught the word ' string ' and knelt down at once, and the men came up and found a dead girl lying on a bier, with a ring on her finger. And as one of the young men took hold of her hand to pull off the ring, he knocked out the man-eater's finger-nail, which had stuck there, and the maiden sat up and said, ' Let him live who gave me life, and slay him who slew me ! ' And when the camel heard the maiden speak, it turned and carried her back to her brothers.

Now the brothers were still seated in the court be-wailing their sister, and their eyes were dim with weeping

[1] ' Riemen.'

so that they could hardly see. And when the camel stood
before them they said, ' Perhaps it has brought back our
sister ! ' and rose to give it a beating. But the camel
knelt down and the girl dismounted, and they flung
themselves on her neck and wept more than ever for
gladness.

'Tell me,' said the eldest, as soon as he could speak,
' how it all came about, and what killed you.'

' I was waiting in the upper chamber,' said she, 'and
a nail of the man-eater's stuck under my nail, and I fell
dead upon the ground. That is all I know.'

'But who pulled out the nail?' asked he.

'A man took hold of my hand and tried to pull off my
ring, and the nail jumped out and I was alive again.
And when the camel heard me say "Let him live who
gave me life, slay him who slew me!" it turned and
brought me back to the castle. That is my story.'

She was silent and the eldest brother spoke. ' Will
you listen to what I have to say, my brothers?'

And they replied, ' How should we not hear you?
Are you not our father as well as our brother?'

'Then this is my advice. Let us take our sister back
to our father and mother, that we may see them once
more before they die.'

And the young men agreed, and they mounted their
horses and placed their sister in a litter on the camel.
So they set out.

At the end of five days' journey they reached the old
home where their father and mother dwelt alone. And
the heart of their father rejoiced, and he said to them,
' Dear sons, why did you go away and leave your mother
and me to weep for you night and day?'

' Dear father,' answered the son, ' let us rest a
little now, and then I will tell you everything from the
beginning.'

' All right,' replied the father, and waited patiently for
three days.

And on the morning of the fourth day the eldest
brother said, 'Dear father, would you like to hear our
adventures ? '

' Certainly I should ! '

' Well, it was our aunt who was the cause of our
leaving home, for we agreed that if the baby was a sister
she should wave a white handkerchief, and if it was a
brother, she should brandish a sickle, for then there would
be nothing to come back for, and we might wander far
away. Now our aunt could not bear us, and hated us to
live in the same house with her, so she brandished the
sickle, and we went away. That is all our story.'

And that is all this story.[1]

[*Märchen und Gedichte aus der Stadt Tripolis.*   Von Hans Stumme.]

THE WHITE WOLF

ONCE upon a time there was a king who had three
daughters; they were all beautiful, but the youngest was
the fairest of the three. Now it happened that one day
their father had to set out for a tour in a distant part
of his kingdom. Before he left, his youngest daughter
made him promise to bring her back a wreath of wild
flowers. When the king was ready to return to his
palace, he bethought himself that he would like to take
home presents to each of his three daughters; so he
went into a jeweller's shop and bought a beautiful neck-
lace for the eldest princess; then he went to a rich
merchant's and bought a dress embroidered in gold and
silver thread for the second princess, but in none of the
flower shops nor in the market could he find the wreath
of wild flowers that his youngest daughter had set her
heart on. So he had to set out on his homeward way
without it. Now his journey led him through a thick
forest. While he was still about four miles distant from
his palace, he noticed a white wolf squatting on the roadside, and, behold! on the head of the wolf, there was a
wreath of wild flowers.

Then the king called to the coachman, and ordered
him to get down from his seat and fetch him the wreath
from the wolf's head. But the wolf heard the order and
said : ' My lord and king, I will let you have the wreath,
but I must have something in return.'

' What do you want?' answered the king. ' I will
gladly give you rich treasure in exchange for it.'

'I do not want rich treasure,' replied the wolf. 'Only promise to give me the first thing that meets you on your way to your castle. In three days I shall come and fetch it.'

And the king thought to himself : 'I am still a good long way from home, I am sure to meet a wild animal or a bird on the road, it will be quite safe to promise.' So he consented, and carried the wreath away with him. But all along the road he met no living creature till he turned into the palace gates, where his youngest daughter was waiting to welcome him home.

That evening the king was very sad, remembering his promise ; and when he told the queen what had happened, she too shed bitter tears. And the youngest princess asked them why they both looked so sad, and why they wept. Then her father told her what a price he would have to pay for the wreath of wild flowers he had brought home to her, for in three days a white wolf would come and claim her and carry her away, and they would never see her again. But the queen thought and thought, and at last she hit upon a plan.

There was in the palace a servant maid the same age and the same height as the princess, and the queen dressed her up in a beautiful dress belonging to her daughter, and determined to give her to the white wolf, who would never know the difference.

On the third day the wolf strode into the palace yard and up the great stairs, to the room where the king and queen were seated.

'I have come to claim your promise,' he said. 'Give me your youngest daughter.'

Then they led the servant maid up to him, and he said to her : 'You must mount on my back, and I will take you to my castle.' And with these words he swung her on to his back and left the palace.

When they reached the place where he had met the king and given him the wreath of wild flowers, he stopped, and told her to dismount that they might rest a little.

So they sat down by the roadside.

'I wonder,' said the wolf, 'what your father would do if this forest belonged to him?'

And the girl answered : 'My father is a poor man, so he would cut down the trees, and saw them into planks, and he would sell the planks, and we should never be poor again ; but would always have enough to eat.'

Then the wolf knew that he had not got the real princess, and he swung the servant-maid on to his back and carried her to the castle. And he strode angrily into the king's chamber, and spoke.

'Give me the real princess at once. If you deceive me again I will cause such a storm to burst over your palace that the walls will fall in, and you will all be buried in the ruins.'

Then the king and the queen wept, but they saw there was no escape. So they sent for their youngest daughter, and the king said to her : 'Dearest child, you must go with the white wolf, for I promised you to him, and I must keep my word.'

So the princess got ready to leave her home ; but first she went to her room to fetch her wreath of wild flowers, which she took with her. Then the white wolf swung her on his back and bore her away. But when they came to the place where he had rested with the servant-maid, he told her to dismount that they might rest for a little at the roadside. Then he turned to her and said : 'I wonder what your father would do if this forest belonged to him?'

And the princess answered : 'My father would cut down the trees and turn it into a beautiful park and gardens, and he and his courtiers would come and wander among the glades in the summer time.'

'This is the real princess,' said the wolf to himself.

But aloud he said : 'Mount once more on my back, and I will bear you to my castle.'

And when she was seated on his back he set out through the woods, and he ran, and ran, and ran, till

THE·WHITE·WOLF·ASKS·THE·PRINCESS·
A·QUESTION·IN·THE·WOOD

at last he stopped in front of a stately courtyard, with massive gates.

'This is a beautiful castle,' said the princess, as the gates swung back and she stepped inside. 'If only I were not so far away from my father and my mother!'

But the wolf answered: 'At the end of a year we will pay a visit to your father and mother.'

And at these words the white furry skin slipped from his back, and the princess saw that he was not a wolf at all, but a beautiful youth, tall and stately ; and he gave her his hand, and led her up the castle stairs.

One day, at the end of half a year, he came into her room and said : ' My dear one, you must get ready for a wedding. Your eldest sister is going to be married, and I will take you to your father's palace. When the wedding is over, I shall come and fetch you home. I will whistle outside the gate, and when you hear me, pay no heed to what your father or mother say, leave your dancing and feasting, and come to me at once ; for if I have to leave without you, you will never find your way back alone through the forests.'

When the princess was ready to start, she found that he had put on his white fur skin, and was changed back into the wolf ; and he swung her on to his back, and set out with her to her father's palace, where he left her, while he himself returned home alone. But, in the evening, he went back to fetch her, and, standing outside the palace gate, he gave a long, loud whistle. In the midst of her dancing the princess heard the sound, and at once she went to him, and he swung her on his back and bore her away to his castle.

Again, at the end of half a year, the prince came into her room, as the white wolf, and said : ' Dear heart, you must prepare for the wedding of your second sister. I will take you to your father's palace to-day, and we will remain there together till to-morrow morning.'

So they went together to the wedding. In the evening, when the two were alone together, he dropped his fur skin, and, ceasing to be a wolf, became a prince again. Now they did not know that the princess's mother was hidden in the room. When she saw the white skin lying on the floor, she crept out of the room, and sent a servant to fetch the skin and to burn it in the kitchen fire. The moment the flames touched the skin there was a fearful clap of thunder heard, and the prince disappeared out of the palace gate in a whirlwind, and returned to his palace alone.

But the princess was heart-broken, and spent the night weeping bitterly. Next morning she set out to find her way back to the castle, but she wandered through the woods and forests, and she could find no path or track to guide her. For fourteen days she roamed in the forest, sleeping under the trees, and living upon wild berries and roots, and at last she reached a little house. She opened the door and went in, and found the wind seated in the room all by himself, and she spoke to the wind and said : ' Wind, have you seen the white wolf ? '

And the wind answered : ' All day and all night I have been blowing round the world, and I have only just come home ; but I have not seen him.'

But he gave her a pair of shoes, in which, he told her, she would be able to walk a hundred miles with every step. Then she walked through the air till she reached a star, and she said : ' Tell me, star, have you seen the white wolf ? '

And the star answered : ' I have been shining all night, and I have not seen him.'

But the star gave her a pair of shoes, and told her that if she put them on she would be able to walk two hundred miles at a stride. So she drew them on, and she walked to the moon, and she said : ' Dear moon, have you not seen the white wolf ? '

But the moon answered, ' All night long I have been sailing through the heavens, and I have only just come home ; but I did not see him.'

But he gave her a pair of shoes, in which she would be able to cover four hundred miles with every stride. So she went to the sun, and said : ' Dear sun, have you seen the white wolf ? '

And the sun answered, ' Yes, I have seen him, and he has chosen another bride, for he thought you had left him, and would never return, and he is preparing for the wedding. But I will help you. Here are a pair of shoes. If you put these on you will be able to walk on glass or ice, and to climb the steepest places. And here is a spinning-wheel, with which you will be able to spin moss into silk. When you leave me you will reach a glass mountain. Put on the shoes that I have given you and with them you will be able to climb it quite easily. At the summit you will find the palace of the white wolf.'

Then the princess set out, and before long she reached the glass mountain, and at the summit she found the white wolf's palace, as the sun had said.

But no one recognised her, as she had disguised herself as an old woman, and had wound a shawl round her head. Great preparations were going on in the palace for the wedding, which was to take place next day. Then the princess, still disguised as an old woman, took out her spinning-wheel, and began to spin moss into silk. And as she spun the new bride passed by, and seeing the moss turn into silk, she said to the old woman : ' Little mother, I wish you would give me that spinning-wheel.'

And the princess answered, ' I will give it to you if you will allow me to sleep to-night on the mat outside the prince's door.'

And the bride replied, ' Yes, you may sleep on the mat outside the door.'

So the princess gave her the spinning-wheel. And that night, winding the shawl all round her, so that no one could recognise her, she lay down on the mat outside the white wolf's door. And when every-one in the palace was asleep she began to tell the whole of her story. She told how she had been one of three sisters, and that she had been the youngest and the fairest of the three, and that her father had betrothed her to a white wolf. And she told how she had gone first to

The Bride wishes to buy
the Spinning Wheel

the wedding of one sister, and then with her husband
to the wedding of the other sister, and how her mother
had ordered the servant to throw the white fur skin into
the kitchen fire. And then she told of her wanderings
through the forest; and of how she had sought the
white wolf weeping; and how the wind and star and
moon and sun had befriended her, and had helped her
to reach his palace. And when the white wolf heard all
the story, he knew that it was his first wife, who had
sought him, and had found him, after such great dangers
and difficulties.

But he said nothing, for he waited till the next day,
when many guests—kings and princes from far countries
—were coming to his wedding. Then, when all the guests
were assembled in the banqueting hall, he spoke to them
and said : ' Hearken to me, ye kings and princes, for I have
something to tell you. I had lost the key of my treasure
casket, so I ordered a new one to be made ; but I have
since found the old one. Now, which of these keys is
the better ? '

Then all the kings and royal guests answered :
' Certainly the old key is better than the new one.'

' Then,' said the wolf, ' if that is so, my former bride
is better than my new one.'

And he sent for the new bride, and he gave her in
marriage to one of the princes who was present, and then
he turned to his guests, and said : ' And here is my
former bride'—and the beautiful princess was led into
the room and seated beside him on his throne. 'I
thought she had forgotten me, and that she would never
return. But she has sought me everywhere, and now
we are together once more we shall never part again.'

MOHAMMED WITH THE MAGIC FINGER

ONCE upon a time, there lived a woman who had a son and a daughter. One morning she said to them: 'I have heard of a town where there is no such thing as death : let us go and dwell there.' So she broke up her house, and went away with her son and daughter.

When she reached the city, the first thing she did was to look about and see if there was any churchyard, and when she found none, she exclaimed, 'This is a delightful spot. We will stay here for ever.'

By-and-by, her son grew to be a man, and he took for a wife a girl who had been born in the town. But after a little while he grew restless, and went away on his travels, leaving his mother, his wife, and his sister behind him.

He had not been gone many weeks when one evening his mother said, 'I am not well, my head aches dreadfully.'

'What did you say?' inquired her daughter-in-law.

'My head feels ready to split,' replied the old woman.

The daughter-in-law asked no more questions, but left the house, and went in haste to some butchers in the next street.

'I have got a woman to sell; what will you give me for her?' said she.

The butchers answered that they must see the woman first, and they all returned together.

Then the butchers took the woman and told her they must kill her.

'But why?' she asked.

'Because,' they said, 'it is always our custom that when persons are ill and complain of their head they should be killed at once. It is a much better way than leaving them to die a natural death.'

'Very well,' replied the woman. 'But leave, I pray you, my lungs and my liver untouched, till my son comes back. Then give both to him.'

But the men took them out at once, and gave them to the daughter-in-law, saying: 'Put away these things till your husband returns.' And the daughter-in-law took them, and hid them in a secret place.

When the old woman's daughter, who had been in the woods, heard that her mother had been killed while she was out, she was filled with fright, and ran away as fast as she could. At last she reached a lonely spot far from the town, where she thought she was safe, and sat down on a stone, and wept bitterly. As she was sitting, sobbing, a man passed by.

'What is the matter, little girl? Answer me! I will be your friend.'

'Ah, sir, they have killed my mother; my brother is far away, and I have nobody.'

'Will you come with me?' asked the man.

'Thankfully,' said she, and he led her down, down, under the earth, till they reached a great city. Then he married her, and in course of time she had a son. And the baby was known throughout the city as 'Mohammed with the magic finger,' because, whenever he stuck out his little finger, he was able to see anything that was happening for as far as two days' distance.

By-and-by, as the boy was growing bigger, his uncle returned from his long journey, and went straight to his wife.

'Where are my mother and sister?' he asked; but his wife answered: 'Have something to eat first, and then I will tell you.'

But he replied: 'How can I eat till I know what has become of them?'

Then she fetched, from the upper chamber, a box full of money, which she laid before him, saying, 'That is the price of your mother. She sold well.'

'What do you mean?' he gasped.

'Oh, your mother complained one day that her head was aching, so I got in two butchers and they agreed to take her. However, I have got her lungs and liver hidden, till you came back, in a safe place.'

'And my sister?'

'Well, while the people were chopping up your mother she ran away, and I heard no more of her.'

'Give me my mother's liver and lungs,' said the young man. And she gave them to him. Then he put them in his pocket, and went away, saying: 'I can stay no longer in this horrible town. I go to seek my sister.'

Now, one day, the little boy stretched out his finger and said to his mother, 'My uncle is coming!'

'Where is he?' she asked.

'He is still two days' journey off: looking for us; but he will soon be here.' And in two days, as the boy had foretold, the uncle had found the hole in the earth, and arrived at the gate of the city. All his money was spent, and not knowing where his sister lived, he began to beg of all the people he saw.

'Here comes my uncle,' called out the little boy.

'Where?' asked his mother.

'Here at the house door;' and the woman ran out and embraced him, and wept over him. When they could both speak, he said: 'My sister, were you by when they killed my mother?'

'I was absent when they slew her,' replied she, 'and as I could do nothing, I ran away. But you, my brother, how did you get here?'

'By chance,' he said, 'after I had wandered far; but I did not know I should find you!'

'My little boy told me you were coming,' she explained, 'when you were yet two days distant; he alone of all men has that great gift.'

But she did not tell him that her husband could change himself into a serpent, a dog, or a monster, when-

MY UNCLE IS COMING

ever he pleased. He was a very rich man, and possessed large herds of camels, goats, sheep, cattle, horses and asses; all the best of their kind. And the next morning, the sister said: 'Dear brother, go and watch our sheep, and when you are thirsty, drink their milk!'

'Very well,' answered he, and he went.

Soon after, she said again, 'Dear brother, go and watch our goats.'

'But why? I like tending sheep better!'

'Oh, it is much nicer to be a goatherd,' she said; so he took the goats out.

When he was gone, she said to her husband, 'You must kill my brother, for I cannot have him living here with me.'

'But, my dear, why should I? He has done me no harm.'

'I wish you to kill him,' she answered, 'or if not I will leave.'

'Oh, all right, then,' said he; 'to-morrow I will change myself into a serpent, and hide myself in the date barrel; and when he comes to fetch dates I will sting him in the hand.'

'That will do very well,' said she.

When the sun was up next day, she called to her brother, 'Go and mind the goats.'

'Yes, of course,' he replied; but the little boy called out: 'Uncle, I want to come with you.'

'Delighted,' said the uncle, and they started together.

After they had got out of sight of the house the boy said to him, 'Dear uncle, my father is going to kill you. He has changed himself into a serpent, and has hidden himself in the date barrel. My mother has told him to do it.'

'And what am I to do?' asked the uncle.

'I will tell you. When we bring the goats back to the house, and my mother says to you, "I am sure you must be hungry: get a few dates out of the cask," just say to me, "I am not feeling very well, Mohammed, you go and get them for me."'

So, when they reached the house the sister came out to meet them, saying, 'Dear brother, you must certainly be hungry: go and get a few dates.'

But he answered, 'I am not feeling very well. Mohammed, you go and get them for me.'

'Of course I will,' replied the little boy, and ran at once to the cask.

'No, no,' his mother called after him; 'come here directly! Let your uncle fetch them himself!'

But the boy would not listen, and crying out to her, 'I would rather get them,' thrust his hand into the date cask.

Instead of the fruit, it struck against something cold and slimy, and he whispered softly, 'Keep still; it is I, your son!'

Then he picked up his dates and went away to his uncle.

'Here they are, dear uncle; eat as many as you want.' And his uncle ate them.

When he saw that the uncle did not mean to come near the cask, the serpent crawled out and regained his proper shape.

'I am thankful I did not kill him,' he said to his wife; 'for, after all, he is my brother-in-law, and it would have been a great sin!'

'Either you kill him or I leave you,' said she.

'Well, well!' sighed the man, 'to-morrow I will do it.'

The woman let that night go by without doing anything further, but at daybreak she said to her brother, 'Get up, brother; it is time to take the goats to pasture!'

'All right,' cried he.

'I will come with you, uncle,' called out the little boy.

'Yes, come along,' replied he.

But the mother ran up, saying, 'The child must not go out in this cold or he will be ill;' to which he only answered, 'Nonsense! I am going, so it is no use your talking! I *am* going! I am! I am!'

'Then go!' she said.

And so they started, driving the goats in front of them.

When they reached the pasture the boy said to his uncle : ' Dear uncle, this night my father means to kill you. While we are away he will creep into your room and hide in the straw. Directly we get home my mother will say to you, " Take that straw and give it to the sheep," and, if you do, he will bite you.'

' Then what am I to do?' asked the man.

'Oh, do not be afraid, dear uncle! I will kill my father myself.'

' All right,' replied the uncle.

As they drove back the goats towards the house, the sister cried : ' Be quick, dear brother, go and get me some straw for the sheep.'

' Let me go,' said the boy.

'You are not big enough; your uncle will get it,' replied she.

' We will both get it,' answered the boy ; ' come, uncle, let us go and fetch that straw ! '

' All right,' replied the uncle, and they went to the door of the room.

' It seems very dark,' said the boy ; ' I must go and get a light ; ' and when he came back with one, he set fire to the straw, and the serpent was burnt.

Then the mother broke into sobs and tears. ' Oh, you wretched boy! What have you done? Your father was in that straw, and you have killed him ! '

' Now, how was I to know that my father was lying in that straw, instead of in the kitchen?' said the boy.

But his mother only wept the more, and sobbed out, ' From this day you have no father. You must do without him as best you can ! '

' Why did you marry a serpent?' asked the boy. ' I thought he was a man! How did he learn those odd tricks?'

As the sun rose, she woke her brother, and said, ' Go and take the goats to pasture ! '

'I will come too,' said the little boy.

'Go then!' said his mother, and they went together.

On the way the boy began : 'Dear uncle, this night my mother means to kill both of us, by poisoning us with the bones of the serpent, which she will grind to powder and sprinkle in our food.'

'And what are we to do?' asked the uncle.

'I will kill *her*, dear uncle. I do not want either a father or a mother like that!'

When they came home in the evening they saw the woman preparing supper, and secretly scattering the powdered bones of the serpent on one side of the dish. On the other, where she meant to eat herself, there was no poison.

And the boy whispered to his uncle, 'Dear uncle, be sure you eat from the same side of the dish as I do!'

'All right,' said the uncle.

So they all three sat down to the table, but before they helped themselves the boy said, 'I am thirsty, mother ; will you get me some milk?'

'Very well,' said she, 'but you had better begin your supper.'

And when she came back with the milk they were both eating busily.

'Sit down and have something too,' said the boy, and she sat down and helped herself from the dish, but at the very first moment she sank dead upon the ground.

'She has got what she meant for us,' observed the boy ; 'and now we will sell all the sheep and cattle.'

So the sheep and cattle were sold, and the uncle and nephew took the money and went to see the world.

For ten days they travelled through the desert, and then they came to a place where the road parted in two.

'Uncle!' said the boy.

'Well, what is it?' replied he.

'You see these two roads? You must take one, and I the other ; for the time has come when we must part.'

But the uncle cried, 'No, no, my boy, we will keep together always.'

'Alas! that cannot be,' said the boy; 'so tell me which way you will go.'

'I will go to the west,' said the uncle.

'One word before I leave you,' continued the boy. 'Beware of any man who has red hair and blue eyes. Take no service under him.'

'All right,' replied the uncle, and they parted.

For three days the man wandered on without any food, till he was very hungry. Then, when he was almost fainting, a stranger met him and said, 'Will you work for me?'

'By contract?' asked the man.

'Yes, by contract,' replied the stranger, 'and whichever of us breaks it, shall have a strip of skin taken from his body.'

'All right,' replied the man; 'what shall I have to do?'

'Every day you must take the sheep out to pasture, and carry my old mother on your shoulders, taking great care her feet shall never touch the ground. And, besides that, you must catch, every evening, seven singing birds for my seven sons.'

'That is easily done,' said the man.

Then they went back together, and the stranger said, 'Here are your sheep; and now stoop down, and let my mother climb on your back.'

'Very good,' answered Mohammed's uncle.

The new shepherd did as he was told, and returned in the evening with the old woman on his back, and the seven singing birds in his pocket, which he gave to the seven boys, when they came to meet him. So the days passed, each one exactly like the other.

At last, one night, he began to weep, and cried: 'Oh, what have I done, that I should have to perform such hateful tasks?'

And his nephew Mohammed saw him from afar, and thought to himself, 'My uncle is in trouble—I must go and help him;' and the next morning he went to his master and said: 'Dear master, I must go to my

· HOW · MOHAMMED ·
· FINDS · HIS · UNCLE ·

uncle, and I wish to send him here instead of myself, while I serve under his master. And that you may know it is he and no other man, I will give him my staff, and put my mantle on him.'

'All right,' said the master.

Mohammed set out on his journey, and in two days
he arrived at the place where his uncle was standing
with the old woman on his back, trying to catch the
birds as they flew past. And Mohammed touched him
on the arm, and spoke : ' Dear uncle, did I not warn
you never to take service under any blue-eyed red-haired
man ? '

' But what could I do ? ' asked the uncle. ' I was
hungry, and he passed, and we signed a contract.'

' Give the contract to me ! ' said the young man.

' Here it is,' replied the uncle, holding it out.

' Now,' continued Mohammed, ' let the old woman
get down from your back.'

' Oh no, I mustn't do that ! ' cried he.

But the nephew paid no attention, and went on
talking : ' Do not worry yourself about the future. I see
my way out of it all. And, first, you must take my stick
and my mantle, and leave this place. After two days'
journey, straight before you, you will come to some tents
which are inhabited by shepherds. Go in there, and
wait.'

' All right ! ' answered the uncle.

Then Mohammed with the Magic Finger picked up a
stick and struck the old woman with it, saying, ' Get
down, and look after the sheep ; I want to go to sleep.'

' Oh, certainly ! ' replied she.

So Mohammed lay down comfortably under a tree
and slept till evening. Towards sunset he woke up and
said to the old woman : ' Where are the singing birds
which you have got to catch ? '

' You never told me anything about that,' replied she.

' Oh, didn't I ? ' he answered. ' Well, it is part of your
business, and if you don't do it, I shall just kill you.'

' Of course I will catch them ! ' cried she in a
hurry, and ran about the bushes after the birds, till
thorns pierced her foot, and she shrieked from pain
and exclaimed, ' Oh dear, how unlucky I am ! and how

abominably this man is treating me!' However, at last she managed to catch the seven birds, and brought them to Mohammed, saying, ' Here they are! '

' Then now we will go back to the house,' said he.

When they had gone some way he turned to her sharply :

' Be quick and drive the sheep home, for I do not know where their fold is.' And she drove them before her. By-and-by the young man spoke :

' Look here, old hag ; if you say anything to your son about my having struck you, or about my not being the old shepherd, I'll kill you ! '

' Oh, no, of course I won't say anything ! '

When they got back, the son said to his mother : ' That is a good shepherd I've got, isn't he ? '

' Oh, a splendid shepherd ! ' answered she. ' Why, look how fat the sheep are, and how much milk they give ! '

' Yes, indeed ! ' replied the son, as he rose to get supper for his mother and the shepherd.

In the time of Mohammed's uncle, the shepherd had had nothing to eat but the scraps left by the old woman ; but the new shepherd was not going to be content with that.

' You will not touch the food till I have had as much as I want,' whispered he.

' Very good ! ' replied she. And when he had had enough, he said :

' Now, eat ! ' But she wept, and cried : ' That was not written in your contract. You were only to have what I left ! '

' If you say a word more, I will kill you ! ' said he.

The next day he took the old woman on his back, and drove the sheep in front of him till he was some distance from the house, when he let her fall, and said : ' Quick ! go and mind the sheep ! '

Then he took a ram, and killed it. He lit a fire and broiled some of its flesh, and called to the old woman :

'Come and eat with me!' and she came. But instead of letting her eat quietly, he took a large lump of the meat and rammed it down her throat with his crook, so that she died. And when he saw she was dead, he said : ' That is what you have got for tormenting my uncle!' and left her lying where she was, while he went after the singing birds. It took him a long time to catch them; but at length he had the whole seven hidden in the pockets of his tunic, and then he threw the old woman's body into some bushes, and drove the sheep before him, back to their fold. And when they drew near the house the seven boys came to meet him, and he gave a bird to each.

' Why are you weeping?' asked the boys, as they took their birds.

' Because your grandmother is dead!' And they ran and told their father. Then the man came up and said to Mohammed : ' What was the matter? How did she die?'

And Mohammed answered : ' I was tending the sheep when she said to me, " Kill me that ram; I am hungry!" So I killed it, and gave her the meat. But she had no teeth, and it choked her.'

' But why did you kill the ram, instead of one of the sheep?' asked the man.

' What was I to do?' said Mohammed. ' I had to obey orders!'

' Well, I must see to her burial!' said the man; and the next morning Mohammed drove out the sheep as usual, thinking to himself, ' Thank goodness I've got rid of the old woman! Now for the boys!'

All day long he looked after the sheep, and towards evening he began to dig some little holes in the ground, out of which he took six scorpions. These he put in his pockets, together with one bird which he caught. After this he drove his flock home.

When he approached the house the boys came out to meet him as before, saying : ' Give me my bird!' and he put a scorpion into the hand of each, and it stung him, and he died. But to the youngest only he gave a bird.

As soon as he saw the boys lying dead on the ground, Mohammed lifted up his voice and cried loudly : ' Help, help ! the children are dead ! '

And the people came running fast, saying : ' What has happened ? How have they died ? '

And Mohammed answered : ' It was your own fault ! The boys had been accustomed to birds, and in this bitter cold their fingers grew stiff, and could hold nothing, so that the birds flew away, and their spirits flew with them. Only the youngest, who managed to keep tight hold of his bird, is still alive.'

And the father groaned, and said, ' I have borne enough ! Bring no more birds, lest I lose the youngest also ! '

' All right,' said Mohammed.

As he was driving the sheep out to grass he said to his master : ' Out there is a splendid pasture, and I will keep the sheep there for two or, perhaps, three days, so do not be surprised at our absence.'

' Very good ! ' said the man ; and Mohammed started. For two days he drove them on and on, till he reached his uncle, and said to him, ' Dear uncle, take these sheep and look after them. I have killed the old woman and the boys, and the flock I have brought to you ! '

Then Mohammed returned to his master ; and on the way he took a stone and beat his own head with it till it bled, and bound his hands tight, and began to scream. The master came running and asked, ' What is the matter ? '

And Mohammed answered : ' While the sheep were grazing, robbers came and drove them away, and because I tried to prevent them, they struck me on the head and bound my hands. See how bloody I am ! '

' What shall we do ? ' said the master ; ' are the animals far off ?

'So far that you are not likely ever to see them again,' replied Mohammed. 'This is the fourth day since the robbers came down. How should you be able to overtake them?'

'Then go and herd the cows!' said the man.

'All right!' replied Mohammed, and for two days he went. But on the third day he drove the cows to his uncle, first cutting off their tails. Only one cow he left behind him.

'Take these cows, dear uncle,' said he. 'I am going to teach that man a lesson.'

'Well, I suppose you know your own business best,' said the uncle. 'And certainly he almost worried me to death.'

So Mohammed returned to his master, carrying the cows' tails tied up in a bundle on his back. When he came to the sea-shore, he stuck all the tails in the sand, and went and buried the one cow, whose tail he had not cut off, up to her neck, leaving the tail projecting After he had got everything ready, he began to shriek and scream as before, till his master and all the other servants came running to see what was the matter.

'What in the world has happened?' they cried

'The sea has swallowed up the cows,' said Mohammed, 'and nothing remains but their tails. But if you are quick and pull hard, perhaps you may get them out again!'

The master ordered each man instantly to take hold of a tail, but at the first pull they nearly tumbled backwards, and the tails were left in their hands.

'Stop,' cried Mohammed, 'you are doing it all wrong. You have just pulled off their tails, and the cows have sunk to the bottom of the sea.'

'See if you can do it any better,' said they; and Mohammed ran to the cow which he had buried in the rough grass, and took hold of her tail and dragged the animal out at once.

'There! that is the way to do it!' said he, 'I told you you knew nothing about it!'

The men slunk away, much ashamed of themselves; but the master came up to Mohammed. 'Get you gone!' he said, 'there is nothing more for you to do! You have killed my mother, you have slain my children, you have stolen my sheep, you have drowned my cows; I have now no work to give you.'

'First give me the strip of your skin which belongs to me of right, as you have broken your contract!'

'That a judge shall decide,' said the master; 'we will go before him.'

'Yes, we will,' replied Mohammed. And they went before the judge.

'What is your case?' asked the judge of the master.

'My lord,' said the man, bowing low, 'my shepherd here has robbed me of everything. He has killed my children and my old mother; he has stolen my sheep, he has drowned my cows in the sea.'

The shepherd answered: 'He must pay me what he owes me, and then I will go.'

'Yes, that is the law,' said the judge.

'Very well,' returned the master, 'let him reckon up how long he has been in my service.'

'That won't do,' replied Mohammed, 'I want my strip of skin, as we agreed in the contract.'

Seeing there was no help for it, the master cut a bit of skin, and gave it to Mohammed, who went off at once to his uncle.

'Now we are rich, dear uncle,' cried he; 'we will sell our cows and sheep and go to a new country. This one is no longer the place for us.'

The sheep were soon sold, and the two comrades started on their travels. That night they reached some Bedouin tents, where they had supper with the Arabs. Before they lay down to sleep, Mohammed called the owner of the tent aside. 'Your greyhound will eat my strip of leather,' he said to the Arab.

'No; do not fear.'

'But supposing he does?'

'Well, then, I will give him to you in exchange,' replied the Arab.

Mohammed waited till everyone was fast asleep, then he rose softly, and tearing the bit of skin in pieces, threw it down before the greyhound, setting up wild shrieks as he did so.

'Oh, master, said I not well that your dog would eat my thong?'

'Be quiet, don't make such a noise, and you shall have the dog.'

So Mohammed put a leash round his neck, and led him away.

In the evening they arrived at the tents of some more Bedouin, and asked for shelter. After supper Mohammed said to the owner of the tent, 'Your ram will kill my greyhound.'

'Oh, no, he won't.'

'And supposing he does?'

'Then you can take him in exchange.'

So in the night Mohammed killed the greyhound, and laid his body across the horns of the ram. Then he set up shrieks and yells, till he roused the Arab, who said: 'Take the ram and go away.'

Mohammed did not need to be told twice, and at sunset he reached another Bedouin encampment. He was received kindly, as usual, and after supper he said to his host: 'Your daughter will kill my ram.'

'Be silent, she will do nothing of the sort; my daughter does not need to steal meat, she has some every day.'

'Very well, I will go to sleep; but if anything happens to my ram I will call out.'

'If my daughter touches anything belonging to my

guest I will kill her,' said the Arab, and went to his bed.

When everybody was asleep, Mohammed got up, killed the ram, and took out his liver, which he broiled on the fire. He placed a piece of it in the girl's hands, and laid some more on her night-dress while she slept and knew nothing about it. After this he began to cry out loudly.

'What is the matter? be silent at once!' called the Arab.

'How can I be silent, when my ram, which I loved like a child, has been slain by your daughter?'

'But my daughter is asleep,' said the Arab.

'Well, go and see if she has not some of the flesh about her.'

'If she has, you may take her in exchange for the ram;' and as they found the flesh exactly as Mohammed had foretold, the Arab gave his daughter a good beating, and then told her to get out of sight, for she was now the property of this stranger.

They wandered in the desert till, at nightfall, they came to a Bedouin encampment, where they were hospitably bidden to enter. Before lying down to sleep, Mohammed said to the owner of the tent: 'Your mare will kill my wife.'

'Certainly not.'

'And if she does?'

'Then you shall take the mare in exchange.'

When everyone was asleep, Mohammed said softly to his wife: 'Maiden, I have got such a clever plan! I am going to bring in the mare and put it at your feet, and I will cut you, just a few little flesh wounds, so that you may be covered with blood, and everybody will suppose you to be dead. But remember that you must not make a sound, or we shall both be lost.'

This was done, and then Mohammed wept and wailed louder than ever.

The Arab hastened to the spot and cried, ' Oh, cease making that terrible noise ! Take the mare and go ; but carry off the dead girl with you. She can lie quite easily across the mare's back.'

Then Mohammed and his uncle picked up the girl, and, placing her on the mare's back, led it away, being very careful to walk one on each side, so that she might not slip down and hurt herself. After the Arab tents could be seen no longer, the girl sat up on the saddle and looked about her, and as they were all hungry they tied up the mare, and took out some dates to eat. When they had finished, Mohammed said to his uncle : ' Dear uncle, the maiden shall be your wife ; I give her to you. But the money we got from the sheep and cows we will divide between us. You shall have two-thirds and I will have one. For you will have a wife, but I never mean to marry. And now, go in peace, for never more will you see me. The bond of bread and salt is at an end between us.'

So they wept, and fell on each other's necks, and asked forgiveness for any wrongs in the past. Then they parted and went their ways.

[*Märchen und Gedichte aus der Stadt Tripolis.* Von Hans Stumme.]

BOBINO

ONCE on a time there was a rich merchant, who had an only son called Bobino. Now, as the boy was clever, and had a great desire for knowledge, his father sent him to be under a master, from whom he thought he would learn to speak all sorts of foreign languages. After some years with this master, Bobino returned to his home.

One evening, as he and his father were walking in the garden, the sparrows in the trees above their heads began such a twittering, that they found it impossible to hear each other speak. This annoyed the merchant very much, so, to soothe him, Bobino said : ' Would you like me to explain to you what the sparrows are saying to each other ? '

The merchant looked at his son in astonishment, and answered : ' What can you mean? How can you explain what the sparrows say ? Do you consider yourself a soothsayer or a magician ? '

' I am neither a soothsayer nor a magician,' answered Bobino ; ' but my master taught me the language of all the animals.'

' Alas ! for my good money ! ' exclaimed the merchant. ' The master has certainly mistaken my intention. Of course I meant you to learn the languages that human beings talk, and not the language of animals.'

' Have patience,' answered the son. ' My master thought it best to begin with the language of animals, and later to learn the languages of human beings.'

On their way into the house the dog ran to meet
them, barking furiously.

' What can be the matter with the beast? ' said the
merchant. ' Why should he bark at me like that, when
he knows me quite well? '

'Shall I explain to you what he is saying?' said
Bobino.

' Leave me in peace, and don't trouble me with your
nonsense,' said the merchant quite crossly. 'How my
money has been wasted! '

A little later, as they sat down to supper, some frogs
in a neighbouring pond set up such a croaking as had
never been heard. The noise so irritated the merchant
that he quite lost his temper and exclaimed : ' This only
was wanting to add the last drop to my discomfort and
disappointment.'

' Shall I explain to you? ' began Bobino.

' Will you hold your tongue with your explanations? '
shouted the merchant. ' Go to bed, and don't let me see
your face again! '

So Bobino went to bed and slept soundly. But his
father, who could not get over his disappointment at the
waste of his money, was so angry, that he sent for two
servants, and gave them orders, which they were to
carry out on the following day.

Next morning one of the servants awakened Bobino
early, and made him get into a carriage that was waiting
for him. The servant placed himself on the seat beside
him, while the other servant rode alongside the carriage
as an escort. Bobino could not understand what they
were going to do with him, or where he was being taken ;
but he noticed that the servant beside him looked very
sad, and his eyes were all swollen with crying.

Curious to know the reason he said to him : ' Why
are you so sad? and where are you taking me? '

But the servant would say nothing. At last, moved
by Bobino's entreaties, he said : ' My poor boy, I am

taking you to your death, and, what is worse, I am doing
so by the order of your father.'

'But why,' exclaimed Bobino, 'does he want me to
die? What evil have I done him, or what fault have I
committed that he should wish to bring about my death?'

'You have done him no evil,' answered the servant,
'neither have you committed any fault; but he is half
mad with anger because, in all these years of study, you
have learnt nothing but the language of animals. He
expected something quite different from you, that is why
he is determined you shall die.'

'If that is the case, kill me at once,' said Bobino.
'What is the use of waiting, if it must be done?'

'I have not the heart to do it,' answered the servant.
'I would rather think of some way of saving your life,
and at the same time of protecting ourselves from your
father's anger. By good luck the dog has followed us.
We will kill it, and cut out the heart and take it back to
your father. He will believe it is yours, and you, in the
meantime, will have made your escape.'

When they had reached the thickest part of the wood,
Bobino got out of the carriage, and having said good-bye
to the servants set out on his wanderings.

On and on he walked, till at last, late in the evening,
he came to a house where some herdsmen lived. He
knocked at the door and begged for shelter for the night.
The herdsmen, seeing how gentle a youth he seemed,
made him welcome, and bade him sit down and share
their supper.

While they were eating it, the dog in the courtyard
began to bark. Bobino walked to the window, listened
attentively for a minute, and then turning to the herdsmen said: 'Send your wives and daughters at once to
bed, and arm yourselves as best you can, because at midnight a band of robbers will attack this house.'

The herdsmen were quite taken aback, and thought
that the youth must have taken leave of his senses.

'How can you know,' they said, 'that a band of robbers mean to attack us? Who told you so?'

'I know it from the dog's barking,' answered Bobino. 'I understand his language, and if I had not been here, the poor beast would have wasted his breath to no purpose. You had better follow my advice, if you wish to save your lives and property.'

The herdsmen were more and more astonished, but they decided to do as Bobino advised. They sent their wives and daughters upstairs, then, having armed themselves, they took up their position behind a hedge, waiting for midnight.

Just as the clock struck twelve they heard the sound of approaching footsteps, and a band of robbers cautiously advanced towards the house. But the herdsmen were on the look-out; they sprang on the robbers from behind the hedge, and with blows from their cudgels soon put them to flight.

You may believe how grateful they were to Bobino, to whose timely warning they owed their safety. They begged him to stay and make his home with them; but as he wanted to see more of the world, he thanked them warmly for their hospitality, and set out once more on his wanderings. All day he walked, and in the evening he came to a peasant's house. While he was wondering whether he should knock and demand shelter for the night, he heard a great croaking of frogs in a ditch behind the house. Stepping to the back he saw a very strange sight. Four frogs were throwing a small bottle about from one to the other, making a great croaking as they did so. Bobino listened for a few minutes, and then knocked at the door of the house. It was opened by the peasant, who asked him to come in and have some supper.

When the meal was over, his host told him that they were in great trouble, as his eldest daughter was so ill, that they feared she could not recover. A great doctor,

The Townspeople make
Bobino King. . . . .

who had been passing that way some time before, had
promised to send her some medicine that would have
cured her, but the servant to whom he had entrusted the
medicine had let it drop on the way back, and now there
seemed no hope for the girl.

Then Bobino told the father of the small bottle he
had seen the frogs play with, and that he knew that was
the medicine which the doctor had sent to the girl. The
peasant asked him how he could be sure of this, and
Bobino explained to him that he understood the language
of animals, and had heard what the frogs said as they
tossed the bottle about. So the peasant fetched the
bottle from the ditch, and gave the medicine to his
daughter. In the morning she was much better, and the
grateful father did not know how to thank Bobino enough.
But Bobino would accept nothing from him, and having
said good-bye, set out once more on his wanderings.

One day, soon after this, he came upon two men resting under a tree in the heat of the day. Being tired he
stretched himself on the ground at no great distance
from them, and soon they all three began to talk to one
another. In the course of conversation, Bobino asked
the two men where they were going; and they replied
that they were on their way to a neighbouring town,
where, that day, a new ruler was to be chosen by the
people.

While they were still talking, some sparrows settled
on the tree under which they were lying. Bobino was
silent, and appeared to be listening attentively. At the
end of a few minutes he said to his companions, ' Do you
know what those sparrows are saying? They are saying
that to-day one of us will be chosen ruler of that town.'

The men said nothing, but looked at each other. A
few minutes later, seeing that Bobino had fallen asleep,
they stole away, and made with all haste for the town,
where the election of a new ruler was to take place.

A great crowd was assembled in the market-place,

waiting for the hour when an eagle should be let loose from a cage, for it had been settled that on whose-soever house the eagle alighted, the owner of that house should become ruler of the town. At last the hour arrived ; the eagle was set free, and all eyes were strained to see where it would alight. But circling over the heads of the crowd, it flew straight in the direction of a young man, who was at that moment entering the town. This was none other than Bobino, who had awakened soon after his companions had left him, and had followed in their footsteps. All the people shouted and proclaimed that he was their future ruler, and he was conducted by a great crowd to the Governor's house, which was for the future to be his home. And here he lived happily, and ruled wisely over the people.

THE DOG AND THE SPARROW

THERE was once upon a time a sheep-dog whose master was so unkind that he starved the poor beast, and ill-treated him in the cruellest manner. At last the dog determined to stand this ill-usage no longer, and, one day, he ran away from home. As he was trotting along the road he met a sparrow, who stopped him and said : 'Brother, why do you look so sad ? '

The dog answered : 'I am sad because I am hungry, and have nothing to eat.'

'If that's all, dear brother,' said the sparrow, 'come to the town with me, and I'll soon get food for you.'

So they went together to the town, and when they came to a butcher's shop, the sparrow said to the dog : 'You stand still and I'll peck down a piece of meat for you.'

First she looked all round to see that no one was watching her, and then she set to work to peck at a piece of meat that lay on the edge of a shelf, till at last it fell down. The dog seized it ravenously, and ran with it to a dark corner where he gobbled it up in a very few minutes.

When he had finished it, the sparrow said : ' Now come with me to another shop, and I will get you a second piece, so that your hunger may be satisfied.' When the dog had finished the second piece of meat, the sparrow asked him : 'Brother, have you had enough now ? '

'Yes,' replied the dog, 'I've had quite enough meat, but I haven't had any bread yet.'

The sparrow said : 'You shall have as much bread as you like, only come with me.' Then she led him to a baker's shop, and pecked so long at two rolls on a shelf that at last they fell down, and the dog ate them up.

But still his hunger was not appeased; so the sparrow took him to another baker's shop, and got some more rolls for him. Then she asked him : ' Well, brother, are you satisfied? '

' Yes,' he replied ; ' and now let us go for a little walk outside the town.'

So the two went for a stroll into the country; but the day was very hot, and after they had gone a short distance the dog said : ' I am very tired, and would like to go to sleep.'

' Sleep, then,' said the sparrow, ' and I will keep watch meantime on the branch of a tree.'

So the dog lay down in the middle of the road, and was soon fast asleep. While he was sleeping a carter passed by, driving a waggon drawn by three horses, and laden with two barrels of wine. The sparrow noticed that the man was not going out of his way to avoid the dog, but was driving right in the middle of the road where the poor animal lay ; so she called out : ' Carter, take care what you are about, or I shall make you suffer for it.'

But the carter merely laughed at her words, and, cracking his whip, he drove his waggon right over the dog, so that the heavy wheels killed him.

Then the sparrow called out : ' You have caused my brother's death, and your cruelty will cost you your waggon and horses.'

' Waggon and horses, indeed,' said the carter ; ' I'd like to know how you could rob me of them ! '

The sparrow said nothing, but crept under the cover of the waggon and pecked so long at the bunghole of one of the barrels that at last she got the cork away, and all the wine ran out without the carter's noticing it.

But at last he turned round and saw that the bottom of the cart was wet, and when he examined it, he found that one of the barrels was quite empty. ' Oh ! what an unlucky fellow I am ! ' he exclaimed.

'You'll have worse luck still,' said the sparrow, as she perched on the head of one of the horses and pecked out its eyes.

The Dog & the Sparrow
How the Carter killed his horse.

When the carter saw what had happened, he seized an axe and tried to hit the sparrow with it, but the little bird flew up into the air, and the carter only hit the blind horse on the head, so that it fell down dead. 'Oh! what an unlucky fellow I am!' he exclaimed again.

'You'll have worse luck yet,' said the sparrow; and when the carter drove on with his two horses she crept under the covering again, and pecked away at the cork of the second barrel till she got it away, and all the wine poured out on to the road.

When the carter perceived this fresh disaster he called out once more: 'Oh! what an unlucky fellow I am!'

But the sparrow answered: 'Your bad luck is not over yet,' and flying on to the head of the second horse she pecked out its eyes.

The carter jumped out of the waggon and seized his axe, with which he meant to kill the sparrow; but the little bird flew high into the air, and the blow fell on the poor blind horse instead, and killed it on the spot. Then the carter exclaimed: 'Oh! what an unlucky fellow I am!'

'You've not got to the end of your bad luck yet,' sang the sparrow; and, perching on the head of the third horse, she pecked out its eyes.

The carter, blind with rage, let his axe fly at the bird; but once more she escaped the blow, which fell on the only remaining horse, and killed it. And again the carter called out: 'Oh! what an unlucky fellow I am!'

'You'll have worse luck yet,' said the sparrow, 'for now I mean to make your home desolate.'

The carter had to leave his waggon on the road, and he went home in a towering passion. As soon as he saw his wife, he called out: 'Oh! what bad luck I have had! all my wine is spilt, and my horses are all three dead.'

'My dear husband,' replied his wife, 'your bad luck pursues you, for a wicked little sparrow has assembled all the other birds in the world, and they are in our barn eating everything up.'

The carter went out to the barn where he kept his corn and found it was just as his wife had said. Thousands and thousands of birds were eating up the grain, and in the middle of them sat the little sparrow. When he saw his old enemy, the carter cried out : ' Oh ! what an unlucky fellow I am ! '

' Not unlucky enough yet,' answered the sparrow ; ' for, mark my words, carter, your cruel conduct will cost you your life ; ' and with these words she flew into the air.

The carter was much depressed by the loss of all his worldly goods, and sat down at the fire plotting vengeance on the sparrow, while the little bird sat on the window ledge and sang in mocking tones : ' Yes, carter, your cruel conduct will cost you your life.'

Then the carter seized his axe and threw it at the sparrow, but he only broke the window panes, and did not do the bird a bit of harm. She hopped in through the broken window and, perching on the mantelpiece, she called out : ' Yes, carter, it will cost you your life.'

The carter, quite beside himself with rage, flew at the sparrow again with his axe, but the little creature always eluded his blows, and he only succeeded in destroying all his furniture. At last, however, he managed to catch the bird in his hands. Then his wife called out : ' Shall I wring her neck ? '

' Certainly not,' replied her husband, ' that would be far too easy a death for her ; she must die in a far crueller fashion than that. I will eat her alive ; ' and he suited the action to his words. But the sparrow fluttered and struggled inside him till she got up into the man's mouth, and then she popped out her head and said : ' Yes, carter, it will cost you your life.'

The carter handed his wife the axe, and said : ' Wife, kill the bird in my mouth dead.'

The woman struck with all her might, but she missed the bird and hit the carter right on the top of his head, so that he fell down dead. But the sparrow escaped out of his mouth and flew away into the air.

[From the German, *Kletke*.]

THE STORY OF THE THREE SONS OF HALI

TILL his eighteenth birthday the young Neangir lived happily in a village about forty miles from Constantinople, believing that Mohammed and Zinebi his wife, who had brought him up, were his real parents.

Neangir was quite content with his lot, though he was neither rich nor great, and unlike most young men of his age had no desire to leave his home. He was therefore completely taken by surprise when one day Mohammed told him with many sighs that the time had now come for him to go to Constantinople, and fix on a profession for himself. The choice would be left to him, but he would probably prefer either to be a soldier or one of the doctors learned in the law, who explain the Koran to the ignorant people. 'You know the holy book nearly by heart,' ended the old man, 'so that in a very short time you would be fitted to teach others. But write to us and tell us how you pass your life, and we, on our side, will promise never to forget you.'

So saying, Mohammed gave Neangir four piastres to start him in the great city, and obtained leave for him to join a caravan which was about to set off for Constantinople.

The journey took some days, as caravans go very slowly, but at last the walls and towers of the capital appeared in the distance. When the caravan halted the travellers went their different ways, and Neangir was left, feeling very strange and rather lonely. He had plenty of

courage and made friends very easily; still, not only was
it the first time he had left the village where he had been
brought up, but no one had ever spoken to him of Constantinople, and he did not so much as know the name
of a single street or of a creature who lived in it.

Wondering what he was to do next, Neangir stood
still for a moment to look about him, when suddenly a
pleasant-looking man came up, and bowing politely, asked
if the youth would do him the honour of staying in his
house till he had made some plans for himself. Neangir,
not seeing anything else he could do, accepted the
stranger's offer and followed him home.

They entered a large room, where a girl of about twelve
years old was laying three places at the table.

' Zelida,' said the stranger, ' was I not quite right
when I told you that I should bring back a friend to sup
with us ? '

' My father,' replied the girl, ' you are always right in
what you say, and what is better still, you never mislead
others.' As she spoke, an old slave placed on the table
a dish called pillau, made of rice and meat, which is a
great favourite among people in the East, and setting
down glasses of sherbet before each person, left the room
quietly.

During the meal the host talked a great deal upon all
sorts of subjects; but Neangir did nothing but look at
Zelida, as far as he could without being positively rude.

The girl blushed and grew uncomfortable, and at
last turned to her father. ' The stranger's eyes never
wander from me,' she said in a low and hesitating voice.
' If Hassan should hear of it, jealousy will make him
mad.'

' No, no,' replied the father, ' you are certainly not for
this young man. Did I not tell you before that I intend
him for your sister Argentine. I will at once take
measures to fix his heart upon her,' and he rose and
opened a cupboard, from which be took some fruits and a

jug of wine, which he put on the table, together with a small silver and mother-of-pearl box.

'Taste this wine,' he said to the young man, pouring some into a glass.

'Give me a little, too,' cried Zelida.

'Certainly not,' answered her father, 'you and Hassan both had as much as was good for you the other day.'

'Then drink some yourself,' replied she, 'or this young man will think we mean to poison him.'

'Well, if you wish, I will do so,' said the father; 'this elixir is not dangerous at my age, as it is at yours.'

When Neangir had emptied his glass, his host opened the mother-of-pearl box and held it out to him. Neangir was beside himself with delight at the picture of a young maiden more beautiful than anything he had ever dreamed of. He stood speechless before it, while his breast swelled with a feeling quite new to him.

His two companions watched him with amusement, until at last Neangir roused himself. 'Explain to me, I pray you,' he said, 'the meaning of these mysteries. Why did you ask me here? Why did you force me to drink this dangerous liquid which has set fire to my blood? Why have you shown me this picture which has almost deprived me of reason?'

'I will answer some of your questions,' replied his host, 'but all, I may not. The picture that you hold in your hand is that of Zelida's sister. It has filled your heart with love for her; therefore, go and seek her. When you find her, you will find yourself.'

'But where *shall* I find her?' cried Neangir, kissing the charming miniature on which his eyes were fixed.

'I am unable to tell you more,' replied his host cautiously.

'But I can' interrupted Zelida eagerly. 'To-morrow you must go to the Jewish bazaar, and buy a watch from the second shop on the right hand. And at midnight——'

But what was to happen at midnight Neangir did

not hear, for Zelida's father hastily laid his hand over
her mouth, crying: 'Oh, be silent, child! Would
you draw down on you by imprudence the fate of

NEANGIR SEES THE PICTURE OF ARGENTINE

your unhappy sisters?' Hardly had he uttered the
words, when a thick black vapour rose about him, proceeding from the precious bottle, which his rapid
movement had overturned. The old slave rushed in and

shrieked loudly, while Neangir, upset by this strange adventure, left the house.

He passed the rest of the night on the steps of a mosque, and with the first streaks of dawn he took his picture out of the folds of his turban. Then, remembering Zelida's words, he inquired the way to the bazaar, and went straight to the shop she had described.

In answer to Neangir's request to be shown some watches, the merchant produced several and pointed out the one which he considered the best. The price was three gold pieces, which Neangir readily agreed to give him; but the man made a difficulty about handing over the watch unless he knew where his customer lived.

'That is more than I know myself,' replied Neangir. ' I only arrived in the town yesterday and cannot find the way to the house where I went first.'

' Well,' said the merchant, ' come with me, and I will take you to a good Mussulman, where you will have everything you desire at a small charge.'

Neangir consented, and the two walked together through several streets till they reached the house recommended by the Jewish merchant. By his advice the young man paid in advance the last gold piece that remained to him for his food and lodging.

As soon as Neangir had dined he shut himself up in his room, and thrusting his hand into the folds of his turban, drew out his beloved portrait. As he did so, he touched a sealed letter which had apparently been hidden there without his knowledge, and seeing it was written by his foster-mother, Zinebi, he tore it eagerly open. Judge of his surprise when he read these words :

' My dearest Child,—This letter, which you will some day find in your turban, is to inform you that you are not really our son. We believe your father to have been a great lord in some distant land, and inside this packet is a letter from him, threatening to be avenged on us if you are not restored to him at once. We shall always love you, but do not seek us or even write to us. It will be useless.'

In the same wrapper was a roll of paper with a few words as follows, traced in a hand unknown to Neangir:

'Traitors, you are no doubt in league with those magicians who have stolen the two daughters of the unfortunate Siroco, and have taken from them the talisman given them by their father. You have kept my son from me, but I have found out your hiding-place and swear by the Holy Prophet to punish your crime. The stroke of my scimitar is swifter than the lightning.'

The unhappy Neangir on reading these two letters— of which he understood absolutely nothing—felt sadder and more lonely than ever. It soon dawned on him that he must be the son of the man who had written to Mohammed and his wife, but he did not know where to look for him, and indeed thought much more about the people who had brought him up and whom he was never to see again.

To shake off these gloomy feelings, so as to be able to make some plans for the future, Neangir left the house and walked briskly about the city till darkness had fallen. He then retraced his steps and was just crossing the threshold when he saw something at his feet sparkling in the moonlight. He picked it up, and discovered it to be a gold watch shining with precious stones. He gazed up and down the street to see if there was anyone about to whom it might belong, but there was not a creature visible. So he put it in his sash, by the side of a silver watch which he had bought from the Jew that morning.

The possession of this piece of good fortune cheered Neangir up a little, 'for,' thought he, 'I can sell these jewels for at least a thousand sequins, and that will certainly last me till I have found my father.' And consoled by this reflection he laid both watches beside him and prepared to sleep.

In the middle of the night he awoke suddenly and

heard a soft voice speaking, which seemed to come from one of the watches.

'Aurora, my sister,' it whispered gently. 'Did they remember to wind you up at midnight?'

'No, dear Argentine,' was the reply. 'And you?'

'They forgot me, too,' answered the first voice, 'and it is now one o'clock, so that we shall not be able to leave our prison till to-morrow—if we are not forgotten again—then.'

'We have nothing now to do here,' said Aurora. 'We must resign ourselves to our fate—let us go.'

Filled with astonishment Neangir sat up in bed, and beheld by the light of the moon the two watches slide to the ground and roll out of the room past the cats' quarters. He rushed towards the door and on to the staircase, but the watches slipped downstairs without his seeing them, and into the street. He tried to unlock the door and follow them, but the key refused to turn, so he gave up the chase and went back to bed.

The next day all his sorrows returned with tenfold force. He felt himself lonelier and poorer than ever, and in a fit of despair he thrust his turban on his head, stuck his sword in his belt, and left the house determined to seek an explanation from the merchant who had sold him the silver watch.

When Neangir reached the bazaar he found the man he sought was absent from his shop, and his place filled by another Jew.

'It is my brother you want,' said he; 'we keep the shop in turn, and in turn go into the city to do our business.'

'Ah! *what* business?' cried Neangir in a fury. 'You are the brother of a scoundrel who sold me yesterday a watch that ran away in the night. But I will find it somehow, or else you shall pay for it, as you are his brother!'

'What is that you say?' asked the Jew, around whom

a crowd had rapidly gathered. 'A watch that ran away.
If it had been a cask of wine, your story might be true,
but a watch——! That is hardly possible!'

'The Cadi shall say whether it is possible or not,' replied
Neangir, who at that moment perceived the other Jew
enter the bazaar. Darting up, he seized him by the arm
and dragged him to the Cadi's house; but not before the
man whom he had found in the shop contrived to whisper
to his brother, in a tone loud enough for Neangir to hear,
' Confess nothing, or we shall both be lost.'

When the Cadi was informed of what had taken place
he ordered the crowd to be dispersed by blows, after the
Turkish manner, and then asked Neangir to state his
complaint. After hearing the young man's story, which
seemed to him most extraordinary, he turned to question
the Jewish merchant, who instead of answering raised
his eyes to heaven and fell down in a dead faint.

The judge took no notice of the swooning man, but
told Neangir that his tale was so singular he really could
not believe it, and that he should have the merchant
carried back to his own house. This so enraged Neangir
that he forgot the respect due to the Cadi, and exclaimed
at the top of his voice, ' Recover this fellow from his
fainting fit, and force him to confess the truth,' giving
the Jew as he spoke a blow with his sword which caused
him to utter a piercing scream.

' You see for yourself,' said the Jew to the Cadi, ' that
this young man is out of his mind. I forgive him his
blow, but do not, I pray you, leave me in his power.'

At that moment the Bassa chanced to pass the Cadi's
house, and hearing a great noise, entered to inquire
the cause. When the matter was explained he looked
attentively at Neangir, and asked him gently how all
these marvels could possibly have happened.

' My lord,' replied Neangir, ' I swear I have spoken
the truth, and perhaps you will believe me when I tell
you that I myself have been the victim of spells wrought

by people of this kind, who should be rooted out from the earth. For three years I was changed into a three-legged pot, and only returned to man's shape when one day a turban was laid upon my lid.'

At these words the Bassa rent his robe for joy, and embracing Neangir, he cried, ' Oh, my son, my son, have I found you at last? Do you not come from the house of Mohammed and Zinebi? '

' Yes, my lord,' replied Neangir, ' it was they who took care of me during my misfortune, and taught me by their example to be less worthy of belonging to you.'

' Blessed be the Prophet,' said the Bassa, ' who has restored one of my sons to me, at the time I least expected it ! You know,' he continued, addressing the Cadi, ' that during the first years of my marriage I had three sons by the beautiful Zambac. When he was three years old a holy dervish gave the eldest a string of the finest coral, saying " Keep this treasure carefully, and be faithful to the Prophet, and you will be happy." To the second, who now stands before you, he presented a copper plate on which the name of Mahomet was engraved in seven languages, telling him never to part from his turban, which was the sign of a true believer, and he would taste the greatest of all joys ; while on the right arm of the third the dervish clasped a bracelet with the prayer that his right hand should be pure and the left spotless, so that he might never know sorrow.

' My eldest son neglected the counsel of the dervish and terrible troubles fell on him, as also on the youngest. To preserve the second from similar misfortunes I brought him up in a lonely place, under the care of a faithful servant named Gouloucou, while I was fighting the enemies of our Holy Faith. On my return from the wars I hastened to embrace my son, but both he and Gouloucou had vanished, and it is only a few months since that I learned that the boy was living with a man called Mohammed, whom I suspected of having stolen him.

Tell me, my son, how it came about that you fell into his hands.'

'My lord,' replied Neangir, 'I can remember little of the early years of my life, save that I dwelt in a castle by the seashore with an old servant. I must have been about twelve years old when one day as we were out walking we met a man whose face was like that of this

ZINEBI PUTS THE TURBAN ON THE POT

Jew, coming dancing towards us. Suddenly I felt myself growing faint. I tried to raise my hands to my head, but they had become stiff and hard. In a word, I had been changed into a copper pot, and my arms formed the handle. What happened to my companion I know not, but I was conscious that someone had picked me up, and was carrying me quickly away.

'After some days, or so it seemed to me, I was placed

on the ground near a thick hedge, and when I heard my
captor snoring beside me I resolved to make my escape
So I pushed my way among the thorns as well as I could,
and walked on steadily for about an hour.

'You cannot imagine, my lord, how awkward it is
to walk with three legs, especially when your knees are
as stiff as mine were. At length after much difficulty I
reached a market-garden, and hid myself deep down
among the cabbages, where I passed a quiet night.

'The next morning, at sunrise, I felt some one stooping over me and examining me closely. "What have
you got there, Zinebi?" said the voice of a man a little
way off.

'"The most beautiful pot in the whole world," answered
the woman beside me, "and who would have dreamed of
finding it among my cabbages!"

'Mohammed lifted me from the ground and looked
at me with admiration. That pleased me, for everyone
likes to be admired, even if he is only a pot! And I was
taken into the house and filled with water, and put on
the fire to boil.

'For three years I led a quiet and useful life, being
scrubbed bright every day by Zinebi, then a young and
beautiful woman.

'One morning Zinebi set me on the fire, with a fine
fillet of beef inside me to cook for dinner. Being afraid
that some of the steam would escape through the lid, and
that the taste of her stew would be spoilt, she looked
about for something to put over the cover, but could see
nothing handy but her husband's turban. She tied it
firmly round the lid, and then left the room. For the
first time during three years I began to feel the fire
burning the soles of my feet, and moved away a little—
doing this with a great deal more ease than I had felt
when making my escape to Mohammed's garden. I was
somehow aware, too, that I was growing taller; in fact
in a few minutes I was a man again.

THERE APPEARED
IN THE DOORWAY
A LOVELY JEWESS

' After the third hour of prayer Mohammed and Zinebi both returned, and you can guess their surprise at finding a young man in the kitchen instead of a copper pot ! I told them my story, which at first they refused to believe, but in the end I succeeded in persuading them that I was speaking the truth. For two years more I lived with them, and was treated like their own son, till the day when they sent me to this city to seek my fortune. And now, my lords, here are the two letters which I found in my turban. Perhaps they may be another proof in favour of my story.'

Whilst Neangir was speaking, the blood from the Jew's wound had gradually ceased to flow ; and at this moment there appeared in the doorway a lovely Jewess, about twenty-two years old, her hair and her dress all disordered, as if she had been flying from some great danger. In one hand she held two crutches of white wood, and was followed by two men. The first man Neangir knew to be the brother of the Jew he had struck with his sword, while in the second the young man thought he recognised the person who was standing by when he was changed into a pot. Both of these men had a wide linen band round their thighs and held stout sticks.

The Jewess approached the wounded man and laid the two crutches near him ; then, fixing her eyes on him, she burst into tears.

' Unhappy Izouf,' she murmured, ' why do you suffer yourself to be led into such dangerous adventures ? Look at the consequences, not only to yourself, but to your two brothers,' turning as she spoke to the men who had come in with her, and who had sunk down on the mat at the feet of the Jew.

The Bassa and his companions were struck both with the beauty of the Jewess and also with her words, and begged her to give them an explanation.

' My lords,' she said, ' my name is Sumi, and I am the daughter of Moïzes, one of our most famous rabbis. I

am the victim of my love for Izaf,' pointing to the man
who had entered last, ' and in spite of his ingratitude, I
cannot tear him from my heart. Cruel enemy of my life,'
she continued turning to Izaf, ' tell these gentlemen your
story and that of your brothers, and try to gain your
pardon by repentance.'

'We all three were born at the same time,' said the
Jew, obeying the command of Sumi at a sign from the
Cadi, ' and are the sons of the famous Nathan Ben-Sadi,
who gave us the names of Izif, Izouf, and Izaf. From
our earliest years we were taught the secrets of magic, and
as we were all born under the same stars we shared
the same happiness and the same troubles.

' Our mother died before I can remember, and when
we were fifteen our father was seized with a dangerous
illness which no spells could cure. Feeling death draw
near, he called us to his bedside and took leave of us in
these words :

' " My sons, I have no riches to bequeath to you ; my
only wealth was those secrets of magic which you know.
Some stones you already have, engraved with mystic signs,
and long ago I taught you how to make others. But you still
lack the most precious of all talismans—the three rings
belonging to the daughters of Siroco. Try to get possession of them, but take heed on beholding these young
girls that you do not fall under the power of their beauty.
Their religion is different from yours, and further, they
are the betrothed brides of the sons of the Bassa of the Sea.
And to preserve you from a love which can bring you
nothing but sorrow, I counsel you in time of peril to seek
out the daughter of Moïzes the Rabbi, who cherishes
a hidden passion for Izaf, and possesses the Book of
Spells, which her father himself wrote with the sacred
ink that was used for the Talmud." So saying, our
father fell back on his cushions and died, leaving us
burning with desire for the three rings of the daughters
of Siroco.

ZELIDA DISCOVERS THE WRITING ON THE FLASK

' No sooner were our sad duties finished than we began to make inquiries where these young ladies were to be found, and we learned after much trouble that Siroco, their father, had fought in many wars, and that his daughters, whose beauty was famous throughout all the land, were named Aurora, Argentine, and Zelida.'

At the second of these names, both the Bassa and his son gave a start of surprise, but they said nothing and Izaf went on with his story.

' The first thing to be done was to put on a disguise, and it was in the dress of foreign merchants that we at length approached the young ladies, taking care to carry with us a collection of fine stones which we had hired for the occasion. But alas! it was to no purpose that Nathan Ben-Sadi had warned us to close our hearts against their charms! The peerless Aurora was clothed in a garment of golden hue, studded all over with flashing jewels; the fair-haired Argentine wore a dress of silver, and the young Zelida, loveliest of them all, the costume of a Persian lady.

' Among other curiosities that we had brought with us, was a flask containing an elixir which had the quality of exciting love in the breasts of any man or woman who drank of it. This had been given me by the fair Sumi, who had used it herself and was full of wrath because I refused to drink it likewise, and so return her passion. I showed this liquid to the three maidens who were engaged in examining the precious stones, and choosing those that pleased them best; and I was in the act of pouring some in a crystal cup, when Zelida's eyes fell on a paper wrapped round the flask containing these words. "Beware lest you drink this water with any other man than him who will one day be your husband." "Ah, traitor!" she exclaimed, "what snare have you laid for me?" and glancing where her finger pointed I recognised the writing of Sumi.

' By this time my two brothers had already got

possession of the rings of Aurora and Argentine in exchange for some merchandise which they coveted, and no sooner had the magic circles left their hands than the two sisters vanished completely, and in their place nothing was to be seen but a watch of gold and one of silver. At this instant the old slave whom we had bribed to let us enter the house, rushed into the room announcing the return of Zelida's father. My brothers, trembling with fright, hid the watches in their turbans, and while the slave was attending to Zelida, who had sunk fainting to the ground, we managed to make our escape.

'Fearing to be traced by the enraged Siroco, we did not dare to go back to the house where we lodged, but took refuge with Sumi.

'"Unhappy wretches!" cried she, "is it thus that you have followed the counsels of your father? This very morning I consulted my magic books, and saw you in the act of abandoning your hearts to the fatal passion which will one day be your ruin. No, do not think I will tamely bear this insult! It was I who wrote the letter which stopped Zelida in the act of drinking the elixir of love! As for you," she went on, turning to my brothers, "you do not yet know what those two watches will cost you! But you can learn it now, and the knowledge of the truth will only serve to render your lives still more miserable."

'As she spoke she held out the sacred book written by Moïzes, and pointed to the following lines:

'"If at midnight the watches are wound with the key of gold and the key of silver, they will resume their proper shapes during the first hour of the day. They will always remain under the care of a woman, and will come back to her wherever they may be. And the woman appointed to guard them is the daughter of Moïzes."

'My brothers were full of rage when they saw themselves outwitted, but there was no help for it. The watches were delivered up to Sumi and they went their way, while I remained behind curious to see what would happen.

'As night wore on Sumi wound up both watches, and when midnight struck Aurora and her sister made their appearance. They knew nothing of what had occurred and supposed they had just awakened from sleep, but when Sumi's story made them understand their terrible fate, they both sobbed with despair and were only consoled when Sumi promised never to forsake them. Then one o'clock sounded, and they became watches again.

'All night long I was a prey to vague fears, and I felt as if something unseen was pushing me on—in what direction I did not know. At dawn I rose and went out, meeting Izif in the street suffering from the same dread as myself. We agreed that Constantinople was no place for us any longer, and calling to Izouf to accompany us, we left the city together, but soon determined to travel separately, so that we might not be so easily recognised by the spies of Siroco.

'A few days later I found myself at the door of an old castle near the sea, before which a tall slave was pacing to and fro. The gift of one or two worthless jewels loosened his tongue, and he informed me that he was in the service of the son of the Bassa of the Sea, at that time making war in distant countries. The youth, he told me, had been destined from his boyhood to marry the daughter of Siroco, whose sisters were to be the brides of his brothers, and went on to speak of the talisman that his charge possessed. But I could think of nothing but the beautiful Zelida, and my passion, which I thought I had conquered, awoke in full force.

'In order to remove this dangerous rival from my path, I resolved to kidnap him, and to this end I began to act a madman, and to sing and dance loudly, crying to the slave to fetch the boy and let him see my tricks. He consented, and both were so diverted with my antics that they laughed till the tears ran down their cheeks, and

even tried to imitate me. Then I declared I felt thirsty
and begged the slave to fetch me some water, and while
he was absent I advised the youth to take off his turban,
so as to cool his head. He complied gladly, and in the
twinkling of an eye was changed into a pot. A cry
from the slave warned me that I had no time to lose if I
would save my life, so I snatched up the pot and fled with
it like the wind.

'You have heard, my lords, what became of the pot,
so I will only say now that when I awoke it had disappeared; but I was partly consoled for its loss by finding
my two brothers fast asleep not far from me. "How did
you get here?" I inquired, "and what has happened to you
since we parted?"

'"Alas!" replied Izouf, "we were passing a wayside inn
from which came sounds of songs and laughter, and fools
that we were—we entered and sat down. Circassian girls
of great beauty were dancing for the amusement of several
men, who not only received us politely, but placed us near
the two loveliest maidens. Our happiness was complete,
and time flew unknown to us, when one of the Circassians
leaned forward and said to her sister, 'Their brother
danced, and they must dance too.' What they meant
by these words I know not, but perhaps you can tell
us?"

'"I understand quite well," I replied. "They were
thinking of the day that I stole the son of the Bassa, and
had danced before him."

'"Perhaps you are right," continued Izouf, "for the two
ladies took our hands and danced with us till we were quite
exhausted, and when at last we sat down a second time to
table we drank more wine than was good for us. Indeed,
our heads grew so confused, that when the men jumped
up and threatened to kill us, we could make no resistance
and suffered ourselves to be robbed of everything we had
about us, including the most precious possession of all,
the two talismans of the daughters of Siroco."

' Not knowing what else to do, we all three returned to Constantinople to ask the advice of Sumi, and found that she was already aware of our misfortunes, having read about them in the book of Moïzes. The kind-hearted creature wept bitterly at our story, but, being poor herself, could give us little help. At last I proposed that every morning we should sell the silver watch into which Argentine was changed, as it would return to Sumi every evening unless it was wound up with the silver key—which was not at all likely. Sumi consented, but only on the condition that we would never sell the watch without ascertaining the house where it was to be found, so that she might also take Aurora thither, and thus Argentine would not be alone if by any chance she was wound up at the mystic hour. For some weeks now we have lived by this means, and the two daughters of Siroco have never failed to return to Sumi each night. Yesterday Izouf sold the silver watch to this young man, and in the evening placed the gold watch on the steps by order of Sumi, just before his customer entered the house ; from which both watches came back early this morning.'

' If I had only known ! ' cried Neangir. ' If I had had more presence of mind, I should have seen the lovely Argentine, and if her portrait is so fair, what must the original be ! '

' It was not your fault,' replied the Cadi, ' you are no magician ; and who could guess that the watch must be wound at such an hour ? But I shall give orders that the merchant is to hand it over to you, and this evening you will certainly not forget.'

' It is impossible to let you have it to-day,' answered Izouf, ' for it is already sold.'

' If that is so,' said the Cadi, ' you must return the three gold pieces which the young man paid.'

The Jew, delighted to get off so easily, put his hand in his pocket, when Neangir stopped him.

' No, no,' he exclaimed, ' it is not money I want,

but the adorable Argentine; without her everything is valueless.'

'My dear Cadi,' said the Bassa, 'he is right. The treasure that my son has lost is absolutely priceless.'

'My lord,' replied the Cadi, 'your wisdom is greater than mine. Give judgment I pray you in the matter.'

So the Bassa desired them all to accompany him to his house, and commanded his slaves not to lose sight of the three Jewish brothers.

When they arrived at the door of his dwelling, he noticed two women sitting on a bench close by, thickly veiled and beautifully dressed. Their wide satin trousers were embroidered in silver, and their muslin robes were of the finest texture. In the hand of one was a bag of pink silk tied with green ribbons, containing something that seemed to move.

At the approach of the Bassa both ladies rose, and came towards him. Then the one who held the bag addressed him saying, 'Noble lord, buy, I pray you, this bag, without asking to see what it contains.'

'How much do you want for it?' asked the Bassa.

'Three hundred sequins,' replied the unknown.

At these words the Bassa laughed contemptuously, and passed on without speaking.

'You will not repent of your bargain,' went on the woman. 'Perhaps if we come back to-morrow you will be glad to give us the four hundred sequins we shall then ask. And the next day the price will be five hundred.'

'Come away,' said her companion, taking hold of her sleeve. 'Do not let us stay here any longer. It may cry, and then our secret will be discovered.' And so saying, the two young women disappeared.

The Jews were left in the front hall under the care of the slaves, and Neangir and Sumi followed the Bassa inside the house, which was magnificently furnished. At one end of a large, brilliantly-lighted room a lady of about thirty-five years old reclined on a couch, still beautiful in spite of the sad expression of her face.

The BASSA laughs at the CIRCASSIANS

'Incomparable Zambac,' said the Bassa, going up to her, 'give me your thanks, for here is the lost son for whom you have shed so many tears,' but before his mother could clasp him in her arms Neangir had flung himself at her feet.

'Let the whole house rejoice with me,' continued the Bassa, 'and let my two sons Ibrahim and Hassan be told, that they may embrace their brother.'

'Alas! my lord!' said Zambac, 'do you forget that this is the hour when Hassan weeps on his hand, and Ibrahim gathers up his coral beads?'

'Let the command of the Prophet be obeyed,' replied the Bassa; 'then we will wait till the evening.'

'Forgive me, noble lord,' interrupted Sumi, 'but what is this mystery? With the help of the Book of Spells perhaps I may be of some use in the matter.'

'Sumi,' answered the Bassa, 'I owe you already the happiness of my life; come with me then, and the sight of my unhappy sons will tell you of our trouble better than any words of mine.'

The Bassa rose fr m his divan and drew aside the hangings leading to a large hall, closely followed by Neangir and Sumi. There they saw two young men, one about seventeen, and the other nineteen years of age. The younger was seated before a table, his forehead resting on his right hand, which he was watering with his tears. He raised his head for a moment when his father entered, and Neangir and Sumi both saw that this hand was of ebony.

The other young man was occupied busily in collecting coral beads which were scattered all over the floor of the room, and as he picked them up he placed them on the same table where his brother was sitting. He had already gathered together ninety-eight beads, and thought they were all there, when they suddenly rolled off the table and he had to begin his work over again.

'Do you see,' whispered the Bassa, 'for three hours daily one collects these coral beads, and for the same space of time the other laments over his hand which has become black, and I am wholly ignorant what is the cause of either misfortune.'

'Do not let us stay here,' said Sumi, 'our presence must add to their grief. But permit me to fetch the Book of Spells, which I feel sure will tell us not only the cause of their malady but also its cure.'

The Bassa readily agreed to Sumi's proposal, but Neangir objected strongly. ' If Sumi leaves us,' he said to his father, 'I shall not see my beloved Argentine when she returns to-night with the fair Aurora. And life is an eternity till I behold her.'

'Be comforted,' replied Sumi. ' I will be back before sunset ; and I leave you my adored Izaf as a pledge.'

Scarcely had the Jewess left Neangir, when the old female slave entered the hall where the three Jews still remained carefully guarded, followed by a man whose splendid dress prevented Neangir from recognising at first as the person in whose house he had dined two days before. But the woman he knew at once to be the nurse of Zelida.

He started eagerly forward, but before he had time to speak the slave turned to the soldier she was conducting. ' My lord,' she said, ' those are the men ; I have tracked them from the house of the Cadi to this palace. They are the same ; I am not mistaken, strike and avenge yourself.'

As he listened the face of the stranger grew scarlet with anger. He drew his sword and in another moment would have rushed on the Jews, when Neangir and the slaves of the Bassa seized hold of him.

'What are you doing?' cried Neangir. 'How dare you attack those whom the Bassa has taken under his protection?'

'Ah, my son,' replied the soldier, 'the Bassa would withdraw his protection if he knew that these wretches have robbed me of all I have dearest in the world. He knows them as little as he knows you.'

'But he knows me very well,' replied Neangir, 'for he has recognised me as his son. Come with me now into his presence.'

The stranger bowed and passed through the curtain held back by Neangir, whose surprise was great at seeing his father spring forward and clasp the soldier in his arms.

'What! is it you, my dear Siroco?' cried he. 'I believed you had been slain in that awful battle when the followers of the Prophet were put to flight. But why do your eyes kindle with the flames they shot forth on that fearful day? Calm yourself and tell me what I can do to help you. See, I have found my son, let that be a good omen for your happiness also.'

'I did not guess,' answered Siroco, 'that the son you have so long mourned had come back to you. Some days since the Prophet appeared to me in a dream, floating in a circle of light, and he said to me, "Go to-morrow at sunset to the Galata Gate, and there you will find a young man whom you must bring home with you. He is the second son of your old friend the Bassa of the Sea, and that you may make no mistake, put your fingers in his turban and you will feel the plaque on which my name is engraved in seven different languages."

'I did as I was bid,' went on Siroco, 'and so charmed was I with his face and manner that I caused him to fall in love with Argentine, whose portrait I gave him. But at the moment when I was rejoicing in the happiness before me, and looking forward to the pleasure of restoring you your son, some drops of the elixir of love were spilt on the table, and caused a thick vapour to arise, which hid everything. When it had cleared away he was gone. This morning my old slave informed me that she had discovered the traitors who had stolen my daughters from me, and I hastened hither to avenge them. But I place myself in your hands, and will follow your counsel.'

'Fate will favour us, I am sure,' said the Bassa, 'for

SUMI SHOWS HASSAN THE BOOK OF MAGIC

H. J. FORD

this very right I expect to secure both the silver and
the gold watch. So send at once and pray Zelida to
join us.'

A rustling of silken stuffs drew their eyes to the door,
and Ibrahim and Hassan, whose daily penance had by
this time been performed, entered to embrace their
brother. Neangir and Hassan, who had also drunk of the
elixir of love, could think of nothing but the beautiful
ladies who had captured their hearts, while the spirits of
Ibrahim had been cheered by the news that the daughter
of Moïzes hoped to find in the Book of Spells some charm
to deliver him from collecting the magic beads.

It was some hours later that Sumi returned, bringing
with her the sacred book.

'See,' she said, beckoning to Hassan, 'your destiny is
written here.' And Hassan stooped and read these words
in Hebrew: 'His right hand has become black as ebony
from touching the fat of an impure animal, and will
remain so till the last of its race is drowned in the sea.'

'Alas!' sighed the unfortunate youth. 'It now comes
back to my memory. One day the slave of Zambac was
making a cake. She warned me not to touch, as the
cake was mixed with lard, but I did not heed her,
and in an instant my hand became the ebony that it
now is.'

'Holy dervish!' exclaimed the Bassa, 'how true were
your words! My son has neglected the advice you gave
him on presenting him the bracelet, and he has been
severely punished. But tell me, O wise Sumi, where I
can find the last of the accursed race who has brought
this doom on my son?'

'It is written here,' replied Sumi, turning over some
leaves. 'The little black pig is in the pink bag carried
by the two Circassians.'

When he read this the Bassa sank on his cushions in
despair.

'Ah,' he said, 'that is the bag that was offered me

this morning for three hundred sequins. Those must be the women who caused Izif and Izouf to dance, and took from them the two talismans of the daughters of Siroco. They only can break the spell that has been cast on us. Let them be found and I will gladly give them the half of my possessions. Idiot that I was to send them away!'

While the Bassa was bewailing his folly, Ibrahim in his turn had opened the book, and blushed deeply as he read the words : 'The chaplet of beads has been defiled by the game of "Odd and Even." Its owner has tried to cheat by concealing one of the numbers. Let the faithless Moslem seek for ever the missing bead.'

'O heaven,' cried Ibrahim, 'that unhappy day rises up before me. I had cut the thread of the chaplet, while playing with Aurora. Holding the ninety-nine beads in my hand she guessed " Odd," and in order that she might lose I let one bead fall from my hand. Since then I have sought it daily, but it never has been found.'

'Holy dervish!' cried the Bassa, 'how true were your words! From the time that the sacred chaplet was no longer complete, my son has borne the penalty. But may not the Book of Spells teach us how to deliver Ibrahim also ?'

'Listen,' said Sumi, 'this is what I find : " The coral bead lies in the fifth fold of the dress of yellow brocade."'

'Ah, what good fortune!' exclaimed the Bassa; 'we shall shortly see the beautiful Aurora, and Ibrahim shall at once search in the fifth fold of her yellow brocade. For it is she no doubt of whom the book speaks.'

As the Jewess closed the Book of Moïzes, Zelida appeared, accompanied by a whole train of slaves and her old nurse. At her entrance Hassan, beside himself with joy, flung himself on his knees and kissed her hand.

'My lord,' he said to the Bassa, 'pardon me these transports. No elixir of love was needed to inflame my heart! Let the marriage rite make us speedily one.'

'My son, are you mad?' asked the Bassa. 'As long
as the misfortunes of your brothers last, shall you alone

THE CIRCASSIANS DANCE INTO THE BASSA'S GARDEN

be happy? And whoever heard of a bridegroom with a
black hand? Wait yet a little longer, till the black pig is
drowned in the sea.'

'Yes! dear Hassan,' said Zelida, 'our happiness will be increased tenfold when my sisters have regained their proper shapes. And here is the elixir which I have brought with me, so that their joy may equal ours.' And she held out the flask to the Bassa, who had it closed in his presence.

Zambac was filled with joy at the sight of Zelida, and embraced her with delight. Then she led the way into the garden, and invited all her friends to seat themselves under the thick overhanging branches of a splendid jessamine tree. No sooner, however, were they comfortably settled, than they were astonished to hear a man's voice, speaking angrily on the other side of the wall.

'Ungrateful girls!' it said, 'is this the way you treat me? Let me hide myself for ever! This cave is no longer dark enough or deep enough for me.'

A burst of laughter was the only answer, and the voice continued, 'What have I done to earn such contempt? Was this what you promised me when I managed to get for you the talismans of beauty? Is this the reward I have a right to expect when I have bestowed on you the little black pig, who is certain to bring you good luck?'

At these words the curiosity of the listeners passed all bounds, and the Bassa commanded his slaves instantly to tear down the wall. It was done, but the man was nowhere to be seen, and there were only two girls of extraordinary beauty, who seemed quite at their ease, and came dancing gaily on to the terrace. With them was an old slave in whom the Bassa recognised Gouloucou, the former guardian of Neangir.

Gouloucou shrank with fear when he saw the Bassa, as he expected nothing less than death at his hands for allowing Neangir to be snatched away. But the Bassa made him signs of forgiveness, and asked him how he had escaped death when he had thrown himself from the cliff. Gouloucou explained that he had been picked up by a dervish who had cured his wounds, and had then given him as slave to the two young ladies now before the company, and in their service he had remained ever since.

' But,' said the Bassa, ' where is the little black pig of which the voice spoke just now? '

' My lord,' answered one of the ladies, ' when at your command the wall was thrown down, the man whom you heard speaking was so frightened at the noise that he caught up the pig and ran away.'

' Let him be pursued instantly,' cried the Bassa ; but the ladies smiled.

' Do not be alarmed, my lord,' said one, ' he is sure to return. Only give orders that the entrance to the cave shall be guarded, so that when he is once in he shall not get out again.'

By this time night was falling and they all went back to the palace, where coffee and fruits were served in a splendid gallery, near the women's apartments. The Bassa then ordered the three Jews to be brought before him, so that he might see whether these were the two damsels who had forced them to dance at the inn, but to his great vexation it was found that when their guards had gone to knock down the wall the Jews had escaped.

At this news the Jewess Sumi turned pale, but glancing at the Book of Spells her face brightened, and she said half aloud, ' There is no cause for disquiet ; they will capture the dervish,' while Hassan lamented loudly that as soon as fortune appeared on one side she fled on the other !

On hearing this reflection one of the Bassa's pages broke into a laugh. ' This fortune comes to us dancing, my lord,' said he, ' and the other leaves us on crutches. Do not be afraid. She will not go very far.'

The Bassa, shocked at his impertinent interference, desired him to leave the room and not to come back till he was sent for.

'My lord shall be obeyed,' said the page, 'but when I return, it shall be in such good company that you will welcome me gladly.' So saying, he went out.

When they were alone, Neangir turned to the fair strangers and implored their help. 'My brothers and myself,' he cried, 'are filled with love for three peerless maidens, two of whom are under a cruel spell. If their fate happened to be in your hands, would you not do all in your power to restore them to happiness and liberty?'

But the young man's appeal only stirred the two ladies to anger. 'What,' exclaimed one, 'are the sorrows of lovers to us? Fate has deprived us of our lovers, and if it depends on us the whole world shall suffer as much as we do!'

This unexpected reply was heard with amazement by all present, and the Bassa entreated the speaker to tell them her story. Having obtained permission of her sister, she began :

THE STORY OF THE FAIR CIRCASSIANS

'WE were born in Circassia of poor people, and my sister's name is Tezila and mine Dely. Having nothing but our beauty to help us in life, we were carefully trained in all the accomplishments that give pleasure. We were both quick to learn, and from our childhood could play all sorts of instruments, could sing, and above all could dance. We were besides, lively and merry, as in spite of our misfortunes we are to this day.

'We were easily pleased and quite content with our lives at home, when one morning the officials who had been sent to find wives for the Sultan saw us, and were struck with our beauty. We had always expected something of the sort, and were resigned to our lot, when we chanced to see two young men enter our house. The elder, who was about twenty years of age, had black hair and very bright eyes. The other could not have been more than fifteen, and was so fair that he might easily have passed for a girl.

'They knocked at the door with a timid air and begged our parents to give them shelter, as they had lost their way. After some hesitation their request was granted, and they were invited into the room in which we were. And if our parents' hearts were touched by their beauty, our own were not any harder, so that our departure for the palace, which had been arranged for the next day, suddenly became intolerable to us.

'Night came, and I awoke from my sleep to find the

younger of the two strangers sitting at my bedside and felt him take my hand.

' " Fear nothing, lovely Dely," he whispered, "from one who never knew love till he saw you. My name," he went on, "is Prince Delicate, and I am the son of the king of the Isle of Black Marble. My friend, who travels with me, is one of the richest nobles of my country, and the secrets which he knows are the envy of the Sultan himself. And we left our native country because my father wished me to marry a lady of great beauty, but with one eye a trifle smaller than the other."

' My vanity was flattered at so speedy a conquest, and I was charmed with the way the young man had declared his passion. I turned my eyes slowly on him, and the look I gave him caused him almost to lose his senses. He fell fainting forward, and I was unable to move till Tezila, who had hastily put on a dress, ran to my assistance together with Thelamis, the young noble of whom the Prince had spoken.

' As soon as we were all ourselves again we began to bewail our fate, and the journey that we were to take that very day to Constantinople. But we felt a little comforted when Thelamis assured us that he and the prince would follow in our steps, and would somehow contrive to speak to us. Then they kissed our hands, and left the house by a side-way.

' A few moments later our parents came to tell us that the escort had arrived, and having taken farewell of them we mounted the camels, and took our seats in a kind of box that was fixed to the side of the animal. These boxes were large enough for us to sleep in comfortably, and as there was a window in the upper part, we were able to see the country through which we passed.

' For several days we journeyed on, feeling sad and anxious as to what might become of us, when one day as I was looking out of the window of our room, I heard my name called, and beheld a beautifully dressed girl jumping out of the box on the other side of our camel. One glance told me that it was the prince, and my heart bounded with joy. It was, he said, Thelamis's idea to disguise him like this, and that he himself had assumed the character of a slave-dealer who was taking this peerless maiden as a present to the Sultan. Thelamis had also persuaded the officer in charge of the caravan to let him hire the vacant box, so it was easy for the prince to scramble out of his own window and approach ours.

This ingenious trick enchanted us, but our agreeable conversation was soon interrupted by the attendants, who perceived that the camel was walking in a crooked manner and came to find out what was wrong. Luckily they were slow in their movements, and the prince had just time to get back to his own box and restore the balance, before the trick was discovered.

' But neither the prince nor his friend had any intention of allowing us to enter the Sultan's palace, though it was difficult to know how we were to escape, and what was to become of us when once we *had* escaped. At length, one day as we were drawing near Constantinople, we learned from the prince that Thelamis had made acquaintance with a holy dervish whom he had met on the road, and had informed him that we were his sisters, who were being sold as slaves against his will. The good man was interested in the story, and readily agreed to find us shelter if we could manage to elude the watchfulness of our guards. The risk was great, but it was our only chance.

' That night, when the whole caravan was fast asleep, we raised the upper part of our boxes and by the help of Thelamis climbed silently out. We next went back some distance along the way we had come, then, striking into another road, reached at last the retreat prepared for us by the dervish. Here we found food and rest, and I need not say what happiness it was to be free once more.

'The dervish soon became a slave to our beauty, and the day after our escape he proposed that we should allow him to conduct us to an inn situated at a short distance, where we should find two Jews, owners of precious talismans which did not really belong to them. "Try," said the dervish, "by some means to get possession of them."

'The inn, though not on the direct road to Constantinople, was a favourite one with merchants, owing to the excellence of the food, and on our arrival we discovered at least six or eight other people who had stopped for refreshment. They greeted us politely, and we sat down to table together.

'In a short time the two men described by the dervish entered the room, and at a sign from him my sister made room at her side for one, while I did the same for the other.

'Now the dervish had happened to mention that "their brother had danced." At the moment we paid no attention to this remark, but it came back to our minds now, and we determined that they should dance also. To accomplish this we used all our arts and very soon bent them to our wills, so that they could refuse us nothing. At the end of the day we remained possessors of the talismans and had left them to their fate, while the prince and Thelamis fell more in love with us than ever, and declared that we were more lovely than any women in the world.

'The sun had set before we quitted the inn, and we had made no plans as to where we should go next, so we readily consented to the prince's proposal that we should embark without delay for the Isle of Black Marble. What a place it was! Rocks blacker than jet towered above its shores and shed thick darkness over the country. Our sailors had not been there before and were nearly as frightened as ourselves, but thanks to Thelamis, who undertook to be our pilot, we landed safely on the beach.

'When we had left the coast behind us, with its walls of jet, we entered a lovely country where the fields were greener, the streams clearer, and the sun brighter than anywhere else. The people crowded round to welcome their prince, whom they loved dearly, but they told him that the king was still full of rage at his son's refusal to marry his cousin the Princess Okimpare, and also at his flight. Indeed, they all begged him not to visit the capital, as his life would hardly be safe. So, much as I should have enjoyed seeing the home of my beloved prince, I implored him to listen to this wise advice and to let us all go to Thelamis's palace in the middle of a vast forest.

'To my sister and myself, who had been brought up in a cottage, this house of Thelamis's seemed like fairyland. It was built of pink marble, so highly polished that the flowers and streams surrounding it were reflected as in a mirror. One set of rooms was furnished especially for me in yellow silk and silver, to suit my black hair. Fresh dresses were provided for us every day, and we had slaves to wait on us. Ah, why could not this happiness have lasted for ever!

'The peace of our lives was troubled by Thelamis's jealousy of my sister, as he could not endure to see her on friendly terms with the prince, though knowing full well that his heart was mine. Every day we had scenes of tender reproaches and of explanations, but Tezila's tears never failed to bring Thelamis to his knees, with prayers for forgiveness.

'We had been living in this way for some months when one day the news came that the king had fallen dangerously ill. I begged the prince to hurry at once to the Court, both to see his father and also to show himself to the senators and nobles, but as his love for me was greater than his desire of a crown, he hesitated as if foreseeing all that afterwards happened. At last Tezila spoke to him so seriously in Thelamis's presence, that he determined to go, but promised that he would return before night.

' Night came but no prince, and Tezila, who had been the cause of his departure, showed such signs of uneasiness that Thelamis's jealousy was at once awakened. As for me, I cannot tell what I suffered. Not being able to sleep I rose from my bed and wandered into the forest, along the road which he had taken so many hours before. Suddenly I heard in the distance the sound of a horse's hoofs, and in a few moments the prince had flung himself down and was by my side. " Ah, how I adore you ! " he exclaimed ; " Thelamis's love will never equal mine." The words were hardly out of his mouth when I heard a slight noise behind, and before we could turn round both our heads were rolling in front of us, while the voice of Thelamis cried :

' " Perjured wretches, answer me ; and you, faithless Tezila, tell me why you have betrayed me like this ? "

' Then I understood what had happened, and that, in his rage, he had mistaken me for my sister.

' " Alas," replied my head in weak tones, " I am not Tezila, but Dely, whose life you have destroyed, as well as that of your friend." At this Thelamis paused and seemed to reflect for an instant.

' " Be not frightened," he said more quietly, "I can make you whole again," and laying a magic powder on our tongues he placed our heads on our necks. In the twinkling of an eye our heads were joined to our bodies without leaving so much as a scar ; only that, blinded with rage as he still was, Thelamis had placed my head on the prince's body, and his on mine !

' I cannot describe to you how odd we both felt at this strange transformation. We both instinctively put up our hands—he to feel his hair, which was, of course, dressed like a woman's, and I to raise the turban which pressed heavily on my forehead. But we did not know what had happened to us, for the night was still dark.

' At this point Tezila appeared, followed by a troop of slaves bearing flowers. It was only by the light of their

THE WRONG HEADS
ON THE WRONG BODIES

torches that we understood what had occurred. Indeed the first thought of both of us was that we must have changed clothes.

' Now in spite of what we may say, we all prefer our own bodies to those of anybody else, so notwithstanding our love for each other, at first we could not help feeling a little cross with Thelamis. However, so deep was the prince's passion for me, that very soon he began to congratulate himself on the change. " My happiness is perfect," he said ; " my heart, beautiful Dely, has always been yours, and now I have your head also."

' But though the prince made the best of it, Thelamis was much ashamed of his stupidity. " I have," he said hesitatingly, " two other pastilles which have the same magic properties as those I used before. Let me cut off your heads again, and that will put matters straight." The proposal sounded tempting, but was a little risky, and after consulting together we decided to let things remain as they were. " Do not blame me then," continued Thelamis, " if you will not accept my offer. But take the two pastilles, and if it ever happens that you are decapitated a second time, make use of them in the way I have shown you, and each will get back his own head." So saying he presented us with the pastilles, and we all returned to the castle.

' However, the troubles caused by the unfortunate exchange were only just beginning. My head, without thinking what it was doing, led the prince's body to my apartments. But my women, only looking at the dress, declared I had mistaken the corridor, and called some slaves to conduct me to his highness's rooms. This was bad enough, but when—as it was still night—my servants began to undress me, I nearly fainted from surprise and confusion, and no doubt the prince's head was suffering in the same manner at the other end of the castle !

' By the next morning—you will easily guess that we

slept but little—we had grown partly accustomed to our strange situation, and when we looked in the mirror, the prince had become brown-skinned and black-haired, while my head was covered with his curly golden locks. And after that first day, everyone in the palace had become so accustomed to the change that they thought no more about it.

'Some weeks after this, we heard that the king of the Isle of Black Marble was dead. The prince's head, which once was mine, was full of ambitious desires, and he longed to ride straight to the capital and proclaim himself king. But then came the question as to whether the nobles would recognise the prince with a girl's body, and indeed, when we came to think of it, which was prince and which was girl?

'At last, after much argument, my head carried the day and we set out; but only to find that the king had declared the Princess Okimpare his successor. The greater part of the senators and nobles openly professed that they would much have preferred the rightful heir, but as they could not recognise him either in the prince or me, they chose to consider us as impostors and threw us into prison.

'A few days later Tezila and Thelamis, who had followed us to the capital, came to tell us that the new queen had accused us of high treason, and had herself been present at our trial—which was conducted without us. They had been in mortal terror as to what would be our sentence, but by a piece of extraordinary luck we had been condemned to be beheaded.

'I told my sister that I did not see exactly where the luck came in, but Thelamis interrupted me rudely:

' " What ! " he cried, " of course I shall make use of the pastilles, and——" but here the officers arrived to lead us to the great square where the execution was to take place—for Okimpare was determined there should be no delay.

' The square was crowded with people of all ages and all ranks, and in the middle a platform had been erected on which was the scaffold, with the executioner, in a black mask, standing by. At a sign from him I mounted first, and in a moment my head was rolling at his feet. With a bound my sister and Thelamis were beside me, and like lightning Thelamis seized the sabre from the headsman, and cut off the head of the prince. And before the multitude had recovered from their astonishment at these strange proceedings, our bodies were joined to our right heads, and the pastilles placed on our tongues. Then Thelamis led the prince to the edge of the platform and presented him to the people, saying, " Behold your lawful king."

' Shouts of joy rent the air at the sound of Thelamis's words, and the noise reached Okimpare in the palace. Smitten with despair at the news, she fell down unconcious on her balcony, and was lifted up by the slaves and taken back to her own house.

' Meanwhile our happiness was all turned to sorrow. I had rushed up to the prince to embrace him fondly, when he suddenly grew pale and staggered.

' " I die faithful to you," he murmured, turning his eyes towards me, " and I die a king ! " and leaning his head on my shoulder he expired quietly, for one of the arteries in his neck had been cut through.

' Not knowing what I did I staggered towards the sabre which was lying near me, with the intention of following my beloved prince as speedily as possible. And when Thelamis seized my hand (but only just in time), in my madness I turned the sabre upon him, and he fell struck through the heart at my feet.'

The whole company were listening to the story with breathless attention, when it became plain that Dely could go no further, while Tezila had flung herself on a heap of cushions and hidden her face. Zambac ordered her women to give them all the attention possible, and desired they should be carried into her own rooms.

When the two sisters were in this condition, Ibrahim, who was a very prudent young man, suggested to his parents that, as the two Circassians were both unconscious, it would be an excellent opportunity to search them and see if the talismans belonging to the daughters of Siroco were concealed about their persons. But the Bassa, shocked at the notion of treating his guests in so inhospitable a manner, refused to do anything of the kind, adding that the next day he hoped to persuade them to give the talismans up of their own free will.

By this time it was nearly midnight and Neangir, who was standing near the Jewess Sumi, drew out the portrait of Argentine, and heard with delight that she was even more beautiful than her picture. Everyone was waiting on tip-toe for the appearance of the two watches, who were expected when the clock struck twelve to come in search of Sumi, and that there might be no delay the Bassa ordered all the doors to be flung wide open. It was done, and there entered not the longed-for watches, but the page who had been sent away in disgrace.

Then the Bassa arose in wrath. 'Azemi,' he said, ' did I not order you to stand no more in my presence?'

' My lord,' replied Azemi, modestly, 'I was hidden outside the door, listening to the tale of the two Circassians. And as I know you are fond of stories, give me also leave to tell you one. I promise you it shall not be long.'

'Speak on,' replied the Bassa, 'but take heed what you say.'

' My lord,' began Azemi, 'this morning I was walking in the town when I noticed a man going in the same direction followed by a slave. He entered a baker's shop, where he bought some bread which he gave to the slave to carry. I watched him and saw that he purchased many other kinds of provisions at other places, and when the slave could carry no more his master commanded him to return home and have supper ready at midnight.

'When left alone the man went up the street, and turning into a jeweller's shop, brought out a watch that as far as I could see was made of silver. He walked on a few steps, then stooped and picked up a gold watch which lay at his feet. At this point I ran up and told him that if he did not give me half its price I would report him to the Cadi ; he agreed, and conducting me to his house produced four hundred sequins, which he said was my share, and having got what I wanted I went away.

' As it was the hour for attending on my lord I returned home and accompanied you to the Cadi, where I heard the story of the three Jews and learned the importance of the two watches I had left at the stranger's. I hastened to his house, but he had gone out, and I could only find the slave, whom I told that I was the bearer of important news for his master. Believing me to be one of his friends, he begged me to wait, and showed me into a room where I saw the two watches lying on the table. I put them in my pocket, leaving the four hundred sequins in place of the gold watch and three gold pieces which I knew to be the price of the other. As you know the watches never remain with the person who buys them, this man may think himself very lucky to get back his money. I have wound them both up, and at this instant Aurora and Argentine are locked safely into my own room.'

Everybody was so delighted to hear this news that Azemi was nearly stifled with their embraces, and Neangir could hardly be prevented from running to break in the door, though he did not even know where the page slept.

But the page begged to have the honour of fetching the ladies himself, and soon returned leading them by the hand.

For some minutes all was a happy confusion, and
Ibrahim took advantage of it to fall on his knees before
Aurora, and search in the fifth fold of her dress for the
missing coral bead. The Book of Spells had told the
truth ; there it was, and as the chaplet was now complete
the young man's days of seeking were over.

In the midst of the general rejoicing Hassan alone
bore a gloomy face.

' Alas ! ' he said, ' everyone is happy but the miserable being you see before you. I have lost the only
consolation in my grief, which was to feel that I had a
brother in misfortune ! '

' Be comforted,' replied the Bassa ; ' sooner or later the
dervish who stole the pink bag is sure to be found.'

Supper was then served, and after they had all eaten
of rare fruits which seemed to them the most delicious in
the whole world, the Bassa ordered the flask containing
the elixir of love to be brought and the young people to
drink of it. Then their eyes shone with a new fire, and
they swore to be true to each other till death.

This ceremony was scarcely over when the clock
struck one, and in an instant Aurora and Argentine had
vanished, and in the place where they stood lay two
watches. Silence fell upon all the company—they had
forgotten the enchantment ; then the voice of Azemi was
heard asking if he might be allowed to take charge of the
watches till the next day, pledging his head to end their
enchantment. With the consent of Sumi, this was
granted, and the Bassa gave Azemi a purse containing a
thousand sequins, as a reward for the services he had
already rendered to them. After this everybody went to
his own apartment.

Azemi had never possessed so much money before,
and never closed his eyes for joy the whole night long.
Very early he got up and went into the garden, thinking
how he could break the enchantment of the daughters of
Siroco. Suddenly the soft tones of a woman fell on his

The Dervish drowning the Pigs

ear, and peeping through the bushes he saw Tezila, who was arranging flowers in her sister's hair. The rustling of the leaves caused Dely to start ; she jumped up as if to fly, but Azemi implored her to remain and begged her to tell him what happened to them after the death of their lovers, and how they had come to find the dervish.

'The punishment decreed to us by the Queen Okimpare,' answered Dely, ' was that we were to dance and sing in the midst of our sorrow, at a great fête which was to be held that very day for all her people. This cruel command nearly turned our brains, and we swore a solemn oath to make all lovers as wretched as we were ourselves. In this design we succeeded so well that in a short time the ladies of the capital came in a body to Okimpare, and prayed her to banish us from the kingdom, before their lives were made miserable for ever. She consented, and commanded us to be placed on board a ship, with our slave Gouloucou.

' On the shore we saw an old man who was busily engaged in drowning some little black pigs, talking to them all the while, as if they could understand him.

' " Accursed race," said he, " it is you who have caused all the misfortunes of him to whom I gave the magic bracelet. Perish all of you ! "

' We drew near from curiosity, and recognised in him the dervish who had sheltered us on our first escape from the caravan.

' When the old man discovered who we were he was beside himself with pleasure, and offered us a refuge in the cave where he lived. We gladly accepted his offer, and to the cave we all went, taking with us the last little pig, which he gave us as a present.

' " The Bassa of the Sea," he added, " will pay you anything you like to ask for it."

' Without asking why it was so precious I took the pig and placed it in my work bag, where it has been ever since. Only yesterday we offered it to the Bassa, who laughed at us, and this so enraged us against the dervish that we cut off his beard when he was asleep, and now he dare not show himself.'

'Ah,' exclaimed the page, 'it is not fitting that such beauty should waste itself in making other people miserable. Forget the unhappy past and think only of the future. And accept, I pray you, this watch, to mark the brighter hours in store.' So saying he laid the watch upon her knee. Then he turned to Tezila. 'And you fair maiden, permit me to offer you this other watch. True it is only of silver, but it is all I have left to give. And I feel quite sure that you must have somewhere a silver seal, that will be exactly the thing to go with it.'

'Why, so you have,' cried Dely; 'fasten your silver seal to your watch, and I will hang my gold one on to mine.'

The seals were produced, and, as Azemi had guessed, they were the talismans which the two Circassians had taken from Izif and Izouf, mounted in gold and silver. As quick as lightning the watches slid from the hands of Tezila and her sister, and Aurora and Argentine stood before them, each with her talisman on her finger.

At first they seemed rather confused themselves at the change which had taken place, and the sunlight which they had not seen for so long, but when gradually they understood that their enchantment had come to an end, they could find no words to express their happiness.

The Circassians could with difficulty be comforted for the loss of the talismans, but Aurora and Argentine entreated them to dry their tears, as their father, Siroco, who was governor of Alexandria, would not fail to reward them in any manner they wished. This promise was soon confirmed by Siroco himself, who came into the garden with the Bassa and his two sons, and was speedily joined by the ladies of the family. Only Hassan was absent. It was the hour in which he was condemned to bewail his ebony hand.

To the surprise of all a noise was at this moment heard in a corner of the terrace, and Hassan himself appeared surrounded by slaves, clapping his hands and shouting with joy. ' I was weeping as usual,' cried he, ' when all at once the tears refused to come to my eyes, and on looking down at my hand I saw that its blackness had vanished. And now, lovely Zelida, nothing prevents me any longer from offering you the hand, when the heart has been yours always.'

But though Hassan never thought of asking or caring what had caused his cure, the others were by no means so indifferent. It was quite clear that the little black pig must be dead—but how, and when ? To this the slaves answered that they had seen that morning a man pursued by three others, and that he had taken refuge in the cavern which they had been left to guard. Then, in obedience to orders, they had rolled a stone over the entrance.

Piercing shrieks interrupted their story, and a man, whom the Circassians saw to be the old dervish, rushed round the corner of the terrace with the three Jews behind him. When the fugitive beheld so many people collected together, he turned down another path, but the slaves captured all four and brought them before their master.

What was the surprise of the Bassa when he beheld in the old dervish the man who had given the chaplet, the copper plaque, and the bracelet to his three sons. ' Fear nothing, holy father,' he said, ' you are safe with me. But tell us, how came you here ? '

' My lord,' explained the dervish, ' when my beard was cut off during my sleep by the two Circassians, I was ashamed to appear before the eyes of men, and fled, bearing with me the pink silk bag. In the night these three men fell in with me, and we passed some time in conversation, but at dawn, when it was light enough to see each other's faces, one of them exclaimed that I was the dervish travelling with the two Circassians who had stolen the talismans from the Jews. I jumped up and tried to fly to my cave, but they were too quick for me, and just as we reached your garden they snatched the bag which contained the little black pig and flung it into the sea. By this act, which delivers your son, I would pray you to forgive them for any wrongs they may have done you—nay more, that you will recompense them for it.'

The Bassa granted the holy man's request, and seeing that the two Jews had fallen victims to the charms of the Circassian ladies, gave his consent to their union, which was fixed to take place at the same time as that of Izaf with the wise Sumi. The Cadi was sent for, and the Jews exchanged the hats of their race for the turbans of the followers of the Prophet. Then, after so many misfortunes, the Bassa's three sons entreated their father to delay their happiness no longer, and the six marriages were performed by the Cadi at the hour of noon.

[Cabinet des Fées.]

THE JACKAL AND THE SPRING

ONCE upon a time all the streams and rivers ran so dry that the animals did not know how to get water. After a very long search, which had been quite in vain, they found a tiny spring, which only wanted to be dug deeper so as to yield plenty of water. So the beasts said to each other, ' Let us dig a well, and then we shall not fear to die of thirst ; ' and they all consented except the jackal, who hated work of any kind, and generally got somebody to do it for him.

When they had finished their well, they held a council as to who should be made the guardian of the well, so that the jackal might not come near it, for, they said, ' he would not work, therefore he shall not drink.'

After some talk it was decided that the rabbit should be left in charge ; then all the other beasts went back to their homes.

When they were out of sight the jackal arrived. ' Good morning ! Good morning, rabbit ! ' and the rabbit politely said, ' Good morning ! ' Then the jackal un-fastened the little bag that hung at his side, and pulled out of it a piece of honeycomb which he began to eat, and turning to the rabbit he remarked :

' As you see, rabbit, I am not thirsty in the least, and this is nicer than any water.'

' Give me a bit,' asked the rabbit. So the jackal handed him a very little morsel.

' Oh, how good it is ! ' cried the rabbit ; ' give me a little more, dear friend ! '

But the jackal answered, 'If you really want me to give you some more, you must have your paws tied behind you, and lie on your back, so that I can pour it into your mouth.'

The rabbit did as he was bid, and when he was tied tight and popped on his back, the jackal ran to the spring and drank as much as he wanted. When he had quite finished he returned to his den.

In the evening the animals all came back, and when they saw the rabbit lying with his paws tied, they said to him : ' Rabbit, how did you let yourself be taken in like this ? '

' It was all the fault of the jackal,' replied the rabbit ; 'he tied me up like this, and told me he would give me something nice to eat. It was all a trick just to get at our water.'

' Rabbit, you are no better than an idiot to have let the jackal drink our water when he would not help to find it. Who shall be our next watchman ? We must have somebody a little sharper than you ! ' and the little hare called out, ' I will be the watchman.'

The following morning the animals all went their various ways, leaving the little hare to guard the spring. When they were out of sight the jackal came back. ' Good morning! good morning, little hare,' and the little hare politely said, ' Good morning.'

' Can you give me a pinch of snuff ? ' said the jackal.

' I am so sorry, but I have none,' answered the little hare.

The jackal then came and sat down by the little hare, and unfastened his little bag, pulling out of it a piece of honeycomb. He licked his lips and exclaimed, ' Oh, little hare, if you only knew how good it is ! '

' What is it ? ' asked the little hare.

' It is something that moistens my throat so deliciously,' answered the jackal, ' that after I have eaten it I don't feel thirsty any more, while I am sure that all you other beasts are for ever wanting water.'

'Give me a bit, dear friend,' asked the little hare.

'Not so fast,' replied the jackal. 'If you really wish to enjoy what you are eating, you must have your paws tied behind you, and lie on your back, so that I can pour it into your mouth.'

'You can tie them, only be quick,' said the little hare, and when he was tied tight and popped on his back, the jackal went quietly down to the well, and drank as much as he wanted. When he had quite finished he returned to his den.

In the evening the animals all came back ; and when they saw the little hare with his paws tied, they said to him : 'Little hare, how did you let yourself be taken in like this? Didn't you boast you were very sharp? You undertook to guard our water ; now show us how much is left for us to drink!'

'It is all the fault of the jackal,' replied the little hare. 'He told me he would give me something nice to eat if I would just let him tie my hands behind my back.'

Then the animals said, 'Who can we trust to mount guard now?' And the panther answered, 'Let it be the tortoise.'

The following morning the animals all went their various ways, leaving the tortoise to guard the spring. When they were out of sight the jackal came back. 'Good morning, tortoise ; good morning.'

But the tortoise took no notice.

'Good morning, tortoise ; good morning.' But still the tortoise pretended not to hear.

Then the jackal said to himself, 'Well, to-day I have only got to manage a bigger idiot than before. I shall just kick him on one side, and then go and have a drink.' So he went up to the tortoise and said to him in a soft voice, 'Tortoise! tortoise!' but the tortoise took no notice. Then the jackal kicked him out of the way, and went to the well and began to drink, but scarcely had he touched the water, than the tortoise seized him by the leg. The jackal shrieked out : 'Oh, you will break my leg!' but the tortoise only held on the tighter. The jackal then took his bag and tried to make the tortoise smell the honeycomb he had inside ; but the tortoise turned away his head and smelt nothing. At last the jackal said to the tortoise, 'I should like to give you my bag and everything in it,' but the only answer the tortoise made was to grasp the jackal's leg tighter still.

So matters stood when the other animals came back. The moment he saw them, the jackal gave a violent tug, and managed to free his leg, and then took to his heels as fast as he could. And the animals all said to the tortoise :

'Well done, tortoise, you have proved your courage ; now we can drink from our well in peace, as you have got the better of that thieving jackal!'

[*Contes Populaires des Bassoutos*, recueillis et traduits par E. Jacottet. Paris : Leroux, éditeur.]

THE BEAR

ONCE on a time there was a king who had an only daughter. He was so proud and so fond of her, that he was in constant terror that something would happen to her if she went outside the palace, and thus, owing to his great love for her, he forced her to lead the life of a prisoner, shut up within her own rooms.

The princess did not like this at all, and one day she complained about it very bitterly to her nurse. Now, the nurse was a witch, though the king did not know it. For some time she listened and tried to soothe the princess; but when she saw that she would not be comforted, she said to her: 'Your father loves you very dearly, as you know. Whatever you were to ask from him he would give you. The one thing he will not grant you is permission to leave the palace. Now, do as I tell you. Go to your father and ask him to give you a wooden wheel-barrow, and a bear's skin. When you have got them bring them to me, and I will touch them with my magic wand. The wheel-barrow will then move of itself, and will take you at full speed wherever you want to go, and the bear's skin will make such a covering for you, that no one will recognise you.'

So the princess did as the witch advised her. The king, when he heard her strange request, was greatly astonished, and asked her what she meant to do with a wheel-barrow and a bear's skin. And the princess answered, 'You never let me leave the house—at least you might grant me this request.' So the king granted it, and the princess went back to her nurse, taking the barrow and the bear's skin with her.

As soon as the witch saw them, she touched them with her magic wand, and in a moment the barrow began to move about in all directions. The princess next put on the bear's skin, which so completely changed her appearance, that no one could have known that she was a girl and not a bear. In this strange attire she seated herself on the barrow, and in a few minutes she found herself far away from the palace, and moving rapidly through a great forest. Here she stopped the barrow with a sign that the witch had shown her, and hid herself and it in a thick grove of flowering shrubs.

Now it happened that the prince of that country was hunting with his dogs in the forest. Suddenly he caught sight of the bear hiding among the shrubs, and calling his dogs, hounded them on to attack it. But the girl, seeing what peril she was in, cried, ' Call off your dogs, or they will kill me. What harm have I ever done to you?' At these words, coming from a bear, the prince was so startled that for a moment he stood stock-still, then he said quite gently, ' Will you come with me? I will take you to my home.'

' I will come gladly,' replied the bear; and seating herself on the barrow it at once began to move in the direction of the prince's palace. You may imagine the surprise of the prince's mother when she saw her son return accompanied by a bear, who at once set about doing the house-work better than any servant that the queen had ever seen.

Now it happened that there were great festivities going on in the palace of a neighbouring prince, and at dinner, one day, the prince said to his mother : ' This evening there is to be a great ball, to which I must go.'

And his mother answered, ' Go and dance, and enjoy yourself.'

Suddenly a voice came from under the table, where

the bear had rolled itself, as was its wont : ' Let me come to the ball ; I, too, would like to dance.'

But the only answer the prince made was to give the bear a kick, and to drive it out of the room.

In the evening the prince set off for the ball. As soon as he had started, the bear came to the queen and implored to be allowed to go to the ball, saying that she would hide herself so well that no one would know she was there. The kind-hearted queen could not refuse her.

The Prince Kicks the Bear out of the Room

Then the bear ran to her barrow, threw off her bear's skin, and touched it with the magic wand that the witch had given her. In a moment the skin was changed into an exquisite ball dress woven out of moon-beams, and the wheel-barrow was changed into a carriage drawn by two prancing steeds. Stepping into the carriage the princess drove to the grand entrance of the palace. When she entered the ball-room, in her wondrous dress of moon-beams, she looked so lovely, so different from all the other guests, that everyone wondered who she was, and no one could tell where she had come from.

From the moment he saw her, the prince fell desperately in love with her, and all the evening he would dance with no one else but the beautiful stranger.

When the ball was over, the princess drove away in her carriage at full speed, for she wished to get home in time to change her ball dress into the bear's skin, and the carriage into the wheel-barrow, before anyone discovered who she was.

The prince, putting spurs into his horse, rode after her, for he was determined not to let her out of his sight. But suddenly a thick mist arose and hid her from him. When he reached his home he could talk to his mother of nothing else but the beautiful stranger with whom he had danced so often, and with whom he was so much in love. And the bear beneath the table smiled to itself, and muttered : ' I am the beautiful stranger ; oh, how I have taken you in ! '

The next evening there was a second ball, and, as you may believe, the prince was determined not to miss it, for he thought he would once more see the lovely girl, and dance with her and talk to her, and make her talk to him, for at the first ball she had never opened her lips.

And, sure enough, as the music struck up the first dance, the beautiful stranger entered the room, looking even more radiant than the night before, for this time her dress was woven out of the rays of the sun. All evening the prince danced with her, but she never spoke a word.

When the ball was over he tried once more to follow her carriage, that he might know whence she came, but suddenly a great waterspout fell from the sky, and the blinding sheets of rain hid her from his sight.

When he reached his home he told his mother that he had again seen the lovely girl, and that this time she had been even more beautiful than the night before. And again the bear smiled beneath the table, and muttered : 'I have taken him in a second time, and he has no idea that I am the beautiful girl with whom he is so much in love.'

On the next evening, the prince returned to the palace for the third ball. And the princess went too, and this time she had changed her bear's skin into a dress woven out of the star-light, studded all over with gems, and she looked so dazzling and so beautiful, that everyone wondered at her, and said that no one so beautiful had ever been seen before. And the prince danced with her, and, though he could not induce her to speak, he succeeded in slipping a ring on her finger.

When the ball was over, he followed her carriage, and rode at such a pace that for long he kept it in sight. Then suddenly a terrible wind arose between him and the carriage, and he could not overtake it.

When he reached his home he said to his mother, 'I do not know what is to become of me ; I think I shall go mad, I am so much in love with that girl, and I have no means of finding out who she is. I danced with her and I gave her a ring, and yet I do not know her name, nor where I am to find her.'

Then the bear laughed beneath the table and muttered to itself.

And the prince continued: 'I am tired to death. Order some soup to be made for me, but I don't want that bear to meddle with it. Every time I speak of my love the brute mutters and laughs, and seems to mock at me. I hate the sight of the creature !'

When the soup was ready, the bear brought it to the prince ; but before handing it to him, she dropped into the plate the ring the prince had given her the night before at the ball. The prince began to eat his soup very slowly and languidly, for he was sad at heart, and all his thoughts were busy, wondering how and where he could see the lovely stranger again. Suddenly he noticed the ring at the bottom of the plate. In a moment he recognised it, and was dumb with surprise.

Then he saw the bear standing beside him, looking at him with gentle, beseeching eyes, and something in the eyes of the bear made him say : 'Take off that skin, some mystery is hidden beneath it.'

And the bear's skin dropped off, and the beautiful girl stood before him, in the dress woven out of the starlight, and he saw that she was the stranger with whom he had fallen so deeply in love. And now she appeared to him a thousand times more beautiful than ever, and he led her to his mother. And the princess told them her story, and how she had been kept shut up by her father in his palace, and how she had wearied of her imprisonment. And the prince's mother loved her, and rejoiced that her son should have so good and beautiful a wife.

So they were married, and lived happily for many years, and reigned wisely over their kingdom.

THE SUNCHILD

ONCE there was a woman who had no children, and this made her very unhappy. So she spoke one day to the Sunball, saying : 'Dear Sunball, send me only a little girl now, and when she is twelve years old you may take her back again.'

So soon after this the Sunball sent her a little girl, whom the woman called Letiko, and watched over with great care till she was twelve years old. Soon after that, while Letiko was away one day gathering herbs, the Sunball came to her, and said : 'Letiko, when you go home, tell your mother that she must bethink herself of what she promised me.'

Then Letiko went straight home, and said to her mother : 'While I was gathering herbs a fine tall gentleman came to me and charged me to tell you that you should remember what you promised him.'

When the woman heard that she was sore afraid, and immediately shut all the doors and windows of the house, stopped up all the chinks and holes, and kept Letiko hidden away, that the Sunball should not come and take her away. But she forgot to close up the keyhole, and through it the Sunball sent a ray into the house, which took hold of the little girl and carried her away to him.

One day, the Sunball having sent her to the straw shed to fetch straw, the girl sat down on the piles of straw and bemoaned herself, saying : 'As sighs this straw under my feet so sighs my heart after my mother.'

And this caused her to be so long away that the

Sunball asked her, when she came back : ' Eh, Letiko, where have you been so long ? '

She answered : ' My slippers are too big, and I could not go faster.'

Then the Sunball made the slippers shorter.

Another time he sent her to fetch water, and when she came to the spring, she sat down and lamented, saying : ' As flows the water even so flows my heart with longing for my mother.'

Thus she again remained so long away that the Sunball asked her : ' Eh, Letiko, why have you remained so long away ? '

And she answered : ' My petticoat is too long and hinders me in walking.'

Then the Sunball cut her petticoat to make it shorter.

Another time the Sunball sent her to bring him a pair of sandals, and as the girl carried these in her hand she began to lament, saying : ' As creaks the leather so creaks my heart after my little mother.'

When she came home the Sunball asked her again : ' Eh, Letiko, why do you come home so late ? '

' My red hood is too wide, and falls over my eyes, therefore I could not go fast.'

Then he made the hood narrower.

At last, however, the Sunball became aware how sad Letiko was. He sent her a second time to bring straw, and, slipping in after her, he heard how she lamented for her mother. Then he went home, called two foxes to him, and said : ' Will you take Letiko home ? '

' Yes, why not ? '

' But what will you eat and drink if you should become hungry and thirsty by the way ? '

' We will eat her flesh and drink her blood.'

When the Sunball heard that, he said : ' You are not suited for this affair.'

Then he sent them away, and called two hares to him, and said : ' Will you take Letiko home to her mother ? '

'Yes, why not?'

'What will you eat and drink if you should become hungry and thirsty by the way?'

'We will eat grass and drink from streamlets.'

'Then take her, and bring her home.'

Then the hares set out, taking Letiko with them, and because it was a long way to her home they became hungry by the way. Then they said to the little girl: 'Climb this tree, dear Letiko, and remain there till we have finished eating.'

So Letiko climbed the tree, and the hares went grazing.

It was not very long, however, before a lamia came under the tree and called out: 'Letiko, Letiko, come down and see what beautiful shoes I have on.'

'Oh! my shoes are much finer than yours.'

LETIKO · LETIKO · COME · DOWN

AND SEE WHAT A BEAUTIFUL APRON I HAVE

'Come down. I am in a hurry, for my house is not yet swept.'

'Go home and sweep it then, and come back when you are ready.'

Then the lamia went away and swept her house, and when she was ready she came back and called out: 'Letiko, Letiko, come down and see what a beautiful apron I have.'

'Oh! my apron is much finer than yours.'

'If you will not come down I will cut down the tree and eat you.'

'Do so, and then eat me.'

Then the lamia hewed with all her strength at the tree, but could not cut it down. And when she saw that, she called out: 'Letiko, Letiko, come down, for I must feed my children.'

'Go home then and feed them, and come back when you are ready.'

When the lamia was gone away, Letiko called out: 'Little hares! little hares!'

Then said one hare to the other: 'Listen, Letiko is calling;' and they both ran back to her as fast as they could go. Then Letiko came down from the tree, and they went on their way.

The lamia ran as fast as she could after them, to catch them up, and when she came to a field where people were working she asked them: 'Have you seen anyone pass this way?'

They answered: 'We are planting beans.'

'Oh! I did not ask about that; but if anyone had passed this way.'

But the people only answered the louder: 'Are you deaf? It is beans, beans, beans we are planting.'

When Letiko had nearly reached her home the dog knew her, and called out, 'Bow wow! see here comes Letiko!'

And the mother said, 'Hush! thou beast of ill-omen! wilt thou make me burst with misery?'

Next the cat on the roof saw her, and called out 'Miaouw! miaouw! see here comes Letiko!'

And the mother said, 'Keep silence! thou beast of ill-omen! wilt thou make me burst with misery?'

Then the cock spied, and called out: 'Cock-a-doodle-do! see here comes Letiko!'

And the mother said again: 'Be quiet! thou bird of ill-omen! wilt thou make me burst with misery?'

LETIKO GETS HOME SAFE AFTER ALL

The nearer Letiko and the two hares came to the house the nearer also came the lamia, and when the hare was about to slip in by the house door she caught it by its little tail and tore it out.

When the hare came in the mother stood up and said to it: 'Welcome, dear little hare; because you have brought me back Letiko I will silver your little tail.'

And she did so; and lived ever after with her daughter in happiness and content.

THE DAUGHTER OF BUK ETTEMSUCH

ONCE upon a time there lived a man who had seven daughters. For a long time they dwelt quite happily at home together, then one morning the father called them all before him and said :

'Your mother and I are going on a journey, and as we do not know how long we may be away, you will find enough provisions in the house to last you three years. But see you do not open the door to anyone till we come home again.'

'Very well, dear father,' replied the girls.

For two years they never left the house or unlocked the door ; but one day, when they had washed their clothes, and were spreading them out on the roof to dry, the girls looked down into the street where people were walking to and fro, and across to the market, with its stalls of fresh meat, vegetables, and other nice things.

'Come here,' cried one. 'It makes me quite hungry ! Why should not we have our share? Let one of us go to the market, and buy meat and vegetables.'

'Oh, we mustn't do that ! ' said the youngest. 'You know our father forbade us to open the door till he came home again.'

Then the eldest sister sprang at her and struck her, the second spit at her, the third abused her, the fourth pushed her, the fifth flung her to the ground, and the sixth tore her clothes. Then they left her lying on the floor, and went out with a basket.

In about an hour they came back with the basket full

of meat and vegetables, which they put in a pot, and set on the fire, quite forgetting that the house door stood wide open. The youngest sister, however, took no part in all this, and when dinner was ready and the table laid, she stole softly out to the entrance hall, and hid herself behind a great cask which stood in one corner.

Now, while the other sisters were enjoying their feast, a witch passed by, and catching sight of the open door, she walked in. She went up to the eldest girl, and said : ' Where shall I begin on you, you fat bolster ? '

' You must begin,' answered she, ' with the hand which struck my little sister.'

So the witch gobbled her up, and when the last scrap had disappeared, she came to the second and asked : ' Where shall I begin on you, my fat bolster ? '

And the second answered, ' You must begin on my mouth, which spat on my sister.'

And so on to the rest; and very soon the whole six had disappeared. And as the witch was eating the last mouthful of the last sister, the youngest, who had been crouching, frozen with horror, behind the barrel, ran out through the open door into the street. Without looking behind her, she hastened on and on, as fast as her feet would carry her, till she saw an ogre's castle standing in front of her. In a corner near the door she spied a large pot, and she crept softly up to it and pulled the cover over it, and went to sleep.

By-and-by the ogre came home. ' Fee, Fo, Fum,' cried he, ' I smell the smell of a man. What ill fate has brought him here ? ' And he looked through all the rooms, and found nobody. ' Where are you ? ' he called. ' Do not be afraid, I will do you no harm.'

But the girl was still silent.

' Come out, I tell you,' repeated the ogre. ' Your life is quite safe. If you are an old man, you shall be my father. If you are a boy, you shall be my son. If your years are as many as mine, you shall be my brother. If you are an old woman, you shall be my mother. If you are a young one, you shall be my daughter. If you are middle-aged, you shall be my wife. So come out, and fear nothing.'

Then the maiden came out of her hiding-place, and stood before him.

'Fear nothing,' said the ogre again; and when he went away to hunt he left her to look after the house. In the evening he returned, bringing with him hares, partridges, and gazelles, for the girl's supper; for himself he only cared for the flesh of men, which she cooked for him. He also gave into her charge the keys of six rooms, but the key of the seventh he kept himself.

And time passed on, and the girl and the ogre still lived together.

She called him 'Father,' and he called her 'Daughter,' and never once did he speak roughly to her.

One day the maiden said to him, 'Father, give me the key of the upper chamber.'

'No, my daughter,' replied the ogre. 'There is nothing there that is any use to you.'

'But I want the key,' she repeated again.

However the ogre took no notice, and pretended not to hear. The girl began to cry, and said to herself: 'To-night, when he thinks I am asleep, I will watch and see where he hides it'; and after she and the ogre had supped, she bade him good-night, and left the room. In a few minutes she stole quietly back, and watched from behind a curtain. In a little while she saw the ogre take the key from his pocket, and hide it in a hole in the ground before he went to bed. And when all was still she took out the key, and went back to the house.

The next morning the ogre awoke with the first ray of light, and the first thing he did was to look for the key. It was gone, and he guessed at once what had become of it.

But instead of getting into a great rage, as most ogres

The Maiden creeps out of the Pot

would have done, he said to himself, 'If I wake the maiden up I shall only frighten her. For to-day she shall keep the key, and when I return to-night it will be time enough to take it from her.' So he went off to hunt.

The moment he was safe out of the way, the girl ran upstairs and opened the door of the room, which was quite bare. The one window was closed, and she threw back the lattice and looked out. Beneath lay a garden which belonged to the prince, and in the garden was an ox, who was drawing up water from the well all by himself—for there was nobody to be seen anywhere. The ox raised his head at the noise the girl made in opening the lattice, and said to her, 'Good morning, O daughter of Buk Ettemsuch! Your father is feeding you up till you are nice and fat, and then he will put you on a spit and cook you.'

These words so frightened the maiden that she burst into tears and ran out of the room. All day she wept, and when the ogre came home at night, no supper was ready for him.

'What are you crying for?' said he. 'Where is my supper, and is it you who have opened the upper chamber?'

'Yes, I opened it,' answered she.

'And what did the ox say to you?'

'He said, "Good morning, O daughter of Buk Ettemsuch. Your father is feeding you up till you are nice and fat, and then he will put you on a spit and cook you."'

'Well, to-morrow you can go to the window and say, "My father is feeding me up till I am nice and fat, but he does not mean to eat me. If I had one of your eyes I would use it for a mirror, and look at myself before and behind; and your girths should be loosened, and you should be blind—seven days and seven nights."'

'All right,' replied the girl, and the next morning, when the ox spoke to her, she answered him as she had been told, and he fell down straight upon the ground, and lay there seven days and seven nights. But the flowers in the garden withered, for there was no one to water them.

When the prince came into his garden he found nothing but yellow stalks; in the midst of them the ox was lying. With a blow from his sword he killed the animal, and, turning to his attendants, he said, ' Go and fetch another ox!' And they brought in a great beast, and he drew the water out of the well, and the flowers revived, and the grass grew green again. Then the prince called his attendants and went away.

The next morning the girl heard the noise of the water-wheel, and she opened the lattice and looked out of the window.

'Good morning, O daughter of Buk Ettemsuch!' said the new ox. 'Your father is feeding you up till you are nice and fat, and then he will put you on a spit and cook you.'

And the maiden answered: 'My father is feeding me up till I am nice and fat, but he does not mean to eat me. If I had one of your eyes I would use it for a mirror, and look at myself before and behind; and your girths should be loosened, and you should be blind—seven days and seven nights.'

Directly she uttered these words the ox fell to the ground and lay there, seven days and seven nights. Then he arose and began to draw the water from the well. He had only turned the wheel once or twice, when the prince took it into his head to visit his garden and see how the new ox was getting on. When he entered the ox was working busily; but in spite of that the flowers and grass were dried up. And the prince drew his sword, and rushed at the ox to slay him, as he had done the other. But the ox fell on his knees and said:

' My lord, only spare my life, and let me tell you how it happened.'

'How what hap-
pened?' asked the
prince.

'My lord, a girl
looked out of that
window and spoke a
few words to me, and
I fell to the ground.
For seven days and
seven nights I lay
there, unable to move.
But, O my lord, it is
not given to us twice
to behold beauty such
as hers.'

'It is a lie,' said
the prince. 'An ogre
dwells there. Is it
likely that he keeps a
maiden in his upper
chamber?'

'Why not?' replied
the ox 'But if you
come here at dawn to-
morrow, and hide be-
hind that tree, you will
see for yourself.'

'So I will,' said the
prince; 'and if I find
that you have not
spoken truth, I will kill
you.'

The prince left the
garden, and the ox went
on with his work.
Next morning the
prince came early to

the garden, and found the ox busy with the water-wheel.

' Has the girl appeared yet ? ' he asked.

' Not yet ; but she will not be long. Hide yourself in the branches of that tree, and you will soon see her.'

The prince did as he was told, and scarcely was he seated when the maiden threw open the lattice.

' Good morning, O daughter of Buk Ettemsuch ! ' said the ox. ' Your father is feeding you up till you are nice and fat, and then he will put you on a spit and cook you.'

' My father is feeding me up till I am nice and fat, but he does not mean to eat me. If I had one of your eyes I would use it for a mirror, and look at myself before and behind ; and your girths should be loosened, and you should be blind—seven days and seven nights.' And hardly had she spoken when the ox fell on the ground, and the maiden shut the lattice and went away. But the prince knew that what the ox had said was true, and that she had not her equal in the whole world. And he came down from the tree, his heart burning with love.

' Why has the ogre not eaten her ? ' thought he. ' This night I will invite him to supper in my palace and question him about the maiden, and find out if she is his wife.'

So the prince ordered a great ox to be slain and roasted whole, and two huge tanks to be made, one filled with water and the other with wine. And towards evening he called his attendants and went to the ogre's house to wait in the courtyard till he came back from hunting. The ogre was surprised to see so many people assembled in front of his house ; but he bowed politely and said, ' Good morning, dear neighbours ! To what do I owe the pleasure of this visit ? I have not offended you, I hope ? '

' Oh, certainly not ! ' answered the prince.

' Then,' continued the ogre, ' What has brought you to my house to-day for the first time ? '

'We should like to have supper with you,' said the prince.

'Well, supper is ready, and you are welcome,' replied the ogre, leading the way into the house, for he had had a good day, and there was plenty of game in the bag over his shoulder.

A table was quickly prepared, and the prince had already taken his place, when he suddenly exclaimed, 'After all, Buk Ettemsuch, suppose you come to supper with me?'

'Where?' asked the ogre.

'In my house. I know it is all ready.'

'But it is so far off—why not stay here?'

'Oh, I will come another day; but this evening I must be your host.'

So the ogre accompanied the prince and his attendants back to the palace. After a while the prince turned to the ogre and said :

'It is as a wooer that I appear before you. I seek a wife from an honourable family.'

'But I have no daughter,' replied the ogre.

'Oh, yes you have, I saw her at the window.'

'Well, you can marry her if you wish,' said he.

So the prince's heart was glad as he and his attendants rode back with the ogre to his house. And as they parted, the prince said to his guest, 'You will not forget the bargain we have made?'

'I am not a young man, and never break my promises,' said the ogre, and went in and shut the door.

Upstairs he found the maiden, waiting till he returned to have her supper, for she did not like eating by herself.

'I have had my supper,' said the ogre, 'for I have been spending the evening with the prince.'

'Where did you meet him?' asked the girl.

'Oh, we are neighbours, and grew up together, and to-night I promised that you should be his wife.'

'I don't want to be any man's wife,' answered she;

but this was only pretence, for her heart too was glad.

Next morning early came the prince, bringing with him bridal gifts, and splendid wedding garments, to carry the maiden back to his palace.

But before he let her go the ogre called her to him, and said, ' Be careful, girl, never to speak to the prince; and when he speaks to you, you must be dumb, unless he swears " by the head of Buk Ettemsuch." Then you may speak.'

' Very well,' answered the girl.

They set out; and when they reached the palace, the prince led his bride to the room he had prepared for her, and said ' Speak to me, my wife,' but she was silent; and by-and-by he left her, thinking that perhaps she was shy. The next day the same thing happened, and the next.

At last he said, ' Well, if you won't speak, I shall go and get another wife who will.' And he did.

Now when the new wife was brought to the palace the daughter of Buk Ettemsuch rose, and spoke to the ladies who had come to attend on the second bride. ' Go and sit down. I will make ready the feast.' And the ladies sat down as they were told, and waited.

The maiden sat down too, and called out, ' Come here, firewood,' and the firewood came. ' Come here, fire,' and the fire came and kindled the wood. ' Come here, pot.' ' Come here, oil ; ' and the pot and the oil came. ' Get into the pot, oil ! ' said she, and the oil did it. When the oil was boiling, the maiden dipped all her fingers in it, and they became ten fried fishes. ' Come here, oven,' she cried next, and the oven came. ' Fire, heat the oven.' And the fire heated it. When it was hot enough, the maiden jumped in, just as she was, with her beautiful silver and gold dress, and all her jewels. In a minute or two she had turned into a snow-white loaf, that made your mouth water.

Said the loaf to the ladies, ' You can eat now ; do not

stand so far off;' but they only stared at each other, speechless with surprise.

'What are you staring at?' asked the new bride.

'At all these wonders,' replied the ladies.

'Do you call *these* wonders?' said she scornfully; 'I can do that too,' and she jumped straight into the oven, and was burnt up in a moment.

Then they ran to the prince and said : 'Come quickly, your wife is dead!'

'Bury her, then!' returned he. 'But why did she do it? I am sure I said nothing to make her throw herself into the oven.'

Accordingly the burnt woman was buried, but the prince would not go to the funeral as all his thoughts were still with the wife who would not speak to him. The next night he said to her, 'Dear wife, are you afraid that something dreadful will happen if you speak to me? If you still persist in being dumb, I shall be forced to get another wife.' The poor girl longed to speak, but dread of the ogre kept her silent, and the prince did as he had said, and brought a fresh bride into the palace. And when she and her ladies were seated in state, the maiden planted a sharp stake in the ground, and sat herself down comfortably on it, and began to spin.

'What are you staring at so?' said the new bride to her ladies. 'Do you think that is anything wonderful? Why, I can do as much myself!'

'I am sure you can't,' said they, much too surprised to be polite.

Then the maid sprang off the stake and left the room, and instantly the new wife took her place. But the sharp stake ran through, and she was dead in a moment. So they sent to the prince and said, 'Come quickly, and bury your wife.'

'Bury her yourselves,' he answered. 'What did she do it for? It was not by my orders that she impaled herself on the stake.'

So they buried her; and in the evening the prince came to the daughter of Buk Ettemsuch, and said to her, ' Speak to me, or I shall have to take another wife.' But she was afraid to speak to him.

The following day the prince hid himself in the room and watched. And soon the maiden woke, and said to the pitcher and to the water-jug, ' Quick! go down to the spring and bring me some water; I am thirsty.'

And they went. But as they were filling themselves at the spring, the water-jug knocked against the pitcher and broke off its spout. And the pitcher burst into tears, and ran to the maiden, and said: ' Mistress, beat the water-jug, for he has broken my spout!'

' By the head of Buk Ettemsuch, I implore you not to beat me!'

' Ah,' she replied, ' if only my husband had sworn by that oath, I could have spoken to him from the beginning, and he need never have taken another wife. But now he will never say it, and he will have to go on marrying fresh ones.'

And the prince, from his hiding-place, heard her words, and he jumped up and ran to her and said, ' By the head of Buk Ettemsuch, speak to me.'

So she spoke to him, and they lived happily to the end of their days, because the girl kept the promise she had made to the ogre.

[*Märchen und Gedichte aus der Stadt Tripolis.* Von Hans Stumme.]

LAUGHING EYE AND WEEPING EYE, OR
THE LIMPING FOX

(SERVIAN STORY)

ONCE upon a time there lived a man whose right eye
always smiled, and whose left eye always cried; and this
man had three sons, two of them very clever, and the
third very stupid. Now these three sons were very
curious about the peculiarity of their father's eyes, and
as they could not puzzle out the reason for themselves,
they determined to ask their father why he did not have
eyes like other people.

So the eldest of the three went one day into his
father's room and put the question straight out; but,
instead of answering, the man flew into a fearful rage,
and sprang at him with a knife. The young fellow ran
away in a terrible fright, and took refuge with his
brothers, who were awaiting anxiously the result of the
interview.

'You had better go yourselves,' was all the reply they
got, 'and see if you will fare any better.'

Upon hearing this, the second son entered his father's
room, only to be treated in the same manner as his
brother; and back he came telling the youngest, the fool
of the family, that it was his turn to try his luck.

Then the youngest son marched boldly up to his
father and said to him, 'My brothers would not let me
know what answer you had given to their question. But

now, do tell me why your right eye always laughs and your left eye always weeps.'

As before, the father grew purple with fury, and rushed forwards with his knife. But the simpleton did not stir a step; he knew that he had really nothing to fear from his father.

'Ah, now I see who is my true son,' exclaimed the old man; 'the others are mere cowards. And as you have shown me that you are brave, I will satisfy your curiosity. My right eye laughs because I am glad to have a son like you; my left eye weeps because a precious treasure has been stolen from me. I had in my garden a vine that yielded a tun of wine every hour—someone has managed to steal it, so I weep its loss.'

The simpleton returned to his brothers and told them of their father's loss, and they all made up their minds to set out at once in search of the vine. They travelled together till they came to some cross roads, and there they parted, the two elder ones taking one road, and the simpleton the other.

'Thank goodness we have got rid of that idiot,' exclaimed the two elder. 'Now let us have some breakfast.' And they sat down by the roadside and began to eat.

They had only half finished, when a lame fox came out of a wood and begged them to give him something to eat. But they jumped up and chased him off with their sticks, and the poor fox limped away on his three pads. As he ran he reached the spot where the youngest son was getting out the food he had brought with him, and the fox asked him for a crust of bread. The simpleton had not very much for himself, but he gladly gave half of his meal to the hungry fox.

'Where are you going, brother?' said the fox, when he had finished his share of the bread; and the young man told him the story of his father and the wonderful vine.

LIMPING·FOX·ADVISES
THE·SIMPLETON·TO
KEEP·THE·GOLDEN
GIRL·HIMSELF·

'Dear me, how lucky!' said the fox. 'I know what has become of it. Follow me!' So they went on till they came to the gate of a large garden.

'You will find here the vine that you are seeking, but it will not be at all easy to get it. You must listen carefully to what I am going to say. Before you reach the vine you will have to pass twelve outposts, each consisting of two guards. If you see these guards looking straight at you, go on without fear, for they are asleep. But if their eyes are shut then beware, for they are wide awake. If you once get to the vine, you will find two shovels, one of wood and the other of iron. Be sure not to take the iron one ; it will make a noise and rouse the guards, and then you are lost.'

The young man got safely through the garden without any adventures till he came to the vine which yielded a tun of wine an hour. But he thought he should find it impossible to dig the hard earth with only a wooden shovel, so picked up the iron one instead. The noise it made soon awakened the guards. They seized the poor simpleton and carried him to their master.

'Why do you try to steal my vine?' demanded he ; 'and how did you manage to get past the guards?'

'The vine is not yours ; it belongs to my father, and if you will not give it to me now, I will return and get it somehow.'

'You shall have the vine if you will bring me in exchange an apple off the golden apple-tree that flowers every twenty-four hours, and bears fruit of gold.' So saying, he gave orders that the simpleton should be released, and this done, the youth hurried off to consult the fox.

'Now you see,' observed the fox, 'this comes of not following my advice. However, I will help you to get the golden apple. It grows in a garden that you will easily recognise from my description. Near the apple-tree are two poles, one of gold, the other of wood.

Take the wooden pole, and you will be able to reach the apple.'

Master Simpleton listened carefully to all that was told him, and after crossing the garden, and escaping as before from the men who were watching it, soon arrived at the apple-tree. But he was so dazzled by the sight of the beautiful golden fruit, that he quite forgot all that the fox had said. He seized the golden pole, and struck the branch a sounding blow. The guards at once awoke, and conducted him to their master. Then the simpleton had to tell his story.

'I will give you the golden apple,' said the owner of the garden, 'if you will bring me in exchange a horse which can go round the world in four-and-twenty hours.' And the young man departed, and went to find the fox.

This time the fox was really angry, and no wonder.

'If you had listened to me, you would have been home with your father by this time. However I am willing to help you once more. Go into the forest, and you will find the horse with two halters round his neck. One is of gold, the other of hemp. Lead him by the hempen halter, or else the horse will begin to neigh, and will waken the guards. Then all is over with you.'

So Master Simpleton searched till he found the horse, and was struck dumb at its beauty.

'What!' he said to himself, 'put the hempen halter on an animal like that? Not I, indeed!'

Then the horse neighed loudly; the guards seized our young friend and conducted him before their master.

'I will give you the golden horse,' said he, 'if you will bring me in exchange a golden maiden who has never yet seen either sun or moon.

'But if I am to bring you the golden maiden you must lend me first the golden steed with which to seek for her.

'Ah,' replied the owner of the golden horse, 'but who will undertake that you will ever come back?'

'I swear on the head of my father,' answered the young man, 'that I will bring back either the maiden or the horse.' And he went away to consult the fox.

Now, the fox who was always patient and charitable to other people's faults, led him to the entrance of a deep grotto, where stood a maiden all of gold, and beautiful as the day. He placed her on his horse and prepared to mount.

'Are you not sorry,' said the fox, 'to give such a lovely maiden in exchange for a horse? Yet you are bound to do it, for you have sworn by the head of your father. But perhaps I could manage to take her place. So saying, the fox transformed himself into another golden maiden, so like the first that hardly anyone could tell the difference between them.

The simpleton took her straight to the owner of the horse, who was enchanted with her.

And the young man got back his father's vine and married the *real* golden maiden into the bargain.

[*Contes Populaires Slaves.* Traduits par Louis Léger. Paris : Ernest Leroux, éditeur.]

THE UNLOOKED-FOR PRINCE

(POLISH STORY)

A LONG time ago there lived a king and queen who had
no children, although they both wished very much for a
little son. They tried not to let each other see how
unhappy they were, and pretended to take pleasure
in hunting and hawking and all sorts of other sports ;
but at length the king could bear it no longer, and
declared that he must go and visit the furthest corners
of his kingdom, and that it would be many months before
he should return to his capital.

By that time he hoped he would have so many things
to think about that he would have forgotten to trouble
about the little son who never came.

The country the king reigned over was very large, and
full of high, stony mountains and sandy deserts, so that it
was not at all easy to go from one place to another. One
day the king had wandered out alone, meaning to go only
a little distance, but everything looked so alike he could
not make out the path by which he had come. He walked
on and on for hours, the sun beating hotly on his head,
and his legs trembling under him, and he might have died
of thirst if he had not suddenly stumbled on a little well,
which looked as if it had been newly dug. On the
surface floated a silver cup with a golden handle, but
as it bobbed about whenever the king tried to seize it, he
was too thirsty to wait any longer and knelt down and
drank his fill.

When he had finished he began to rise from his knees, but somehow his beard seemed to have stuck fast in the water, and with all his efforts he could not pull it out. After two or three jerks to his head, which only hurt him without doing any good, he called out angrily, ' Let go at once! Who is holding me ? '

' It is I, the King Kostieï,' said a voice from the well, and looking up through the water was a little man with green eyes and a big head. ' You have drunk from my spring, and I shall not let you go until you promise to give me the most precious thing your palace contains, which was not there when you left it.'

Now the only thing that the king much cared for in his palace was the queen herself, and as she was weeping bitterly on a pile of cushions in the great hall when he had ridden away, he knew that Kostieï's words could not apply to her. So he cheerfully gave the promise asked for by the ugly little man, and in the twinkling of an eye, man, spring, and cup had disappeared, and the king was left kneeling on the dry sand, wondering if it was all a dream. But as he felt much stronger and better he made up his mind that this strange adventure must really have happened, and he sprang on his horse and rode off with a light heart to look for his companions.

In a few weeks they began to set out on their return home, which they reached one hot day, eight months after they had all left. The king was greatly beloved by his people, and crowds lined the roads, shouting and waving their hats as the procession passed along. On the steps of the palace stood the queen, with a splendid golden cushion in her arms, and on the cushion the most beautiful boy that ever was seen, wrapped about in a cloud of lace. In a moment Kostieï's words rushed into the king's mind, and he began to weep bitterly, to the surprise of every-body, who had expected him nearly to die of joy at the sight of his son. But try as he would and work as hard as he might he could never forget his promise, and every

time he let the baby out of his sight he thought that he
had seen it for the last time.

However, years passed on and the prince grew first into
a big boy, and then into a fine young man. Kostieï made
no sign, and gradually even the anxious king thought less
and less about him, and in the end forgot him altogether.

There was no family in the whole kingdom happier
than the king and queen and prince, until one day when
the youth met a little old man as he was hunting in a
lonely part of the woods.

'How are you my unlooked-for Prince?' he said.
'You kept them waiting a good long time!'

'And who are you?' asked the prince.

'You will know soon enough. When you go home
give my compliments to your father and tell him that I
wish he would square accounts with me. If he neglects
to pay his debts he will bitterly repent it.'

So saying the old man disappeared, and the prince
returned to the palace and told his father what had
happened.

The king turned pale and explained to his son the
terrible story.

'Do not grieve over it, father,' answered the prince.
It is nothing so dreadful after all! I will find some way
to force Kostieï to give up his rights over me. But if I
do not come back in a year's time, you must give up all
hopes of ever seeing me.'

Then the prince began to prepare for his journey. His
father gave him a complete suit of steel armour, a sword,
and a horse, while his mother hung round his neck a
cross of gold. So, kissing him tenderly, with many tears
they let him go.

He rode steadily on for three days, and at sunset on
the fourth day he found himself on the seashore. On
the sand before him lay twelve white dresses, dazzling as
the snow, yet as far as his eyes could reach there was no
one in sight to whom they could belong. Curious to see

what would happen, he took up one of the garments, and leaving his horse loose, to wander about the adjoining fields, he hid himself among some willows and waited. In a few minutes a flock of geese which had been paddling about in the sea approached the shore, and put on the dresses, struck the sand with their feet and were transformed in the twinkling of an eye into eleven beautiful young girls, who flew away as fast as they could. The twelfth and youngest remained in the water, stretching out her long white neck and looking about her anxiously. Suddenly, among the willows, she perceived the king's son, and called out to him with a human voice :

'Oh Prince, give me back my dress, and I shall be for ever grateful to you.'

The prince hastened to lay the dress on the sand, and walked away. When the maiden had thrown off the goose-skin and quickly put on her proper clothes, she came towards him and he saw that none had ever seen or told of such beauty as hers. She blushed and held out her hand, saying to him in a soft voice :

'I thank you, noble Prince, for having granted my request. I am the youngest daughter of Kostieï the immortal, who has twelve daughters and rules over the kingdoms under the earth. Long time my father has waited for you, and great is his anger. But trouble not yourself and fear nothing, only do as I bid you. When you see the King Kostieï, fall straightway upon your knees and heed neither his threats nor his cry, but draw near to him boldly. That which will happen after, you will know in time. Now let us go.'

At these words she struck the ground with her foot and a gulf opened, down which they went right into the heart of the earth. In a short time they reached Kostieï's palace, which gives light, with a light brighter than the sun, to the dark kingdoms below. And the prince, as he had been bidden, entered boldly into the hall.

Kostieï, with a shining crown upon his head, sat in

the centre upon a golden throne. His green eyes glittered
like glass, his hands were as the claws of a crab. When
he caught sight of the prince he uttered piercing yells,
which shook the walls of the palace. The prince took
no notice, but continued his advance on his knees
towards the throne. When he had almost reached it,
the king broke out into a laugh and said :

'It has been very lucky for you that you have
been able to make me laugh. Stay with us in our underground empire, only first you will have to do three things.
To-night it is late. Go to sleep; to-morrow I will tell
you.'

Early the following morning the prince received a
message that Kostieï was ready to see him. He got up
and dressed, and hastened to the presence chamber,
where the little king was seated on his throne. When
the prince appeared, bowing low before him, Kostieï
began :

'Now, Prince, this is what you have to do. By to-night
you must build me a marble palace, with windows of
crystal and a roof of gold. It is to stand in the middle
of a great park, full of streams and lakes. If you are
able to build it you shall be my friend. If not, off with
your head.'

The prince listened in silence to this startling speech,
and then returning to his room set himself to think
about the certain death that awaited him. He was quite
absorbed in these thoughts, when suddenly a bee flew
against the window and tapped, saying, ' Let me come in.'
He rose and opened the window, and there stood before
him the youngest princess.

' What are you dreaming about, Prince ? '

' I was dreaming of your father, who has planned my
death.'

' Fear nothing. You may sleep in peace, and to-
morrow morning when you awake you will find the
palace all ready.'

What she said, she did. The next morning when the prince left his room he saw before him a palace more beautiful than his fancy had ever pictured. Kostieï for his part could hardly believe his eyes, and pondered deeply how it had got there.

'Well, this time you have certainly won; but you are not going to be let off so easily. To-morrow all my twelve daughters shall stand in a row before you, and if you cannot tell me which of them is the youngest, off goes your head.'

'What! Not recognise the youngest princess!' said the Prince to himself, as he entered his room, 'a likely story!'

'It is such a difficult matter that you will never be able to do it without my help,' replied the bee, who was buzzing about the ceiling. 'We are all so exactly alike, that even our father scarcely knows the difference between us.'

'Then what must I do?'

'This. The youngest is she who will have a ladybird on her eyelid. Be very careful. Now good-bye.'

Next morning King Kostieï again sent for the prince. The young princesses were all drawn up in a row, dressed precisely in the same manner, and with their eyes all cast down. As the prince looked at them, he was amazed at their likeness. Twice he walked along the line, without being able to detect the sign agreed upon. The third time his heart beat fast at the sight of a tiny speck upon the eyelid of one of the girls.

'This one is the youngest,' he said.

'How in the world did you guess?' cried Kostieï in a fury. 'There is some jugglery about it! But you are not going to escape me so easily. In three hours you shall come here and give me another proof of your cleverness. I shall set alight a handful of straw, and before it is burnt up you will have turned it into a pair of boots. If not, off goes your head.'

So the prince returned sadly into his room, but the bee was there before him.

'Why do you look so melancholy, my handsome Prince?'

'How can I help looking melancholy when your father has ordered me to make him a pair of boots? Does he take me for a shoemaker?'

'What do you think of doing?'

'Not of making boots, at any rate! I am not afraid of death. One can only die once after all.'

'No, Prince, you shall not die. I will try to save you. And we will fly together or die together.'

As she spoke she spat upon the ground, and then drawing the prince after her out of the room, she locked the door behind her and threw away the key. Holding each other tight by the hand, they made their way up into the sunlight, and found themselves by the side of the same sea, while the prince's horse was still quietly feeding in the neighbouring meadow. The moment he saw his master, the horse whinnied and galloped towards him. Without losing an instant the prince sprang into the saddle, swung the princess behind him, and away they went like an arrow from a bow.

When the hour arrived which Kostieï had fixed for the prince's last trial, and there were no signs of him, the king sent to his room to ask why he delayed so long. The servants, finding the door locked, knocked loudly and received for answer, 'In one moment.' It was the spittle, which was imitating the voice of the prince.

The answer was taken back to Kostieï. He waited; still no prince. He sent the servants back again, and the same voice replied, 'Immediately.'

'He is making fun of me!' shrieked Kostieï in a rage. 'Break in the door, and bring him to me!'

The servants hurried to do his bidding. The door was broken open. Nobody inside; but just the spittle in fits of laughter! Kostieï was beside himself with rage, and commanded his guards to ride after the fugitives. If the guards returned without the fugitives, their heads should pay for it.

By this time the prince and princess had got a good start, and were feeling quite happy, when suddenly they heard the sound of a gallop far behind them. The prince sprang from the saddle, and laid his ear to the ground.

'They are pursuing us,' he said.

'Then there is no time to be lost,' answered the princess; and as she spoke she changed herself into a river, the prince into a bridge, the horse into a crow, and divided the wide road beyond the bridge into three little ones. When the soldiers came up to the bridge, they paused uncertainly. How were they to know which of the three roads the fugitives had taken? They gave it up in despair and returned in trembling to Kostieï.

'Idiots!' he exclaimed, in a passion. 'They *were* the bridge and the river, of course! Do you mean to say you never thought of that? Go back at once!' and off they galloped like lightning.

But time had been lost, and the prince and princess were far on their way.

'I hear a horse,' cried the princess.

The prince jumped down and laid his ear to the ground.

'Yes,' he said, 'they are not far off now.'

In an instant prince, princess, and horse had all disappeared, and instead was a dense forest, crossed and recrossed by countless paths. Kostieï's soldiers dashed hastily into the forest, believing they saw before them the flying horse with its double burden. They seemed close upon them, when suddenly horse, wood, everything disappeared, and they found themselves at the place where they started. There was nothing for it but to return to Kostieï, and tell him of this fresh disaster.

'A horse! a horse!' cried the king. 'I will go after

them myself. *This* time they shall *not* escape.' And he galloped off, foaming with anger.

'I think I hear someone pursuing us,' said the princess.

'Yes, so do I.'

'And this time it is Kostieï himself. But his power only reaches as far as the first church, and he can go no farther. Give me your golden cross.' So the prince unfastened the cross which was his mother's gift, and the princess hastily changed herself into a church, the prince into a priest, and the horse into a belfry.

It was hardly done when Kostieï came up.

'Greeting, monk. Have you seen some travellers on horseback pass this way?'

'Yes, the prince and Kostieï's daughter have just gone by. They have entered the church, and told me to give you their greetings if I met you.'

Then Kostieï knew that he had been hopelessly beaten, and the prince and princess continued their journey without any more adventures.

[*Contes Populaires Slaves.* Traduits par Louis Léger. Paris : Leroux, éditeur.]

THE SIMPLETON

THERE lived, once upon a time, a man who was as rich
as he could be ; but as no happiness in this world is ever
quite complete, he had an only son who was such a
simpleton that he could barely add two and two together.
At last his father determined to put up with his stupidity
no longer, and giving him a purse full of gold, he sent
him off to seek his fortune in foreign lands, mindful of
the adage :

> How much a fool that's sent to roam
> Excels a fool that stays at home.

Moscione, for this was the youth's name, mounted a
horse, and set out for Venice, hoping to find a ship there
that would take him to Cairo.   After he had ridden for
some time he saw a man standing at the foot of a poplar
tree, and said to him : ' What's your name, my friend ;
where do you come from, and what can you do ? '
    The man replied, ' My name is Quick-as-Thought, I
come from Fleet-town, and I can run like lightning.'
    ' I should like to see you,' returned Moscione.
    'Just wait a minute, then,' said Quick-as-Thought,
' and I will soon show you that I am speaking the truth.'
    The words were hardly out of his mouth when a
young doe ran right across the field they were standing
in.
    Quick-as-Thought let her run on a short distance, in
order to give her a start, and then pursued her so quickly

and so lightly that you could not have tracked his footsteps if the field had been strewn with flour. In a very few springs he had overtaken the doe, and had so impressed Moscione with his fleetness of foot that he begged Quick-as-Thought to go with him, promising at the same time to reward him handsomely.

Quick-as-Thought agreed to his proposal, and they continued on their journey together. They had hardly gone a mile when they met a young man, and Moscione stopped and asked him : ' What's your name, my friend ; where do you come from, and what can you do ? '

The man thus addressed answered promptly, ' I am called Hare's-ear, I come from Curiosity Valley, and if I lay my ear on the ground, without moving from the spot, I can hear everything that goes on in the world, the plots and intrigues of court and cottage, and all the plans of mice and men.'

' If that's the case,' replied Moscione, ' just tell me what's going on in my own home at present.'

The youth laid his ear to the ground and at once reported : ' An old man is saying to his wife, " Heaven be praised that we have got rid of Moscione, for perhaps, when he has been out in the world a little, he may gain some common sense, and return home less of a fool than when he set out." '

' Enough, enough,' cried Moscione. ' You speak the truth, and I believe you. Come with us, and your fortune's made.'

The young man consented ; and after they had gone about ten miles, they met a third man, to whom Moscione said : ' What's your name, my brave fellow ; where were you born, and what can you do ? '

The man replied, ' I am called Hit-the-Point, I come from the city of Perfect-aim, and I draw my bow so exactly that I can shoot a pea off a stone.'

' I should like to see you do it, if you've no objection,' said Moscione.

The man at once placed a pea on a stone, and, drawing his bow, he shot it in the middle with the greatest possible ease.

When Moscione saw that he had spoken the truth, he immediately asked Hit-the-Point to join his party.

After they had all travelled together for some days, they came upon a number of people who were digging a trench in the blazing sun.

Moscione felt so sorry for them, that he said : ' My dear friends, how can you endure working so hard in heat that would cook an egg in a minute ? '

But one of the workmen answered : ' We are as fresh as daisies, for we have a young man among us who blows on our backs like the west wind.'

' Let me see him,' said Moscione.

The youth was called, and Moscione asked him : ' What's your name ; where do you come from, and what can you do ? '

He answered : ' I am called Blow-Blast, I come from Wind-town, and with my mouth I can make any winds you please. If you wish a west wind I can raise it for you in a second, but if you prefer a north wind I can blow these houses down before your eyes.'

' Seeing is believing,' returned the cautious Moscione.

Blow-Blast at once began to convince him of the truth of his assertion. First he blew so softly that it seemed like the gentle breeze at evening, and then he turned round and raised such a mighty storm, that he blew down a whole row of oak trees.

When Moscione saw this he was delighted, and begged Blow-Blast to join his company. And as they went on their way they met another man, whom Moscione addressed as usual : ' What's your name ; where do you come from, and what can you do ? '

' I am called Strong-Back ; I come from Power-borough, and I possess such strength that I can take a mountain on my back, and it seems a feather to me.'

'If that's the case,' said Moscione, 'you are a clever fellow ; but I should like some proof of your strength.'

Then Strong-Back loaded himself with great boulders of rock and trunks of trees, so that a hundred waggons could not have taken away all that he carried on his back.

When Moscione saw this he prevailed on Strong-Back to join his troop, and they all continued their journey till they came to a country called Flower Vale. Here there reigned a king whose only daughter ran as quickly as the wind, and so lightly that she could run over a field of young oats without bending a single blade. The king had given out a proclamation that anyone who could beat the princess in a race should have her for a wife, but that all who failed in the competition should lose their head.

As soon as Moscione heard of the Royal Proclamation, he hastened to the king and challenged the princess to race with him. But on the morning appointed for the trial he sent word to the king that he was not feeling well, and that as he could not run himself he would supply someone to take his place.

'It's just the same to me,' said Canetella, the princess ; 'let anyone come forward that likes, I am quite prepared to meet him.'

At the time appointed for the race the whole place was crowded with people anxious to see the contest, and, punctual to the moment, Quick-as-Thought, and Canetella dressed in a short skirt and very lightly shod, appeared at the starting-point.

Then a silver trumpet sounded, and the two rivals started on their race, looking for all the world like a greyhound chasing a hare.

But Quick-as-Thought, true to his name, outran the princess, and when the goal was reached the people all clapped their hands and shouted, 'Long live the stranger !'

The Princess beaten by Quick-as-Thought

Canetella was much depressed by her defeat; but, as the race had to be run a second time, she determined she would not be beaten again. Accordingly she went home and sent Quick-as-Thought a magic ring, which prevented the person who wore it, not only from running, but even from walking, and begged that he would wear it for her sake.

Early next morning the crowd assembled on the race-course, and Canetella and Quick-as-Thought began their trial afresh. The princess ran as quickly as ever, but poor Quick-as-Thought was like an overloaded donkey, and could not go a step.

Then Hit-the-Point, who had heard all about the princess's deception from Hare's-ear, when he saw the danger his friend was in, seized his bow and arrow and shot the stone out of the ring Quick-as-Thought was wearing. In a moment the youth's legs became free again, and in five bounds he had overtaken Canetella and won the race.

The king was much disgusted when he saw that he must acknowledge Moscione as his future son-in-law, and summoned the wise men of his court to ask if there was no way out of the difficulty. The council at once decided that Canetella was far too dainty a morsel for the mouth of such a travelling tinker, and advised the king to offer Moscione a present of gold, which no doubt a beggar like him would prefer to all the wives in the world.

The king was delighted at this suggestion, and calling Moscione before him, he asked him what sum of money he would take instead of his promised bride.

Moscione first consulted with his friends, and then answered: ' I demand as much gold and precious stones as my followers can carry away.'

The king thought he was being let off very easily, and produced coffers of gold, sacks of silver, and chests of precious stones ; but the more Strong-Back was loaded with the treasure the straighter he stood.

At last the treasury was quite exhausted, and the king had to send his courtiers to his subjects to collect all the gold and silver they possessed. But nothing was of any avail, and Strong-Back only asked for more.

When the king's counsellors saw the unexpected result of their advice, they said it would be more than foolish to let some strolling thieves take so much treasure out of the country, and urged the king to send a troop of soldiers after them, to recover the gold and precious stones.

So the king sent a body of armed men on foot and horse, to take back the treasure Strong-Back was carrying away with him.

But Hare's-ear, who had heard what the counsellors had advised the king, told his companions just as the dust of their pursuers was visible on the horizon.

No sooner had Blow-Blast taken in their danger than he raised such a mighty wind that all the king's army was blown down like so many nine-pins, and as they were quite unable to get up again, Moscione and his companions proceeded on their way without further let or hindrance.

As soon as they reached his home, Moscione divided his spoil with his companions, at which they were much delighted. He, himself, stayed with his father, who was obliged at last to acknowledge that his son was not quite such a fool as he looked

[From the Italian, *Kletke*.]

THE STREET MUSICIANS

A MAN once possessed a donkey which had served him faithfully for many years, but at last the poor beast grew old and feeble, and every day his work became more of a burden. As he was no longer of any use, his master made up his mind to shoot him; but when the donkey learnt the fate that was in store for him, he determined not to die, but to run away to the nearest town and there to become a street musician.

When he had trotted along for some distance he came upon a greyhound lying on the road, and panting for dear life. 'Well, brother,' said the donkey, 'what's the matter with you? You look rather tired.'

'So I am,' replied the dog, 'but because I am getting old and am growing weaker every day, and cannot go out hunting any longer, my master wanted to poison me; and, as life is still sweet, I have taken leave of him. But how I am to earn my own livelihood I haven't a notion.'

'Well,' said the donkey, 'I am on my way to the nearest big town, where I mean to become a street musician. Why don't you take up music as a profession and come along with me? I'll play the flute and you can play the kettle-drum.'

The greyhound was quite pleased at the idea, and the two set off together. When they had gone a short distance they met a cat with a face as long as three rainy days. 'Now, what has happened to upset your happiness, friend puss?' inquired the donkey

'It's impossible to look cheerful when one feels depressed,' answered the cat. 'I am well up in years now, and have lost most of my teeth; consequently I prefer sitting in front of the fire to catching mice, and so my old mistress wanted to drown me. I have no wish to die yet, so I ran away from her; but good advice is expensive, and I don't know where I am to go to, or what I am to do.'

'Come to the nearest big town with us,' said the donkey, 'and try your fortune as a street musician. I know what sweet music you make at night, so you are sure to be a success.'

The cat was delighted with the donkey's proposal, and they all continued their journey together. In a short time they came to the courtyard of an inn, where they found a cock crowing lustily. 'What in the world is the matter with you?' asked the donkey. 'The noise you are making is enough to break the drums of our ears.'

'I am only prophesying good weather,' said the cock; 'for to-morrow is a feast day, and just because it is a holiday and a number of people are expected at the inn, the landlady has given orders for my neck to be wrung to-night, so that I may be made into soup for to-morrow's dinner.'

'I'll tell you what, redcap,' said the donkey; 'you had much better come with us to the nearest town. You have got a good voice, and could join a street band we are getting up.' The cock was much pleased with the idea, and the party proceeded on their way.

But the nearest big town was a long way off, and it took them more than a day to reach it. In the evening they came to a wood, and they made up their minds to go no further, but to spend the night there. The donkey and the greyhound lay down under a big tree, and the cat and the cock got up into the branches, the cock flying right up to the topmost twig, where he thought he would be safe from all danger. Before he went to sleep he looked round the four points of the compass, and saw a little spark burning in the distance. He called out to his companions that he was sure there must be a house not far off, for he could see a light shining.

When he heard this, the donkey said at once : ' Then we must get up, and go and look for the house, for this is very poor shelter.' And the greyhound added : ' Yes ; I feel I'd be all the better for a few bones and a scrap or two of meat.'

So they set out for the spot where the light was to be seen shining faintly in the distance, but the nearer they approached it the brighter it grew, till at last they came to a brilliantly lighted house. The donkey being the biggest of the party, went to the window and looked in.

' Well, greyhead, what do you see ? ' asked the cock.

' I see a well-covered table,' replied the donkey, ' with excellent food and drink, and several robbers are sitting round it, enjoying themselves highly.'

' I wish we were doing the same,' said the cock.

' So do I,' answered the donkey. ' Can't we think of some plan for turning out the robbers, and taking possession of the house ourselves ? '

So they consulted together what they were to do, and at last they arranged that the donkey should stand at the window with his fore-feet on the sill, that the greyhound should get on his back, the cat on the dog's shoulder, and the cock on the cat's head. When they had grouped themselves in this way, at a given signal, they all began their different forms of music. The donkey brayed, the greyhound barked, the cat miawed, and the cock crew. Then they all scrambled through the window into the room, breaking the glass into a thousand pieces as they did so.

The robbers were all startled by the dreadful noise, and thinking that some evil spirits at the least were entering the house, they rushed out into the wood, their hair standing on end with terror. The four companions, delighted with the success of their trick, sat down at the table, and ate and drank all the food and wine that the robbers had left behind them.

When they had finished their meal they put out the lights, and each animal chose a suitable sleeping-place. The donkey lay down in the courtyard outside the house, the dog behind the door, the cat in front of the fire, and the cock flew up on to a high shelf, and, as they were all tired after their long day, they soon went to sleep.

Shortly after midnight, when the robbers saw that no light was burning in the house and that all seemed quiet, the captain of the band said : ' We were fools to let ourselves be so easily frightened away ; ' and, turning to one of his men, he ordered him to go and see if all was safe.

The man found everything in silence and darkness, and going into the kitchen he thought he had better strike a light. He took a match, and mistaking the fiery eyes of the cat for two glowing coals, he tried to light his match with them. But the cat didn't see the joke, and sprang at his face, spitting and scratching him in the most vigorous manner. The man was terrified out of his life, and tried to run out by the back door ; but he stumbled over the greyhound, which bit him in the leg. Yelling with pain he ran across the courtyard only to receive a kick from the donkey's hind leg as he passed him. In the meantime the cock had been roused from his slumbers, and feeling very cheerful he called out, from the shelf where he was perched, ' Kikeriki ! '

Then the robber hastened back to his captain and said : ' Sir, there is a dreadful witch in the house, who spat at me and scratched my face with her long fingers ; and before the door there stands a man with a long knife, who cut my leg severely. In the courtyard outside lies a black monster, who fell upon me with a huge wooden club ; and that is not all, for, sitting on the roof,

is a judge, who called out : " Bring the rascal to me." So
I fled for dear life.'

After this the robbers dared not venture into the
house again, and they abandoned it for ever. But the
four street musicians were so delighted with their
lodgings that they determined to take up their abode in
the robbers' house, and, for all I know to the contrary,
they may be living there to this day.

[From the German, *Kletke*.]

THE TWIN BROTHERS

ONCE there was a fisherman who had plenty of money but no children. One day an old woman came to his wife and said : 'What use is all your prosperity to you when you have no children ? '

'It is God's will,' answered the fisherman's wife.

'Nay, my child, it is not God's will, but the fault of your husband ; for if he would but catch the little gold-fish you would surely have children. To-night, when he comes home, tell him he must go back and catch the little fish. He must then cut it in six pieces—one of these you must eat, and your husband the second, and soon after you will have two children. The third piece you must give to the dog, and she will have two puppies. The fourth piece give to the mare, and she will have two foals. The fifth piece bury on the right of the house door, and the sixth on the left, and two cypress trees will spring up there.'

When the fisherman came home at evening his wife told him all that the old woman had advised, and he promised to bring home the little gold-fish. Next morning, therefore, he went very early to the water, and caught the little fish. Then they did as the old woman had ordered, and in due time the fisherman's wife had two sons, so like each other that no one could tell the difference. The dog had two puppies exactly alike, the mare had two foals, and on each side of the front door there sprang up two cypress trees precisely similar.

When the two boys were grown up, they were not content to remain at home, though they had wealth in plenty; but they wished to go out into the world, and make a name for themselves. Their father would not allow them both to go at once, as they were the only children he had. He said: 'First one shall travel, and when he is come back then the other may go.'

So the one took his horse and his dog, and went, saying to his brother: 'So long as the cypress trees are green, that is a sign that I am alive and well; but if one begins to wither, then make haste and come to me.' So he went forth into the world.

One day he stopped at the house of an old woman, and as at evening he sat before the door, he perceived in front of him a castle standing on a hill. He asked the old woman to whom it belonged, and her answer was: 'My son, it is the castle of the Fairest in the Land!'

'And I am come here to woo her!'

'That, my son, many have sought to do, and have lost their lives in the attempt; for she has cut off their heads and stuck them on the post you see standing there.'

'And the same will she do to me, or else I shall be victor, for to-morrow I go there to court her.'

Then he took his zither and played upon it so beautifully that no one in all that land had ever heard the like, and the princess herself came to the window to listen.

The next morning the Fairest in the Land sent for the old woman and asked her, 'Who is it that lives with you, and plays the zither so well?'

'It is a stranger, princess, who arrived yesterday evening,' answered the old woman.

And the princess then commanded that the stranger should be brought to her.

When he appeared before the princess she questioned

him about his home and his family, and about this and that ; and confessed at length that his zither-playing gave her great pleasure, and that she would take him for her husband. The stranger replied that it was with that intent he had come.

The princess then said : ' You must now go to my father, and tell him you desire to have me to wife, and when he has put the three problems before you, then come back and tell me.'

The stranger then went straight to the king, and told him that he wished to wed his daughter.

And the king answered : ' I shall be well pleased, provided you can do what I impose upon you ; if not you will lose your head. Now, listen ; out there on the ground, there lies a thick log, which measures more than two fathoms ; if you can cleave it in two with one stroke of your sword, I will give you my daughter to wife. If you fail, then it will cost you your head.'

Then the stranger withdrew, and returned to the house of the old woman sore distressed, for he could believe nothing but that next day he must atone to the king with his head. And so full was he of the idea of how to set about cleaving the log that he forgot even his zither.

In the evening came the princess to the window to listen to his playing, and behold all was still. Then she called to him : ' Why are you so cast down this evening, that you do not play on your zither?'

And he told her his trouble.

But she laughed at it, and called to him : ' And you grieve over that? Bring quickly your zither, and play something for my amusement, and early to-morrow come to me.'

Then the stranger took his zither and played the whole evening for the amusement of the princess.

Next morning she took a hair from her locks and gave it to him, saying : ' Take this hair, and wind it round your sword, then you will be able to cleave the log in two.'

Then the stranger went forth, and with one blow cleft the log in two.

But the king said : ' I will impose another task upon you, before you can wed my daughter.'

' Speak on,' said the stranger.

' Listen, then,' answered the king ; ' you must mount a horse and ride three miles at full gallop, holding in each hand a goblet full of water. If you spill no drop then I shall give you my daughter to wife, but should you not succeed then I will take your life.'

Then the stranger returned to the house of the old woman, and again he was so troubled as to forget his zither.

In the evening the princess came to the window as before to listen to the music, but again all was still ; and she called to him : ' What is the matter that you do not play on your zither ? '

Then he related all that the king had ordered him to do, and the princess answered : ' Do not let yourself be disturbed, only play now, and come to me to-morrow morning.'

Then next morning he went to her, and she gave him her ring, saying : ' Throw this ring into the water and it will immediately freeze, so that you will not spill any.'

The stranger did as the princess bade him, and carried the water all the way.

Then the king said : ' Now I will give you a third task, and this shall be the last. I have a negro who will fight with you to-morrow, and if you are the conqueror you shall wed my daughter.'

The stranger returned, full of joy, to the house of the old woman, and that evening was so merry that the princess called to him : ' You seem very cheerful this evening ; what has my father told you that makes you so glad ? '

He answered : ' Your father has told me that to-morrow I must fight with his negro. He is only another man like myself, and I hope to subdue him, and to gain the contest.'

But the princess answered : ' This is the hardest of all. I myself am the black man, for I swallow a drink that changes me into a negro of unconquerable strength. Go to-morrow morning to the market, buy twelve buffalo hides and wrap them round your horse ; fasten this cloth round you, and when I am let loose upon you to-morrow show it to me, that I may hold myself back and may not kill you. Then when you fight me you must try to hit my horse between the eyes, for when you have killed it you have conquered me.'

Next morning, therefore, he went to the market and bought the twelve buffalo hides which he wrapped round his horse. Then he began to fight with the black man, and when the combat had already lasted a long time, and eleven hides were torn, then the stranger hit the negro's horse between the eyes, so that it fell dead, and the black man was defeated.

Then said the king : ' Because you have solved the three problems I take you for my son-in-law.'

But the stranger answered : ' I have some business to conclude first ; in fourteen days I will return and bring the bride home.'

So he arose and went into another country, where he came to a great town, and alighted at the house of an old woman. When he had had supper he begged of her some water to drink, but she answered : ' My son, I have no water ; a giant has taken possession of the spring, and only lets us draw from it once a year, when we bring him a maiden. He eats her up, and then he lets us draw water ; just now it is the lot of the king's daughter, and to-morrow she will be led forth.'

The next day accordingly the princess was led forth to the spring, and bound there with a golden chain. After that all the people went away and she was left alone.

When they had gone the stranger went to the maiden and asked her what ailed her that she lamented so much, and she answered that the reason was because the giant would come and eat her up. And the stranger promised that he would set her free if she would take him for her husband, and the princess joyfully consented.

When the giant appeared the stranger set his dog at him, and it took him by the throat and throttled him till he died ; so the princess was set free.

Now when the king heard of it he gladly consented to the marriage, and the wedding took place with great rejoicings. The young bridegroom abode in the palace one hundred and one weeks. Then he began to find it too dull, and he desired to go out hunting. The king would fain have prevented it, but in this he could not succeed. Then he begged his son-in-law at least to take sufficient escort with him, but this, too, the young man evaded, and took only his horse and his dog.

He had ridden already a long way, when he saw in the distance a hut, and rode straight towards it in order to get some water to drink. There he found an old woman from whom he begged the water. She answered that first he should allow her to beat his dog with her little wand, that it might not bite her while she fetched the water. The hunter consented ; and as soon as she had touched the dog with her wand it immediately turned to stone. Thereupon she touched the hunter and also his horse, and both turned to stone. As soon as that had happened, the cypress trees in front of his father's house began to wither. And when the other brother saw this, he immediately set out in search of his twin. He came first to the town where his brother had slain the giant, and there fate led him to the same old woman where his brother had lodged. When she saw him she took him for his twin brother, and said to him : ' Do not take it amiss of me, my son, that I did not come to wish you joy on your marriage with the king's daughter.'

The stranger perceived what mistake she had made, but only said : ' That does not matter, old woman,' and rode on, without further speech, to the king's palace, where the king and the princess both took him for his twin brother, and called out : ' Why have you tarried so long away ? We thought something evil had befallen you.'

When night came and he slept with the princess, who still believed him to be her husband, he laid his sword between them, and when morning came he rose early and went out to hunt. Fate led him by the same way which his brother had taken, and from a distance he saw him and knew that he was turned to stone. Then he entered the hut and ordered the old woman to disenchant his brother. But she answered : ' Let me first touch your dog with my wand, and then I will free your brother.'

He ordered the dog, however, to take hold of her, and bite her up to the knee, till she cried out : ' Tell your dog to let me go and I will set your brother free ! '

But he only answered : ' Tell me the magic words that I may disenchant him myself ; ' and as she would not he ordered his dog to bite her up to the hip.

Then the old woman cried out : ' I have two wands, with the green one I turn to stone, and with the red one I bring to life again.'

So the hunter took the red wand and disenchanted his brother, also his brother's horse, and his dog, and ordered his own dog to eat the old woman up altogether.

While the brothers went on their way back to the castle of the king, the one brother related to the other how the cypress tree had all at once dried up and withered, how he had immediately set out in search of his twin, and how he had come to the castle of his father-in-law, and had claimed the princess as his wife. But the other brother became furious on hearing this, and smote him over the forehead till he died, and returned alone to the house of his father-in-law.

THE TWIN BROTHERS

THE BROTHER COMES TO THE RESCUE

When night came and he was in bed the princess asked him : ' What was the matter with you last night, that you never spoke a word to me ? '

Then he cried out : 'That was not me, but my brother, and I have slain him, because he told me by the way that he had claimed you for his wife ! '

' Do you know the place where you slew him ? ' asked the princess, ' and can you find the body ? '

' I know the place exactly.'

' Then to-morrow we shall ride thither,' said the princess.

Next morning accordingly they set out together, and when they had come to the place, the princess drew forth a small bottle that she had brought with her, and sprinkled the body with some drops of the water so that immediately he became alive again.

When he stood up, his brother said to him : ' Forgive me, dear brother, that I slew you in my anger.' Then they embraced and went together to the Fairest in the Land, whom the unmarried brother took to wife.

Then the brothers brought their parents to live with them, and all dwelt together in joy and happiness.

CANNETELLA

THERE was once upon a time a king who reigned over a country called 'Bello Puojo.' He was very rich and powerful, and had everything in the world he could desire except a child. But at last, after he had been married for many years, and was quite an old man, his wife Renzolla presented him with a fine daughter, whom they called Cannetella.

She grew up into a beautiful girl, and was as tall and straight as a young fir-tree. When she was eighteen years old her father called her to him and said : ' You are of an age now, my daughter, to marry and settle down ; but as I love you more than anything else in the world, and desire nothing but your happiness, I am determined to leave the choice of a husband to yourself. Choose a man after your own heart, and you are sure to satisfy me.' Cannetella thanked her father very much for his kindness and consideration, but told him that she had not the slightest wish to marry, and was quite determined to remain single.

The king, who felt himself growing old and feeble, and longed to see an heir to the throne before he died, was very unhappy at her words, and begged her earnestly not to disappoint him.

When Cannetella saw that the king had set his heart on her marriage, she said : ' Very well, dear father, I will marry to please you, for I do not wish to appear ungrateful for all your love and kindness ; but you must find me a husband handsomer, cleverer, and more charming than anyone else in the world.'

The king was overjoyed by her words, and from early in the morning till late at night he sat at the window and looked carefully at all the passers-by, in the hopes of finding a son-in-law among them.

One day, seeing a very good-looking man crossing the street, the king called his daughter and said : ' Come quickly, dear Cannetella, and look at this man, for I think he might suit you as a husband.'

They called the young man into the palace, and set a sumptuous feast before him, with every sort of delicacy you can imagine. In the middle of the meal the youth let an almond fall out of his mouth, which, however, he picked up again very quickly and hid under the table-cloth.

When the feast was over the stranger went away, and the king asked Cannetella : ' Well, what did you think of the youth ? '

' I think he was a clumsy wretch,' replied Cannetella. ' Fancy a man of his age letting an almond fall out of his mouth ! '

When the king heard her answer he returned to his watch at the window, and shortly afterwards a very handsome young man passed by. The king instantly called his daughter to come and see what she thought of the new comer.

' Call him in,' said Cannetella, ' that we may see him close.'

Another splendid feast was prepared, and when the stranger had eaten and drunk as much as he was able, and had taken his departure, the king asked Cannetella how she liked him.

' Not at all, ' replied his daughter; ' what could you do with a man who requires at least two servants to help him on with his cloak, because he is too awkward to put it on properly himself ? '

' If that's all you have against him,' said the king, ' I

see how the land lies. You are determined not to have a husband at all; but marry someone you shall, for I do not mean my name and house to die out.'

'Well, then, my dear parent,' said Cannetella, 'I must tell you at once that you had better not count upon me, for I never mean to marry unless I can find a man with a gold head and gold teeth.'

The king was very angry at finding his daughter so obstinate; but as he always gave the girl her own way in everything, he issued a proclamation to the effect that any man with a gold head and gold teeth might come forward and claim the princess as his bride, and the kingdom of Bello Puojo as a wedding gift.

Now the king had a deadly enemy called Scioravante, who was a very powerful magician. No sooner had this man heard of the proclamation than he summoned his attendant spirits and commanded them to gild his head and teeth. The spirits said, at first, that the task was beyond their powers, and suggested that a pair of golden horns attached to his forehead would both be easier to make and more comfortable to wear; but Scioravante would allow no compromise, and insisted on having a head and teeth made of the finest gold. When it was fixed on his shoulders he went for a stroll in front of the palace. And the king, seeing the very man he was in search of, called his daughter, and said: 'Just look out of the window, and you will find exactly what you want.'

Then, as Scioravante was hurrying past, the king shouted out to him: 'Just stop a minute, brother, and don't be in such desperate haste. If you will step in here you shall have my daughter for a wife, and I will send attendants with her, and as many horses and servants as you wish.'

'A thousand thanks,' returned Scioravante; 'I shall be delighted to marry your daughter, but it is quite unnecessary to send anyone to accompany her. Give me a horse and I will carry off the princess in front

SCIORAVANTE LEAVES
CANNETELLA IN THE STABLE

of my saddle, and will bring her to my own kingdom, where there is no lack of courtiers or servants, or, indeed, of anything your daughter can desire.'

At first the king was very much against Cannetella's departing in this fashion ; but finally Scioravante got his way, and placing the princess before him on his horse, he set out for his own country.

Towards evening he dismounted, and entering a stable he placed Cannetella in the same stall as his horse, and said to her : 'Now listen to what I have to say. I am going to my home now, and that is a seven years' journey from here ; you must wait for me in this stable, and never move from the spot, or let yourself be seen by a living soul. If you disobey my commands, it will be the worse for you.'

The princess answered meekly : 'Sir, I am your servant, and will do exactly as you bid me ; but I should like to know what I am to live on till you come back ? '

'You can take what the horses leave,' was Scioravante's reply.

When the magician had left her Cannetella felt very miserable, and bitterly cursed the day she was born. She spent all her time weeping and bemoaning the cruel fate that had driven her from a palace into a stable, from soft down cushions to a bed of straw, and from the dainties of her father's table to the food that the horses left.

She led this wretched life for a few months, and during that time she never saw who fed and watered the horses, for it was all done by invisible hands.

One day, when she was more than usually unhappy, she perceived a little crack in the wall, through which she could see a beautiful garden, with all manner of delicious fruits and flowers growing in it. The sight and smell of such delicacies were too much for poor Cannetella, and she said to herself, ' I will slip quietly out, and pick a few oranges and grapes, and I don't care what happens. Who is there to tell my husband what I do? and even if he should hear of my disobedience, he cannot make my life more miserable than it is already.'

So she slipped out and refreshed her poor, starved body with the fruit she plucked in the garden.

But a short time afterwards her husband returned unexpectedly, and one of the horses instantly told him that Cannetella had gone into the garden, in his absence, and had stolen some oranges and grapes.

Scioravante was furious when he heard this, and seizing a huge knife from his pocket he threatened to kill his wife for her disobedience. But Cannetella threw herself at his feet and implored him to spare her life, saying that hunger drove even the wolf from the wood. At last she succeeded in so far softening her husband's heart that he said, 'I will forgive you this time, and spare your life; but if you disobey me again, and I hear, on my return, that you have as much as moved out of the stall, I will certainly kill you. So, beware; for I am going away once more, and shall be absent for seven years.'

With these words he took his departure, and Cannetella burst into a flood of tears, and, wringing her hands, she moaned : ' Why was I ever born to such a hard fate ? Oh ! father, how miserable you have made your poor daughter ! But, why should I blame my father? for I have only myself to thank for all my sufferings. I got the cursed head of gold, and it has brought all this misery on me. I am indeed punished for not doing as my father wished ! '

When a year had gone by, it chanced, one day, that the king's cooper passed the stables where Cannetella was kept prisoner. She recognised the man, and called him to come in. At first he did not know the poor princess, and could not make out who it was that called him by name. But when he heard Cannetella's tale of woe, he hid her in a big empty barrel he had with him,

CANNETELLA COMES OUT OF THE CASK

partly because he was sorry for the poor girl, and, even more, because he wished to gain the king's favour. Then he slung the barrel on a mule's back, and in this way the princess was carried to her own home. They arrived at the palace about four o'clock in the morning, and the cooper knocked loudly at the door. When the servants came in haste and saw only the cooper standing at the gate, they were very indignant, and scolded him soundly for coming at such an hour and waking them all out of their sleep.

The king hearing the noise and the cause of it, sent for the cooper, for he felt certain the man must have some important business, to have come and disturbed the whole palace at such an early hour.

The cooper asked permission to unload his mule, and Cannetella crept out of the barrel. At first the king refused to believe that it was really his daughter, for she had changed so terribly in a few years, and had grown so thin and pale, that it was pitiful to see her. At last the princess showed her father a mole she had on her right arm, and then he saw that the poor girl was indeed his long-lost Cannetella. He kissed her a thousand times, and instantly had the choicest food and drink set before her.

After she had satisfied her hunger, the king said to her: 'Who would have thought, my dear daughter, to have found you in such a state? What, may I ask, has brought you to this pass?'

Cannetella replied: 'That wicked man with the gold head and teeth treated me worse than a dog, and many a time, since I left you, have I longed to die. But I couldn't tell you all that I have suffered, for you would never believe me. It is enough that I am once more with you, and I shall never leave you again, for I would rather be a slave in your house than queen in any other.'

In the meantime Scioravante had returned to the

stables, and one of the horses told him that Cannetella had been taken away by a cooper in a barrel.

When the wicked magician heard this he was beside himself with rage, and, hastening to the kingdom of Bello Puojo, he went straight to an old woman who lived exactly opposite the royal palace, and said to her: 'If you will let me see the king's daughter, I will give you whatever reward you like to ask for.'

The woman demanded a hundred ducats of gold, and Scioravante counted them out of his purse and gave them to her without a murmur. Then the old woman led him to the roof of the house, where he could see Cannetella combing out her long hair in a room in the top story of the palace.

The princess happened to look out of the window, and when she saw her husband gazing at her, she got such a fright that she flew downstairs to the king, and said: 'My lord and father, unless you shut me up instantly in a room with seven iron doors, I am lost.'

'If that's all,' said the king, 'it shall be done at once.' And he gave orders for the doors to be closed on the spot.

When Scioravante saw this he returned to the old woman, and said: 'I will give you whatever you like if you will go into the palace, hide under the princess's bed, and slip this little piece of paper beneath her pillow, saying, as you do so: "May everyone in the palace, except the princess, fall into a sound sleep."'

The old woman demanded another hundred golden ducats, and then proceeded to carry out the magician's wishes. No sooner had she slipped the piece of paper under Cannetella's pillow, than all the people in the palace fell fast asleep, and only the princess remained awake.

Then Scioravante hurried to the seven doors and opened them one after the other. Cannetella screamed with terror when she saw her husband, but no one came to her help, for all in the palace lay as if they were dead. The magician seized her in the bed on which she lay, and was going to carry her off with him, when the little piece of paper which the old woman had placed under her pillow fell on the floor.

In an instant all the people in the palace woke up, and as Cannetella was still screaming for help, they rushed to her rescue. They seized Scioravante and put him to death ; so he was caught in the trap which he had laid for the princess—and, as is so often the case in this world, the biter himself was bit.

[From the Italian, *Kletke*.]

THE OGRE

THERE lived, once upon a time, in the land of Marigliano, a poor woman called Masella, who had six pretty daughters, all as upright as young fir-trees, and an only son called Antonio, who was so simple as to be almost an idiot. Hardly a day passed without his mother saying to him, 'What are you doing, you useless creature? If you weren't too stupid to look after yourself, I would order you to leave the house and never to let me see your face again.'

Every day the youth committed some fresh piece of folly, till at last Masella, losing all patience, gave him a good beating, which so startled Antonio that he took to his heels and never stopped running till it was dark and the stars were shining in the heavens. He wandered on for some time, not knowing where to go, and at last he came to a cave, at the mouth of which sat an ogre, uglier than anything you can conceive.

He had a huge head and wrinkled brow—eyebrows that met, squinting eyes, a flat broad nose, and a great gash of a mouth from which two huge tusks stuck out. His skin was hairy, his arms enormous, his legs like sword blades, and his feet as flat as ducks'. In short, he was the most hideous and laughable object in the world.

But Antonio, who, with all his faults, was no coward, and was moreover a very civil-spoken lad, took off his hat, and said : 'Good-day, sir ; I hope you are pretty well.

Could you kindly tell me how far it is from here to the place where I wish to go?'

ANTONIO · IS · NOT · AFRAID · OF · THE OGRE

When the ogre heard this extraordinary question he burst out laughing, and as he liked the youth's polite manners he said to him : 'Will you enter my service?'

'What wages do you give?' replied Antonio.

'If you serve me faithfully,' returned the ogre, 'I'll be bound you'll get enough wages to satisfy you.'

So the bargain was struck, and Antonio agreed to become the ogre's servant. He was very well treated, in every way, and he had little or no work to do, with the result that in a few days he became as fat as a quail, as round as a barrel, as red as a lobster, and as impudent as a bantam-cock.

But, after two years, the lad got weary of this idle life, and longed desperately to visit his home again. The ogre, who could see into his heart and knew how unhappy he was, said to him one day: 'My dear Antonio, I know how much you long to see your mother and sisters again, and because I love you as the apple of my eye, I am willing to allow you to go home for a visit. Therefore, take this donkey, so that you may not have to go on foot; but see that you never say "Bricklebrit" to him, for if you do you'll be sure to regret it.'

Antonio took the beast without as much as saying thank you, and jumping on its back he rode away in great haste; but he hadn't gone two hundred yards when he dismounted and called out 'Bricklebrit.'

No sooner had he pronounced the word than the donkey opened its mouth and poured forth rubies, emeralds, diamonds and pearls, as big as walnuts.

Antonio gazed in amazement at the sight of such wealth, and joyfully filling a huge sack with the precious stones, he mounted the donkey again and rode on till he came to an inn. Here he got down, and going straight to the landlord, he said to him: 'My good man, I must ask you to stable this donkey for me. Be sure you give the poor beast plenty of oats and hay, but beware of saying the word "Bricklebrit" to him, for if you do I can promise you will regret it. Take this heavy sack, too, and put it carefully away for me.'

The landlord, who was no fool, on receiving this strange warning, and seeing the precious stones sparkling through the canvas of the sack, was most anxious to see what would happen if he used the forbidden word. So he gave Antonio an excellent dinner, with a bottle of fine old wine, and prepared a comfortable bed for him. As soon as he saw the poor simpleton close his eyes and had heard his lusty snores, he hurried to the stables and said to the donkey 'Bricklebrit,' and the animal as usual poured out any number of precious stones.

When the landlord saw all these treasures he longed to get possession of so valuable an animal, and determined to steal the donkey from his foolish guest. As soon as it was light next morning Antonio awoke, and having rubbed his eyes and stretched himself about a hundred times he called the landlord and said to him : 'Come here, my friend, and produce your bill, for short reckonings make long friends.'

When Antonio had paid his account he went to the stables and took out his donkey, as he thought, and fastening a sack of gravel, which the landlord had substituted for his precious stones, on the creature's back, he set out for his home.

No sooner had he arrived there than he called out : 'Mother, come quickly, and bring table-cloths and sheets with you, and spread them out on the ground, and you will soon see what wonderful treasures I have brought you.'

His mother hurried into the house, and opening the linen-chest where she kept her daughters' wedding outfits, she took out table-cloths and sheets made of the finest linen, and spread them flat and smooth on the ground. Antonio placed the donkey on them, and called out 'Bricklebrit.' But this time he met with no success, for the donkey took no more notice of the magic word than he would have done if a lyre had been twanged in his ear. Two, three, and four times did Antonio pronounce

'Bricklebrit,' but all in vain, and he might as well have spoken to the wind.

Disgusted and furious with the poor creature, he seized a thick stick and began to beat it so hard that he nearly broke every bone in its body. The miserable donkey was so distracted at such treatment that, far from pouring out precious stones, it only tore and dirtied all the fine linen.

When poor Masella saw her table-cloths and sheets being destroyed, and that instead of becoming rich she had only been made a fool of, she seized another stick and belaboured Antonio so unmercifully with it, that he fled before her, and never stopped till he reached the ogre's cave.

When his master saw the lad returning in such a sorry plight, he understood at once what had happened to him, and making no bones about the matter, he told Antonio what a fool he had been to allow himself to be so imposed upon by the landlord, and to let a worthless animal be palmed off on him instead of his magic donkey.

Antonio listened humbly to the ogre's words, and vowed solemnly that he would never act so foolishly again. And so a year passed, and once more Antonio was overcome by a fit of home-sickness, and felt a great longing to see his own people again.

Now the ogre, although he was so hideous to look upon, had a very kind heart, and when he saw how restless and unhappy Antonio was, he at once gave him leave to go home on a visit. At parting he gave him a beautiful table-cloth, and said : 'Give this to your mother ; but see that you don't lose it as you lost the donkey, and till you are safely in your own house beware of saying "Table-cloth, open," and "Table-cloth, shut." If you do, the misfortune be on your own head, for I have given you fair warning.'

Antonio set out on his journey, but hardly had he got

out of sight of the cave than he laid the table-cloth on the ground and said, ' Table-cloth, open.' In an instant the table-cloth unfolded itself and disclosed a whole mass of precious stones and other treasures.

When Antonio perceived this he said, ' Table-cloth, shut,' and continued his journey. He came to the same inn again, and calling the landlord to him, he told him to put the table-cloth carefully away, and whatever he did not to say ' Table-cloth, open,' or ' Table-cloth, shut,' to it.

The landlord, who was a regular rogue, answered, ' Just leave it to me, I will look after it as if it were my own.'

After he had given Antonio plenty to eat and drink, and had provided him with a comfortable bed, he went straight to the table-cloth and said, ' Table-cloth, open.' It opened at once, and displayed such costly treasures that the landlord made up his mind on the spot to steal it.

When Antonio awoke next morning, the host handed him over a table-cloth exactly like his own, and carrying it carefully over his arm, the foolish youth went straight to his mother's house, and said : ' Now we shall be rich beyond the dreams of avarice, and need never go about in rags again, or lack the best of food.'

With these words he spread the table-cloth on the ground and said, ' Table-cloth, open.'

But he might repeat the injunction as often as he pleased, it was only waste of breath, for nothing happened. When Antonio saw this he turned to his mother and said : ' That old scoundrel of a landlord has done me once more ; but he will live to repent it, for if I ever enter his inn again, I will make him suffer for the loss of my donkey and the other treasures he has robbed me of.'

Masella was in such a rage over her fresh disappointment that she could not restrain her impatience, and, turning on Antonio, she abused him soundly, and told him to get out of her sight at once, for she would never acknowledge him as a son of hers again. The poor boy was very depressed by her words, and slunk back to his master like a dog with his tail between his legs. When the ogre saw him, he guessed at once what had happened. He gave Antonio a good scolding, and said, 'I don't know what prevents me smashing your head in, you useless ne'er-do-well! You blurt everything out, and your long tongue never ceases wagging for a moment. If you had remained silent in the inn this misfortune would never have overtaken you, so you have only yourself to blame for your present suffering.'

Antonio listened to his master's words in silence, looking for all the world like a whipped dog. When he had been three more years in the ogre's service he had another bad fit of home-sickness, and longed very much to see his mother and sisters again.

So he asked for permission to go home on a visit, and it was at once granted to him. Before he set out on his journey the ogre presented him with a beautifully carved stick and said, 'Take this stick as a remembrance of me; but beware of saying, "Rise up, Stick," and "Lie down, Stick," for if you do, I can only say I wouldn't be in your shoes for something.'

Antonio took the stick and said, 'Don't be in the least alarmed, I'm not such a fool as you think, and know better than most people what two and two make.'

'I'm glad to hear it,' replied the ogre, 'but words are women, deeds are men. You have heard what I said, and forewarned is forearmed.'

This time Antonio thanked his master warmly for all his kindness, and started on his homeward journey in great spirits; but he had not gone half a mile when he said 'Rise up, Stick.'

The words were hardly out of his mouth when the stick rose and began to rain down blows on poor Antonio's back with such lightning-like rapidity that he had hardly strength to call out, ' Lie down, Stick ; but as soon as he uttered the words the stick lay down, and ceased beating his back black and blue.

Although he had learnt a lesson at some cost to himself, Antonio was full of joy, for he saw a way now of revenging himself on the wicked landlord. Once more he arrived at the inn, and was received in the most friendly and hospitable manner by his host. Antonio greeted him cordially, and said : ' My friend, will you kindly take care of this stick for me ? But, whatever you do, don't say " Rise up, Stick." If you do, you will be sorry for it, and you needn't expect any sympathy from me.'

The landlord, thinking he was coming in for a third piece of good fortune, gave Antonio an excellent supper ; and after he had seen him comfortably to bed, he ran to the stick, and calling to his wife to come and see the fun, he lost no time in pronouncing the words ' Rise up, Stick.'

The moment he spoke the stick jumped up and beat the landlord so unmercifully that he and his wife ran screaming to Antonio, and, waking him up, pleaded for mercy.

When Antonio saw how successful his trick had been, he said : ' I refuse to help you, unless you give me all that you have stolen from me, otherwise you will be beaten to death.'

The landlord, who felt himself at death's door already, cried out : ' Take back your property, only release me from this terrible stick ; ' and with these words he ordered the donkey, the table-cloth, and other treasures to be restored to their rightful owner.

As soon as Antonio had recovered his belongings he said ' Stick, lie down,' and it stopped beating the landlord at once.

Then he took his donkey and table-cloth and arrived safely at his home with them. This time the magic words had the desired effect, and the donkey and table-cloth provided the family with treasures untold.   Antonio very soon married off his sister, made his mother rich for life, and they all lived happily for ever after.

[From the Italian, *Kletke.*]

A FAIRY'S BLUNDER

ONCE upon a time there lived a fairy whose name
was Dindonette. She was the best creature in the
world, with the kindest heart; but she had not much
sense, and was always doing things, to benefit people,
which generally ended in causing pain and distress to
everybody concerned. No one knew this better than
the inhabitants of an island far off in the midst of the
sea, which, according to the laws of fairyland, she had
taken under her special protection, thinking day and
night of what she could do to make the isle the
pleasantest place in the whole world, as it was the most
beautiful.

Now what happened was this :

As the fairy went about, unseen, from house to house,
she heard everywhere children longing for the time when
they would be ' grown-up,' and able, they thought, to do
as they liked ; and old people talking about the past, and
sighing to be young again.

' Is there no way of satisfying these poor things ? ' she
thought. And then one night an idea occurred to her.
' Oh, yes, of course ! It has been tried before ; but I will
manage better than the rest, with their old Fountain of
Youth, which, after all, only made people young again. I
will enchant the spring that bubbles up in the middle of
the orchard, and the children that drink of it shall at
once become grown men and women, and the old people
return to the days of their childhood.'

And without stopping to consult one single other fairy, who might have given her good advice, off rushed Dindonette, to cast her spell over the fountain.

It was the only spring of fresh water in the island, and at dawn was crowded with people of all ages, come to drink at its source. Delighted at her plan for making them all happy, the fairy hid herself behind a thicket of roses, and peeped out whenever footsteps came that way. It was not long before she had ample proof of the success of her enchantments. Almost before her eyes the children put on the size and strength of adults, while the old men and women instantly became helpless, tiny babies. Indeed, so pleased was she with the result of her work, that she could no longer remain hidden, and went about telling everybody what she had done, and enjoying their gratitude and thanks.

But after the first outburst of delight at their wishes being granted, people began to be a little frightened at the rapid effects of the magic water. It was delicious to feel yourself at the height of your power and beauty, but you would wish to keep so always! Now this was exactly what the fairy had been in too much of a hurry to arrange, and no sooner had the children become grown up, and the men and women become babies, than they all rushed on to old age at an appalling rate! The fairy only found out her mistake when it was too late to set it right.

When the inhabitants of the island saw what had befallen them, they were filled with despair, and did everything they could think of to escape from such a dreadful fate. They dug wells in their places, so that they should no longer need to drink from the magic spring; but the sandy soil yielded no water, and the rainy season was already past. They stored up the dew that fell, and the juice of fruits and of herbs, but all this was as a drop in the ocean of their wants. Some threw themselves into the sea, trusting that the current might carry them to other shores—they had no boats—and a few, still more impatient, put themselves to death on the spot. The rest submitted blindly to their destiny.

Perhaps the worst part of the enchantment was, that the change from one age to another was so rapid that the person had no time to prepare himself for it. It would not have mattered so much if the man who stood up in the assembly of the nation, to give his advice as to peace or war, had looked like a baby, as long as he spoke with the knowledge and sense of a full-grown man. But, alas! with the outward form of an infant, he had taken on its helplessness and foolishness, and there was no one who could train him to better things. The end of it all was, that before a month had passed the population had died out, and the fairy Dindonette, ashamed and grieved at the effects of her folly, had left the island for ever.

Many centuries after, the fairy Selnozoura, who had fallen into bad health, was ordered by her doctors to make the tour of the world twice a week for change of air, and in one of these journeys she found herself at Fountain Island. Selnozoura never made these trips alone, but always took with her two children, of whom she was very fond —Cornichon, a boy of fourteen, bought in his childhood at a slave-market, and Toupette, a few months younger, who had been entrusted to the care of the fairy by her guardian, the genius Kristopo. Cornichon and Toupette were intended by Selnozoura to become husband and wife, as soon as they were old enough. Meanwhile, they travelled with her in a little vessel, whose speed through the air was just a thousand nine hundred and fifty times greater than that of the swiftest of our ships.

Struck with the beauty of the island, Selnozoura ran the vessel to ground, and leaving it in the care of the dragon which lived in the hold during the voyage, stepped on shore with her two companions. Surprised at the sight of a large town whose streets and houses were absolutely desolate, the fairy resolved to put her

magic arts in practice to find out the cause. While she
was thus engaged, Cornichon and Toupette wandered
away by themselves, and by-and-by arrived at the
fountain, whose bubbling waters looked cool and delicious on such a hot day. Scarcely had they each
drunk a deep draught, when the fairy, who by this
time had discovered all she wished to know, hastened to
the spot.

'Oh, beware! beware!' she cried, the moment she saw
them. 'If you drink that deadly poison you will be
ruined for ever!'

'Poison?' answered Toupette. 'It is the most refresh-
ing water I have ever tasted, and Cornichon will say so
too!'

'Unhappy children, then I am too late! Why did
you leave me? Listen, and I will tell you what has
befallen the wretched inhabitants of this island, and what
will befall you too. The power of fairies is great,' she
added, when she had finished her story, 'but they cannot
destroy the work of another fairy. Very shortly you will
pass into the weakness and silliness of extreme old age,
and all I can do for you is to make it as easy to you as
possible, and to preserve you from the death that others
have suffered, from having no one to look after them.
But the charm is working already! Cornichon is taller
and more manly than he was an hour ago, and Toupette
no longer looks like a little girl.'

It was true; but this fact did not seem to render the
young people as miserable as it did Selnozoura.

'Do not pity us,' said Cornichon. 'If we are fated to
grow old so soon, let us no longer delay our marriage.
What matter if we anticipate our decay, if we only anticipate our happiness too?'

The fairy felt that Cornichon had reason on his side,
and seeing by a glance at Toupette's face that there was
no opposition to be feared from her, she answered, 'Let
it be so, then. But not in this dreadful place. We will

return at once to Bagota, and the festivities shall be the
most brilliant ever seen.'

They all returned to the vessel, and in a few hours the
four thousand five hundred miles that lay between the
island and Bagota were passed. Everyone was surprised
to see the change which the short absence had made in
the young people, but as the fairy had promised absolute
silence about the adventure, they were none the wiser,
and busied themselves in preparing their dresses for the
marriage, which was fixed for the next night.

Early on the following morning the genius Kristopo
arrived at the Court, on one of the visits he was in the
habit of paying his ward from time to time. Like the
rest, he was astonished at the sudden improvement in the
child. He had always been fond of her, and in a moment
he fell violently in love. Hastily demanding an audience
of the fairy, he laid his proposals before her, never doubt-
ing that she would give her consent to so brilliant a
match. But Selnozoura refused to listen, and even hinted
that in his own interest Kristopo had better turn his
thoughts elsewhere. The genius pretended to agree, but,
instead, he went straight to Toupette's room, and flew
away with her through the window, at the very instant
that the bridegroom was awaiting her below.

When the fairy discovered what had happened, she was
furious, and sent messenger after messenger to the genius
in his palace at Ratibouf, commanding him to restore
Toupette without delay, and threatening to make war in
case of refusal.

Kristopo gave no direct answer to the fairy's envoys,
but kept Toupette closely guarded in a tower, where the
poor girl used all her powers of persuasion to induce him
to put off their marriage. All would, however, have been
quite vain if, in the course of a few days, sorrow, joined
to the spell of the magic water, had not altered her appearance so completely that Kristopo was quite alarmed,
and declared that she needed amusement and fresh air,

and that, as his presence seemed to distress her, she should be left her own mistress. But one thing he declined to do, and that was to send her back to Bagota.

In the meantime both sides had been busily collecting armies, and Kristopo had given the command of his to a famous general, while Selnozoura had placed Cornichon at the head of her forces. But before war was actually declared, Toupette's parents, who had been summoned by the genius, arrived at Ratibouf. They had never seen their daughter since they parted from her as a baby, but from time to time travellers to Bagota had brought back accounts of her beauty. What was their amazement, therefore, at finding, instead of a lovely girl, a middle-aged woman, handsome indeed, but quite faded—looking, in fact, older than themselves. Kristopo, hardly less astonished than they were at the sudden change, thought that it was a joke on the part of one of his courtiers, who had hidden Toupette away, and put this elderly lady in her place. Bursting with rage, he sent instantly for all the servants and guards of the town, and inquired who had the insolence to play him such a trick, and what had become of their prisoner. They replied that since Toupette had been in their charge she had never left her rooms unveiled, and that during her walks in the surrounding gardens, her food had been brought in and placed on her table ; as she preferred to eat alone no one had ever seen her face, or knew what she was like.

The servants were clearly speaking the truth, and Kristopo was obliged to believe them. 'But,' thought he, 'if they have not had a hand in this, it must be the work of the fairy,' and in his anger he ordered the army to be ready to march.

On her side, Selnozoura of course knew what the genius had to expect, but was deeply offended when she heard of the base trick which she was believed to have invented. Her first desire was to give battle to Kristopo at once, but with great difficulty her ministers induced her to pause, and to send an ambassador to Kristopo to try to arrange matters.

So the Prince Zeprady departed for the court of Rati-bouf, and on his way he met Cornichon, who was en-camped with his army just outside the gates of Bagota. The prince showed him the fairy's written order that for the present peace must still be kept, and Cornichon, filled with longing to see Toupette once more, begged to be allowed to accompany Zeprady on his mission to Rati-bouf.

By this time the genius's passion for Toupette, which had caused all these troubles, had died out, and he willingly accepted the terms of peace offered by Zeprady, though he informed the prince that he still believed the fairy to be guilty of the dreadful change in the girl. To this the prince only replied that on that point he had a witness who could prove, better than anyone else, if it was Toupette or not, and desired that Cornichon should be sent for.

When Toupette was told that she was to see her old lover again, her heart leapt with joy ; but soon the recollec-tion came to her of all that had happened, and she re-membered that Cornichon would be changed as well as she. The moment of their meeting was not all happiness, es-pecially on the part of Toupette, who could not forget her lost beauty, and the genius, who was present, was at last convinced that he had not been deceived, and went out to sign the treaty of peace, followed by his attendants.

'Ah, Toupette : my dear Toupette !' cried Cornichon, as soon as they were left alone ; 'now that we are once more united, let our past troubles be forgotten.'

'Our *past* troubles !' answered she, 'and what do you call our lost beauty and the dreadful future before us ? You are looking fifty years older than when I saw you last, and I know too well that fate has treated me no better !'

'Ah, do not say that,' replied Cornichon, clasping her hand. 'You are different, it is true ; but every age has its graces, and surely no woman of sixty was ever handsomer than you! If your eyes had been as bright as of yore they would have matched badly with your faded skin. The wrinkles which I notice on your forehead explain the increased fulness of your cheeks, and your throat in withering is elegant in decay. Thus the harmony shown by your features, even as they grow old, is the best proof of their former beauty.'

'Oh, monster!' cried Toupette, bursting into tears, 'is that all the comfort you can give me?'

'But, Toupette,' answered Cornichon, 'you used to declare that you did not care for beauty, as long as you had my heart.'

'Yes, I know,' said she, 'but how can you go on caring for a person who is as old and plain as I?'

'Toupette, Toupette,' replied Cornichon, 'you are only talking nonsense. My heart is as much yours as ever it was, and nothing in the world can make any difference.'

At this point of the conversation the Prince Zeprady entered the room, with the news that the genius, full of regret for his behaviour, had given Cornichon full permission to depart for Bagota as soon as he liked, and to take Toupette with him; adding that, though he begged they would excuse his taking leave of them before they went, he hoped, before long, to visit them at Bagota.

Neither of the lovers slept that night—Cornichon from joy at returning home, Toupette from dread of the blow to her vanity which awaited her at Bagota. It was hopeless for Cornichon to try to console her during the journey with the reasons he had given the day before. She only grew worse and worse, and when they reached the palace went straight to her old apartments, entreating the fairy to allow both herself and Cornichon to remain concealed, and to see no one.

For some time after their arrival the fairy was taken up with the preparations for the rejoicings which were to celebrate the peace, and with the reception of the genius, who was determined to do all in his power to regain Selnozoura's lost friendship. Cornichon and Toupette were therefore left entirely to themselves, and though this was only what they wanted, still, they began to feel a little neglected.

At length, one morning, they saw from the windows that the fairy and the genius were approaching, in state, with all their courtiers in attendance. Toupette instantly hid herself in the darkest corner of the room, but Cornichon, forgetting that he was now no longer a boy of fourteen, ran to meet them. In so doing he tripped and fell, bruising one of his eyes severely. At the sight of her lover lying helpless on the floor, Toupette hastened to his side; but her feeble legs gave way under her, and she fell almost on top of him, knocking out three of her loosened teeth against his forehead. The fairy, who entered the room at this moment, burst into tears, and listened in silence to the genius, who hinted that by-and-by everything would be put right.

'At the last assembly of the fairies,' he said, 'when the doings of each fairy were examined and discussed, a proposal was made to lessen, as far as possible, the mischief caused by Dindonette by enchanting the fountain. And it was decided that, as she had meant nothing but kindness, she should have the power of undoing one half of the spell. Of course she might always have destroyed the fatal fountain, which would have been best of all; but this she never thought of. Yet, in spite of this, her heart is so good, that I am sure that the moment she hears that she is wanted she will fly to help. Only, before she comes, it is for you, Madam, to make up your mind which of the two shall regain their former strength and beauty.'

At these words the fairy's soul sank. Both Cornichon and Toupette were equally dear to her, and how could she favour one at the cost of the other? As to the courtiers, none of the men were able to understand why she hesitated a second to declare for Toupette; while the ladies were equally strong on the side of Cornichon.

But, however undecided the fairy might be, it was quite different with Cornichon and Toupette.

'Ah, my love,' exclaimed Cornichon, 'at length I shall be able to give you the best proof of my devotion by showing you how I value the beauties of your mind above those of your body! While the most charming women of the court will fall victims to my youth and strength, I shall think of nothing but how to lay them at your feet, and pay heart-felt homage to your age and wrinkles.'

'Not so fast,' interrupted Toupette, 'I don't see why you should have it all. Why do you heap such humiliations upon me? But I will trust to the justice of the fairy, who will not treat me so.'

Then she entered her own rooms, and refused to leave them, in spite of the prayers of Cornichon, who begged her to let him explain.

No one at the court thought or spoke of any other subject during the few days before the arrival of Dindonette, whom everybody expected to set things right in a moment. But, alas! she had no idea herself what was best to be done, and always adopted the opinion of the person she was talking to. At length a thought struck her, which seemed the only way of satisfying both parties, and she asked the fairy to call together all the court and the people to hear her decision.

'Happy is he,' she began, 'who can repair the evil he has caused, but happier he who has never caused any.'

As nobody contradicted this remark, she continued :

'To me it is only allowed to undo one half of the mischief I have wrought. I could restore you your youth,' she said to Cornichon, 'or your beauty,' turning to Toupette. 'I will do both ; and I will do neither.'

A murmur of curiosity arose from the crowd, while Cornichon and Toupette trembled with astonishment.

'No,' went on Dindonette, 'never should I have the cruelty to leave one of you to decay, while the other enjoys the glory of youth. And as I cannot restore you both at once to what you were, one half of each of your bodies shall become young again, while the other half goes on its way to decay. I will leave it to you to choose which half it shall be—if I shall draw a line round the waist, or a line straight down the middle of the body.'

She looked about her proudly, expecting applause for her clever idea. But Cornichon and Toupette were shaking with rage and disappointment, and everyone else broke into shouts of laughter. In pity for the unhappy lovers, Selnozoura came forward.

'Do you not think,' she said, 'that instead of what you propose, it would be better to let them take it in turns to enjoy their former youth and beauty for a fixed time? I am sure you could easily manage that.'

'What an excellent notion!' cried Dindonette. 'Oh, yes, of course that is best! Which of you shall I touch first?'

'Touch her,' replied Cornichon, who was always ready to give way to Toupette. 'I know her heart too well to fear any change.'

So the fairy bent forward and touched her with her magic ring, and in one instant the old woman was a girl again. The whole court wept with joy at the sight, and Toupette ran up to Cornichon, who had fallen down in his surprise, promising to pay him long visits, and tell him of all her balls and water parties.

The two fairies went to their own apartments, where the genius followed them to take his leave.

'Oh, dear!' suddenly cried Dindonette, breaking in to the farewell speech of the genius. 'I quite forgot to fix the time when Cornichon should in his turn grow young. How stupid of me! And now I fear it is too late, for I ought to have declared it before I touched Toupette with the ring. Oh, dear! oh, dear! why did nobody warn me?'

'You were so quick,' replied Selnozoura, who had long been aware of the mischief the fairy had again done, 'and we can only wait now till Cornichon shall have reached the utmost limits of his decay, when he will drink of the water, and become a baby once more, so that Toupette will have to spend her life as a nurse, a wife, and a caretaker.'

After the anxiety of mind and the weakness of body to which for so long Toupette had been a prey, it seemed as if she could not amuse herself enough, and it was seldom indeed that she found time to visit poor Cornichon, though she did not cease to be fond of him, or to be kind to him. Still, she was perfectly happy without him, and this the poor man did not fail to see, almost blind and deaf from age though he was.

But it was left to Kristopo to undo at last the work of Dindonette, and give Cornichon back the youth he had lost, and this the genius did all the more gladly, as he discovered, quite by accident, that Cornichon was in fact his son. It was on this plea that he attended the great yearly meeting of the fairies, and prayed that, in consideration of his services to so many of the members, this one boon might be granted him. Such a request had never before been heard in fairyland, and was objected to by some of the older fairies ; but both Kristopo and Selnozoura were held in such high honour that the murmurs of disgust were set aside, and the latest victim to the enchanted fountain was pronounced to be free of the spell. All that the genius asked in return was that he might accompany the fairy back to Bagota, and be present when his son assumed his proper shape.

They made up their minds they would just tell Toupette that they had found a husband for her, and give her a pleasant surprise at her wedding, which was fixed for the following night. She heard the news with astonishment, and many pangs for the grief which Cornichon would certainly feel at his place being taken by another; but she did not dream of disobeying the fairy, and spent the whole day wondering who the bridegroom could be.

At the appointed hour, a large crowd assembled at the fairy's palace, which was decorated with the sweetest flowers, known only to fairyland. Toupette had taken her place, but where was the bridegroom?

'Fetch Cornichon!' said the fairy to her chamberlain.

But Toupette interposed: 'Oh, Madam, spare him, I entreat you, this bitter pain, and let him remain hidden and in peace.'

'It is necessary that he should be here,' answered the fairy, 'and he will not regret it.'

And, as she spoke, Cornichon was led in, smiling with the foolishness of extreme old age at the sight of the gay crowd.

'Bring him here,' commanded the fairy, waving her hand towards Toupette, who started back from surprise and horror.

Selnozoura then took the hand of the poor old man, and the genius came forward and touched him three times with his ring, when Cornichon was transformed into a handsome young man.

'May you live long,' the genius said, 'to enjoy happiness with your wife, and to love your father.'

And that was the end of the mischief wrought by the fairy Dindonette!

[*Cabinet des Fées.*]

LONG, BROAD, AND QUICKEYE

(A BOHEMIAN STORY)

ONCE upon a time there lived a king who had an only son whom he loved dearly. Now one day the king sent for his son and said to him :

' My dearest child, my hair is grey and I am old, and soon I shall feel no more the warmth of the sun, or look upon the trees and flowers. But before I die I should like to see you with a good wife; therefore marry, my son, as speedily as possible.'

' My father,' replied the prince, ' now and always, I ask nothing better than to do your bidding, but I know of no daughter-in-law that I could give you.'

On hearing these words the old king drew from his pocket a key of gold, and gave it to his son, saying :

' Go up the staircase, right up to the top of the tower. Look carefully round you, and then come and tell me which you like best of all that you see.'

So the young man went up. He had never before been in the tower, and had no idea what it might contain.

The staircase wound round and round and round, till the prince was almost giddy, and every now and then he caught sight of a large room that opened out from the side. But he had been told to go to the top, and to the top he went. Then he found himself in a hall, which had an iron door at one end. This door he unlocked with his golden key, and he passed through into a vast

the sadness of her face seemed
to pass into his heart.

HJ FORD

chamber which had a roof of blue sprinkled with golden
stars, and a carpet of green silk soft as turf. Twelve
windows framed in gold let in the light of the sun, and
on every window was painted the figure of a young
girl, each more beautiful than the last. While the prince
gazed at them in surprise, not knowing which he liked
best, the girls began to lift their eyes and smile at him.
He waited, expecting them to speak, but no sound
came.

Suddenly he noticed that one of the windows was
covered by a curtain of white silk.

He lifted it, and saw before him the image of a maiden
beautiful as the day and sad as the tomb, clothed in a
white robe, having a girdle of silver and a crown of pearls.
The prince stood and gazed at her, as if he had been
turned into stone, but as he looked the sadness which
was on her face seemed to pass into his heart, and he
cried out:

'This one shall be my wife. This one and no other.'

As he said the words the young girl blushed and hung
her head, and all the other figures vanished.

The young prince went quickly back to his father, and
told him all he had seen and which wife he had chosen.
The old man listened to him full of sorrow, and then he
spoke:

'You have done ill, my son, to search out that which
was hidden, and you are running to meet a great danger.
This young girl has fallen into the power of a wicked
sorcerer, who lives in an iron castle. Many young men
have tried to deliver her, and none have ever come back.
But what is done is done! You have given your word,
and it cannot be broken. Go, dare your fate, and return
to me safe and sound.'

So the prince embraced his father, mounted his horse,
and set forth to seek his bride. He rode on gaily for
several hours, till he found himself in a wood where he
had never been before, and soon lost his way among its

winding paths and deep valleys. He tried in vain to see
where he was : the thick trees shut out the sun, and he
could not tell which was north and which was south,
so that he might know what direction to make for. He
felt in despair, and had quite given up all hope of getting
out of this horrible place, when he heard a voice calling
to him.

'Hey ! hey ! stop a minute ! '

The prince turned round and saw behind him a
very tall man, running as fast as his legs would carry
him.

'Wait for me,' he panted, 'and take me into your
service. If you do, you will never be sorry.'

'Who are you ? ' asked the prince, 'and what can
you do ? '

'Long is my name, and I can lengthen my body at
will. Do you see that nest up there on the top of that
pine-tree ? Well, I can get it for you without taking the
trouble of climbing the tree,' and Long stretched himself
up and up and up, till he was very soon as tall as the
pine itself. He put the nest in his pocket, and before
you could wink your eyelid he had made himself small
again, and stood before the prince.

'Yes ; you know your business,' said he, 'but birds'
nests are no use to me. I am too old for them. Now
if you were only able to get me out of this wood, you
would indeed be good for something.'

'Oh, there's no difficulty about that,' replied Long,
and he stretched himself up and up and up till he was
three times as tall as the tallest tree in the forest. Then
he looked all round and said, 'We must go in this
direction in order to get out of the wood,' and shortening
himself again, he took the prince's horse by the bridle,
and led him along. Very soon they got clear of the
forest, and saw before them a wide plain ending in a pile
of high rocks, covered here and there with trees, and very
much like the fortifications of a town.

As they left the wood behind, Long turned to the prince and said, 'My lord, here comes my comrade. You should take him into your service too, as you will find him a great help.'

'Well, call him then, so that I can see what sort of a man he is.'

'He is a little too far off for that,' replied Long. 'He would hardly hear my voice, and he couldn't be here for some time yet, as he has so much to carry. I think I had better go and bring him myself,' and this time he

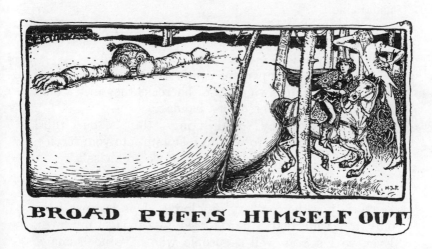

BROAD PUFFS HIMSELF OUT

stretched himself to such a height that his head was lost in the clouds. He made two or three strides, took his friend on his back, and set him down before the prince. The new-comer was a very fat man, and as round as a barrel.

'Who are you?' asked the prince, 'and what can you do?'

'Your worship, Broad is my name, and I can make myself as wide as I please.'

'Let me see how you manage it.'

'Run, my lord, as fast as you can, and hide yourself

in the wood,' cried Broad, and he began to swell himself out.

The prince did not understand why he should run to the wood, but when he saw Long flying towards it, he thought he had better follow his example. He was only just in time, for Broad had so suddenly inflated himself that he very nearly knocked over the prince and his horse too. He covered all the space for acres round. You would have thought he was a mountain!

At length Broad ceased to expand, drew a deep breath that made the whole forest tremble, and shrank into his usual size.

'You have made me run away,' said the prince. 'But it is not every day one meets with a man of your sort. I will take you into my service.'

So the three companions continued their journey, and when they were drawing near the rocks they met a man whose eyes were covered by a bandage.

'Your excellency,' said Long, 'this is our third comrade. You will do well to take him into your service, and, I assure you, you will find him worth his salt.'

'Who are you?' asked the prince. 'And why are your eyes bandaged? You can never see your way!'

'It is just the contrary, my lord! It is because I see only too well that I am forced to bandage my eyes. Even so I see as well as people who have no bandage. When I take it off my eyes pierce through everything. Everything I look at catches fire, or, if it cannot catch fire, it falls into a thousand pieces. They call me Quickeye.'

And so saying he took off his bandage and turned towards the rock. As he fixed his eyes upon it a crack was heard, and in a few moments it was nothing but a heap of sand. In the sand something might be detected glittering brightly. Quickeye picked it up and brought it to the prince. It turned out to be a lump of pure gold.

'You are a wonderful creature,' said the prince, 'and I should be a fool not to take you into my service. But since your eyes are so good, tell me if I am very far from the Iron Castle, and what is happening there just now.'

'If you were travelling alone,' replied Quickeye, 'it would take you at least a year to get to it; but as we are with you, we shall arrive there to-night. Just now they are preparing supper.'

'There is a princess in the castle. Do you see her?'

'A wizard keeps her in a high tower, guarded by iron bars.'

'Ah, help me to deliver her!' cried the prince.

And they promised they would.

Then they all set out through the grey rocks, by the breach made by the eyes of Quickeye, and passed over great mountains and through deep woods. And every time they met with any obstacle the three friends contrived somehow to put it aside. As the sun was setting, the prince beheld the towers of the Iron Castle, and before it sank beneath the horizon he was crossing the iron bridge which led to the gates. He was only just in time, for no sooner had the sun disappeared altogether, than the bridge drew itself up and the gates shut themselves.

There was no turning back now!

The prince put up his horse in the stable, where everything looked as if a guest was expected, and then the whole party marched straight up to the castle. In the court, in the stables, and all over the great halls, they saw a number of men richly dressed, but every one turned into stone. They crossed an endless set of rooms, all opening into each other, till they reached the dining-hall. It was brilliantly lighted; the table was covered with wine and fruit, and was laid for four. They waited a few minutes expecting someone to come, but as nobody did, they sat down and began to eat and drink, for they were very hungry.

When they had done their supper they looked about for some place to sleep. But suddenly the door burst open, and the wizard entered the hall. He was old and hump-backed, with a bald head and a grey beard that fell to his knees. He wore a black robe, and instead of a belt three iron circlets clasped his waist. He led by the hand a lady of wonderful beauty, dressed in white, with a girdle of silver and a crown of pearls, but her face was pale and sad as death itself.

The prince knew her in an instant, and moved eagerly forward ; but the wizard gave him no time to speak, and said :

'I know why you are here. Very good ; you may have her if for three nights following you can prevent her making her escape. If you fail in this, you and your servants will all be turned into stone, like those who have come before you.' And offering the princess a chair, he left the hall.

The prince could not take his eyes from the princess, she was so lovely! He began to talk to her, but she neither answered nor smiled, and sat as if she were made of marble. He seated himself by her, and determined not to close his eyes that night, for fear she should escape him. And in order that she should be doubly guarded, Long stretched himself like a strap all round the room, Broad took his stand by the door and puffed himself out, so that not even a mouse could slip by, and Quickeye leant against a pillar which stood in the middle of the floor and supported the roof. But in half a second they were all sound asleep, and they slept sound the whole night long.

In the morning, at the first peep of dawn, the prince awoke with a start. But the princess was gone. He aroused his servants and implored them to tell him what he must do.

'Calm yourself, my lord,' said Quickeye. 'I have

found her already.   A hundred miles from here there is a
forest.   In the middle of the forest, an old oak, and on
the top of the oak, an acorn.   This acorn is the princess.
If Long will take me on his shoulders, we shall soon
bring her back.'   And sure enough, in less time than it
takes to walk round a cottage, they had returned from
the forest, and Long presented the acorn to the prince.

'Now, your excellency, throw it on the ground.'

The prince obeyed, and was enchanted to see the princess
appear at his side.   But when the sun peeped for the first
time over the mountains, the door burst open as before,
and the wizard entered with a loud laugh.   Suddenly he
caught sight of the princess ; his face darkened, he
uttered a low growl, and one of the iron circlets gave
way with a crash.   He seized the young girl by the hand
and bore her away with him.

All that day the prince wandered about the castle,
studying the curious treasures it contained, but everything
looked as if life had suddenly come to a standstill.   In
one place he saw a prince who had been turned into stone
in the act of brandishing a sword round which his two
hands were clasped.   In another, the same doom had fallen
upon a knight in the act of running away.   In a third, a
serving man was standing eternally trying to convey a
piece of beef to his mouth, and all around them were
others, still preserving for evermore the attitudes they were
in when the wizard had commanded ' From henceforth be
turned into marble.'   In the castle, and round the castle,
all was dismal and desolate.   Trees there were, but without leaves ; fields there were, but no grass grew on them.
There was one river, but it never flowed and no fish
lived in it.   No flowers blossomed, and no birds sang.

Three times during the day food appeared, as if by
magic, for the prince and his servants.   And it was not
until supper was ended that the wizard appeared, as on
the previous evening, and delivered the princess into the
care of the prince.

All four determined that this time they would keep awake at any cost. But it was no use. Off they went as they had done before, and when the prince awoke the next morning the room was again empty.

With a pang of shame, he rushed to find Quickeye. 'Awake! Awake! Quickeye! Do you know what has become of the princess?'

Quickeye rubbed his eyes and answered: 'Yes, I see her. Two hundred miles from here there is a mountain. In this mountain is a rock. In the rock, a precious stone. This stone is the princess. Long shall take me there, and we will be back before you can turn round.'

So Long took him on his shoulders and they set out. At every stride they covered twenty miles, and as they drew near Quickeye fixed his burning eyes on the mountain; in an instant it split into a thousand pieces, and in one of these sparkled the precious stone. They picked it up and brought it to the prince, who flung it hastily down, and as the stone touched the floor the princess stood before him. When the wizard came, his eyes shot forth flames of fury. Cric-crac was heard, and another of his iron bands broke and fell. He seized the princess by the hand and led her off, growling louder than ever.

All that day things went on exactly as they had done the day before. After supper the wizard brought back the princess, and looking him straight in the eyes he said, 'We shall see which of us two will gain the prize after all!'

That night they struggled their very hardest to keep awake, and even walked about instead of sitting down. But it was quite useless. One after another they had to give in, and for the third time the princess slipped through their fingers.

When morning came, it was as usual the prince who awoke the first, and as usual, the princess being gone, he rushed to Quickeye.

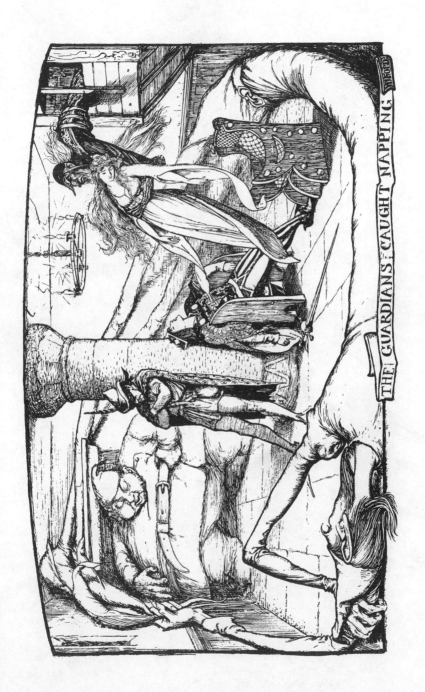

THE GUARDIANS CAUGHT NAPPING

'Get up, get up, Quickeye, and tell me where is the princess ? '

Quickeye looked about for some time without answering. ' Oh, my lord, she is far, very far. Three hundred miles away there lies a black sea. In the middle of this sea there is a little shell, and in the middle of the shell is fixed a gold ring. That gold ring is the princess. But do not vex your soul ; we will get her. Only to-day, Long must take Broad with him. He will be wanted badly.'

So Long took Quickeye on one shoulder, and Broad on the other, and they set out. At each stride they left thirty miles behind them. When they reached the black sea, Quickeye showed them the spot where they must seek the shell. But though Long stretched down his hand as far as it would go, he could not find the shell, for it lay at the bottom of the sea.

' Wait a moment, comrades, it will be all right. I will help you,' said Broad.

Then he swelled himself out so that you would have thought the world could hardly have held him, and stooping down he drank. He drank so much at every mouthful, that only a minute or so passed before the water had sunk enough for Long to put his hand to the bottom. He soon found the shell, and pulled the ring out. But time had been lost, and Long had a double burden to carry. The dawn was breaking fast before they got back to the castle, where the prince was waiting for them in an agony of fear.

Soon the first rays of the sun were seen peeping over the tops of the mountains. The door burst open, and finding the prince standing alone the wizard broke into peals of wicked laughter. But as he laughed a loud crash was heard, the window fell into a thousand pieces, a gold ring glittered in the air, and the princess stood before the enchanter. For Quickeye, who was watching from afar, had told Long of the terrible danger now threatening the prince, and Long, summoning all his strength for one gigantic effort, had thrown the ring right through the window.

The wizard shrieked and howled with rage, till the whole castle trembled to its foundations. Then a crash was heard, the third band split in two, and a crow flew out of the window.

Then the princess at length broke the enchanted silence, and blushing like a rose, gave the prince her thanks for her unlooked-for deliverance.

But it was not only the princess who was restored to life by the flight of the wicked black crow. The marble figures became men once more, and took up their occupations just as they had left them off. The horses neighed in the stables, the flowers blossomed in the garden, the birds flew in the air, the fish darted in the water. Everywhere you looked, all was life, all was joy!

And the knights who had been turned into stone came in a body to offer their homage to the prince who had set them free.

'Do not thank me,' he said, 'for I have done nothing. Without my faithful servants, Long, Broad, and Quickeye, I should even have been as one of you.'

With these words he bade them farewell, and departed with the princess and his faithful companions for the kingdom of his father.

The old king, who had long since given up all hope, wept for joy at the sight of his son, and insisted that the wedding should take place as soon as possible.

All the knights who had been enchanted in the Iron Castle were invited to the ceremony, and after it had taken place, Long, Broad, and Quickeye took leave of the young couple, saying that they were going to look for more work.

The prince offered them all their hearts could desire if they would only remain with him, but they replied that an idle life would not please them, and that they could never be happy unless they were busy, so they went away to seek their fortunes, and for all I know are seeking still.

[*Contes populaires.* Traduits par Louis Léger. Paris : Leroux, éditeur.]

PRUNELLA

THERE was once upon a time a woman who had an only daughter. When the child was about seven years old she used to pass every day, on her way to school, an orchard where there was a wild plum tree, with delicious ripe plums hanging from the branches. Each morning the child would pick one, and put it into her pocket to eat at school. For this reason she was called Prunella. Now, the orchard belonged to a witch. One day the witch noticed the child gathering a plum, as she passed along the road. Prunella did it quite innocently, not knowing that she was doing wrong in taking the fruit that hung close to the roadside. But the witch was furious, and next day hid herself behind the hedge, and when Prunella came past, and put out her hand to pluck the fruit, she jumped out and seized her by the arm.

'Ah! you little thief!' she exclaimed. 'I have caught you at last. Now you will have to pay for your misdeeds.'

The poor child, half dead with fright, implored the old woman to forgive her, assuring her that she did not know she had done wrong, and promising never to do it again. But the witch had no pity, and she dragged Prunella into her house, where she kept her till the time should come when she could have her revenge.

As the years passed Prunella grew up into a very beautiful girl. Now her beauty and goodness, instead of softening the witch's heart, aroused her hatred and jealousy.

One day she called Prunella to her, and said : ' Take this basket, go to the well, and bring it back to me filled with water. If you don't I will kill you.'

The girl took the basket, went and let it down into the well again and again. But her work was lost labour. Each time, as she drew up the basket, the water streamed out of it. At last, in despair, she gave it up, and leaning against the well she began to cry bitterly, when suddenly she heard a voice at her side saying ' Prunella, why are you crying? '

Turning round she beheld a handsome youth, who looked kindly at her, as if he were sorry for her trouble.

' Who are you,' she asked, ' and how do you know my name ? '

' I am the son of the witch,' he replied, ' and my name is Bensiabel. I know that she is determined that you shall die, but I promise you that she shall not carry out her wicked plan. Will you give me a kiss, if I fill your basket? '

' No,' said Prunella, ' I will not give you a kiss, because you are the son of a witch.'

' Very well,' replied the youth sadly. ' Give me your basket and I will fill it for you.' And he dipped it into the well, and the water stayed in it. Then the girl returned to the house, carrying the basket filled with water. When the witch saw it, she became white with rage, and exclaimed ' Bensiabel must have helped you.' And Prunella looked down, and said nothing.

' Well, we shall see who will win in the end,' said the witch, in a great rage.

The following day she called the girl to her and said : ' Take this sack of wheat. I am going out for a little ; by the time I return I shall expect you to have made it into bread. If you have not done it I will kill you.' Having said this she left the room, closing and locking the door behind her.

Poor Prunella did not know what to do. It was

impossible for her to grind the wheat, prepare the dough, and bake the bread, all in the short time that the witch would be away. At first she set to work bravely, but when she saw how hopeless her task was, she threw herself on a chair, and began to weep bitterly. She was roused from her despair by hearing Bensiabel's voice at her side saying : ' Prunella, Prunella, do not weep like that. If you will give me a kiss I will make the bread, and you will be saved.'

' I will not kiss the son of a witch,' replied Prunella.

But Bensiabel took the wheat from her, and ground it, and made the dough, and when the witch returned the bread was ready baked in the oven.

Turning to the girl, with fury in her voice, she said : ' Bensiabel must have been here and helped you ; ' and Prunella looked down, and said nothing.

' We shall see who will win in the end,' said the witch, and her eyes blazed with anger.

Next day she called the girl to her and said : ' Go to my sister, who lives across the mountains. She will give you a casket, which you must bring back to me.' This she said knowing that her sister, who was a still more cruel and wicked witch than herself, would never allow the girl to return, but would imprison her and starve her to death. But Prunella did not suspect anything, and set out quite cheerfully. On the way she met Bensiabel.

' Where are you going, Prunella ? ' he asked.

' I am going to the sister of my mistress, from whom I am to fetch a casket.'

' Oh poor, poor girl ! ' said Bensiabel. ' You are being sent straight to your death. Give me a kiss, and I will save you.'

But again Prunella answered as before, ' I will not kiss the son of a witch.'

' Nevertheless, I will save your life,' said Bensiabel, ' for I love you better than myself. Take this flagon of

oil, this loaf of bread, this piece of rope, and this broom.
When you reach the witch's house, oil the hinges of the
door with the contents of the flagon, and throw the loaf
of bread to the great fierce mastiff, who will come to
meet you. When you have passed the dog, you will see
in the courtyard a miserable woman trying in vain to
let down a bucket into the well with her plaited hair.
You must give her the rope. In the kitchen you will
find a still more miserable woman trying to clean the
hearth with her tongue; to her you must give the
broom. You will see the casket on the top of a cupboard, take it as quickly as you can, and leave the house
without a moment's delay. If you do all this exactly as I
have told you, you will not be killed.'

So Prunella, having listened carefully to his instructions, did just what he had told her. She reached the
house, oiled the hinges of the door, threw the loaf to the
dog, gave the poor woman at the well the rope, and the
woman in the kitchen the broom, caught up the casket
from the top of the cupboard, and fled with it out of the
house. But the witch heard her as she ran away, and
rushing to the window called out to the woman in the
kitchen : ' Kill that thief, I tell you ! '

But the woman replied: ' I will not kill her, for she
has given me a broom, whereas you forced me to clean
the hearth with my tongue.'

Then the witch called out in fury to the woman at
the well : ' Take the girl, I tell you, and fling her into
the water, and drown her ! '

But the woman answered : ' No, I will not drown her,
for she gave me this rope, whereas you forced me to use
my hair to let down the bucket to draw water.'

Then the witch shouted to the dog to seize the girl
and hold her fast; but the dog answered : ' No, I will not
seize her, for she gave me a loaf of bread, whereas you
let me starve with hunger.'

The witch was so angry that she nearly choked, as

she called out : ' Door, bang upon her, and keep her a
prisoner.'

But the door answered : ' I won't, for she has oiled my
hinges, so that they move quite easily, whereas you left
them all rough and rusty.'

And so Prunella escaped, and, with the casket under
her arm, reached the house of her mistress, who, as you
may believe, was as angry as she was surprised to see
the girl standing before her, looking more beautiful than
ever. Her eyes flashed, as in furious tones she asked her,
' Did you meet Bensiabel ? '

But Prunella looked down, and said nothing.

' We shall see,' said the witch, ' who will win in the
end.   Listen, there are three cocks in the hen-house ; one
is yellow, one black, and the third is white.   If one of
them crows during the night you must tell me which one
it is.   Woe to you if you make a mistake.   I will gobble
you up in one mouthful.'

Now Bensiabel was in the room next to the one
where Prunella slept.   At midnight she awoke hearing a
cock crow.

' Which one was that ? ' shouted the witch.

Then, trembling, Prunella knocked on the wall and
whispered : ' Bensiabel, Bensiabel, tell me, which cock
crowed ? '

' Will you give me a kiss if I tell you ? ' he whispered
back through the wall.

But she answered ' No.'

Then he whispered back to her : ' Nevertheless, I will
tell you.   It was the yellow cock that crowed.'

The witch, who had noticed the delay in Prunella's
answer, approached her door calling angrily : ' Answer at
once, or I will kill you.'

So Prunella answered : ' It was the yellow cock that
crowed.'

And the witch stamped her foot and gnashed her
teeth.

Soon after another cock crowed. 'Tell me now which one it is,' called the witch. And, prompted by Bensiabel, Prunella answered : 'That is the black cock.'

A few minutes after the crowing was heard again, and the voice of the witch demanding 'Which one was that ? '

And again Prunella implored Bensiabel to help her. But this time he hesitated, for he hoped that Prunella might forget that he was a witch's son, and promise to give him a kiss. And as he hesitated he heard an agonised cry from the girl : ' Bensiabel, Bensiabel, save me ! The witch is coming, she is close to me, I hear the gnashing of her teeth ! '

With a bound Bensiabel opened his door and flung himself against the witch. He pulled her back with such force that she stumbled, and falling headlong, dropped down dead at the foot of the stairs.

Then, at last, Prunella was touched by Bensiabel's goodness and kindness to her, and she became his wife, and they lived happily ever after.

A CATALOGUE OF SELECTED DOVER BOOKS
IN ALL FIELDS OF INTEREST

A CATALOGUE OF SELECTED DOVER
BOOKS IN ALL FIELDS OF INTEREST

CONDITIONED REFLEXES, Ivan P. Pavlov. Full translation of most complete statement of Pavlov's work; cerebral damage, conditioned reflex, experiments with dogs, sleep, similar topics of great importance. 430pp. 5⅜ x 8½. 60614-7 Pa. $4.50

NOTES ON NURSING: WHAT IT IS, AND WHAT IT IS NOT, Florence Nightingale. Outspoken writings by founder of modern nursing. When first published (1860) it played an important role in much needed revolution in nursing. Still stimulating. 140pp. 5⅜ x 8½. 22340-X Pa. $2.50

HARTER'S PICTURE ARCHIVE FOR COLLAGE AND ILLUSTRATION, Jim Harter. Over 300 authentic, rare 19th-century engravings selected by noted collagist for artists, designers, decoupeurs, etc. Machines, people, animals, etc., printed one side of page. 25 scene plates for backgrounds. 6 collages by Harter, Satty, Singer, Evans. Introduction. 192pp. 8⅞ x 11¾. 23659-5 Pa. $5.00

MANUAL OF TRADITIONAL WOOD CARVING, edited by Paul N. Hasluck. Possibly the best book in English on the craft of wood carving. Practical instructions, along with 1,146 working drawings and photographic illustrations. Formerly titled *Cassell's Wood Carving*. 576pp. 6½ x 9¼. 23489-4 Pa. $7.95

THE PRINCIPLES AND PRACTICE OF HAND OR SIMPLE TURNING, John Jacob Holtzapffel. Full coverage of basic lathe techniques— history and development, special apparatus, softwood turning, hardwood turning, metal turning. Many projects—billiard ball, works formed within a sphere, egg cups, ash trays, vases, jardiniers, others—included. 1881 edition. 800 illustrations. 592pp. 6⅛ x 9¼. 23365-0 Clothbd. $15.00

THE JOY OF HANDWEAVING, Osma Tod. Only book you need for hand weaving. Fundamentals, threads, weaves, plus numerous projects for small board-loom, two-harness, tapestry, laid-in, four-harness weaving and more. Over 160 illustrations. 2nd revised edition. 352pp. 6½ x 9¼. 23458-4 Pa. $5.00

THE BOOK OF WOOD CARVING, Charles Marshall Sayers. Still finest book for beginning student in wood sculpture. Noted teacher, craftsman discusses fundamentals, technique; gives 34 designs, over 34 projects for panels, bookends, mirrors, etc. "Absolutely first-rate"—E. J. Tangerman. 33 photos. 118pp. 7¾ x 10⅝. 23654-4 Pa. $3.50

THE COMPLETE BOOK OF DOLL MAKING AND COLLECTING, Catherine Christopher. Instructions, patterns for dozens of dolls, from rag doll on up to elaborate, historically accurate figures. Mould faces, sew clothing, make doll houses, etc. Also collecting information. Many illustrations. 288pp. 6 x 9. 22066-4 Pa. $4.50

THE DAGUERREOTYPE IN AMERICA, Beaumont Newhall. Wonderful portraits, 1850's townscapes, landscapes; full text plus 104 photographs. The basic book. Enlarged 1976 edition. 272pp. 8¼ x 11¼. 23322-7 Pa. $7.95

CRAFTSMAN HOMES, Gustav Stickley. 296 architectural drawings, floor plans, and photographs illustrate 40 different kinds of "Mission-style" homes from *The Craftsman* (1901-16), voice of American style of simplicity and organic harmony. Thorough coverage of Craftsman idea in text and picture, now collector's item. 224pp. 8⅛ x 11. 23791-5 Pa. $6.00

PEWTER-WORKING: INSTRUCTIONS AND PROJECTS, Burl N. Osborn. & Gordon O. Wilber. Introduction to pewter-working for amateur craftsman. History and characteristics of pewter; tools, materials, step-by-step instructions. Photos, line drawings, diagrams. Total of 160pp. 7⅞ x 10¾. 23786-9 Pa. $3.50

THE GREAT CHICAGO FIRE, edited by David Lowe. 10 dramatic, eye-witness accounts of the 1871 disaster, including one of the aftermath and rebuilding, plus 70 contemporary photographs and illustrations of the ruins—courthouse, Palmer House, Great Central Depot, etc. Introduction by David Lowe. 87pp. 8¼ x 11. 23771-0 Pa. $4.00

SILHOUETTES: A PICTORIAL ARCHIVE OF VARIED ILLUSTRATIONS, edited by Carol Belanger Grafton. Over 600 silhouettes from the 18th to 20th centuries include profiles and full figures of men and women, children, birds and animals, groups and scenes, nature, ships, an alphabet. Dozens of uses for commercial artists and craftspeople. 144pp. 8⅜ x 11¼. 23781-8 Pa. $4.00

ANIMALS: 1,419 COPYRIGHT-FREE ILLUSTRATIONS OF MAMMALS, BIRDS, FISH, INSECTS, ETC., edited by Jim Harter. Clear wood engravings present, in extremely lifelike poses, over 1,000 species of animals. One of the most extensive copyright-free pictorial sourcebooks of its kind. Captions. Index. 284pp. 9 x 12. 23766-4 Pa. $7.95

INDIAN DESIGNS FROM ANCIENT ECUADOR, Frederick W. Shaffer. 282 original designs by pre-Columbian Indians of Ecuador (500-1500 A.D.). Designs include people, mammals, birds, reptiles, fish, plants, heads, geometric designs. Use as is or alter for advertising, textiles, leathercraft, etc. Introduction. 95pp. 8¾ x 11¼. 23764-8 Pa. $3.50

SZIGETI ON THE VIOLIN, Joseph Szigeti. Genial, loosely structured tour by premier violinist, featuring a pleasant mixture of reminiscenes, insights into great music and musicians, innumerable tips for practicing violinists. 385 musical passages. 256pp. 5⅝ x 8¼. 23763-X Pa. $3.50

HOUSEHOLD STORIES BY THE BROTHERS GRIMM. All the great Grimm stories: "Rumpelstiltskin," "Snow White," "Hansel and Gretel," etc., with 114 illustrations by Walter Crane. 269pp. 5⅜ x 8½.
21080-4 Pa. $3.00

SLEEPING BEAUTY, illustrated by Arthur Rackham. Perhaps the fullest, most delightful version ever, told by C. S. Evans. Rackham's best work. 49 illustrations. 110pp. 7⅞ x 10¾. 22756-1 Pa. $2.50

AMERICAN FAIRY TALES, L. Frank Baum. Young cowboy lassoes Father Time; dummy in Mr. Floman's department store window comes to life; and 10 other fairy tales. 41 illustrations by N. P. Hall, Harry Kennedy, Ike Morgan, and Ralph Gardner. 209pp. 5⅜ x 8½. 23643-9 Pa. $3.00

THE WONDERFUL WIZARD OF OZ, L. Frank Baum. Facsimile in full color of America's finest children's classic. Introduction by Martin Gardner. 143 illustrations by W. W. Denslow. 267pp. 5⅜ x 8½.
20691-2 Pa. $3.50

THE TALE OF PETER RABBIT, Beatrix Potter. The inimitable Peter's terrifying adventure in Mr. McGregor's garden, with all 27 wonderful, full-color Potter illustrations. 55pp. 4¼ x 5½. (Available in U.S. only)
22827-4 Pa. $1.25

THE STORY OF KING ARTHUR AND HIS KNIGHTS, Howard Pyle. Finest children's version of life of King Arthur. 48 illustrations by Pyle. 131pp. 6⅛ x 9¼. 21445-1 Pa. $4.95

CARUSO'S CARICATURES, Enrico Caruso. Great tenor's remarkable caricatures of self, fellow musicians, composers, others. Toscanini, Puccini, Farrar, etc. Impish, cutting, insightful. 473 illustrations. Preface by M. Sisca. 217pp. 8⅜ x 11¼. 23528-9 Pa. $6.95

PERSONAL NARRATIVE OF A PILGRIMAGE TO ALMADINAH AND MECCAH, Richard Burton. Great travel classic by remarkably colorful personality. Burton, disguised as a Moroccan, visited sacred shrines of Islam, narrowly escaping death. Wonderful observations of Islamic life, customs, personalities. 47 illustrations. Total of 959pp. 5⅜ x 8½.
21217-3, 21218-1 Pa., Two-vol. set $12.00

INCIDENTS OF TRAVEL IN YUCATAN, John L. Stephens. Classic (1843) exploration of jungles of Yucatan, looking for evidences of Maya civilization. Travel adventures, Mexican and Indian culture, etc. Total of 669pp. 5⅜ x 8½. 20926-1, 20927-X Pa., Two-vol. set $7.90

AMERICAN LITERARY AUTOGRAPHS FROM WASHINGTON IRVING TO HENRY JAMES, Herbert Cahoon, et al. Letters, poems, manuscripts of Hawthorne, Thoreau, Twain, Alcott, Whitman, 67 other prominent American authors. Reproductions, full transcripts and commentary. Plus checklist of all American Literary Autographs in The Pierpont Morgan Library. Printed on exceptionally high-quality paper. 136 illustrations. 212pp. 9⅛ x 12¼. 23548-3 Pa. $7.95

AMERICAN BIRD ENGRAVINGS, Alexander Wilson et al. All 76 plates. from Wilson's *American Ornithology* (1808-14), most important ornithological work before Audubon, plus 27 plates from the supplement (1825-33) by Charles Bonaparte. Over 250 birds portrayed. 8 plates also reproduced in full color. 111pp. 9⅜ x 12½. 23195-X Pa. $6.00

CRUICKSHANK'S PHOTOGRAPHS OF BIRDS OF AMERICA, Allan D. Cruickshank. Great ornithologist, photographer presents 177 closeups, groupings, panoramas, flightings, etc., of about 150 different birds. Expanded *Wings in the Wilderness*. Introduction by Helen G. Cruickshank. 191pp. 8¼ x 11. 23497-5 Pa. $6.00

AMERICAN WILDLIFE AND PLANTS, A. C. Martin, et al. Describes food habits of more than 1000 species of mammals, birds, fish. Special treatment of important food plants. Over 300 illustrations. 500pp. 5⅜ x 8½. 20793-5 Pa. $4.95

THE PEOPLE CALLED SHAKERS, Edward D. Andrews. Lifetime of research, definitive study of Shakers: origins, beliefs, practices, dances, social organization, furniture and crafts, impact on 19th-century USA, present heritage. Indispensable to student of American history, collector. 33 illustrations. 351pp. 5⅜ x 8½. 21081-2 Pa. $4.00

OLD NEW YORK IN EARLY PHOTOGRAPHS, Mary Black. New York City as it was in 1853-1901, through 196 wonderful photographs from N.-Y. Historical Society. Great Blizzard, Lincoln's funeral procession, great buildings. 228pp. 9 x 12. 22907-6 Pa. $7.95

MR. LINCOLN'S CAMERA MAN: MATHEW BRADY, Roy Meredith. Over 300 Brady photos reproduced directly from original negatives, photos. Jackson, Webster, Grant, Lee, Carnegie, Barnum; Lincoln; Battle Smoke, Death of Rebel Sniper, Atlanta Just After Capture. Lively commentary. 368pp. 8⅜ x 11¼. 23021-X Pa. $8.95

TRAVELS OF WILLIAM BARTRAM, William Bartram. From 1773-8, Bartram explored Northern Florida, Georgia, Carolinas, and reported on wild life, plants, Indians, early settlers. Basic account for period, entertaining reading. Edited by Mark Van Doren. 13 illustrations. 141pp. 5⅜ x 8½. 20013-2 Pa. $4.50

THE GENTLEMAN AND CABINET MAKER'S DIRECTOR, Thomas Chippendale. Full reprint, 1762 style book, most influential of all time; chairs, tables, sofas, mirrors, cabinets, etc. 200 plates, plus 24 photographs of surviving pieces. 249pp. 9⅞ x 12¾. 21601-2 Pa. $6.50

AMERICAN CARRIAGES, SLEIGHS, SULKIES AND CARTS, edited by Don H. Berkebile. 168 Victorian illustrations from catalogues, trade journals, fully captioned. Useful for artists. Author is Assoc. Curator, Div. of Transportation of Smithsonian Institution. 168pp. 8½ x 9½. 23328-6 Pa. $5.00

A MAYA GRAMMAR, Alfred M. Tozzer. Practical, useful English-language grammar by the Harvard anthropologist who was one of the three greatest American scholars in the area of Maya culture. Phonetics, grammatical processes, syntax, more. 301pp. 5⅜ x 8½. 23465-7 Pa. $4.00

THE JOURNAL OF HENRY D. THOREAU, edited by Bradford Torrey, F. H. Allen. Complete reprinting of 14 volumes, 1837-61, over two million words; the sourcebooks for *Walden*, etc. Definitive. All original sketches, plus 75 photographs. Introduction by Walter Harding. Total of 1804pp. 8½ x 12¼. 20312-3, 20313-1 Clothbd., Two-vol. set $50.00

CLASSIC GHOST STORIES, Charles Dickens and others. 18 wonderful stories you've wanted to reread: "The Monkey's Paw," "The House and the Brain," "The Upper Berth," "The Signalman," "Dracula's Guest," "The Tapestried Chamber," etc. Dickens, Scott, Mary Shelley, Stoker, etc. 330pp. 5⅜ x 8½. 20735-8 Pa. $3.50

SEVEN SCIENCE FICTION NOVELS, H. G. Wells. Full novels. *First Men in the Moon, Island of Dr. Moreau, War of the Worlds, Food of the Gods, Invisible Man, Time Machine, In the Days of the Comet.* A basic science-fiction library. 1015pp. 5⅜ x 8½. (Available in U.S. only) 20264-X Clothbd. $8.95

ARMADALE, Wilkie Collins. Third great mystery novel by the author of *The Woman in White* and *The Moonstone.* Ingeniously plotted narrative shows an exceptional command of character, incident and mood. Original magazine version with 40 illustrations. 597pp. 5⅜ x 8½. 23429-0 Pa. $5.00

MASTERS OF MYSTERY, H. Douglas Thomson. The first book in English (1931) devoted to history and aesthetics of detective story. Poe, Doyle, LeFanu, Dickens, many others, up to 1930. New introduction and notes by E. F. Bleiler. 288pp. 5⅜ x 8½. (Available in U.S. only) 23606-4 Pa. $4.00

FLATLAND, E. A. Abbott. Science-fiction classic explores life of 2-D being in 3-D world. Read also as introduction to thought about hyperspace. Introduction by Banesh Hoffmann. 16 illustrations. 103pp. 5⅜ x 8½. 20001-9 Pa. $1.75

THREE SUPERNATURAL NOVELS OF THE VICTORIAN PERIOD, edited, with an introduction, by E. F. Bleiler. Reprinted complete and unabridged, three great classics of the supernatural: *The Haunted Hotel* by Wilkie Collins, *The Haunted House at Latchford* by Mrs. J. H. Riddell, and *The Lost Stradivarious* by J. Meade Falkner. 325pp. 5⅜ x 8½. 22571-2 Pa. $4.00

AYESHA: THE RETURN OF "SHE," H. Rider Haggard. Virtuoso sequel featuring the great mythic creation, Ayesha, in an adventure that is fully as good as the first book, *She.* Original magazine version, with 47 original illustrations by Maurice Greiffenhagen. 189pp. 6½ x 9¼. 23649-8 Pa. $3.50

THE CURVES OF LIFE, Theodore A. Cook. Examination of shells, leaves, horns, human body, art, etc., in *"the* classic reference on how the golden ratio applies to spirals and helices in nature . . . . "—Martin Gardner. 426 illustrations. Total of 512pp. 5⅜ x 8½.   23701-X Pa. $5.95

AN ILLUSTRATED FLORA OF THE NORTHERN UNITED STATES AND CANADA, Nathaniel L. Britton, Addison Brown. Encyclopedic work covers 4666 species, ferns on up. Everything. Full botanical information, illustration for each. This earlier edition is preferred by many to more recent revisions. 1913 edition. Over 4000 illustrations, total of 2087pp. 6⅛ x 9¼.   22642-5, 22643-3, 22644-1 Pa., Three-vol. set $24.00

MANUAL OF THE GRASSES OF THE UNITED STATES, A. S. Hitchcock, U.S. Dept. of Agriculture. The basic study of American grasses, both indigenous and escapes, cultivated and wild. Over 1400 species. Full descriptions, information. Over 1100 maps, illustrations. Total of 1051pp. 5⅜ x 8½.   22717-0, 22718-9 Pa., Two-vol. set $15.00

THE CACTACEAE,, Nathaniel L. Britton, John N. Rose. Exhaustive, definitive. Every cactus in the world. Full botanical descriptions. Thorough statement of nomenclatures, habitat, detailed finding keys. The one book needed by every cactus enthusiast. Over 1275 illustrations. Total of 1080pp. 8 x 10¼.   21191-6, 21192-4 Clothbd., Two-vol. set $35.00

AMERICAN MEDICINAL PLANTS, Charles F. Millspaugh. Full descriptions, 180 plants covered: history; physical description; methods of preparation with all chemical constituents extracted; all claimed curative or adverse effects. 180 full-page plates. Classification table. 804pp. 6½ x 9¼.   23034-1 Pa. $10.00

A MODERN HERBAL, Margaret Grieve. Much the fullest, most exact, most useful compilation of herbal material. Gigantic alphabetical encyclopedia, from aconite to zedoary, gives botanical information, medical properties, folklore, economic uses, and much else. Indispensable to serious reader. 161 illustrations. 888pp. 6½ x 9¼. (Available in U.S. only)   22798-7, 22799-5 Pa., Two-vol. set $12.00

THE HERBAL or GENERAL HISTORY OF PLANTS, John Gerard. The 1633 edition revised and enlarged by Thomas Johnson. Containing almost 2850 plant descriptions and 2705 superb illustrations, Gerard's *Herbal* is a monumental work, the book all modern English herbals are derived from, the one herbal every serious enthusiast should have in its entirety. Original editions are worth perhaps $750. 1678pp. 8½ x 12¼.   23147-X Clothbd. $50.00

MANUAL OF THE TREES OF NORTH AMERICA, Charles S. Sargent. The basic survey of every native tree and tree-like shrub, 717 species in all. Extremely full descriptions, information on habitat, growth, locales, economics, etc. Necessary to every serious tree lover. Over 100 finding keys. 783 illustrations. Total of 986pp. 5⅜ x 8½.   20277-1, 20278-X Pa., Two-vol. set $10.00

THE DEPRESSION YEARS AS PHOTOGRAPHED BY ARTHUR ROTH-STEIN, Arthur Rothstein. First collection devoted entirely to the work of outstanding 1930s photographer: famous dust storm photo, ragged children, unemployed, etc. 120 photographs. Captions. 119pp. 9¼ x 10¾.
23590-4 Pa. $5.00

CAMERA WORK: A PICTORIAL GUIDE, Alfred Stieglitz. All 559 illustrations and plates from the most important periodical in the history of art photography, Camera Work (1903-17). Presented four to a page, reduced in size but still clear, in strict chronological order, with complete captions. Three indexes. Glossary. Bibliography. 176pp. 8⅜ x 11¼.
23591-2 Pa. $6.95

ALVIN LANGDON COBURN, PHOTOGRAPHER, Alvin L. Coburn. Revealing autobiography by one of greatest photographers of 20th century gives insider's version of Photo-Secession, plus comments on his own work. 77 photographs by Coburn. Edited by Helmut and Alison Gernsheim. 160pp. 8⅛ x 11.
23685-4 Pa. $6.00

NEW YORK IN THE FORTIES, Andreas Feininger. 162 brilliant photographs by the well-known photographer, formerly with Life magazine, show commuters, shoppers, Times Square at night, Harlem nightclub, Lower East Side, etc. Introduction and full captions by John von Hartz. 181pp. 9¼ x 10¾.
23585-8 Pa. $6.00

GREAT NEWS PHOTOS AND THE STORIES BEHIND THEM, John Faber. Dramatic volume of 140 great news photos, 1855 through 1976, and revealing stories behind them, with both historical and technical information. Hindenburg disaster, shooting of Oswald, nomination of Jimmy Carter, etc. 160pp. 8¼ x 11.
23667-6 Pa. $5.00

THE ART OF THE CINEMATOGRAPHER, Leonard Maltin. Survey of American cinematography history and anecdotal interviews with 5 masters—Arthur Miller, Hal Mohr, Hal Rosson, Lucien Ballard, and Conrad Hall. Very large selection of behind-the-scenes production photos. 105 photographs. Filmographies. Index. Originally Behind the Camera. 144pp. 8¼ x 11.
23686-2 Pa. $5.00

DESIGNS FOR THE THREE-CORNERED HAT (LE TRICORNE), Pablo Picasso. 32 fabulously rare drawings—including 31 color illustrations of costumes and accessories—for 1919 production of famous ballet. Edited by Parmenia Migel, who has written new introduction. 48pp. 9⅜ x 12¼. (Available in U.S. only)
23709-5 Pa. $5.00

NOTES OF A FILM DIRECTOR, Sergei Eisenstein. Greatest Russian filmmaker explains montage, making of Alexander Nevsky, aesthetics; comments on self, associates, great rivals (Chaplin), similar material. 78 illustrations. 240pp. 5⅜ x 8½.
22392-2 Pa. $4.50

AN AUTOBIOGRAPHY, Margaret Sanger. Exciting personal account of hard-fought battle for woman's right to birth control, against prejudice, church, law. Foremost feminist document. 504pp. 5⅜ x 8½.
20470-7 Pa. $5.50

MY BONDAGE AND MY FREEDOM, Frederick Douglass. Born as a slave, Douglass became outspoken force in antislavery movement. The best of Douglass's autobiographies. Graphic description of slave life. Introduction by P. Foner. 464pp. 5⅜ x 8½.
22457-0 Pa. $5.50

LIVING MY LIFE, Emma Goldman. Candid, no holds barred account by foremost American anarchist: her own life, anarchist movement, famous contemporaries, ideas and their impact. Struggles and confrontations in America, plus deportation to U.S.S.R. Shocking inside account of persecution of anarchists under Lenin. 13 plates. Total of 944pp. 5⅜ x 8½.
22543-7, 22544-5 Pa., Two-vol. set $11.00

LETTERS AND NOTES ON THE MANNERS, CUSTOMS AND CONDITIONS OF THE NORTH AMERICAN INDIANS, George Catlin. Classic account of life among Plains Indians: ceremonies, hunt, warfare, etc. Dover edition reproduces for first time all original paintings. 312 plates. 572pp. of text. 6⅛ x 9¼. 22118-0, 22119-9 Pa., Two-vol. set $11.50

THE MAYA AND THEIR NEIGHBORS, edited by Clarence L. Hay, others. Synoptic view of Maya civilization in broadest sense, together with Northern, Southern neighbors. Integrates much background, valuable detail not elsewhere. Prepared by greatest scholars: Kroeber, Morley, Thompson, Spinden, Vaillant, many others. Sometimes called Tozzer Memorial Volume. 60 illustrations, linguistic map. 634pp. 5⅜ x 8½.
23510-6 Pa. $7.50

HANDBOOK OF THE INDIANS OF CALIFORNIA, A. L. Kroeber. Foremost American anthropologist offers complete ethnographic study of each group. Monumental classic. 459 illustrations, maps. 995pp. 5⅜ x 8½.
23368-5 Pa. $10.00

SHAKTI AND SHAKTA, Arthur Avalon. First book to give clear, cohesive analysis of Shakta doctrine, Shakta ritual and Kundalini Shakti (yoga). Important work by one of world's foremost students of Shaktic and Tantric thought. 732pp. 5⅜ x 8½. (Available in U.S. only)
23645-5 Pa. $7.95

AN INTRODUCTION TO THE STUDY OF THE MAYA HIEROGLYPHS, Syvanus Griswold Morley. Classic study by one of the truly great figures in hieroglyph research. Still the best introduction for the student for reading Maya hieroglyphs. New introduction by J. Eric S. Thompson. 117 illustrations. 284pp. 5⅜ x 8½.
23108-9 Pa. $4.00

A STUDY OF MAYA ART, Herbert J. Spinden. Landmark classic interprets Maya symbolism, estimates styles, covers ceramics, architecture, murals, stone carvings as artforms. Still a basic book in area. New introduction by J. Eric Thompson. Over 750 illustrations. 341pp. 8⅜ x 11¼.
21235-1 Pa. $6.95

CATALOGUE OF DOVER BOOKS

THE COMPLETE BOOK OF DOLL MAKING AND COLLECTING, Catherine Christopher. Instructions, patterns for dozens of dolls, from rag doll on up to elaborate, historically accurate figures. Mould faces, sew clothing, make doll houses, etc. Also collecting information. Many illustrations. 288pp. 6 x 9. 22066-4 Pa. $4.50

THE DAGUERREOTYPE IN AMERICA, Beaumont Newhall. Wonderful portraits, 1850's townscapes, landscapes; full text plus 104 photographs. The basic book. Enlarged 1976 edition. 272pp. 8¼ x 11¼. 23322-7 Pa. $7.95

CRAFTSMAN HOMES, Gustav Stickley. 296 architectural drawings, floor plans, and photographs illustrate 40 different kinds of "Mission-style" homes from The Craftsman (1901-16), voice of American style of simplicity and organic harmony. Thorough coverage of Craftsman idea in text and picture, now collector's item. 224pp. 8⅛ x 11. 23791-5 Pa. $6.00

PEWTER-WORKING: INSTRUCTIONS AND PROJECTS, Burl N. Osborn. & Gordon O. Wilber. Introduction to pewter-working for amateur craftsman. History and characteristics of pewter; tools, materials, step-by-step instructions. Photos, line drawings, diagrams. Total of 160pp. 7⅞ x 10¾. 23786-9 Pa. $3.50

THE GREAT CHICAGO FIRE, edited by David Lowe. 10 dramatic, eyewitness accounts of the 1871 disaster, including one of the aftermath and rebuilding, plus 70 contemporary photographs and illustrations of the ruins—courthouse, Palmer House, Great Central Depot, etc. Introduction by David Lowe. 87pp. 8¼ x 11. 23771-0 Pa. $4.00

SILHOUETTES: A PICTORIAL ARCHIVE OF VARIED ILLUSTRATIONS, edited by Carol Belanger Grafton. Over 600 silhouettes from the 18th to 20th centuries include profiles and full figures of men and women, children, birds and animals, groups and scenes, nature, ships, an alphabet. Dozens of uses for commercial artists and craftspeople. 144pp. 8⅜ x 11¼. 23781-8 Pa. $4.00

ANIMALS: 1,419 COPYRIGHT-FREE ILLUSTRATIONS OF MAMMALS, BIRDS, FISH, INSECTS, ETC., edited by Jim Harter. Clear wood engravings present, in extremely lifelike poses, over 1,000 species of animals. One of the most extensive copyright-free pictorial sourcebooks of its kind. Captions. Index. 284pp. 9 x 12. 23766-4 Pa. $7.95

INDIAN DESIGNS FROM ANCIENT ECUADOR, Frederick W. Shaffer. 282 original designs by pre-Columbian Indians of Ecuador (500-1500 A.D.). Designs include people, mammals, birds, reptiles, fish, plants, heads, geometric designs. Use as is or alter for advertising, textiles, leathercraft, etc. Introduction. 95pp. 8¾ x 11¼. 23764-8 Pa. $3.50

SZIGETI ON THE VIOLIN, Joseph Szigeti. Genial, loosely structured tour by premier violinist, featuring a pleasant mixture of reminiscenes, insights into great music and musicians, innumerable tips for practicing violinists. 385 musical passages. 256pp. 5⅝ x 8¼. 23763-X Pa. $3.50

THE AMERICAN SENATOR, Anthony Trollope. Little known, long unavailable Trollope novel on a grand scale. Here are humorous comment on American vs. English culture, and stunning portrayal of a heroine/villainess. Superb evocation of Victorian village life. 561pp. 5⅜ x 8½.
23801-6 Pa. $6.00

WAS IT MURDER? James Hilton. The author of *Lost Horizon* and *Goodbye, Mr. Chips* wrote one detective novel (under a pen-name) which was quickly forgotten and virtually lost, even at the height of Hilton's fame. This edition brings it back—a finely crafted public school puzzle resplendent with Hilton's stylish atmosphere. A thoroughly English thriller by the creator of Shangri-la. 252pp. 5⅜ x 8. (Available in U.S. only)
23774-5 Pa. $3.00

CENTRAL PARK: A PHOTOGRAPHIC GUIDE, Victor Laredo and Henry Hope Reed. 121 superb photographs show dramatic views of Central Park: Bethesda Fountain, Cleopatra's Needle, Sheep Meadow, the Blockhouse, plus people engaged in many park activities: ice skating, bike riding, etc. Captions by former Curator of Central Park, Henry Hope Reed, provide historical view, changes, etc. Also photos of N.Y. landmarks on park's periphery. 96pp. 8½ x 11. 23750-8 Pa. $4.50

NANTUCKET IN THE NINETEENTH CENTURY, Clay Lancaster. 180 rare photographs, stereographs, maps, drawings and floor plans recreate unique American island society. Authentic scenes of shipwreck, lighthouses, streets, homes are arranged in geographic sequence to provide walking-tour guide to old Nantucket existing today. Introduction, captions. 160pp. 8⅞ x 11¾. 23747-8 Pa. $6.95

STONE AND MAN: A PHOTOGRAPHIC EXPLORATION, Andreas Feininger. 106 photographs by *Life* photographer Feininger portray man's deep passion for stone through the ages. Stonehenge-like megaliths, fortified towns, sculpted marble and crumbling tenements show textures, beauties, fascination. 128pp. 9¼ x 10¾. 23756-7 Pa. $5.95

CIRCLES, A MATHEMATICAL VIEW, D. Pedoe. Fundamental aspects of college geometry, non-Euclidean geometry, and other branches of mathematics: representing circle by point. Poincare model, isoperimetric property, etc. Stimulating recreational reading. 66 figures. 96pp. 5⅝ x 8¼.
63698-4 Pa. $2.75

THE DISCOVERY OF NEPTUNE, Morton Grosser. Dramatic scientific history of the investigations leading up to the actual discovery of the eighth planet of our solar system. Lucid, well-researched book by well-known historian of science. 172pp. 5⅜ x 8½. 23726-5 Pa. $3.00

THE DEVIL'S DICTIONARY. Ambrose Bierce. Barbed, bitter, brilliant witticisms in the form of a dictionary. Best, most ferocious satire America has produced. 145pp. 5⅜ x 8½. 20487-1 Pa. $2.00

HOLLYWOOD GLAMOUR PORTRAITS, edited by John Kobal. 145 photos capture the stars from 1926-49, the high point in portrait photography. Gable, Harlow, Bogart, Bacall, Hedy Lamarr, Marlene Dietrich, Robert Montgomery, Marlon Brando, Veronica Lake; 94 stars in all. Full background on photographers, technical aspects, much more. Total of 160pp. 8⅜ x 11¼. 23352-9 Pa. $6.00

THE NEW YORK STAGE: FAMOUS PRODUCTIONS IN PHOTO-GRAPHS, edited by Stanley Appelbaum. 148 photographs from Museum of City of New York show 142 plays, 1883-1939. *Peter Pan, The Front Page, Dead End, Our Town,* O'Neill, hundreds of actors and actresses, etc. Full indexes. 154pp. 9½ x 10. 23241-7 Pa. $6.00

MASTERS OF THE DRAMA, John Gassner. Most comprehensive history of the drama, every tradition from Greeks to modern Europe and America, including Orient. Covers 800 dramatists, 2000 plays; biography, plot summaries, criticism, theatre history, etc. 77 illustrations. 890pp. 5⅜ x 8½. 20100-7 Clothbd. $10.00

THE GREAT OPERA STARS IN HISTORIC PHOTOGRAPHS, edited by James Camner. 343 portraits from the 1850s to the 1940s: Tamburini, Mario, Caliapin, Jeritza, Melchior, Melba, Patti, Pinza, Schipa, Caruso, Farrar, Steber, Gobbi, and many more—270 performers in all. Index. 199pp. 8⅜ x 11¼. 23575-0 Pa. $6.50

J. S. BACH, Albert Schweitzer. Great full-length study of Bach, life, background to music, music, by foremost modern scholar. Ernest Newman translation. 650 musical examples. Total of 928pp. 5⅜ x 8½. (Available in U.S. only) 21631-4, 21632-2 Pa., Two-vol. set $10.00

COMPLETE PIANO SONATAS, Ludwig van Beethoven. All sonatas in the fine Schenker edition, with fingering, analytical material. One of best modern editions. Total of 615pp. 9 x 12. (Available in U.S. only) 23134-8, 23135-6 Pa., Two-vol. set $15.00

KEYBOARD MUSIC, J. S. Bach. Bach-Gesellschaft edition. For harpsichord, piano, other keyboard instruments. English Suites, French Suites, Six Partitas, Goldberg Variations, Two-Part Inventions, Three-Part Sinfonias. 312pp. 8⅛ x 11. (Available in U.S. only) 22360-4 Pa. $6.95

FOUR SYMPHONIES IN FULL SCORE, Franz Schubert. Schubert's four most popular symphonies: No. 4 in C Minor ("Tragic"); No. 5 in B-flat Major; No. 8 in B Minor ("Unfinished"); No. 9 in C Major ("Great"). Breitkopf & Hartel edition. Study score. 261pp. 9⅜ x 12¼. 23681-1 Pa. $6.50

THE AUTHENTIC GILBERT & SULLIVAN SONGBOOK, W. S. Gilbert, A. S. Sullivan. Largest selection available; 92 songs, uncut, original keys, in piano rendering approved by Sullivan. Favorites and lesser-known fine numbers. Edited with plot synopses by James Spero. 3 illustrations. 399pp. 9 x 12. 23482-7 Pa. $7.95

CATALOGUE OF DOVER BOOKS

AMERICAN ANTIQUE FURNITURE, Edgar G. Miller, Jr. The basic coverage of all American furniture before 1840: chapters per item chronologically cover all types of furniture, with more than 2100 photos. Total of 1106pp. 7⅞ x 10¾. 21599-7, 21600-4 Pa., Two-vol. set $17.90

ILLUSTRATED GUIDE TO SHAKER FURNITURE, Robert Meader. Director, Shaker Museum, Old Chatham, presents up-to-date coverage of all furniture and appurtenances, with much on local styles not available elsewhere. 235 photos. 146pp. 9 x 12. 22819-3 Pa. $5.00

ORIENTAL RUGS, ANTIQUE AND MODERN, Walter A. Hawley. Persia, Turkey, Caucasus, Central Asia, China, other traditions. Best general survey of all aspects: styles and periods, manufacture, uses, symbols and their interpretation, and identification. 96 illustrations, 11 in color. 320pp. 6⅛ x 9¼. 22366-3 Pa. $6.95

CHINESE POTTERY AND PORCELAIN, R. L. Hobson. Detailed descriptions and analyses by former Keeper of the Department of Oriental Antiquities and Ethnography at the British Museum. Covers hundreds of pieces from primitive times to 1915. Still the standard text for most periods. 136 plates, 40 in full color. Total of 750pp. 5⅜ x 8½. 23253-0 Pa. $10.00

THE WARES OF THE MING DYNASTY, R. L. Hobson. Foremost scholar examines and illustrates many varieties of Ming (1368-1644). Famous blue and white, polychrome, lesser-known styles and shapes. 117 illustrations, 9 full color, of outstanding pieces. Total of 263pp. 6⅛ x 9¼. (Available in U.S. only) 23652-8 Pa. $6.00

Prices subject to change without notice.

Available at your book dealer or write for free catalogue to Dept. GI, Dover Publications, Inc., 180 Varick St., N.Y., N.Y. 10014. Dover publishes more than 175 books each year on science, elementary and advanced mathematics, biology, music, art, literary history, social sciences and other areas.